Spellbound by Murder

Also available by Stacie Ramey

Switching Fates

It's My Life

The Secrets We Bury

The Homecoming

The Sister Pact

Spellbound by Murder

A MYSTIC HOLLOW BOOKSHOP MYSTERY

Stacie Ramey

NEW YORK

Books should be disposed of and recycled according to local requirements.
All paper materials used are FSC compliant.

Published in the United States by Crooked Lane Books, an imprint of The Quick Brown Fox & Company LLC.

Crooked Lane Books and its logo are trademarks of The Quick Brown Fox & Company LLC.

Library of Congress Catalog-in-Publication data available upon request.

ISBN (hardcover): 979-8-89242-412-7
ISBN (paperback): 979-8-89242-413-4
ISBN (ebook): 979-8-89242-414-1

Cover design by Lucy Rose

Printed in the United States.

www.crookedlanebooks.com

Crooked Lane Books
34 West 27th St., 10th Floor
New York, NY 10001

First Edition: March 2026

The authorized representative in the EU for product safety and compliance is eucomply OÜPärnu mnt 139b-14, 11317 Tallinn, Estonia, hello@eucompliancepartner.com, +33757690241

10 9 8 7 6 5 4 3 2 1

For babygirls everywhere,
especially mine.

Chapter One

It's not a great idea to move to New England all the way from the southern tip of Florida during hurricane season, but I've never been terrific at planning. Even though the mystical devotee in me believes that sometimes you need a storm to stir up your life, being caught in evacuation traffic on the only route out of the tip of this peninsula with a truly pissed off teenager does not make for a pleasant trip.

"You want to track up a playlist?" I offer, which, honestly feels like a pretty significant move toward detente on my part.

Phoebe leans her head against the window and stares at the parking lot the turnpike has become. "No thanks."

I point to her iPad. "You could play one of your romcoms. I downloaded all of them."

She ignores me so hard it hurts.

"I know the timing isn't ideal but . . ."

"Waze says it's going to take eight hours to get to Orlando. Eight!"

"We could listen to a book on tape. I've got *With Anyone Else*."

"They're called audiobooks, Mom." Scoff. "Plus, you know I'm into retro romcoms. Vintage."

She likes the eighties movies. Most times as a suggestion for how to set me up. Why she's obsessed with this mission is beyond me. Why she's stuck in the eighties is even more confounding.

"We'll probably run out of gas and have to rely on our car snacks for sustenance, which is sad because all we've got are Takis and birthday cake Oreos."

"That can't be right." But I admit, at first, I'm concerned. Did I forget to pack food? I fumble through my purse and pull out a Kind bar. "See? Nutritious and delicious. Plus, I'm certain there are apple slices and peanut butter in the cooler."

A heavy sigh. I am not making inroads here.

"She needs us." I cut a quick look at my daughter. "I can't not help."

"I know," Phoebe says, and that gives me hope. "I want to help Gran too."

"It's just for now," I offer. "We can always come back."

"Just what I want—to move twice in high school."

"You are going to love fall. Real fall." I pivot. "Plus, according to local lore, Mystic Hollow is full of witches. It'll be like living in a *Sabrina* episode." I shoot her my best encouraging smile.

Phoebe scoffs. "Riiiight." Phoebe wants to believe in magic, I know. It fits her overly romantic view on life, as well as fuels her *Narnia* and *Harry Potter* devotion, but she didn't have my grandmother as her best friend growing up like I did. Now she'll get that chance. They can make magic together.

Gran has owned Mystic Hollow Books for forty years. It was supposed to go to me before I'd bailed on New England. With Mom living in Paris since Dad died, I am Gran's only backup. Plus, her life in the Hollow is exactly the kind of idyll people get nostalgic for, especially me. It's a small town where you can walk to get coffee or pizza or cupcakes. Where you can soak up the New England charm. I am a sucker for New England charm.

It's weird how things always seem to line up. When trouble at Phoebe's school went down, it seemed like a good time to get her out of there. Then our rental was going condo and I couldn't afford to buy. When Gran called, frantic because she'd fallen at work, I had to admit it seemed like divine intervention. "Tripped over a stack of books," she'd told me with a small chuckle. "I am becoming ridiculous."

"You are anything but that," I'd told her. "Of course we'll come." What I hadn't asked is why she'd left a stack of books on the floor to begin with. Gran was meticulous. Orderly. Unlike my chaotic self. Very much like Phoebe, though.

The thought of the two of them getting to know each other warmed me as much as the thought of hot chocolate on a real fall day as opposed to the faux fall South Florida served up—sixty degrees for one day in December if you were lucky. When all the girls ran out to get their favorite peppermint mocha in cardigans and Uggs.

"You can finally write that book," Gran had said. "The store practically runs itself."

It was exactly the kind of turn of phrase she used with me. Playing with my fervent hope for magical muses as well as hinting at a life that I wanted. Manifestation at its finest.

Bluetooth alerts me to an incoming call from a Mystic Hollow number. "Hello?"

"Mrs. Blackthorne?" A crisp voice says. "Veronica Blackthorne?"

I bristle at the formal tone. "Yes?"

"I'm Almira Leach. The store manager of Fox N Sox Books in Norwalk."

"Hello," I say a little hesitant based on her tone. "So nice of you to reach out, both of us being in the book biz and all." I do a little laugh. Cringy but hopefully disarming.

Phoebe gestures for me to put the call on speaker. I comply because somehow it feels like maybe I need a witness. Plus, Phoebe being on my team against anyone else is just what this mother-daughter duo needs to get back on track.

Almira's voice slips into a decidedly salesy tone. Assertive and wise, and that puts me on high alert.

"That's why I'm calling. I've heard your grandmother has been sidelined. Too bad." She coos. "I'm worried she's left you with quite a mess to clean up and if it were me, I'd appreciate a head's up."

Phoebe covers her mouth so I'm guessing my read on Almira as a potential frenemy is accurate. It always helps to get confirmation in these situations. "Really?" I play along. "I guess thanks are in order?"

"I'm surprised the store survived this long. It's hard to keep one like that going for as long as your grandmother has. It's commendable."

Ah, yes. Gran told me she'd been approached by potential buyers. Some were friendly, but others were relentless—scouts for big-box store chains who want to extend their reach into small towns using fictitious names as a way to hide their ties to a big parent company.

"Listen, I know it's a family business. Sort of, right? I mean, it's not like you even asked her to start it. And soon you will have to take over for her. It's inevitable. Maybe I can help you out of an untenable situation. Yes?"

I'm annoyed by this woman's insinuations, but I don't want to start my new life at war with anyone. "The store is not for sale. But thanks for reaching out."

Leach continues. "This was a courtesy call."

"I'm not sure that word means what you think it does."

Phoebe does a fist pump.

"Like I was trying to say before your conversational skills devolved into petty insults, I am happy to help you with the upcoming Mystic Hollow Festival. The one where your book event is supposed to serve as a huge kickoff. The festival that is, if you don't mind my saying, half-baked and I'm being generous at that."

"You want to help?" I pause. "Thanks, but we've got it."

"You should take the offer. For the help and for the bookstore."

"Yeah. Well, I don't always make stellar decisions. Good day." With that, I hang up. My face heats and my mind races. Damn, my ADHD. Did Gran tell me about this festival? I take a swig of cold brew. "Wow," I say. "She was something, huh?"

"Was that some of that small-town charm you promised?" Phoebe smirks. "But you were awesome."

I allow that rare compliment from my favorite human to warm me for a second before I say, "Book festival? I think Gran mentioned something about that . . ." I reach again for the cup of cold brew filled to the brim when we left but now half gone. Damn. More than half.

"I'll help," Phoebe says. She spends the next few minutes googling the festival. "It looks like Gran maybe started working on it. It doesn't list many attending authors, though, but that should be no problem. You know tons of authors."

She means because I've been attending writing conferences and book festivals for years trying to land on an idea, a mentor, and a contract. "Yeah, I have people I can call."

"Give me your phone," Phoebe says.

"Now?"

"Perfect timing. We've got hours in the car." She looks at the logjam. "Maybe days. May as well put it to good use."

I've got to admit, when she's right, she's right.

Chapter Two

By the time we make it to Mystic Hollow, Phoebe has made a spreadsheet to track our progress on the festival, including generating a list of speakers, their books, their approximate sales records, and social media accounts. "Hmm. It's looking a little grim, Mom."

"We'll spruce," I say.

Mystic Hollow is as cute and quirky as I remembered. There's a pumpkin patch set up in front of a white church with a large steeple. "Ooh, a belfry! We aren't in south Florida anymore, Toto. And look at the brick sidewalks."

Phoebe remains silent, but I can see that she's sitting up straighter. That's a good sign.

We stop at the town's only red light, which Gran said they put in last year, despite the pushback from many of the Mystic Hollow residents. I, for one, am grateful for the pause in motion so I can drink in every bit of this small-town charm I didn't even realize I missed.

A woman pulls one of those red wagons behind her, with two little kids all bundled up, each holding a large pretzel. Suddenly I feel incredibly guilty for having deprived Phoebe of this life.

"Do you forgive me for never pulling you in a Radio Flyer wagon?"

"You still can," she offers.

I flex my bicep. "Maybe after I take some classes. No gym per se, but Kiki runs a fitness group out of the original one-room schoolhouse."

"You're making that up."

"Well, it was a preschool at one point. I think. Or a bike shop. Real estate office? I don't remember, but it's shaped like a barn, and she throws the doors open sometimes so you can feel the air as you yoga. I believe you burn more calories when exercising in an adorable location."

"Yes, that seems real," Phoebe says.

We pass the town square with the tiny post office, a diner, a pizza place, and a gazebo with bales of hay stacked in the corners. The trees are lit from behind as the sun sinks lower, making them look like they're on fire. The light is so different here, almost like it's been filtered. Then, of course, there are the hills with the soft green landscape that sets the stage for the real star of the show—the leaves.

"Talk about your fall foliage," I gush. "Orange and red and brown and yellow—hey, those fall-themed M&M's really didn't do this scene justice. Didn't they only have brown and red and orange? Sad."

"Yes. It's surprising that those all-natural candy-coated chocolates do not accurately reflect nature."

I hold my palm in front of her face. "No negativity."

We pass the tailor, who has a sign saying they also do shoe repair. "A cobbler," I say. "Our town has an actual cobbler."

Phoebe puts her hand over her mouth in feigned excitement.

"A cobbler! Like in a fairy tale. Have you ever met a cobbler?"

"No. But somehow I've lived."

"Wait until you see how big a deal Halloween is here. They have a festival with dunk tanks and hot cider and cider donuts."

"Oh my!"

"There's a jack-o'-lantern decorating contest which, sadly, I have never won."

"Did you enter?"

"Not the point. They could have recruited me."

Phoebe nods. "Yes. Strange. Since you're known for your pumpkin decorating skills."

I ignore the snark and keep going. "In November, they have a turkey trot. But no turkeys are harmed. It's all very plant forward."

"Uh-huh."

"I wonder if they still have that barn dance? Richard Walker once asked me to go, then bailed when a new version of one of his video games came out. Ugh."

We pass the bank, which is mostly brick with white columns. And the entrance to the park.

I point. "There's a statue of Paul Revere in there somewhere."

"He lived here?"

"I think he passed through." I quickly shift topics since I remember it might not be factually accurate. "For Christmas, they make the stores look like gingerbread houses."

A whoosh of memories hits as we drive deeper into town. When I was Phoebe's age, I used to run here as often as I could to escape my life. In the end, it wasn't far enough from my parents' reach, so I ran all the way to Florida, where I met a hot guy, married him at the courthouse, got pregnant, and was abandoned well before Phoebe was born. That was when I decided I'd never depend on anyone ever again. Since then, it's only been me and Phoebe and chocolate and coffee. But now . . . now I'm back and it feels like I should never have left. "Ahh."

"It's fairly disingenuous of you to be gushing about how pretty and romantic the Hollow is when you are totally giving romance-is-dead vibes."

"Disingenuous is *my* word." I cock my head. "But you're wrong. I *do* fall in love. Right now? I'm totally vibing with New England." I hold up my hand like I'm in a dance club and the music is tight. Except I can't remember the last time any of those things were true about me. Still . . . "Woot, woot," I say approximating the raise-the-roof hand gesture of my youth.

Phoebe rolls her eyes.

"I'm still going. I am enamored with fall. I am craving a caramel apple. I am besotted with the town square. And this weather? It's fall, you know, autumn. Like you've only read about or seen in movies." I put the windows down. "Just smell that crisp air. Sweater weather!"

"I've been to my grandmother's house before, remember?"

"When you were three."

"It still counts."

"Cable knits and peacoats and boots. So many boots."

"Eyes on the road, missy." Phoebe points. "Or you'll be sporting a cast along with those argyles."

"Ahh, argyles. And faux leather. And—"

"And she's off," Phoebe opines, but there's a lightness to it that fills me with hope.

We drive by the dry cleaners. The florist. The candy shop, spelled shoppe, complete with the striped awning out front. Finally, we make it to the bookstore. I stop the car, my hands on the steering wheel as I crane my neck to scan from the ground floor up to the old attic where Gran stores the seasonal decorations. I always felt like the place was magical, and Gran agreed.

"That's it?" Phoebe asks.

"That's it."

She also cranes her neck.

"What are *you* looking at?" I ask.

"Gargoyles," she says. "It has gargoyles."

I look again. "I always loved those. But they need cleaning and maybe some restoration. I think one is missing a foot. Put it on the list."

"Definitely."

I swing around back and park in the parking lot, where the paint is peeling and the door is rusted around the edges. That's when my spirits dampen a bit. I don't want to give that Leach person the benefit of the doubt, but the store *does* look a little run down.

Except for the barrels of flowers, the fir trees that hug the outside of the store and extend all the way around back, which is weird since Gran has never been much of a gardener. She used to fill those barrels with yews because they were almost impossible to kill. No way the beautiful asters I see now are her doing, nor is that xeriscape tree and bush arrangement hers. So that begs the question, where did she get money to pay someone to garden if things are as bad as that Leach woman implied?

We walk past the wooden and concrete bench I used to sit on when I was a kid. I have to fight the urge to sit, to feel the cool slats against my legs. There used to be a chalkboard sandwich board out front with funny sayings, but I see none. That goes on the list too.

"Wow," Phoebe says, and I love seeing the store through her eyes. She's not seeing ruin or rot, she's seeing possibilities.

I open the door, and the bell that hangs in the corner struggles to cough out a tiny discordant sound but fails to produce more than a hollow knock, most likely due to corroded clappers. On the list. The lights in the store are dim. Cobwebs collect in the corners. There's a bucket in the corner to collect rain from a leaky roof.

"The Leach was right!" I whisper. "This place needs a makeover of the extreme kind. "

"Don't let her get in your head," Phoebe waves her hands dramatically. "You like spooky. You're all magic is real and embrace the mysticism in Mystic Hollow, remember?"

"You're right." I wind my way around stacks of books and shelves that are haphazardly displayed. Where are the posters? The end caps? Where is the merch? Okay. This just means there's room to improve. "Hello?" I call.

"Hello back." A girl Phoebe's age wearing a long white button-down shirt with a black graphic tee overtop of it calls out without lifting her eyes. She perches on a stool at the front counter completely immersed in a fashion magazine. She plays with the ends of one of her braids as she ignores everything that is not on the two-page spread in front of her black-rimmed glasses.

I put my hands on either side of the glossy and am rewarded with actual eye contact and a shiny smile. "Hello, sorry. Was reading."

"Well, it's a bookstore, isn't it?"

She looks around. "Yup." Then she goes back to reading.

I do a small throat clear. "I guess I'm your new boss. That is, until my grandmother is well enough to return."

Confusion settles in her eyes for just a second before she deliberately shifts into a boisterous tone, framing my face with her hands. "You're the legendary Veronica." She nods in a way that encourages me to join her in the affirmation. "We've been expecting you."

Phoebe appears beside me. "I'm Phoebe, the daughter. Of the granddaughter."

"Cool. Cool. I'm Kim or Kimmie. I'm thinking of trying out Kimberly. Seems more mature." She nods to herself and goes back to perusing the mag.

"Which do you prefer?"

"Kimmie," she says, chewing on her lip like this is an all-encompassing decision. She nods as if to reassure herself. "Makes me sound fun and accessible." She keeps reading.

I like her immediately. "Perfect, Kimmie. Kimmie James, if I'm correct?"

"Actually, let's just go with Kim. That's best, I think. I work here a few days a week, after school usually, unless you're rethinking?"

"Nope. First order of business, where do they keep the chocolate and the coffee?"

Kim looks at the ceiling as if she's dragging information from the corners of her mind. She holds up one finger like a concierge. "Connelly's for chocolate." Pauses. Another finger rises. "The diner for the best cup of coffee. I think Mack puts chicory in it, but he won't confirm."

"They have cold brew?"

"Not actually, that's too new age for the diner. For cold brew you'd want the coffee shop—the Magic Bean."

"The coffee shop doesn't have the best cup of coffee in town?"

"Nope." Her smile spreads. "That's weird, right? But for cold brew it's your best bet."

"Perfect," I say. "Be right back. Get you girls anything?"

Phoebe shoots me a look that tells me I've embarrassed her. Since when is an offer of snacks embarrassing? I step out of the door and the little bell chimes. Weird. Wasn't that just broken? It's been a long two days, I am exhausted, and I need to clear my head and fill it with rejuvenating caffeine. I pass the bakery, the diner, and land at the Magic Bean, which has fall appliques covering the windows and a sign announcing clove and ginger kombucha. I am definitely feeling the fall vibe. I step inside and inhale the heady aroma of roasting coffee beans.

An older man with a gray goatee stands at the counter dressed in a UConn sweatshirt and baggy jeans. "You Veronica?" He asks.

I'm tempted to look at my shirt for some sort of nametag. "How did you know?"

"Small town," he says. "Your gran's been telling everyone about your homecoming."

"Ah." I point to the sign that lists all the flavors of kombucha. "Is the grapefruit good? I'll try that."

He shakes me off like a catcher unhappy with the pitch. Which is about all the sportsball stuff I know. What I do know is that for whatever reason, this dude does not want to serve me a kombucha. "I've got cold brew. I'd do a pistachio foam for you if you like."

My turn to shake him off. I need straight caffeine, hold the frills. "Two large cold brews. Black. And you are . . . ?"

"Rusty." Only he doesn't have red hair so I'm stumped. I must look confused so he adds, "I once stepped on a rusty nail when I was ten. Nickname stuck."

I laugh. Then I realize he's not laughing, so I add hastily, "At least the tetanus didn't stick." I pantomime slapping my knee in hilarity, but he just gives me a patronizing look.

"Florida, right?" As in I'm not from here.

"Only recently. Grew up in Norwalk."

"Ah, city folk."

With nothing left to say, I pay and take my two coffees, no carrier. Got it. We are into saving the planet. Perfect. I take a large sip of my drink. There's so much to consider moving into this next phase. There's registering Phoebe at school. There's moving our things into Gran's. There's the bookstore. The change suddenly feels too big. So I drink more coffee, which is literally my answer to everything. Except, of course, chocolate. I need some of that too. I stop in the bakery and get three slices of coconut chocolate chip cake, waited on by the owner, Lynn, who is a woman in her seventies with a white bun on her head and a sweet smile. "Welcome home, Veronica," she tells me. "No charge for your first order. I insist!"

I almost correct her and tell her this wasn't my home, but instead, I accept the warm feelings that are being aimed at me. "Thank you.'

As I muscle my way through the front door of the bookstore, I see the lights in the store have brightened. Or my eyes have adjusted.

"Hello," a familiar loving voice greets me. I push past the display of huggable pillows with cute slogans on them, which I don't remember seeing earlier. It can't be. I'm imagining it. But no, as I make my way to the front of the store, I see her in all her glory—Gran standing as tall as the last time I saw her. No boot on her foot. No cast. Although she does have one of those wheeled walkers next to her like a prop.

"Gran," I rush to her. "You look amazing."

She hunches over; puts a hand on the small of her back. Maybe a little theatrically?

"How'd you get here?" I ask.

"I heard you were here, so Patrice ran me over."

"You heard?"

"Small town," Kim shrugs.

"It sure is."

Chapter Three

"Who's hungry?" Gran asks, eyeing the bag of cake slices that will now have to wait until after whatever she has waiting for us. Her pantry is extensive, as is her freezer. If I know her, she's already defrosting homemade soup, but we haven't eaten in hours and that's a long time to wait. My stomach growls. I'm already doing the mental math about how quickly we can scarf down these slices on our short drive to her house. Then I remember, there's no room for another person in the car. "The car's sort of packed. Phoebe, you want to—"

"You drive. I'll walk," Gran says.

"What?" Kim asks. "You can't do that. I mean, those cold plunge sessions have been *amazing*, but you're hurt." She does an exaggerated nod in Gran's direction like a parent trying to make a child obey.

"Of course," Gran clears her throat and places her hand on the leg she injured. "I keep forgetting." She does a forced laugh. "I increase my distance a little every day, but walking home? That's too far." She waves the thought away and leans on a small table. Three books fall off. Kim bends to pick them up. "It's the standing that's hard for me. And my hand isn't working so good." Gran stares at the tremor that feels like it's for my benefit. "Also, like

Kim said, Kiki has been giving me a daily massage and use of her plunge pools. That's really helped."

"Kiki the dance teacher?" I ask, memories of being dressed as a swan in an ill-fated recital descend on me, and I blush a little at the thought of how clumsy I was.

"She's now a certified Reiki master." Gran's eyes light with that last proclamation.

"Your grandmother's recovery has been nothing short of charmed," Kim agrees, eating the cake I left for her on the counter. Gran shoots her a look like maybe she's gone too far. She shovels the slice in faster.

Phoebe stares daggers at me. "Aren't you glad Gran's doing so well?"

Gran puffs herself up a little. "Yeah. Aren't you?"

"Of course," I say, feeling like the worst human in the world for believing Gran inflated her injury. I mean, what would that serve? To get me here? That makes no sense. If she'd wanted a visit, she could have just asked. If she'd needed short-term help, she could have said that also. What she'd actually said feels fuzzy in my brain now. I remember the words, *I've fallen.* And the tone—freaked. I remember I'd never heard her sound that small. "Of course. It's wonderful."

"And if we'd been home, look what we'd be dealing with now." Phoebe shows me a video of our neighborhood currently being thrashed by a Cat 5 hurricane.

"Yeah. Well, that's terrible."

"Plus, we have fall here. Real fall."

I stare at Gran and Kim. Which one of them is brainwashing my daughter? And also, do I care if it serves me? Question for future-me. For now, there's a meal in the hopefully very near future and I mean to get to the table as fast as I can.

"I'll drive Gran," Kim offers. "The store can sit empty for two minutes."

"Great idea," Gran says. "See you all at home."

* * *

"Did you know she's part of an heirloom bean club? Heirloom beans!" Phoebe says as she gets in the car.

"Did you know we only have two minutes to scarf this cake down before we get there?" I counter.

But Phoebe is not buying in. "I mean, in some ways it's a little bougie; beans are supposed to be cheap. That's part of the appeal, am I right?"

"Taco Bell certainly thinks so."

"But heirloom beans? I'm so curious."

The feeling of being played is so heavy in the air that I find myself doubting when I should be embracing. Celebrating, even. Gran is better than I thought. Awesome. The store needs an intervention, but maybe that's also not as terrible as I thought. These are good things.

I tell myself to tap into gratitude as I turn into her gravel driveway. The soft sounds the tires make as they roll toward the garage helps by stirring my heart. Gran's house, a cute two-story cottage painted soft New England blue with a sweet white porch, is here waiting for me. I'm really home.

"Not bad," Phoebe says as we walk up the steps together. "Cute."

"This is the first place I felt I really belonged." As soon as I say that the lights on the porch turn on. "Is that weird?" I ask.

Phoebe rolls her eyes. "Timers."

The aroma of lentil soup and bread wafts into the foyer. How is all of this ready so quickly? We walk through the living room, past the dollhouse that was mine growing up. It was the only thing I took from Mom and Dad's house. The only thing I loved. Gran swore to give it a safe place to hang until I could come get it. "I always felt like this dollhouse was a promise of a good life to come. Weird. Right?"

"No," Phoebe says, peering inside. "It's sweet. Do you have figurines?"

"Only a few." I bend to take a closer look. A light in one of the rooms is on. That's new. It's the kitchen that's lit up, and there's a display of fake fruit in a small bowl on the table that looks good enough to eat, if not for its diminutive size. I'm smitten. I pick up the Mom figure. "I've got your grandma. I like her like this. Less judgy."

Phoebe takes her from me. "It looks just like Grandma. Smartly dressed. Full face of makeup."

"We'll call her later," Gran appears in the doorway at just the right time, but it's like a snapshot from all of those times before, reminding me of how at home I feel here. "Your mother," she adds in case I was confused. "Soup's on."

"That was fast," Phoebe says what I'm thinking.

"You must be starved. Patrice helped me get this set up. Had the soup made already. In the freezer. Vegan, dear." She says to Phoebe.

"With the magic beans?"

Gran laughs. Blushes. Then says, "Ohh, the heirloom ones? Yes." Her smile goes all the way to her eyes. "Grab the bowls, would you? The shallow ones in that cabinet."

The kitchen is exactly as I remember, with a small English pub table and mismatched chairs. A bowl of fruit sits on the table like in my dollhouse. So many coincidences layered over so many memories. It's like my brain is an alchemist, magically mixing old and new. Then and now.

As Phoebe rushes to set the table and Gran commands from her station in the corner, leaning against the counter, bread comes out of the oven and petite apple pies go in.

"I'm never leaving here," Phoebe says.

The cool air floats in from the open window. The warm aroma of good home cooking. It hugs me like a blanket as my eyes continue to feast on the room I missed so much. The bookshelf in the corner is still crammed with cookbooks. The ones I loved reading on rainy days. But there are new editions. Piles of new tomes catch my eye. Only, the new additions seem to be all about magical influences. *A Good Girl's Guide to Magic. How to Call Your Ancestors.* Some books by Florence Scovel Shinn. Talk about going old school.

"You join a coven since I last saw you?" I ask.

Gran laughs. Maybe a little nervously. She slices the bread and places pieces in a basket with a towel wrapped around it. "You know I'm not a joiner."

Phoebe brings glasses of water to the table.

"Seriously, Gran, what's going on?"

"Let's sit," she says. Then unable to avoid my stare for long she says, "All is well." Then to Phoebe. "Is your mother always this dramatic?"

"You have no idea," she murmurs.

Great. Now they're colluding. Full time.

I've never witnessed Phoebe so excited for a meal. We usually eat take-out food or frozen pizza in front of the TV, so it's not that I blame her. She washes her hands, serves the soup, and helps Gran to her seat. I am witnessing a makeover of my teen, and it's amazing.

"I heard you spoke with The Leach," Gran says as she butters a piece of sourdough bread.

"She always such a treat?"

Gran makes a face and fake shudders. "Sounds like you met her on a good day."

"Oh, sounds like there's tea. Spill it."

"She's not exactly a fan of some of my business practices," Gran says. "Grab the salt and pepper."

"Your business practices? Are you using coercion to get people to buy books? Blackmail? Other nefarious means?"

"Goodness, no. Although according to her, our sales tactics are, as the kids say . . ." Gran pauses and frames her mouth with her hand, " a little sus."

Phoebe gives her an appreciative look for nailing the correct use of the word.

I am less thrilled and more concerned. "What prompted this?"

Gran passes the bread basket. "She's just mad because a huge shipment of one of the *New York Times* bestselling author's books sort of appeared at the store and even before I could investigate or send them back, the author herself landed on my doorstep. Car trouble."

"Her car broke down in town?"

"In the parking lot. Convenient." Gran shrugs. Then to Phoebe. "We made a killing."

"How huge a killing?" I ask.

"We sold a thousand books." Gran's eyes expertly avoid mine. "Do we need more—"

I put my hand over hers. "How is that possible?"

"Luck?" Gran offers.

"Law of attraction," Phoebe says as if she's been a spiritual person her entire life.

I lean over and grab one of the books, *How to use Attraction Spells*. "Are you sure you didn't do a little . . ."

"A little what, dear?"

I lean in. "Maybe some amateur conjuring?"

Gran acts offended. "I never do amateur anything."

"And the store is . . ."

She cocks her head as she arranges her thoughts. "Coming out of a slump but on solid ground considering the economy. We've had a few lean years, but things are turning around."

"You're sure?"

"I just told you we sold a pallet of books! I'll show you the accounts. Tomorrow. For now, we sup."

Phoebe flips through the attraction book. She is the kind of kid who can inhale information of all kinds. If she'd been born in earlier times, she might have been a professor or a scholar. As it stands now, with the world filled with so many types of information and media, my girl is a content junkie. "Can anyone do it?" she asks.

"Do what?" Gran asks.

"Attract things like good luck or money or people?"

"It helps to have the genes." Gran says. "We have the genes."

"What about our genes?" Phoebe asks.

Gran ignores Phoebe and says to me, "Remember I told you I did one of those DNA tests and found out our line goes back to a coven of witches that were cloistered off of Cape Cod?"

"No," I say. "You most certainly did not." I shoot her a look, but Gran ignores it or doesn't see my very forceful throat slash that should indicate to stop talking about DNA in front of my daughter.

"You did a DNA test?" Phoebe's eyes are wide with awe.

Damn.

"Yup. Swab, swab." Gran imitates the motions required to do one of those tests. "Then stick it in an envelope and off it goes. Zip. Zip."

"Not fair!" Phoebe, obsessed with finding out who her father is, turns on me. "You said those kits collect information on us. You practically went conspiracy theorist on me. And your grandmother did one? If Gran can do one, so can I."

Gran looks pleased with how the conversation has turned, but I'm not letting her off the hook so easily.

I hold up my hand in front of Phoebe. "You are not doing a DNA test. And you," I point to Gran, "are not going to launch a distraction bomb to get out of this. What's going on?"

"You used to be so open-minded," Gran says. "What has Florida done to you?"

"I want answers," I tell her.

"I want pie," Gran says. Then to Phoebe, "We'll try a few practice spells after dinner. Everyone in New England dabbles. It's just for fun."

Phoebe stands up to clear the table without being asked. "Gran," she says. "Look! There's an owl."

Gran gets to her feet fast for a woman who is rehabbing an injury so serious that she needed full-time help at the store. I shoot her a look, but she hobbles (this time on the wrong foot) to the window. "A barn owl. That's good luck."

"That's my favorite kind of owl," Phoebe says. "Will it stay?"

"She. And yes, they usually pick a place and make that their home base," Gran says.

"How can you tell it's a girl?" Phoebe asks.

"The markings, see the spots around the eyes. Oh, and she has one orange foot. Neat," Gran says. "We've never had one so close to the house before, which means she's here for you."

My typically difficult-to-convince daughter doesn't question any of this. She simply leans on the windowsill, clearly smitten. "Stella. That's her name." She smiles at the bird again.

"Told ya this place is magical," I say because I feel I'm owed this one small quip.

She laughs. "Right, Mom, and Sabrina will be in my AP Stats class."

I cock my head. "I'm not sure she's a math girl, but sure. Why not?"

Gran turns to wink at me, and I realize there is no way I'm winning this argument tonight, so I let it go. Gran is Gran and Phoebe is thrilled. I love seeing my girl happy. My *girls* happy. And that's good enough for me. For now.

Chapter Four

The next day as I stock shelves, sweep floors, and place orders, Gran waits on customers. Replacing the light bulbs is a Catch-22—you can see better, but the better you see, the more you notice what needs sprucing. Oh, well. I keep checking my phone for a frantic message from Phoebe on her first day at school, but there is none. I know that's good, but I can't help remaining on guard. Customers seem to trickle in pretty regularly, but when I listen in to the conversation, Gran is busy telling them about me and about Phoebe in absentia. "I feel like an exhibit in the zoo," I text Phoebe. She sends me a head exploding emoji. Meaning she's not supposed to text at school and don't get her in trouble, so I try to be an adult and refrain.

Around two-thirty we get a period of no customers. "Fishbowl, party of one," I say to Gran.

"They're just curious," Gran says. "It's a small town."

"If I had a nickel for every time someone said that here . . . I could save the store!" I mean it to be funny, but it comes off a little heavier than I want. My hands go up in the surrender position. "Kidding!"

I am rewarded for my snark by the door opening. I'm hoping it's Phoebe since school is out, but it's just another customer. We keep working and I keep the grumbling mostly to myself since I get a chance to sneak in the back and eat the pound cake muffin I got at Connelly's earlier. Divine. Especially with a dark chocolate cold brew from the Magic Bean. With my mood back in line, I reemerge.

Gran finishes swiping the card of one more customer as Kim enters and takes her place behind the counter. Gran holds up a book. "Look what just came in!"

At first, I think she's talking about Phoebe, but she's pointing to a box she's just opened.

"Oh. Just books," I say.

"You cannot be in charge of our marketing campaign, dear."

I take a few steps forward. "Oh, is that Adam's newest?" Adam Whitford is one of the it-boys in publishing. Maybe *the* it-boy at the moment. His newest is a thriller about corporate werewolves who trade in commodities and gives *Billions* vibes with the twist of a long lycanthrope bloodline à la *Succession*. It's actually selling more copies than stores can stock. It doesn't hurt that Adam himself is not bad on the eyes.

My mind zips to the last time I saw Adam. It was at a conference. An agent critiqued my first ten pages, and that meant a lot since only the best pieces were sent to the agents. I was half flying and half stunned. Adam saw me, pointed and said, "I'm hearing good things about you."

Then came the rejection from said agent. Plus ten more. Publishing is a game of inches, my critique group told me as we celebrated my near misses. So now I'm thinking about my critique group.

Meanwhile, Gran muses, "He'd be a real game changer, wouldn't he, dear?" Only I am so lost in my thoughts, while stewing in my imposter syndrome that I barely hear her. "Dear?"

Leafing through the pages, I say, "What I wouldn't give to have him headline our event."

"While you were in the back, Carolyn dropped off some coupons from the Candy Shoppe for giveaways."

"She's in town?" I glance at the fliers from the Candy Shoppe. "I hate when people spell words using Old English. It's pretentious."

"Is it?" Gran asks. "I think it's charming. Carolyn is here helping her mother with the store. I think that's nice, don't you?"

"Just coupons, huh? A few lemon drops would be nice. Or those gummies that taste like soda. Or maybe chocolates, if they really wanted to make an impression."

"Who's Carolyn?" Phoebe asks when she finally makes it into the store. "And no hugs, Mom. I am back from school. Not the war."

"Whatever." I consider grabbing Phoebe, anyway, knowing she really wants at least one hug. Or more likely, she'll tolerate one, but she's almost an adult now, so I let her be. "Carolyn was in my year. Except she got to go to Mystic Hollow High like you do, while I was forced to attend Carrington Prep. So, she's on the annoyed-me list."

"You're still keeping those lists, dear?"

"I'm like Daenerys in *Game of Thrones*, Breaker of Chains, Mother of Dragons, only I'm Keeper of Lists."

"I didn't realize it was so ambitious an undertaking, dear. Well, then. Carry on."

"Am I on the list?" Phoebe asks.

"Unsure at this time." She gives me a very short hug. "Okay. You were on the list but now you're not. Plus, her hair did the perfect flip when she turned while mine stayed stubbornly in place."

"This is still Carolyn?" Phoebe asks. When I nod, she says, "The monster!"

"She was so arrogant. Everything she did was better. From her all-organic free-range lunches to her bespoke ringtones. And oh, that revoltingly strong-smelling bug spray her mother doused her with before any outdoor activities." I gag at the memory. "Everybody hated it. And oh my God. She also had this obnoxious charm bracelet which she jingled on purpose just to annoy people."

"Annoy people or annoy you?" Phoebe asks.

"I believe it was personal, yes. Also, you passed the test and took Mommy's side so . . ." I point to the back of the store. "There are two pieces of cake for you girls."

"Yes!" Phoebe does a fist pump. "But how did you know ahead of time I would earn cake?"

I put my hand on her shoulder. "Mommy's psychic."

"Psychic, psycho . . . just two letters separate those two words." Phoebe moves her hands up and down like she's a scale and is weighing the differences. Then, when she sees my frown, she counters with "Joking!"

"Doesn't her mom have one of those preppy New England nicknames?" I muse as the girls vacate.

"You mean Bitsy, dear?"

I laugh louder than would be expected. "You'd think with a name like Bitsy she could have been a bitsy more generous and given us actual candy for the giveaways."

"Bitsy is a nickname for Elizabeth, and it's perfectly acceptable."

"Of course it is." I try to seem sincere but don't quite pull it off. "Seriously though, when we ring people up, are we asking for their socials and other contact info?"

"There's that ADHD that I love."

"Maybe a little sugar rush from sample candies would curtail that. But . . . sadly, Bitsy cheaped out."

"Odds are they'd never have made it into the bags anyway."

I gasp and put my hand over my heart. "Wounded."

"I'm sorry, dear. I may have misjudged you."

"Nah . . . Your assessment was accurate. Sometimes the truth hurts. Hey, maybe we could do some writing workshops here." I look around. "It's the perfect space for a small critique group. I miss my critique group. Plus, this area has to be lousy with writers."

"Love the thought." Gran says. "Let's just hope the writers themselves aren't lousy."

"We will be a beacon of hope for writers of all abilities," I say.

The door opens and a girl I haven't met yet steps in. "That's Tatum. Care to opine on her name?" Gran whispers.

I do the zipping my lips gesture.

"Well, that's a relief. From now on, I'll be certain to have all the women in the Hollow run their baby names by you before deciding."

"I think that's best." I do my most serious-minded nod.

"Look at you being so wise these days."

"I believe my nod *was* sagacious. Even if fake. Fauxgacious."

"Sagacious is a great word!" Gran says. "But I'm not sure you can add faux to it and make it work."

"The kids can. They combine everything these days. Stagflation. Netiquette. And my favorite—cronut. Ugh. Now, I'm hungry."

Gran gives me the look that is part admiration, part love, mixed with a little tiny bit of reproach. "I have my book club. Which means you must fend for yourself for dinner, dears."

Phoebe emerges from the back of the store in time to hear the news. Fend for yourself is what Gran always said when I stayed over and she was busy. I loved it when that happened because that meant I'd get to spend the night in front of the television eating delivery food. The kind of evening that never happened at my house where all the meals were formal and in the dining room.

Now, when she says it, I feel that same feeling of endless possibilities. But then I remember that my Gran may need a little help. "Do you need us to take you?" I ask.

"No, dear. I've got a ride." She wobbles outside faster than I can keep up and climbs into the waiting car of one of her friends, the identity to be revealed later.

"Was that weird?" I ask Phoebe, who looks up from the book she is thumbing through. That's my girl, all day at school and she winds down with a little reading. *Harry Potter and the Half Blood Prince.* This is her fifth time reading this particular title, to my knowledge.

"Sigh, Mom." She puts the book down. "Stop being so suspicious. Why don't we geek out over school supply shopping and mother-daughter time." She shifts into her imitation of me, which is not always flattering. "Remember mother-daughter time?"

She's nailed me. The inflection, the pronunciation, the tone. I can't help but crack up. Besides, she is right. Or technically, I am right. Either way, we are all right. It is definitely time for this mother and daughter to spend some time together.

"I have a supply list," she tells me.

"Let's walk," I say. "It'll give us a chance to really see the town."

I half expect a complaint, but those seem to have been left behind in our Florida life. Whatever the reason, Phoebe is embracing Mystic Hollow. Hallelujah.

It's still daylight, but the light is fading. "Look at the streetlights!" I say. They aren't the behemoth twenty feet tall lights that shone down on us with metal arms and futuristic lights like in Florida. "They look like they are straight out of Narnia. You know, if it were snowing and there were wreaths up. Now it's just pumpkins and horns of plenty."

"Great use of an atypical plural," Phoebe says. "If we'd been playing Grammar Me, you'd have scored big on that one."

Grammar Me is a game we made up to pass the time on long drives. Points for interesting words, use of difficult-to-conjugate plurals, and otherwise exciting turns of phrases. Phoebe usually wins, and I'm annoyed I didn't announce a session so that I could scoop up those points.

"I think we should be allowed to retroactively call for a game of Grammar Me."

"Defeats the purpose. Let's focus on something else for now," she says.

"Sigh. It *is* pretty neat how the entire town resets for every season. Now it's oranges and reds and browns. Rust. Burnt orange. Pale yellow. A perfect palette." I gesture toward the trees.

"So, you are counting nature as a decoration? I mean, theoretically every town up north during fall has leaves of many colors."

"Right." I look around. "But ours seem better, don't they?" I gesture wildly. "And the wrought iron fences around the park. So cute."

I gaze at the awnings on all of the buildings, the same as before, more likely than not, but with ribbons and other ornaments. Tables are set up outside with pumpkins and gourds and cinnamon bundles. Even the newsstand has burlap around the posts. It all seems so inviting.

"Seriously, Mom, you gotta chill with all of this . . ." Then she sees the white owl from our house. Stella, with her orange foot, three lamp posts ahead of us.

"Is that?" I shake my head. "It can't be."

"And yet . . . I think she's following us."

"No, she's leading us," I say.

"That's not possible." Phoebe yanks on my arm, keeping me from gaping at the owl.

But I'm stuck. Planted in front of the Old Candy Shoppe's entrance. Inside, Carolyn is having an animated discussion with a customer. Laughing. "Grr." I say. "Her hair is still better than mine."

"It's not. Yours is superior."

I shake my head. "You know what kills me about her?"

"Do tell."

"Only slightly sarcastic. I'll take it. She is always trying to one-up me, to be better than I am. At everything, as if it were a competition."

"That *is* annoying."

"I'm serious. One time in eleventh grade, she entered a county story writing contest. And won!"

"The nerve!"

"And hers was such a gimmicky, cheap derivative story too. It was so close to an Agatha Christie story, I wondered if it was fanfic."

"Which story?" Phoebe asks.

"Which Agatha story?"

"Right. Which one did she copy so closely that you felt it was stolen?"

"I don't remember. Something about poison. The point is, she stole the story, stole the contest, stole the boy I had a crush on."

"She took your boyfriend too?"

I look down. "Well, it was really a celebrity crush. On Taylor Lautner." I smile. "He had the best abs."

Phoebe gasps. "Let me get this straight. This woman stole your glory and your completely imaginary relationship?"

"Yup."

"That's it. She's at the top of the list. Only those white chocolate chunks in her store look amazing."

"Traitor."

Phoebe points to Odi's store. "School supplies. Remember? First, we shop and then if you still feel like it, we'll plan the best imaginary revenge for the imaginary slights."

"Well, okay then."

The next twenty minutes are spent loading supplies into a cart and then parting with more than a fair chunk of my money, but we are both glowing from our purchases. Who doesn't love school supplies? She's also filled me in on most of her day. Most classes are good. Except her math class, which is a bore. We leave the town store with big bags in each hand. "We are amply supplied."

A hooting alerts me. Stella. Again. It can't be. I point with my bagged hand and inadvertently knock into a woman rushing by with a yoga mat and an attitude. "You might want to watch where you're going."

"I'm so sorry." I whip around to face my accuser but end up whacking the mat out of her hand. The bag breaks, sending Post-it notes, highlighters, and pens flying. Phoebe bends to collect it all.

The woman sneers. Grasps for her water bottle that has somehow been bent into an unnatural shape. "We are so sorry. Let me buy you a new one," I say as Phoebe runs to replace it.

The woman stands. Brushes the dirt off of her legs and arms. "Not necessary."

Another person smirks as she passes the logjam. "Oh, Almira. Better hurry or I'll get your spot."

"Almira?" I ask. "Leach?"

"Yes. And you must be Veronica and Phoebe. Charmed, I'm sure," she practically spits, almost growls, something I associate with Kim Novak in *Bell, Book and Candle* when she threatened Jimmy Stewart's fiancée. Man, I need to watch that again.

I guess I must have spaced out, and one of those awkward conversational pauses that Phoebe's always nailing me for ensues.

"Are you okay?" Almira asks.

"I didn't think you lived in the Hollow," I say.

"You don't have to live here to take the classes with Miss Kiki."

Phoebe comes out of the store with a cold bottle of water.

The Leach sneers. "Plastic? No thanks."

"You have to be adequately hydrated." I insist. "Really."

She snatches the bottle and jogs toward the barn that serves as Miss Kiki's yoga studio.

"Wow," I say. "I think she really likes us."

Phoebe hums the refrain of the Wicked Witch from *The Wizard of Oz* as we meander down the street laughing. "Hungry?" I ask as we come up to the diner.

"I could eat."

A sign displaying a large pie with a border of flowers hangs from the rafters announcing April's Eats.

Phoebe's head tips up. "It has pie, so . . ."

"Pie for dinner?" I ask.

"Maybe."

The place is cute. Small tables mostly. Painted chairs. I just hope they have vegan food for Phoebe. A chalkboard centered on the wall displays the specials. A man who looks so much like Jake Gyllenhaal I have to look again, pours coffee into the mug of one of the customers at the counter.

"Anywhere is fine," the famous Jake look-alike tells us.

We grab a table by a window so we can stash our bags near the wall. The man saunters over and plunks two plastic menus on the table and grabs two waters from a tray a teenager carries behind him.

I make a face. "We were hoping to meet the owner of this little establishment. Seeing as it's our first time and all."

"Well, you've got me. April is buying the food we need."

"Oh," I say, keeping the bit going a little longer. "We'll wait." I close the menu and nod at Phoebe to follow suit.

"I think we should give this gentleman a chance. Since we are starving and it's against the law not to feed your child."

The guy smiles. Dimpled chin and all. He scratches his head with the pencil he uses for the orders. "That's funny. Since I'm actually the sheriff."

I put my hand over my mouth. "Are you confused? Do you think this is the jail?" I mouth to Phoebe. "How sad."

"April's my sister. I help her run the place when she needs to step away."

"Is it reciprocal?"

"Excuse me?" the man asks.

"You cover for her when she's running errands. Does she step in as sheriff when you need?

"Mom," Phoebe says. "I wasn't kidding about those neglect charges. I'm starving."

"You just had cake." To the sheriff. "I swear, she just had a huge piece of cake before this." To Phoebe. "We don't even know this man's name. If he's taken the appropriate food safety courses. In short, if it's safe to let him take our order. It is my duty to protect you."

The man leans in. "The name's Mack. I'm more than qualified to take your order. And it's most likely safer to be served by me than it is to walk to yoga class in your vicinity."

I shoot Phoebe a look. "Small town."

"You know what you want?" he asks.

"What's good?" I ask, looking at a pretty standard diner menu.

"Do you have any vegan options?" Phoebe asks.

I half expect him to give her a hard time—this is a diner and why can't you eat meat—but his face lights up. "I'll be right back." He hustles behind the counter and comes up with a bright green menu. He jogs back and hands it to Phoebe. "I've waited fifteen years for someone to ask." He points. "The mushroom stroganoff is the best thing on here in my opinion."

Phoebe gives him an appreciative look. "I'll take that, then." She points at me. "She'll have the grilled chicken sandwich. Honey mustard. I'm still trying to convert her. Two coffees, black, please."

He smiles, writes our orders on his pad, and disappears.

"He's cute," Phoebe says. Then she gives me a knowing look.

"Oh my God," I say. "Do you see the dry-erase board?"

"Ten thousand nine hundred and forty days have passed since the last serious crime?" Phoebe reads. "Wow. That's . . ."

Mack returns with our coffees. "Thirty years. We've got quite a streak going. I'd like to keep it that way. My father was sheriff before me. Although your assault on Almira almost counts as a crime." He laughs. "And before you ask, April wanted the board in here. She took one of those adult education classes at the community center, and they said businesses should look for opportunities to cross-promote."

I cock my head. "So does that mean you have flyers about the diner in your jail?"

Lynn from Connelly's is seated at the table next to us. She leans over. "They have samples. And menu items named after crimes."

"Oh . . . That's what jailhouse chili referred to. I wasn't going to ask," I say, holding my hand to my mouth like I'm whispering a secret.

"I'd go for the felony French fries. They are a real crowd pleaser," Lynn says.

"I may have to commit a real crime to get a tour of the jail that inspired those dishes. And for the samples."

"Letting that Almira woman suck up to our townspeople is the real crime," Lynn says. "She just wants to get her mitts on our local economy."

"Anyone can take Kiki's classes." Mack gives me a knowing look. "As for you, you're off the hook. This time. Consider it a warning."

Chapter Five

As the furious pace to get ready for the festival renders me incapable of cooking or arranging meals, I am reminded how nice it is to have Gran cook for me. Still, buckets of homemade soup cannot make up for the concern I have that things are not what they seem and Gran is fibbing to me about everything.

When Phoebe's not at school, she helps in the store. Right now, she's in the romance section with Gran right next to her. The two of them are thick as thieves, reading pages from one book, putting it down, then picking up another one. My heart fills with gratitude. My daughter with my gran.

"What are you two up to, anyway?" I ask but can't cross the room at present since I'm busy hanging fairy lights from the bookshelves. Orange colored. For fall.

"Wouldn't you like to know," Phoebe says in a gentle mocking tone.

"Nope. I'm good. You stay in your love zone."

"Sure you won't join?" Gran asks.

"If only," Phoebe conspires with her. "She's got a heart of ice, that one."

Phoebe does something, and Gran says, "Very good. Now try the Latin."

"I thought you were reading romcoms. Since when are those in Latin?"

Giggles. Snickers. No information. Kim comes in the front door, assesses the scene and must believe I'm the one in need of help as she jogs forward, hands in the air, mouth open wide. "You got it?" she asks.

The stepstool I'm standing on starts to wobble a little. Gran puts her hands out. "Oh, dear."

It falls back into place.

Phoebe rushes over. "You okay, Mom?"

"Fine." I climb down.

"Maybe the kids should do this. Better balance," Gran says.

"Nope. I've got it. Just need a sip of coffee, then back to the grind."

I take a mini break in the back of the store. The vent overhead pipes in some of their conversation. Gotta love old buildings. Gran and I used to spy on the customers' conversations sometimes. Innocent stuff. But now I've turned the tables.

I hear Phoebe say something about *Sleepless in Seattle.*

Oh. Great. They *are* conspiring. But about what? The lights blink. We've got to get an electrician in here.

"A movie, not a book?" I hear Gran gasp theatrically.

"Movies can be adapted from books," Phoebe says as if this kind of thing happens every day and it's just another chance to debate her core beliefs with someone who has skin in the game.

"But not that one," Gran argues. "Who knows how that will play out . . . as this is a trial run and all."

What? They are definitely planning something. I race to the front of the store, ready to confront the little conspirators, but Gran is now in the children's section and Phoebe is outside putting up the chalkboard sandwich board in front of the store.

"What?" I ask. "When?"

Gran looks up. "Are you well, dear? You look flustered."

"No. You and Phoebe were just talking. I heard you."

"That's right, dear. Then you went into the back of the store and she took the new sign out front. Great idea bringing that thing back. Kim came up with a great quote to go on it."

"Kim?"

"Yes, dear."

"Where is she?" Suddenly I feel like I'm being set up or punked. Or that I've somehow lost track of time.

"I sent her for cake."

The rest of the fairy lights have been strung. Impossible.

"But I heard you and Phoebe talking while I was in back. About romcom books and movies."

"Sounds like us," Gran says, scooting by me and grabbing my chin, which would annoy me if anyone else did it but feels sweet coming from her. "Look how fantastic things are coming along."

She's right. The store does look good. We've managed to reorganize it and fix a few of the small things that needed fixing. Other things feel like they've fixed themselves, even though I realize that's not possible. The leak in the roof remains stubbornly unfixed. Does that require more than Gran's ability to attract? Where's real magic when you need it?

Still, I'm rattled by all of this. I could have sworn I was only in the back of the store for two minutes, tops, but when I look at my coffee cup, it's completely empty. Did I sit down? Space out? Fall asleep?

"Whatever's bothering you, Veronica, it'll all work out."

"I guess."

"Now catch me up on the festival, dear."

"Right. Phoebe and Kim have crafted social media campaigns that are hysterical and impactful. There's been a lot of interest in premium panels such as author speed dating." Kim suggested an RSVP system, and tickets are selling. Mystic Hollow Books stands to take home a good chunk of the profit, even after the allocation to the town.

"We have a dream team with those two."

Kim bursts through the door with two bags of goodies. "They had coffee crumb today!"

"Wonderful," Gran says. "Shall we?"

Kim hands us our bag, seemingly saving the other one for her and Phoebe. Gran heads for the table in the back, and I follow, silently bemoaning my current lack of coffee.

"No worries, dear. Phoebe went to the Magic Bean."

Fully content after my coffee and cake break, I head back out to the front of the store.

* * *

Kim is seated behind the counter and scarcely looks up from the magazine—this time on musicians—she's thumbing through.

Suddenly, I remember what I wanted to ask her. I lean on the counter. "What's up with the store next door? Accounting and costumes?"

She nods. "Very popular here."

"The costumes or the accounting?"

Kim barely looks up as she answers, "Both."

There's a sign in the window that says closed for tax season (January through May) except by appointment. And another handwritten sign tacked to the door saying the owner, Danetra, is away on a commission and to text her with any needs. "How many costuming needs could one small town need?"

"You'd be surprised," Kim says, still not dragging her attention away from her reading.

"Oh no." I hear Gran. I'm moving before I even think about rushing to her side.

Gran is sitting at the desk looking at her emails, upset. "We've got problems."

"About the festival? I know. I didn't want to concern you, but I'm worried about how we can increase attendance. I am thinking of placing more ads online and in local papers within a fifty-mile radius. We really need a huge name to bring people in. But I've contacted some local high schools with creative writing clubs . . ." It takes me a hot second to focus on Gran's worried expression. "What happened?"

"We have no keynote. Dawn Nightengale was supposed to do it, but she just canceled. She said it was a family emergency."

"Wow. Okay. As for the festival, we'll figure this out." Losing the keynote speaker is *not* good, but I am nothing if not persistent. "Not a problem. We'll get a replacement." Somehow. Maybe. With almost no notice. I stare at my phone. Who could I ask?

"Weren't you just saying how you know Adam Whitford?" Gran offers, a little too slickly. "The ladies in my book club were just talking about him. What a beefcake."

"Gross." I say.

"We need a headliner. Dawn is a good midlister, but she was forced on me by The Leach, who honestly should not be involved with the festival since her store isn't in Mystic Hollow." She makes a sour face. Then brightens. "But that man? *He* is a draw. Plus, not bad eye candy."

"Is it weird that he just reached out to me the other day? Asked if I'd be interested in doing his brother's podcast on aspiring authors."

"I'd say it's fate."

I shoot her a look. Something's afoot, although I realize I can't exactly tie Gran to the need for a new headliner or for the fact that said headliner seemingly out of the blue contacted me. Still, it feels way too coincidental. I recall that happening a lot in this town.

"You two have a history of sorts, am I right?"

"Only the very brief and platonic kind. Many degrees of separation."

"History's history. Of any kind. Why don't you slide into his DMs, as the kids say."

"I don't know. Doesn't that seem a little desperate?"

"We *are* desperate."

"I guess we are." I log on to Instagram and start typing a message to Adam Whitford, the author who became an overnight success after his wife's death, when he mourned publicly. Nothing gets women going more than a vulnerable man. I was writing a story about him for the magazine I worked for in Miami when he'd done a signing at Books & Hooks. He flirted. I wasn't immune. Mostly because he was who I wanted to be—a successful writer.

"Now we wait," I say, but then I get a notification on my phone. From him.

In New England on a small book tour and have no plans for that weekend. Would love to reconnect.

Gran pumps her fist—Phoebe's classic move now added to her repertoire. "Yes!"

"Don't get too excited. Who knows how much he charges to do a keynote."

"We'll figure it out," Gran says. "Ask him."

I do. His response blows me away. *For you, I will do a deep discount. Only $500 and a private meet up with you. I'd do it for free, but my agent would kill me.*

Wow. Uh. Okay. I quickly send an email to the town council to let them know of the changes, hoping this will put us in favor with them. I type out the subject line—A big name is going to keynote! If I've learned anything from Kim and Phoebe, it's that you have to sell yourself.

Gran laughs.

"Don't you dare act smug," I tell her. "This is not a romcom and no amount of conspiring between you and Phoebe will make it one."

She sips her coffee. "I'm sure you're right, dear."

* * *

Later, on the way to town hall to discuss the final details regarding the literary festival, I finally see the owner of the costume shop in the flesh.

"Hello," I stick my hand out. "I'm Veronica Blackthorne, I've been dying to meet you."

"Danetra. Charmed." She's an athletic and tall brown goddess who could pull off any outfit but is currently wearing a tan trench coat over a super white sweater and pleather leggings. "You have a tax question? Need some costumes?"

"No. I just think your shop is so cool. A costume shop in such a small town!"

"Well, in a normal small town maybe not, but here? There are festivals and reenactments and some of the local groups have specific needs. Honestly, I'm busy from August to January for all sorts of costuming. Then I jump right into the accountant mode. Which is breakneck speed for most accountants but is a good respite for me."

"When you put it that way it makes sense."

"It's niche, but it works. Plus, it's fun." Danetra smiles. "How are things going with your grandmother's store? It seems even more charming than usual lately. Your touch?"

"God, no. I am no sprucer." I hesitate to say this next thing, but dive in anyway. "I'm hearing people are worried about some of the store's sales techniques?"

"I wouldn't say worried. I mean, there have been some weird goings on, but this is Mystic Hollow, heavy on the mystic, so nobody is really surprised by a little marketing magic." She emphasizes those words by making gestures that imitate fireworks.

"You mean . . ."

"The store looks the best it's looked in years. Your grandmother was so excited about running the store with you. That chemistry is giving happy vibes. Happy vibes invite customers."

We make it to town hall just in time for Mayor Delores Racker to gavel it to order. "First on the agenda, we have a new business partner. I, for one, am thrilled to have this lady," she angles her head toward a woman with overly straightened hair, perfect bleached teeth, expertly applied lipstick, and a manner that reminds me of Miranda Priestly from *The Devil Wears Prada*, or more accurately, Meryl Streep playing Miranda Priestly. But it's The Leach. The mayor continues. "May I introduce our new director of the festival and brand-new corporate sponsor, Almira Leach from Fox N Sox Books, who has graciously offered to cover all of the vendor fees and advertising costs so more proceeds can go to the town fund!"

Everyone claps. Everyone but me.

The Leach positively beams.

I raise my hand like I'm in a classroom. The mayor waves her pen at me to speak. "I thought you had to be a town resident in order to head the committee. Bylaws and all."

Danetra shoots me a warning look.

"We held an emergency meeting of the business community that allowed the bending of a few ancient bylaws." Her tone indicates my objection has been asked and answered.

"Wait a minute. Gran is part of the business committee, and we were not aware—"

"Oh, that's sad," Almira says, rearranging her papers in front of her so as to not make eye contact.

I'm burning with rage. Fuming. But it's obvious that I'm not going to win this battle.

The mayor bangs the gavel again. Everyone quiets. "To begin with, our new chairwoman has some concerns over the new keynote speaker."

"Of course she does," I think I say in my head but am horrified to see everyone turn toward me, so unless they've all suddenly become mind readers, I must have said it out loud. "Sorry," I say. "Joke! I'm kidding. Um. Go ahead, I'd love to hear your concerns. All of them. We all would, I'm sure." Damn my ADHD.

The Leach grimaces. "If you're through . . ."

"Yes, please . . ." I wave my hand dramatically to indicate it's her rightful turn to speak.

"So, I have just been made aware of a change concerning the speaker. The keynote speaker, no less."

"Yes," I say. "If I may, our keynote had to bow out so I had to find someone right away."

"Everything about this festival must be approved by this board," Almira looks around the room to sycophantic head nods. She continues. "We need to vet this speaker. Be certain he isn't controversial in any way that would keep attendees from coming to your little town."

"He's nationally renowned. I know him personally." I swipe the air as if my confidence cannot be questioned. "I can vouch for him."

"Then you know that there have been allegations of certain . . . improprieties."

"What?" The room feels like it's getting smaller. All eyes go to me.

Almira leans forward, clearly savoring the moment. "Plagiarism."

"I've never heard of anything of the sort."

She clears her throat and sits taller. "I also hear he went on social media to discuss his grief over losing his wife. Some felt it was unseemly."

I take another drink of my cold brew. "He was bringing light to the grieving process."

"Or he was using that as a ploy to sell books, appeal to women. Like in that movie, *Sleepless in Seattle*. In fact, that's what they are calling him." She uses air quotes. "The '*Sleepless* sells author.' Or the 'tragedy to trending author.'"

A few people gasp at that one. I choke on my drink. The coffee shop dude pounds me on my back. "I'm sorry. Who is calling him that?"

"There's a hashtag." She holds up her phone as proof, then passes it around.

"Well, I for one don't think we should let a few unsubstantiated attacks on his character get in the way of a big box-office earner like Adam. He draws a crowd."

Almira puts her hand in front of her mouth, doing a stage whisper, "Especially the cut, paste, cry people. That may be my favorite hashtag yet."

Everyone laughs.

Her phone finally lands in my hand. I inspect the evidence. There is the original although completely anonymous complainant followed by a huge line of people who are outraged on their behalf. It's not a full-blown scandal, but it isn't great. "This is circumstantial. Plus, the festival is in a few days. He gave us a deep discount, so we are paying a big lister less than the mid lister we previously secured, who bowed out at the last minute, I might remind you."

"She had a family emergency," Almira defends her friend. "It would seem like you, of all people, would understand that."

"The point is, we had to move on." I pull out my phone. "We already have two thousand preorders for his books since we announced his attendance just this morning. Oh, wait. More now. Close to three thousand. That's good money."

"Says the owner of the town's only bookstore. Convenient. It's always about money with these people," Almira snipes.

"A percentage of all proceeds goes to the festival. To the town."

Almira scoffs.

The mayor puts her hand out to placate her. "I agree that this will help us grow our festival. Tourism is one of the hallmarks of our industry here."

Almira bows her head slightly. "I want it on record that I am objecting to this all."

"You are on record. And Veronica can monitor the author and keep tabs on the situation."

Almira sneers. "Maybe with those trackers you added, as if we need more technology invading our privacy." She skims the Memorandum of Understanding for the event, which now lists the bracelets, geo tags, air tags, and QR codes attached to promotional materials as well as included in the goodie bags and lanyards for the authors.

"Do we have approval for the use of those?" Mayor Racker asks. "Privacy and all that?"

"Yes. Absolutely," I say. "The QR codes are readily visible on the promo items, including the bracelets. As patrons make their way through the activities, a light and a chime notifies them that they've been tracked. People are allowed to opt out. The authors and other VIP guests have all opted in with the signing of the presenter agreement. It's all above board and transparent."

"Plus drones," Almira says. "Why on earth would we need drones?"

"Clayton offered those to us free of charge, and I think we should take all the help we can get. Drones can grab great aerial footage that we can use to promote the event," I say.

"Of course, Clayton would. He's thinking of stocking those in his general store. Shudder. Like we need more invasion of our privacy." Almira groans.

Danetra shakes her head. "I think it's smart. There's no telling how useful the data will be when planning for next year. We want to grow the festival? We need real numbers about customer experience."

"Data driven decisions," Mayor Racker says. "Makes sense to me. As long as it's legal."

"Speaking of numbers," Danetra says. "I just got the updated sales on Adam's books." She snaps her fingers. "Ka-ching."

I shoot her a grateful look.

"Can we fulfill all of those orders?" The Leach asks.

"We have a pipeline set up with the publisher to deliver as many as we need to fulfill these orders plus sixty percent more."

"That's impressive," Mayor Racker says.

"As long as the keynote doesn't get caught in any other scandals," The Leach says, giving me a pointed look as if I'm in control of the news cycle.

The mayor gavels the meeting closed. I take that as a win.

Chapter Six

It's the day of the festival, and I've had a chance to suss out the scoop on Adam's recent scandal. A woman is saying he critiqued her work at a conference and then stole the idea. It's not unheard of and it definitely scares people, but it's also not as commonplace as the world would believe. It isn't only about the concept. Unless it's groundbreaking. And even then, as an author you have to deliver.

Still, it's not good.

I try to track down the source, but whoever she is, she is remaining hidden behind fake social media accounts and has been super careful not to incriminate herself. I wonder if I could back-track from his calendar and figure it out from there? Then again, even if I knew the source of the rumor, that wouldn't help me. Forward motion is the thing now.

My phone rings. It's got the *Wizard of Oz* ringtone attached to it—courtesy of Phoebe—so I know it's Almira Leach. I grit my teeth and answer. "We are ready to start," she tells me.

"On my way." A walkthrough feels excessive since we've rechecked the plans over and over again, but here we are. Although I admit, seeing the construction of the booths warms me. Aside from the usual festival fare of corn dogs and funnel cakes, we've also got La La's setting up a seafood stand with clam chowder. Yum.

The ice cream booth might be my favorite. Clayton, the guy who runs the general store, is helping his friend Christine run the stand. They are dressed as literary characters—Clayton as Sherlock Holmes, and Christine as Alice from Wonderland. That would be enough for me. But according to the signage, they will be serving Pride and Pistachio, Catcher in the Pie, To Chill a Mockingbird, to name just a few. Extra points for running with the theme.

I get to the town hall entrance and race through the door with my handy cup of cold brew, only to almost run into Mayor Racker. "Well, that was dramatic," she says.

"Sorry," I blurt.

"No damage done," She looks down at her shirt to be certain I hadn't actually spilled on her. "This is my daughter, Laurel." She practically shoves a twentysomething mini version of herself at me like a dance mom. "She's come home from Wellesley to attend."

"Wellesley? That's impressive."

Laurel scoffs. "No big."

"It is big. She's working on her MFA. Top of her class, of course. A shoo-in for the Pen Push Prize—a literary portend for a productive future."

"Mom," Laurel implores before facing me squarely. "Honestly, I'm hoping to learn from you. I cannot believe you landed Adam Whitford. He's huge."

"Are you a fan of his work?" I ask.

"Of sorts. I mean, it's kind of commercial, isn't it? But not bad." She glances at her phone, flips it over quickly, and smiles at me, her teeth gleaming at me like they belong in a toothpaste commercial. When she straightens a poster, I get annoyed. That kind of snobbery is gross, plus I hate when people redo my work.

"Things going well on your end?" Leach interrupts.

"Yup. All good."

"Excellent. See you tonight. I hope this thing runs smoothly, but with a small committee in charge, well, one does what one can."

"It'll be spectacular."

"We'll see."

I try not to growl openly.

"Hey, wait up." I turn to see Danetra in ridiculously high heels running to catch up.

"Slow down, I'll wait," I say.

She links her arm in mine. "I'm actually really excited about the reading tonight." She smiles and that makes me feel proud. "Loving the events, by the way. Inspired."

"Yeah. Want to get everyone excited about reading."

"Author speed date, truth or dare for the YA authors, reader bingo. Really awesome." Then she laughs. "Good call not putting Adam on any of those."

"Trying to keep it under control," I say. "Not that I believe all of the allegations, but we do not need that kind of drama."

"Drama sells, though. Could turn the festival into an urban legend. Bring people back next year hoping to see a little more."

We make it to the town hall entrance where a stage is set up with an amplification system and chairs on the lawn. Food trucks line the periphery. Phoebe's idea. "It's really magical, isn't it?" I breathe.

"Amazing. Good luck, you. Going to mingle."

As she walks away, my phone dings.

Adam: *Here. Excited. Maybe we can meet up later?*

Me: *Sure. When and where?*

Adam: *What's the tallest building you have in town?*

Me: *Why the tallest?*

Adam: *If they're calling me the Sleepless in Seattle author, I may as well play it out.*

That's kind of cute. But I remind myself I am not interested in him. I haven't been interested in anyone since Phoebe's dad. Is it possible to be talked into romantic feelings? Like some sort of group hallucination? I think of *The Crucible* and picture Phoebe and Gran as the girls pointing at me, accusing me, all with the white owl Stella perched on Phoebe's shoulder. Wow. My imagination is really going to the races. Reality check here.

Yes, there are pluses in the pro/con list I constantly generate. First, I am in awe of his success. Second, he's pretty cute—your standard, bookishly attractive individual. Third, there's this glow that surrounds him. Maybe it's just because he's buoyed by a growing fanbase. Maybe it's the success of his books. Maybe it's his obvious charm. Which typically is a turnoff for me, I remind myself. I'm doing a lot of the reminding myself lately.

Me: *The church bell tower. Although that's more like Vertigo.*
Adam: *It can be our Empire State Building if we want it to be.*

That's cheesy but also kind of cute. Why am I letting him talk me into this?

I wave to Joe, the guy who runs the We Care Animal Shelter. He's got a table set up with walls behind it plastered in pictures of adoptable puppies, kittens, and even a ferret. "Nice," I say and he gives me a thumbs up.

Next to him is a booth for the We Mail It store. I didn't even know there was one of those. "Brad," he extends his hand as I stop by to peruse his offerings. He's got a wheel that you spin to win coupons. I do a turn. "Free pound of shredding coupons?" I say. "That's clutch."

He smiles, seemingly happy with my evaluation of his booth. Also available on the wheel are coupons for free shipping, a beanie bear knockoff with a mailbag. Despite my desire to pare down my knickknacks, I can definitely see the appeal of this plushie. "Great merch," I say.

A crowd passes me on their way to finding seats. I hear them talk about how nice everything looks. How good the food is. It feels like a rave so far, even before the main events have started.

The seats up front have been reserved for our dignitaries. The mayor, of course, her daughter, the town council, and a few representatives from the local high school, including the creative writing club teacher, the media specialist, and select students who are in charge of the Battle of the Books campaign.

It's twilight and the white fairy lights we strung up around the square with the pumpkins and other fall decorations really set the stage. Everyone is waiting for Adam. Maybe me, especially. Weirdly. The owner of the Magic Bean gives me the thumbs up. He's opened a pop-up coffee store and is selling hot chocolate and coffee. By the looks of it, business is good.

Phoebe is manning the Mystic Hollow Books stand, which sits right next to the festival's pop-up, selling tickets to all of the special events, including a dinner with the keynote speaker tomorrow night at one of our best restaurants.

We've also got Connelly's bakery offering cake pops and cookies. The Corner Store is represented with their bags of kettle corn and sodas and water on ice.

The Candy Shoppe has a booth manned by Carolyn and her mom, Bitsy. They are selling their usual fare, caramel clusters and gummy worms, but they've also made cups filled with assorted treats labeled Wuthering Bites, My Candy Crush, and Plot Twisties—pretzels dipped in chocolate. I am begrudgingly happy with their setup despite the cheap-out with the coupons, and, of course, Carolyn's high crimes against me in high school. Gran arrives just as Sylvester Van Horn stands in front of his Tricks R 4 Kids toy store booth. He's got a large banner all lit up with white lights. His booth is set up to sell pinwheels and bubbles and sparklers, the latter supposedly only for the bonfire, but based on what I've heard about the guy, he will do as he pleases. I want to go all fire marshal on him, but I'm too busy adding up all the ways the denizens of Mystic Hollow have stepped up for this event. I'll admit, I'm floored.

"Isn't his store name a little unoriginal?" I ask when we are far enough from his booth to not be overheard.

"Good marketing?" Gran answers.

"I guess. I feel like it's sort of cheap."

"Never mind him. He's always running around saying, you're going to hurt yourself. You're going to hurt yourself." Gran's voice takes on a squeaky register and her hands fly around her ears. I have to cover my mouth. I've never seen her imitate anyone. Ever.

"Shh," I say. "He'll hear you."

"I don't care. What a miser. He hates kids but loves toys.".

"That's actually funny," I say. "Wait, didn't he have a little brother a year ahead of me?"

"I believe so. Why?"

I make a face. "He always ate those horrible cheese peanut butter crackers and didn't wash his hands. When it came to pick teams for kickball, he never picked me."

"I don't remember you liking sports, dear."

"I didn't. I was horrible at them, but a girl likes to be asked."

"You're right dear. Miserable family." Gran locks her arm in mine and smiles. Then her face changes to fear, and she says. "Gotta mingle."

"Wait. What?" I ask, but Gran's already skittered away.

Carolyn is suddenly next to me. Ah. Got it. Gran is not fond of confrontations.

"Hello, Veronica. Lovely to see you." Her stupid charm bracelet is jingling, as is her purse. Her purse? She needed more charms?

This woman! I see one in the shape of skis. That reminds me, wasn't she supposed to be in Colorado?

I turn to face her head-on. "As always."

"I'm surprised you're back here," Carolyn says. "I thought you said you'd never return."

"Same," I say. "I thought you were a bonafide West Coaster. Ski instructor, wasn't it?"

Direct hit. She does a small laugh to make it seem like whatever the story is, she's rising above it. "I'm helping my mom. Because I actually like mine." She pauses. Rearranges her face to seem genuine and kind. "I think it's sweet you're here to help your Gran. They say older people suffer more from loneliness than anything else."

We watch Gran hop from one group to the next, smiling, laughing, having the best time.

"I don't think my Gran is suffering from loneliness with or without me."

"Anyway, I wanted to say hello. It seems we are on a similar journey." She takes a small vial of essential oil out of her purse and dabs some behind her ears. "This is perfect for fall," she says. "No annoying mosquitos." She offers it to me. "Want some?"

"I'm good." Except I hear a buzzing next to my ear and now have to work like mad to not display my discomfort at the dive-bombing insects, but no way am I giving into Carolyn's pushy and smug preparedness.

"Suit yourself." With that, she finally walks off and I can swat the bug that's landed on my neck. Gran returns to my side and helps brush the dead bug off of me.

"Never mind whatever that was. You should really be proud of yourself, Veronica. Last year they had card tables and lemonade for sale in fifty-degree weather. There was no literary festival so no books to sell and only local color to promote. This actually could raise enough to save the store."

I admit that I'm feeling weirdly satisfied underneath the nerves. The atmosphere is charming and inviting. The scent of street food wafts through the crowd. Kiki salutes me with a cup from the Magic Bean. Tallulah, Gran's always exuberant next-door neighbor, stands next to her while she nibbles on a caramel apple from the candy store, giving an enthusiastic thumb's up and a huge wattage smile.

The alarm I set goes off, jolting me. "Oh no." Adam goes on in five minutes. "Where is he?"

Just then the crowd parts.

"Like magic," Gran says.

"Sigh."

"Go on, say hello to the man."

"I invited him, so . . ." I jog to where he emerges and force myself into extrovert mode. "Adam." I hold up my hand in acknowledgement. Not too excited. Not too bored.

His wide smile makes me believe he's actually excited to see me. His eyes sparkle. Actually sparkle. I allow him to hug me. He whispers in my ear. "See you later at the bell tower."

Do I smile? I think I do. It's all a blur, because the moment he says that, a coldness comes over me as if a wind were blowing right through me. My hearing goes out, and I have to use my eyes to guide me forward. It's such a disconcerting feeling to see the mouths of the townspeople, talking, laughing, calling out, while not hearing anything. What is this? An owl screech lets me know my hearing has returned. Phoebe's owl, who perches in a tree near her booth. Phoebe stands next to Gran, their arms around each other. I see them smile as if they've been privy to all of the text exchanges, the flirting, the plans. And they approve. That's crazy.

I watch Adam take the stage. See The Leach introduce him so warmly it looks like she's been on board this entire time. He clears his throat. "I am so excited to be here in your quaint little Hollow.

I don't know how many of you know this about me, but I grew up in a town very much like this." Pause. "We had parades for the local football teams from peewee to high school. The band played at all of our events. We even had a pie eating contest at our local fair." Chuckles from the crowd. "What we never had, though, was a literary festival like this." He pauses. Looks around. Smiles warmly. He applauds. "Good on you."

The crowd responds.

"I never won the pie eating contest," he holds up his index finger, "but Lord knows I tried." Everyone hangs on his words. "Nor did I play peewee football." He pulls an inhaler out of his pocket as a little bit of show and tell. Laughs from the crowd. "What I *did* win was the writing contest that our library hosted." Applause. "Mrs. Phelps handed me my certificate as my parents beamed and just before the Kroger boys smashed the pumpkins that lined the walkway to the post office, sending the police racing after them." Laughter.

He pauses. Takes a drink of water. "That's when I knew I wanted to write. How I knew I wanted to reach people. Readers. Like you all. Even the Kroger boys, who, by the way, wrote to me last year and told me I was their favorite author." He places his hand over his heart. "Winning their approval meant more than all the other accolades. Readers matter. You matter."

The crowd leans forward, and I find myself just as enraptured. Adam Whitford as a humble man of the people was not on my bingo card, but here he is pulling it off.

"We must support our bookstores. Stores like your Mystic Hollow Books. What a wonderful establishment." He holds up one of his books. "Firstly, because we must feed our authors." Laughs. "But equally important—we must pair people with the books they didn't even know they needed. Make no mistake, connecting readers with books is a sacred mission."

"Sell it, Adam," Danetra calls out causing him to smile widely.

"Even as we eat our cider donuts." He points to the stand set up by our local orchard. "Or as we try to win a goldfish at the ping-pong ball toss, we're coming together. We are celebrating. We are creating magic, something the town of Mystic Hollow is known for, am I right?"

Hoots and hollers.

"It is my hope that this weekend will lead to more than just memories. More than just friendships rekindled." He looks at me when he says this, and I blush. "Hopefully, we are also making connections. I can't wait to meet as many of you as I can. I can't wait to sign my books for you. To taste your town's local wares. To drink in the mystique of this small, beautiful town. Thank you all for having me. And please, be kind tomorrow during the dunking booth."

Even The Leach seems thrilled with his speech. In fact, she seems really enamored. There's that Adam Whitford magic. Or is The Leach, in her role as a PR genius, a gifted actress? The only person who is less than thrilled is the mayor's daughter. Her lips purse in distaste. Was she hoping for an academic diatribe on the writing process?

Afterwards, I join my grandmother at the Mystic Hollow Books booth. Kim conducts transactions swiftly as I move significant product.

Clayton stops by. He picks up one of Adam's latest. "Not really my thing usually," he says.

"It's my favorite one of his," Gran says. "Has an aquarium and a shark in it."

Clayton's eyes widen. "Wow. That actually sounds good."

Adam is two tables away from me signing books and taking selfies with the townspeople. He shoots me a smile every now and then, and I pretend I don't notice.

The mayor takes the podium. "The bonfire will start in ten minutes."

That event will be in front of the fire department just in case. Good thing, too, since it only has one truck and two volunteer firefighters. The DJ starts the music that drifts all the way here. Mack leans back against a tree, his hands on his waist. I'm wondering if he's here as excited citizen or police officer tonight.

People start peeling off. The wind blows. A chill makes me clutch my coat around me. I look for the moon, lower now, shining down on me as if it's wishing me luck. It's time for the festivities I'm in charge of to be over

The guy my grandmother hired to break down the tables arrives, allowing Phoebe, Kim, Gran, and me to walk back to the store. My phone pings.

Phoebe says, "Who's that, Mom?"

It's from Adam. A selfie of him standing at the top of the tower, pointing to his watch.

"None of your bees," I say, which is one of our things, but we all know who it is. "I'll be back," I say, imitating one of Phoebe's favorite old movies, *Commando*.

She laughs. "Just don't *go* commando."

Kim snorts a laugh. So does Gran. I should have lied.

I have no idea why I am meeting this man. It's not me. Not anymore. But somehow, I feel compelled to—which, by the way, exactly recreates how it was with Phoebe's father. I should go back. Put an end to this nonsense before it even begins.

I stand, halfway to meeting him and halfway to the bookstore. *Go home*, I tell myself. Text him you've got a headache or you have to deal with something. Anything. Don't do this. Yes, that's exactly what I'll do. Then I hear an owl hoot. Once. Twice. Three times. I remember my pledge to be open to new things. My heart softens. What could it hurt?

I wind my way around the booths that are being disassembled. I pass the DJ and the bubbles his machine is blowing. The kids eating kabobs. The parents eating the clam chowder. The soft laughter and the dance music behind me.

By the time I make it to Third Street, I am almost running. I enter the bell tower. Make my way up the spiral staircase. Does that mean something? Aren't spirals a symbol of spiritual growth? Ascension? I feel myself getting carried away with hope. Everything comes to me in snippets as I enter the belfry. First, how dark it is. Second, how large the bells are. Third, that the room is empty. No Adam. My heart sinks.

Oh well, what did I expect? But then I hear a commotion. I go to the window. Look down. A crowd has gathered, surrounding something on the ground. Then I realize it's not something. It's someone. "Oh no," I say.

Faces turn upward and stare at me. I can't make them out, but I do see the sheriff's head. My stomach plummets. Fear grips me. Even my tired and addled brain can figure out that the situation isn't good. Whoever is on the ground—is it Adam? Whoever it is doesn't look alive. Plus, I am the only one at the scene. I've read enough mysteries to know that's not a good look.

Chapter Seven

Everything is black. My sight is gone. I am blind. Then I realize I've closed my eyes. The shock of it hits me. Adam is dead. His body is on the ground. I need to get there. I need to see for myself. I need to be sure. My legs are jelly, and I have to hold on to the metal rail of the staircase to descend safely. By the time I make it to the ground, the sounds are deafening and all around me. So much closer. Red lights flash. An ambulance. Good. Maybe that means he's still got a chance? Maybe the fall wasn't deadly.

"I need everyone to stay back," Mack says in full sheriff mode, but no one listens. He pulls a whistle out of his pocket and blows it. Hard.

"That's loud!" Clayton puts his hands over his ears. "Take it easy, man."

"Everybody back," Rusty says. "You heard the man."

The crowd is enormous and only a block from the bonfire. Danetra is there. As is Almira. The mayor. Her daughter. Joe from the animal shelter. Brad from the We Mail It store. They all stand on the periphery of the most horrible crime scene this town has seen in more than thirty years. Town council members show up with volunteer firefighters and the barricades they retrieved from the police station.

"Sorry, man," I hear one of the firefighters say. "Couldn't find them."

Mack nods. "Don't remember the last time we needed the accessory blockades." He scowls as he says it and his chiseled features look well drawn and strong. He shakes his head.

The firefighters clear the area while Mack and another police officer try to block the body from view. I am pushed behind a barrier with the rest of the crowd, thankfully. I see Phoebe and Kim run toward me.

"Mom, thank God," Phoebe says. "I heard the bell tower and someone said a person fell and . . ." She hugs me hard. After a quick sob, she releases me, faces the spectacle. "Is that . . . ?"

"I'm afraid so." I start to shiver. She throws her arm around me.

"Should we go?" Phoebe asks. "Gran is back at the store."

"Won't they want to speak with me? I was meeting him."

"They'll find you later," Kim says. "It's a small town."

For some reason, that makes me laugh.

Kim nods sagely. "You need coffee and warmth."

The walk back to the store feels much longer and colder than it did just a few minutes ago. Phoebe keeps her arm around me, and Kim holds my arm as if I am unsteady and in need of propping. Maybe I am. Different sensations and memories overwhelm me. I recall the screech of an owl outside the tower. Wait. Did I know Stella was there? The scent of something earthy and fruity. Lemon? Did they just polish the wood floors? Or was it the fir trees with their strong smell? Citrusy for sure, like that diffuser I put in my car. Only this scent smelled better and worse at the same time. Then a sound as I crushed something small on my way out. Finally, a metallic glint when I looked down. More than that, the absence of Adam, the fear when I realized he was gone.

People pass us. Some with unconcerned faces. Gleeful, even, whispering and conversing excitedly. The out-of-towners who are probably unaware of what has happened. Kim peels off before we get to the bookstore. Part of my mind wonders where she's going. Most of me doesn't care. I let Phoebe lead me inside where Gran is waiting for me with open arms. "Oh, dear," she says. "I'm so sorry."

Instantly I'm ten years old and crying because my parents won't let me skip the family trip to Europe for Christmas. I wanted to stay with Gran. Then I'm seventeen, and Mom won't let me apply to the big state college like my friends. Finally, I'm eighteen and pregnant with Phoebe.

The door opens, and Kim enters with a tray of hot drinks. Gran eases me into a chair in the sitting area at the front of the store where we sometimes hold movie nights before taking one herself. Kim hands me a hot cocoa. "I told them to hold the whip so I could get here faster, but you know Rusty . . ."

"The man is obsessed with his accoutrements," Gran nods. "Such a diva." She takes a mug from Kim and sips her hot chocolate. "Although this cinnamon peppermint hot chocolate is genius. I shall never doubt him again."

I stare at my hot cocoa. For once, I have no desire to taste it.

"It'll help if you drink something warm," Gran says. "You've had quite a fright."

"It's freaky," Phoebe says. "Do you think it was on purpose?"

"No," I say. I drink some and despite my lack of appetite, the combination of sugar and heat revive me. "No. Something happened to him."

"What do you remember?" Gran asks.

I drink more but to stall this time. "It's a jumble."

"We need some clarity before you speak with the sheriff."

"Mack?"

"He will be pissed. Someone messed up his no violent crime streak. There will be no placating him."

"That's what he'll be upset about? A man is dead . . ."

"That too," Gran nods. "Of course."

"But he was pretty proud of that streak," Kim adds.

"Maybe it was an accident?" Phoebe offers. "He has vertigo from flying in and an undiagnosed inner ear infection. It happens." She sips her cocoa. Vegan version.

"Maybe," I say, but I'm not convinced. I think someone hurt Adam. "Oh my God," I say. "If someone did this . . . were they in the belfry when I was? Could I have been next?"

Gran pats my knee. "I don't think we're dealing with a serial killer here." She frowns. "Statistically speaking . . . it's not likely."

"Well, that's a relief. I feel so much better now."

Phoebe points to me. "Sarcasm. Her go-to."

"Better not," Gran says, looking around the store. "She likes good vibes. I'm not certain she even understands mockery."

Kim nods.

Phoebe stares at her feet.

I may be a little rattled from tonight's events, but I am not completely oblivious. Something is going on between Phoebe and Gran. They have been conspiring since they reunited. "She?" I ask.

Everybody falls all over themselves trying not to meet my eyes. A hoot brings everything into focus. Phoebe's owl is outside the window peering in.

Phoebe jumps up from her chair to open the window. "She must be nervous. Owls are not fond of drama, especially of the murder-y kind."

I'm about to tell her she can't let that bird in here, but Kim rises on cue as well and disappears behind the counter, bringing a perch out for the owl as if this was a regular occurrence. As if Stella were a pet parrot.

I point as Stella lands. "Is that a little weird—"

"We need to focus, dear," Gran clasps my hands. "We need to figure out what happened to Adam. We don't want you implicated in any kind of . . . scandal."

It's my turn to nod. "Yes, murder is scandalous."

"We don't know that Adam was murdered. We only suspect."

"We do? I'm not sure what I suspect. I only know I went to meet him. He wasn't there. Then he was on the ground. What happened?"

"It's a mystery," Gran says. "But none of it was your fault."

My hand jumps to my throat, which suddenly feels like it's closing. I am choking. Gran pats me on the back. I stand. My body heats. So hot. I fan myself. "My fault? Could it be? I hadn't even thought . . ."

"Of course not, dear. But as I was saying earlier, perhaps we need to start puzzling this out. Don't you agree?" She pulls a little notebook out of her pocket and begins rifling through it. "I could use some illumination." The light on the wall next to her flicks on. I look around. Did Kim do that? Nope. She's busy looking under the counter for something. Phoebe is tending to her owl.

"What is going on around here?" I ask, pointing to the lamp that lit itself. "Do you have some sort of timers or Bluetooth app for those?

"Come here, honey." Gran pats the stool next to her, which sits around a high-top table. "I haven't been completely honest with you."

"You mean about your injury?" I almost scoff but catch myself.

She smiles. "I did need you, Veronica. You have no idea."

"So, tell me," I lean forward, place my cup on the table.

"It's the bookstore. She's magical."

I do a spit take. A really big one. Kim jumps up and rushes forward with napkins. So many napkins. But honestly, I'm not sure there are enough. "She's what?"

"Magical. You've known about magic and mysticism in the Hollow since you were little. I taught you about that. You remember that, right?"

"Did you teach me how to make a money basket on the new moon, yes . . . but not . . . not . . ."

"It's a money *bowl*, dear. And I have told you that there's much more to it than that. Like how we did a healing spell on Tallulah's dog and healed it from that dyspeptic episode."

"Okay. The dog burped." I feel the need to defend myself. "I was young and it was exciting to believe in magic like any child would. But now . . . it feels like it's too far out, maybe."

"You know I've done spells," Gran insists. "You're just overwhelmed now, and your life away from Mystic Hollow allows doubt to creep in. When you aren't here, it feels impossible, dear. But I assure you, it is possible."

Phoebe puts her hand on my arm. "It's real. You can believe in it. I didn't at first until Gran showed me."

"Showed you?"

"Just a spell here and there." When I cross my arms, Gran says, "Okay, one to light a candle with your mind. One to make the plants grow faster and heartier."

"We could save the world!" Phoebe adds.

My mind is racing.

"I've told you in so many ways how this place is special. So many times. I thought you got it. But you always need proof. Trust issues, I think they call that. I don't know where that comes from."

Phoebe nods. "It *is* a struggle."

"You're talking about specific magic? Not loosey goosey associations? Not affirmations and actualizations? Actual real magic?"

"I told you. The candles. The plants. Haven't you noticed the changes since you got here?"

I look around. "Sure. You unboxed more inventory. You spruced." I stare at the spot where the leak has slowed to almost nothing despite the steady rain that started outside.

Gran takes a sip of cocoa but shakes her head. "Not my doing."

"So magical in the sense that the store looks cheerier? But the roof is still leaking? What kind of magic is that?"

Gran shrugs. "Magic is as magic does."

Phoebe starts looking around. "She *does* seem happy we're here. She's brightened."

"Best she's looked in years," Kim says, leaning on the counter, which she has suddenly retreated behind.

I'm a little put off by the use of a pronoun when it comes to the store, but I'm also superstitious enough not to jinx any positive outcomes of the magical sort. Still, I have questions. "Since when has this been a magical bookstore?"

"It was when that nasty Mrs. Leach was trying to buy us out. I was upset and out of the blue I found the spell book in the attic. So that would be about six months ago, wouldn't you say, Kim?"

Kim looks unfazed, palming her cheek, staring at the ceiling. "Yeah. That tracks."

"So why wasn't it enchanted—I'm sorry, is that the word I'm supposed to use? I'm trying to be sensitive here—when we first walked in?"

Gran scoffs. "It requires intention, doesn't it?"

"I don't actually know. Does it?"

"It does, Miss Smarty-Pants. Also, the bookstore requires one of its blood relatives in house to tap into the magic. We have three generations here. Three, that makes it extra potent. It's glowing now, isn't it?"

I look around the store, and it certainly does look brighter. "What kind of magic are we talking about?"

"I'd say the magic in this store operates on the law of attraction, mainly."

"What exactly does it attract?" I ask. "And what price do you pay?"

"It's not like that, exactly," Gran says. "When magic is done with a pure heart and pure intentions, it pays you back, not the other way. Like my garden out front. It fills in every time we do a spell."

I think about the flowers out front and how I wondered who had planted them. Now I know. Still, it feels like there must be a cost of some sort. "May I see this spell book?" I ask.

"Of course. Kim?"

Kim reaches under the counter and lifts a heavy object onto the table. It literally looks like the Book of Shadows from *Charmed* and I feel like I'm reliving my teens. I pull up to the counter and start paging through it. "Can anyone use it?" I ask.

"Nope. Just us," Gran says.

Is it weird that I'm worried Kim is feeling left out? "That seems a little arbitrary, doesn't it? I mean, if we're going to have magic, can't we let everyone partake? Or at least those who work in the magical store? Shouldn't there be some employee benefits?"

Gran stops folding the leftover napkins from my spit take. She makes a face like I'm being completely daft. "It works on our bloodline, and Kim, while an amazing bookseller and assistant, she isn't from our ancestral line."

"No offense," I say to Kim.

Kim shrugs. "I'm cool."

"Wait a minute. Wait one minute. This is too much. You're telling me that you found a magical book. A book that you are using to attract good vibes and *New York Times* bestselling authors. Isn't that a little problematic at the very least?"

Gran scoffs. "It's nothing that indecorous."

"That's a pretty lofty word for an impolite means."

"I never thought of you as a vocabulary elitist," Gran says. "Indecorous is a perfectly good word even for the common folk."

Phoebe bursts out laughing but stops herself when she finds herself on the side of one of Gran's stare-downs.

"Back to the subject at hand." Gran hobbles to the counter. "It's about accepting magic into your life. It's about being open to the universe and all of its wonders. And what better place for that to happen than in a bookstore? Where the power of the word is supreme."

"And yet, a man is dead."

"You can't blame the store for that. Honestly. Magic can't change the course of events exactly. It can only nudge us toward a place of understanding and resolution."

"You are being purposely evasive."

"Ask the question." Gran hobbles over to the stools, and Phoebe helps her onto one before returning to stand beside me.

"What kind of magic have *you* done with this book?"

The book flips pages, stopping abruptly. On the page, there's a picture of a woman sitting at the base of a tree. Wind behind her. Something in her hand.

"It was a simple love spell," Phoebe whispers.

"You didn't!"

"If you say so, dear." Gran says.

"I can't believe you two. You . . . cast a love spell on me and Adam. And now—"

Gran's hands go up in front of her. "We did not cast a spell on Adam. Only you."

"Just so you'd be open to it," Phoebe says. "Don't you think you could use a little love in your life?"

I put one of my hands on her. "I have a little love in my life."

Phoebe ignores me and reads an incantation, which she delivers in a whisper that sounds so reverent, I am shaken with the depth of her feeling. The words themselves are unknown to me—perhaps in another language. I look at Gran.

Latin, she mouths.

"When did you learn to read Latin?"

"It's phonetic."

"Such a pretty spell and it should have worked too," says Gran.

"It did work," I say. "It got me to meet him. I had no idea why I was doing that." My anger starts building.

"Now, now, dear, it was a small intervention. Nobody meant any harm."

"And now, I may be implicated in a—"

"Let's hope not. But since we know the magic worked so well with just the two of us, imagine how powerful it would be with three of us."

The book flips pages wildly at first, then lands open. We gawk at it. Something about this page feels familiar. Then I see it; the illustration goes from blurry to clear. A labyrinth. I remember I'd walked one on at a writing retreat once. The feeling of focus, of sacred potential, was all around me. This feels like that. The air prickles with static electricity.

My hands are drawn to the labyrinth page, and I know without even trying, I won't be able to move them. Nobody else seems to care.

Phoebe starts to read from the book, her finger tracing the spiral of words. "The power of the blood opens the door. The presence of the three ignites the flame. Good fortune will ring out. The cost will be tallied. Help will be provided. Say it and it will be done." The lights in the store flash. A warm wind blows through. The air then stalls, as if readying for something.

With the practiced movement of a server, Kim places a candle and a bell on the counter. The candle somehow lights itself. Of course it does.

"Cost?" I ask. "Don't we need to know what the terms are?"

Gran nods sagely. "There's always a cost, but maybe not to us. Maybe to the person who committed this horrible crime."

That makes sense, but is that just because I want it to? "I'm not sure . . ."

"Whatever it is, we can afford it. After the spell that brought the author to my door, I ended up having to direct the high school's attempt at *Wicked.* It was arduous. And I'd never normally agree to that, but it seemed fair. We need help, Veronica. Ask," Gran whispers.

"What should I ask for?"

"For insight. For help," Phoebe says.

"That's always best." Kim adds, "Those spells work better than most. So I've heard."

I want to ask her what she means. How she knows. If any of this is real. But somehow my lips move. "Please give me insight and help." For the first time in a long time, I feel a sense of peace come over me. The anxiety that hugs my heart and lungs lifts, and I take in a full breath.

Gran murmurs something to Phoebe, which brings me back to the present.

"Right." Phoebe acts like what just happened is the most natural thing. Like she's been a practicing witch for years. She leans forward and blows out the candle, and the book releases its hold on us and slams shut as fast as those vacuum cleaner cord retractor things. Phoebe kisses the first three fingers of her free hand, closes the book, then rings the bell.

Another wind blows through the store. This one carries the scent of one of the springs near here where Gran used to take me on picnics. Despite my patchy memory, that particular recollection is crystal clear, sending me back in time, my seven-year-old feet on springy grass, standing next to the water that everyone from around here believes is magical.

Stella hoots and lifts her wings. Something silver and red falls from her talons as if she'd been holding it the entire time. An amulet attached to a silver string. "Thanks," Phoebe says.

But I'm not certain who Phoebe is thanking—the spirits? The store? The book? Or her owl?

"What just happened?" I ask.

Phoebe shoots me a look like she's worried about me. "We just did a spell. Mom?"

I nod.

"That was an excellent wish." Gran's hand falls on my shoulder. "I can't wait to see how it plays out."

Gran turns to Kim. "Okay to close up?" she asks her.

"Sure."

"I'll close out the accounts tomorrow. Just take care of the customers."

"No prob." Kim puts her magazine away dutifully and adjusts her focus toward stashing the magic regalia behind the counter as if it's a return or a preorder. Nothing special, even though it is definitely extracurricular.

Chapter Eight

My eyes bang open before I can stop them. I rub my neck where I expect there to be tension, but there isn't any. How is that possible? Magic? Man, the chiropractors will be put off by this new cure. My hand goes to the heart-shaped dish next to my bed—Wedgewood, Mom's. In it, I've placed my new amulet. In the light I see it's not solid silver, but it has an owl shape stamped on it, framed by little crystals. Kim told me their names last night, but it was too much information. I try to recall it, but it feels muddled. I pick up the necklace and a voice echoes in my head. Kim's. From last night.

"Quartz for insight. Moonstone for the deepest levels of psychic connection and especially helpful for female intuition. Obsidian for self-reflection like a mirror. Amethyst for psychic intervention."

"A perfect recipe, dear," Gran said at the time.

How am I hearing all of this on replay?

Shouldn't I be more freaked out by this?

Why am I asking myself questions I have no answer to?

I'm still doing it.

I need to stop.

Damn. I was planning to sleep in today since the festival is most likely canceled—who would come to our town now? But as I grab my watch I am surprised to see it's just past six. What? The sun isn't fully up and our town is ready for business, apparently, based on the recent texts and emails from the organizers, the committee, and, of course, The Leach. People aren't canceling and even more have RSVP'd. What?

My head pounds, and I ache for a strong cup of coffee. When I make it down to the kitchen, I am greeted by Gran who is working an espresso machine I didn't know she had.

I point. "You use a little . . ." I use my finger to wiggle my nose like Samantha on *Bewitched*.

She laughs. "You're so dramatic. It's called the get it faster app. I figured you could use a little jolt today. But if you're not interested . . ."

"Nope. No. Do not put that beautiful cup of liquid away." I take the cup she holds out to me and balance it on its small saucer. The get it fast app obviously was fully stocked and somehow also delivered shortbread cookies to dip. "But don't think this means I've forgiven you."

"Of course not, dear. Feel free to hold a grudge for as long as you need."

"How is the festival not canceled?" I whine like I used to when Gran would send me back to my parents.

"Drama sells, apparently."

"People are weird."

"I'm not certain that's the slogan I'd move forward with." Gran sips her espresso. "Your phone is blowing up."

I hold it up. "Damn. I need to be at the diner in half an hour." I race upstairs and take the fastest shower known to man. I throw on pleather pants, a red cowl neck oversized sweater with white stripes on the sleeves and boots I can run in. At the last second, I grab the amulet and clasp it around my neck. I need as much help as is available.

"Get your little accomplice moving," I tell Gran as I exit. "I'm going to need her."

"She's already up and out. Setting up at city hall."

"Little suck-up," I say, but I am actually super grateful. "Kim's with her?"

"Thick as thieves."

A warmth fills me. Kim seems like the kind of kid my kid could be good friends with. Best friends, even. She's never really had that. The kids where we lived were different from Phoebe. She had a group that hung out, but I could tell she was on the edge. Then with that incident at the school, she was completely out. I shake my head. No use dwelling. Besides, I've got to move. Daylight is burning.

Grabbing my jacket from the coat rack, I throw on a scarf and beanie. Layers are going to be essential today. I don't drive—there's no point. I'd never find parking. Besides, the brisk air and the walk help me focus.

My mind is overfilled. With memories from last night, before and after the fall. With sorrow for Adam. With worry that I am somehow responsible, even though I am not guilty. With feelings of being manipulated—okay, that's a strong word. Maybe more like nudged in a particular direction. A direction I wouldn't likely take on my own. By people who love me and want me happy, I concede. This inner conversation I'm holding keeps me from paying attention to anything around me, so I nearly run over our neighbors who are walking their tiny dogs in a stroller. Two dogs are wearing Scottish flannels and one is wearing a beanie. Do they make those for dogs? Well, apparently, they do.

"Where's the fire, honey?" Tallulah calls.

"Sorry." I keep my eyes on the sidewalk and jog to April's Eats. Questions crowd out my memories now. What happened in that belfry before I got there? Was there really another person? If so, did they intentionally hurt Adam? How did they go undetected? Why did it smell so distinctive? Strong like lemon furniture wax, but I don't remember it looking that well maintained. Maybe it's not important—an errant detail that will waylay me. I try to sort through the puzzle in front of me, but it stays stubbornly locked.

Bursting into the diner, a draft slams the door behind me. Not the low profile I was hoping to keep today.

"You Blackthornes know how to make an entrance," a snide voice says. The Leach.

She's seated at the largest table with the mayor, Danetra, Kiki, who in addition to being the dance and yoga instructor, Reiki master, and owner of the plunge baths that have nearly miraculously healed Gran's leg, is also now on the festival committee. Weird?

There's a woman I don't recognize. Maybe in her seventies with long gray hair, the kind of gray that looks natural and gorgeous, and she's wearing these chic tortoiseshell glasses. She extends her hand. "Cassandra Fetterly. The town librarian," she says. "I've just returned from out of town."

"Your timing is impeccable," Kiki does jazz hands. "Just in time for the finale. Of sorts."

"What do you want?" A grumpy voice calls from behind me. Mack.

I square myself to the table. "An iced donut and water."

"Perfect." He walks away, shaking his head.

I swivel to watch his moody departure. "Is he okay?"

"Don't mind him," Cassandra says. "He's just angry he might have to alter his board." She inclines her head toward the dry-erase board with the number of days since a violent crime. "He's waiting for word. Hoping like mad it was an accident and his streak stays alive."

"Is that possible? An accident?" I pick at the donut one of the teens who works at the diner deposits in front of me.

"Anything's possible." The mayor takes a sip of her coffee. "Although not likely."

My heart sinks. Adam. Dead. And I was there. My heart jitterbugs in my chest. Surely no one would suspect me in the event it was foul play. I mean, what would be my motive? I am so consumed with my inner dialogue, I almost miss my cue. Danetra nudges me. "I think the mayor has a question for you."

"I was asking where we are with today's events? The show must indeed go on."

I pull out my iPad. "Everything is sold out. Including all of our stock of Adam's books." A sadness creeps in when I say that. A shudder makes its way into my voice. "Um. We do have a few spots he was supposed to fill later today, although most of his big events were last night, thankfully."

"At least there's that," The Leach says. "Attendance remains high. Maybe even higher. Note for next year's festival, schedule a scandal. Of sorts. Although I'm not certain we could get away with another death." She laughs as she butters her toast.

It takes all I have not to tell her to choke on it, but I do send a silent prayer that the butter clogs her arteries. Danetra puts her hand on mine. The amulet clings to my skin and vibrates.

It's okay, honey. Just keep going.

Wait. What? Did I just hear Danetra's thoughts? Am I a mind reader now? She tilts her head toward my new necklace. The amulet. She knows. Somehow.

This town was built on magic. It can be your friend if you let it.

All of a sudden, I get super hot, but I resist the urge to fan myself. Instead, I drink the water Danetra pushes toward me.

The mayor laughs at something I've missed. I need to get my head back in the game. Kim and Phoebe show up. Mack hands them boxes full of breakfast pastries. I nod at Phoebe, and she gives me a weak smile. *Authors' room*, she mouths.

"Excuse me," I stand. I help Kim and Phoebe load the car, and when Kim goes back into the diner with Mack in tow, I whisper to Phoebe. "I can hear people's thoughts."

"Huh?"

"I think it's the amulet."

"Ooh. That makes sense. Awesome. You have a superpower. Tell me, what am I thinking?"

"It doesn't work that way."

"So maybe you are just picking up on people's vibes and body language. Like those fake psychics you hate."

"No. I'm hearing actual thoughts. Like Danetra earlier."

"What did she think?"

I run the conversation through my mind and realize that Phoebe would attribute that to reading nonverbals.

Kim and Mack come out lugging huge jugs of orange juice, apple juice, and coffee to be brewed at the event. They have to dodge the crowd to do so, even though it's barely seven-thirty. Weirdly, the town is already filled with people, and the first event doesn't start until ten. Mack slams the trunk closed, and Kim and Phoebe wave as they hop in to head to their destination.

I follow Mack inside, carefully since he seems disturbed, to say the least.

"People are insane," Mack says. "Look at them. Vultures. Probably hoping for another murder or something."

"So, it was murder?" I ask.

"Not conclusive but try telling that to the hordes of rubber-neckers. Bunch of jackals, all of them." He points out the window.

The mayor puts her hand up. "You mean tourists."

I take my seat. The cool air has revived me, and I feel like I can tackle the next thing. "Where are we?" I ask.

"We still need to get the authors their angels and assignment folders," The Leach says.

I check my spreadsheet. "I thought Laurel was on that?"

The mayor adds cream to her coffee, stirring it in a mesmerizing swirl. "She's down with a migraine. Poor thing."

I almost say, "Of course she is," like I did at the committee meeting, but the fire of that memory brings color to my cheeks and sows my lips shut. Still, a tiny fragment of annoyance rises in me. Like sand in an oyster. Only that thought brings me back to last night, weirdly. Not the beach, though. Something about the forest. But what? Back to the here and now. Why does the mayor's flaky daughter get to bail while mine is picking up her slack? I decide to add that to the list of things to be annoyed by at a later date.

I shiver. The amulet lays flat against my collarbone, its presence welcome. I'm not sure how much I believed in these mystical things before today. It was something distant, essentially a luxury I afforded myself. Now it's a dire need, so I decide to keep an open mind. To be grateful even. If luck comes to me in the form of magic, so be it.

"Damn it," Mack scowls as he looks at his phone. He curses under his breath, walks to the dry-erase board and, using the back of his hand, erases the number of days since the last violent crime. Then he writes a single unit. Zero. He hangs his head and wipes the counter so hard I'm surprised he doesn't bore a hole through it.

"It's official," Kiki says. "It was murder."

* * *

"Now if we can focus," The Leach says. "Remember those holes in the schedule that we need to fill in."

"Almira," the mayor says. Apparently even she feels it's morbid. "Maybe we should bring in some counselors for the attendees and the authors."

"That's a good idea," I say. "Do we have any resources?"

"The library has a list, sort of like first responders," Cassandra offers. "I'll get on that immediately. Good thinking, you." She excuses herself and pushes her way out the door, moving surprisingly fast for someone of Gran's age.

"She's in incredible shape," Kiki reads my mind. "It's the yoga. And the Reiki."

"And the plunge pools?" I ask without meaning to. My brain filter is definitely clogged at the moment.

She smiles brightly, like she's on stage. "Yes. Does wonders." Then she stares at her unfinished breakfast.

"Back to work, people," The Leach says. "We need to be proactive and fill those spots."

"Maybe we should be sensitive." The mayor inclines her head toward me as if I in particular have been affected by the tragedy.

I hold up my hands. "I barely knew him. But she's right, I am shaken by it. As we should all be."

"I thought you were close," the mayor says. "Sorry if I am mischaracterizing that relationship."

Do I really need people shining a light on that with the current state of affairs? The man's been murdered. Officially.

Almira smirks. Takes a noisy sip of her coffee.

"Who are we thinking of to fill the gaps?" I ask, straightening myself up so that I look more commanding than I feel. I scroll through my spreadsheets. "What about Lana Dellano? *New York Times* bestseller? She's already planning on attending. I could reach out and see if she's available to fill in."

"Of course you want to promote her. After she helped your grandmother's store and all."

My turn to smirk, although I try to tempter it. "It's true that she has a good relationship with Mystic Hollow Books and my grandmother, but I'm really thinking of salvaging what's left of the festival."

Danetra pipes in. "We want people to leave with a favorable impression of our little town with just the hint of mystique. A tiny whiff of murder is fine as long as it's chased with other more palatable experiences."

"Really?" Almira asks.

"Honestly," Danetra takes a cool drink of water. "The public's memory does not last that long. Soon they will only remember that something exciting happened here. It's sad but true. PR works on the premise that this too shall pass. Everything does. So, let's cap off this festival with as much fun as we can. Social media posts are even more important than ever."

I nod.

"Also, get pictures of some of the counselors. We want to assure people that we are taking care of everyone's mental health. We *did* have a tragedy. We are sad. But life goes on and so will we. Maybe even in honor of the deceased," she says.

"You are a marketing genius," I say. "Thank you."

"No worries. Costuming and accounting are all about minimizing risk while maximizing good feelings. This is no different."

"Except it's murder," Kiki says

"*Murder in the Hollow*, maybe that'll be your breakout book, Veronica," The Leach says, guffawing as she does.

"So it will be," Danetra answers. "It is sanctified now." Her smile is bright, and her eyes shine as if she's totally enjoying herself.

In my mind I hear her say, *Watch your back, lady. That one is coming at you full bore.*

I send a message back. *Thanks.* Or at least I think I do. Who knows if Danetra receives it or how any of this works.

We stand. My legs wobble. Danetra's arms steady me. It's been a long time since I've had anyone I can trust. Too long.

"I got you," she says, out loud this time.

I don't answer because I'm a little choked with emotion.

You're not alone.

It's all I can do to keep walking forward. I've never not been alone. Except for Phoebe. And Gran. Now Danetra. Okay, Mystic Hollow, well played. And just like that, the tables turn. Or I do. And I see Mack without his apron. Without the Boston Red Sox sweatshirt he was just wearing. But with his sheriff's uniform.

He motions for me to follow him. "I guess it's my turn," I say.

"Go get 'em girl. We'll go deal with the authors," Danetra says. "Divas, most of them. They may write about high crimes and misdemeanors, but if their matcha latte isn't frothed enough—well. *Apocalypse Now,* baby."

Chapter Nine

When Phoebe's dad left us. I was pretty bitter. I let the anger boil up inside me so much that I knew it wouldn't be good for my growing baby. So I did a stint in group therapy, not being able to afford individual care. One thing the counselor told us over and over again was her favorite motto: *Do the next right thing.*

As in, no matter what is happening in your life. No matter how dire. You simply need to focus on doing the next right thing. Then the next. Then the next. Until sooner or later you'll be standing in a life you don't recognize because it's so good.

That worked for me. More than anything else. I ate healthy for Phoebe's sake. I told my parents and Gran even though I really didn't want to. Besides, Phoebe had a right to know her grandparents, so doing the next right thing meant I brought her to them and let them into her life. Every choice I made was in accordance with that motto.

Now I follow the sheriff down the street to the police station, the building two doors down from the diner. It's the next right thing. I've got the amulet and a vague understanding of how to use it, but I am terrified to even try. He can't think I did this. Can he? I am amazed, literally shocked at how big the station is. I was expecting one or two rooms. It's got a front counter, four desks, two private offices, and two jail cells way in the back.

"This is some setup for a place with no violent crimes."

He glares at me. Opens his door, and motions for me to sit at the chair opposite his desk.

"I feel like I'm in my guidance counselor's office," I say.

"Happy to advise. Don't do drugs. Don't kill people." He swipes the air with a straight, steady motion. "Simple."

"I didn't kill anyone," I say. Then because I'm nervous, I add, "You don't really believe that, do you?"

He grimaces like I'm spoiling all of this. Puts his hand to his temple. There's a knock on the door. "Yes?"

The door opens. A gray-haired woman with a bun on top of her head peeks in. "Does the suspect care for tea or coffee?"

"I never said she was a suspect," Mack answers. "Bring her coffee."

"And water, please," I say, unhooking the amulet and slipping it into my pocket. Yes, it would help me to read his thoughts, but I would feel guilty wearing it, and that would come across.

"Of course," the woman says with a curtness to her tone that wasn't there before.

"Delores," Mack points his knuckle into his temple, rubbing out a knot. "I never said—"

"You're wearing your uniform," Delores says. "That tells me she's a suspect." Then to me. "Don't let him bully you. You know your rights?"

Mack glares at the ceiling, blows out a breath.

"He makes me take a course every year on protocol, and we are supposed to offer you a beverage and ask if you want a lawyer."

"Delores!"

"Well, if you don't want us to take the courses, you shouldn't assign them."

Mack waves at her and she disappears.

"Well, that was entertaining," I point to the door. "More small-town charm, I guess. Only the use of the words *suspect* and *lawyer* will score you down with the judges."

"I never formally said you were a suspect," he says.

I point to his uniform. "It was implied, apparently."

"Just because Delores says—"

I put my hand up. "Not just that. When's the last time you wore that uniform?"

"I'm supposed to be asking the questions here."

"I'd say more than five years. You've got the five-year spread." I point to his shirt. "Women get it all the time, but it's usually in increments of three years. Yay, us. That button is pulling the tiniest bit and I'm assuming that you are far too vain to wear an ill-fitting shirt unless you didn't know it didn't fit anymore." I tilt my head. "Gotta cut down the carbs after thirty."

He shakes his head, but his grin stretches, although it's not exactly the kind of smile that exudes warmth. "I'm wondering if this tactic of constantly insulting me is your best play at this point."

Damn it. He's right. I pretend to zip my lips as Delores comes in with a tray holding two coffee cups, two glasses of water, and a plate of cookies. "For your blood sugar, honey. Anxiety can cause a crash."

Mack puts his feet on his desk, coffee mug in hand. "Next time we're doing this in the interrogation room."

I whip my head around. "Where's that? This place resembles one of those tents in *Harry Potter*. Just unending space. I need to speak with your architect."

Mack sits up, places his mug on his desk. "I have a few questions for you relating to the death of Adam Whitford." He puts his phone next to it. "Do you mind if I record this?"

"I get a choice?"

"Actually, no. I was trying to seem polite. I'm recording this."

"You're lovely," I tell him, sipping my coffee. "And this coffee is amazing! Do you put chicory in it?" I lean forward, resting my chin in my clasped hands. "Do tell."

Big smile on that one but no attempt to answer. Instead, he opens a file and a notebook and clicks his pen. "Would you like to tell me how well you knew Adam?"

"Would I? No. Will I? Yes. We were acquaintances. I wrote a story about one of his book signings in Miami. I also attended conferences where he presented."

"Conferences?"

"You know. Places where people convene to learn stuff. Writing conferences specifically."

I stay quiet as he ruffles through his notes. "You wrote an article about . . ."

"Yes. I wrote for a Miami magazine and newspaper. They asked me to cover his event since I'd met him before. Not that I expected him to remember me. He does a million of those things."

"Did he? Remember you?"

"I don't know. I mean, at that time I wasn't sure. We went for dinner after, but I don't know if that was simply because I was writing an article about him or if he remembered me. Men like that really want the spotlight to shine on them continuously, and they tend to reward the people who are willing to do that."

Mack puts his pen in the dimple on his chin. It's a practiced move, and I wonder if he's even aware he's doing it. "Men like that?"

"Well, to be fair, I have no idea if Adam had always been that way—craving the attention—or if it came with being famous. He won big in terms of advances and publicity. He was a star, and maybe that made him want more in order to keep the entire deal going. I wouldn't know. My fiction hasn't been published yet."

"Did Adam use his position as a star—your word—to get women to . . . or to promise influence in the publishing world?"

"I don't know."

He raises one eyebrow. "Really? You haven't heard anything about that?"

"I have heard things, of course, but I don't know for certain that anything was promised or implied."

Mack nods. "Yes. That's the key, isn't it? What were you doing at the church tower?"

"I don't know if I should have a lawyer for this part."

More nods. "That makes sense." He opens his drawer and pulls out a large evidence bag that holds a phone with a cracked face, a broken lanyard with Adam's name on it, torn brown fabric, and a small crushed tinny thing. He withdraws the phone. "I will tell you that we've already retrieved the messages." He reaches into his drawer and pulls out a transcript which he slides across the table toward me.

I see the back and forth. My face heats. "I'm not usually like that," I say before I can stop myself. "I mean, I don't usually date. I didn't find him attractive in that way before this event."

He holds up his hand. "I'm not certain you should say any more."

"I didn't kill him. I can say that. I didn't even have a motive. You can see by the texts that we hadn't met before this."

"I can imply that much, yes."

"If I was hoping to parlay any interaction with him for help or influence, he would have been more helpful to me alive."

He puts his fingers together and tucks the tips into that chin dimple. "Hmm. Yes, but he was known as a player."

"Not sure how that makes me homicidal. I knew that going in, one might say."

"I'm just spitballing here. Maybe he double booked and that made you feel embarrassed."

"I didn't do it."

"Did you notice anyone else in the belfry?"

"No."

"Did you see anyone leave?"

"No. When I got to the belfry, it was empty. I thought he changed his mind. I was going to go down when I heard the commotion outside. That's when I looked out."

"You were supposed to meet him in the highest building in the Hollow."

"His idea."

"You were the one who brought him to the festival."

"The original keynote speaker canceled last minute. We needed a big name. I reached out to him, thinking he would not do it. Or it would cost too much. But we were desperate."

"Desperate?"

"For the festival to do well. We needed a big draw. The store needed a big win. So did the town. Adam Whitford brought in a big crowd. He agreed to do it for a nominal fee."

"Do you know why he offered that?"

I blush. "He said it was a favor because I'd been so supportive of him."

"In what way?"

"Nothing special. That article I wrote. At conferences. It's a small world, really. Publishing. Those trying to break in. Those already there."

"When he made the plans to be the keynote, did he ask you to meet him privately?"

"Yes."

"Was that typically how you treated other festival guests?"

"This is the first festival I've ever run. But no. Not in the way he implied."

"Were you excited about the implication?"

I have to stop and think. "I don't know. It wasn't like me. But Adam had always been nice. And he wasn't bad looking. And Gran and Phoebe were sort of egging me on . . . So. I guess so." My face heats when I remember the love spell Gran and Phoebe placed on me. They were just trying to help, but at this point, I did, in fact, whether under a spell or not, look like I was as into Adam as all the other lovesick women. That did not make me look good.

"Would you mind showing me your arms and hands?"

I pull my sweater down. I don't have marks on me, but I don't like being asked to bare my skin for anyone. "No. I don't think so."

"Something to hide?"

"It feels improper without an attorney, and if I had suffered any injury from Adam defending his life, it'll still be visible in a day or two when you make it formal."

Mack leans forward and switches off the recording. "Adam's brother, Pete, is coming today, and we have to interview a few more people, but I intend to bring you back as a person of interest."

I pull the sleeves of my sweater over my wrists. A habit I did as a small child that has charmingly found a way back to me now, making me look weak and guilty at the same time. Perfect.

"Your grandmother has been kind to me over the years, so I want to be certain to treat you in the most humane way possible. When I call you back in, you should bring an attorney. Would you like me to give you the number of the public defender?"

I look at my hands. "No. I'll manage."

"Okay," he says.

"Okay," I say, but I grab the cookies. "Parting gifts. Swag."

Mack eyes me like I'm a lunatic, but I don't care. I only care about next steps.

* * *

I stop by the bookstore on the way back to the festival to buy a small notebook and a pen. I need a place to record my thoughts. Tatum is manning the cash register.

"Do you even have to pay?" she asks, her eyes wide like she knows the camera is ready to take her selfie and she doesn't want to look sleepy. Like Amy Adams in *Wedding Crashers*.

"Don't want to be accused of embezzling, do I?" I laugh at my very weak joke.

"Oh," she says. "That makes sense."

Her affirmations feel as fake as her wide-eyed look, but maybe I'm just grumpy. I scoot to the back room to grab one of those frozen PB&J sandwiches with the crusts cut off that I made fun of when they first came out because how hard is it to make a PB&J? Not that hard. Why make the grab-and-go kind? The joke was on me. They are amazing.

Only, when I get back there, I find Gran sitting at the table crying. When I come in, she puts her head in her hands and really starts wailing. "What have I done, Veronica?"

"Gran, what's wrong?"

"Everything." Her eyes flit around the room, finally landing on me. She cups my cheek. "If I hadn't brought you here . . ."

I put my hands on her arms. "It's okay. I'm glad we're here. We wanted to help."

"I may have fibbed a little about my injury," she looks down. "I could have managed without you. Physically."

"Hmm. Really?" My tone is light. "I hadn't realized."

"I'm being serious. I did need your help. For the store. And selfishly I wanted you up here with me."

I sigh. There it is. "Phoebe is loving it here. And so am I. Now, about the bookstore."

"I know. It was in pretty grave shape, but with a few bumps and positive trending . . ."

"You mean when Lana Dellano sold a pallet of books after you did a little—" I wiggle my nose with my finger. "I will never understand how Elizabeth Montgomery could do that."

"No one does. Unless . . ."

"Are you saying Elizabeth Montgomery was really a witch? Because I've never read such an account."

"Celebrities are different. Plus, you don't always know what's going on behind closed doors."

"You're kidding me. Not." I do a snarky smile. Then switch gears. "Gran, do you think she could have done this? Killed Adam?"

"Elizabeth Montgomery? Is she even still alive?"

"Lana Dellano."

"That birdlike woman? I mean, she's all skin and bones. She looks like she can barely lift a spoon to her mouth. Would take a lot of heft to push a man to his death. Right?"

I shiver. "You're right. I hadn't thought of that."

"He'd have to have been facing away from her for a start." Gran stands and pantomimes. She looks over her shoulder. "Push me."

"No, thanks, but I am thinking about what would make a man like Adam vulnerable to attack. And if someone pushed him, why didn't I see anyone? Or hear anything. It would have had to have happened right before I got there."

"These are all good questions. I see you've got yourself a little notebook. Like when you were little."

I blush. I'd forgotten how Gran would always give me something to write in. A small, recycled composition book. Or a moleskin notebook. Until I was disgusted by the name. Gran laughed and told me that was just a description. "Sometimes things can sound like one thing and be another," she'd said.

Or act like something and be something else. That thought is piped in from the ether.

And bam. Just like that I remember how Adam looked right before leaving the book signing. He had a hand to his temple like he was getting a headache. The last book he signed, he had to redo, and it looked like he was having trouble seeing. Someone shined a flashlight on the book to make it easier for him. When he texted me to meet him, I expected him to bail. "He looked bad that night," I tell Gran.

"Adam? I think the general consensus was that he looked yummy."

"Gross. I mean at the end of the book signing. Remember, he kept messing up the signatures."

"It's no big deal. We'll return those to the publisher." Gran waves the concern away.

"No. I mean, it's significant. Maybe. What was he drinking? Who got it for him?"

Gran's eyes lit. "Was he drunk?"

"I don't think so. I mean, he wasn't slurring his words. He didn't gradually get worse. It sort of snuck up on him."

"Oh. You mean someone put something in it? Are they doing a tox screen?"

"No idea. I do know Mack said I was a person of interest—and before you jump in, he did not mean that in a complimentary way."

"Hmm. You and Mack I hadn't thought. I mean, I've never seen him with anyone."

I snap my fingers to bring her back. "There will be none of that. You and Phoebe will not be colluding against me in the future. That stops now."

"Oh, dear, we would never collude against you." She tsk-tsked me.

"You are impossible, but I need my energy to figure this out. Who wanted Adam dead? Did they possibly dose him with something to make it easier to kill him? And how did they know we were meeting in the bell tower?"

"All excellent questions. Did the amulet help?"

My hand goes to my neck, where its absence feels significant. I take it out of my pocket and latch it on. "I was scared to use it with Mack. Felt illegal."

Gran smiles at me. "Aww. What a great meet-cute."

I cross my arms. "None. Of that. Now, do we know who else dabbles in the Hollow?" I ask. "I definitely picked up on some vibes from Danetra."

"Maybe, but it's impolite to ask."

"Witchy etiquette. Interesting. Okay. My phone is blowing up. I gotta go. You coming?"

"Yes. I just need to get my—"

"Your walker. Not buying it."

"You are so suspicious," Gran says. "But I do feel strong enough to make it one block without it. I'll just take my cane if that won't upset you."

"I think that's wise.

Chapter Ten

As we make it to town hall, I head straight to the authors' break room. Lana Dellano is there, thankfully. As are a bunch of other authors. Everyone is discussing Adam's death. When I walk in, the chatter winds down, but the groups of people remain intact—little circles of doom for me, the person who has to get them in the mood to sell themselves while they are likely scared and feeling targeted.

"Good morning, all. How are you all doing?" I wait to test the mood. To see if we have any authors who need emotional triage, but they stay silent.

The Leach speaks up. "We have arranged for some counselors should you need to speak to anyone."

Dan Johnson looks away. He was friends with Adam, I know. They also shared an editor—Nicholas Turner—and an agent, Marilyn Edwards. It was the big talk at one of the conferences years ago when they were both discovered during a table read with Marilyn. She supposedly fawned over Dan's work until Adam read his. Then her attention shifted, as agents are known to do. Still, she requested both manuscripts. She sold Adam's manuscript for a large advance, marketing, and royalties, and while Dan got much less, he did still have a decent midlist career. The two remained friends throughout it all. So the story goes.

"You okay, Dan?" I ask, putting my hand on his arm.

"We started together, "Dan says. "In the same critique group."

"I didn't know that" I tell him, playing with the amulet for extra insight. "I know what those groups are like. Close. Like family."

That makes him laugh. "Like family, all fighting for the lion's share of the Thanksgiving meal."

"Exactly. What was he like back then?"

"He had better premises than I did, but everyone in the group thought my writing was sharper. You know, more compelling. More human." He takes a drink of coffee and I notice small tremors in his hand. Are those from a condition? Is he just emotional? "I had to rewrite so many of his sentences. He was a rough writer."

I put my hand on his arm again. As I do, the amulet vibrates against my skin. I am hit with a wave of feeling. I expect sadness, but what I'm feeling is excitement.

No loss for the masses. His books were formulaic. Nothing special. His face brightens. *My turn now. Finally. Hated sharing Nick with him. Maybe he'll finally push my books.*

My mind searches for purchase. The amulet is doing this. It's no parlor trick. I can read people's minds. Sometimes. Specifically, after I make contact with them. That's how it works. Aha!

Lana approaches, bumping my shoulder. "So sorry," she says. Her hands fall on my arms. "I'm such a klutz."

Her head thoughts are sharper than Dan's. *Horrible man. Finally got his due. Used his wife's death to become the new literary darling. Rigged game.* She pastes a sad look on her face. "So sorry for your loss," she tells me.

I put my hands over hers. "We are all feeling the loss," I say sharply. "No more mine than others. I barely knew him."

Me thinks she doth protest too much?

"Of course. What can I do to help?" Lana the hypocrite asks.

"Just be your wonderful self," I coo, hoping somehow in the depths of her rotten heart she realizes that was meant as a dig.

She blushes. I almost pump my hand and say *Score*, but I stop myself. This mind-reading gift is the best thing ever, and I need to tell Phoebe that the movies and books that use it as a device do not do it justice!

The door opens. Murmurs rise.

Well, look who's here, Dan thinks. At least I think it's Dan.

"Is that who I think it is?" I think out loud.

"Who are *they*?" Danetra asks.

Lana grabs Danetra's arm now in a way that makes it seem like they are close friends instead of just having met. "Adam's editor and agent. Nicholas Turner and Marilyn Edwards in the flesh."

Danetra whispers. "Did they RSVP?"

"I don't think so." I search my spreadsheet for their names. "Ah. Just RSVP'd last night." Interesting. Were they here for his keynote? Were they supposed to meet up with him? None of this makes sense. If they were here last night, why didn't Adam make plans to meet them? Or maybe he did.

"Interesting. No?" Lana purrs.

"A surprise for sure," I say before I can control my outburst. "I mean, it's so great to have them here."

I really need access to my notebook. How will I possibly remember all of this?

Dan leans against the table in the back, and I get the sense that he is purposely not approaching them. *Let them come to me this time*, he thinks, and now I'm privy to those thoughts even from across the room. Does this thing have a range? So many questions.

The two publishing execs beeline to their surviving author, and I am able to hear his smug thoughts. *Now they love me. Now I'm their star.*

The energy he exudes is spiteful with a splash of regret. But what exactly does he regret? Could he be responsible for Adam's death? Could he be a murderer?

The room is bustling with private and semiprivate conversations. All the authors. The committee members. The mayor's daughter, who somehow managed to rebound from her migraine long enough to attend. Cassandra Fetterly. Kiki. The Leach. All the players. Phoebe and Kim are doing the grunt work while we do the schmoozing.

My phone dings. A notification about a write-up online: "Murder in a Sleepy Hollow." Perfect. We've made the mainstream. I show Danetra.

"Yeah. I'm aware. Just keep dancing." *And listening.* "And mingling."

She's right. This power to tune into people is not for nothing. It is a gift at a time where private thoughts may be deadly. I need to try and find out if any of these people did this horrible thing.

If the amulet works on touch, I need to find ways to physically connect with as many people as possible. A light bump. A hand on an arm or back. I manage to make contact with most of the people in the authors' room, but that results in a cacophony of thoughts.

How exciting!

Scary!

Are we safe?

Should I put this on my socials?

Great idea for a book.

Hate her. Hate him.

Do they know? Can they tell?

Stop looking guilty.

I can't tell who is thinking those things. No clue whatsoever, so maybe I should narrow the search. Go person by person.

Dan is speaking with his agent. I insert myself into the conversation as one of the festival committee members and an aspiring author. Either role allows me to pop my hand out. "Veronica Blackthorne," I say.

"We've met, yes?" Marilyn shakes my hand.

I can't help feeling flattered she remembered. "Yes, at a conference."

"I thought so. Thank you so much for your careful stewardship of my authors." I hear her think. *Horrid people. Vultures. All of them.*

Dan slurps his coffee. Then his thoughts flood in. *She means him. Ugh. How can death make him more desirable. He'll probably sell out entirely. Get more print runs. The money will go to his brother. No one else. It's not like he has a family.*

From Nicholas: *Maybe we should do another printing. Death sells. At least I stopped him before he ruined us. Good thing. No coming back from that. Would have been fired for sure. No loyalty.*

Ignorant untalented hack. Brute. From someone else.

Then back to Marilyn. *No idea what he's doing.*

"If you'll excuse me," Marilyn says. "I want to thank Lana for filling in. I heard your last book was a huge success," she coos at the author. "What are your plans for the next one?"

Could this be my break? Would love to be with her. Lana. At least I think it is. I can't exactly zoom in like with a camera.

I'm not surprised. Was bound to happen.

He used people. What an ego.

It's a relief. How can I think that way? A man is dead. I'm the worst. Although . . .

It's like I'm living in a psychic musical. I almost expect people to break out in song, but I am busy deflecting thoughts from the bodies in the room. Who knew authors were so insecure? I guess I should know that. I force myself to shake more hands as I make my way across the room. I pick up feelings now. Sadness. Depression. And something else. An anger. But I can't tell who that belongs to. A rage. In this room, which has doubled in capacity.

The deal's sunk now. Couldn't keep his eye on the prize. Swore he was done with all of that. Waste of my time.

Who thought that? I look around and have no clue. This is all so confusing.

The Leach parts the crowd and crooks her finger. "You're wanted. Something about the angels."

"If you'll excuse me, I have to attend to a few things." I pull Danetra over with my gaze. "Danetra will be happy to answer any and all questions."

I bump my way out of the room, texting Phoebe as I do. Meet me. ASAP. I am sharing my location with her so she'll find me. I'm dizzy from eavesdropping. I need some space. She is more than capable of dealing with the angels—the volunteers in charge of helping the authors.

The last few thoughts hit me as I exit the room:

Got what he deserved.

Couldn't have happened to a nicer dude.

Good riddance to bad rubbage.

Isn't it rubbish? I think. Who said rubbage? This feels important, but I slip out of the room, grateful for the relief from the voices in my head.

"Okay, people. The first panels are starting. Places, everyone," The Leach says.

As I make my way out on a wave of people, the clasp on my amulet somehow releases and it falls to the floor. Before I can do anything it gets kicked down the hallway. I try to catch it, but it skates along the ground, pushed along by festival attendees. Aw. Poor thing. Also, poor me. The only tool I had to figure this out is now gone.

Chapter Eleven

It's only noon in what feels like the longest day ever. The events have been going on for two hours. When Gran and I step outside, there is a bustle of activity. Pop-up tents are set up with tables selling local wares. There's a green market. A cool wind blows, and I hear a hoot. When I scan the trees, I see Stella perched near the library.

"Do owls usually follow their . . . person?"

"Not generally. But then Stella and Phoebe are both exceptional."

I can't argue with that. More hoots. "Is she telling us something?"

"It seems so. Let's not keep her waiting, dear."

Is it weird that my grandmother who is rehabbing an injured leg regardless of the exaggerated severity is literally pulling me across the town square? I've got to try those plunge pools.

When I get to the library, I see Phoebe and Kim. Phoebe rushes to me. "Mom. I was worried." She holds up the amulet. "Found this."

It's smashed. Stomped on. "I don't think that will work anymore."

Kim offers, "Probably not."

I look around. In addition to the planned vendors, there's a new table with a dry-erase sandwich board and coordinated colored pinback buttons. Pink and blue.

"What's this?"

"Don't worry about it, Mom. It's nothing. Small-town nonsense. You know." Phoebe and Kim block the board.

"Move," I say.

Gran sees it first and says, "Oh, dear."

The board is broken up into two categories. Veronica vs. Mack. "What? We're not in a competition."

"I'd say not," Cassandra Fetterly appears next to me. "But take heart, you're new in town."

"Not really," I complain. "I mean, I've been coming here forever."

"I'd say it's closer than it looks." Cassandra shakes the bin of pinback buttons. "There's been an uptick in pink pin requests lately. Don't lose heart."

Gran plunks down a ten-dollar bill.

"Color?"

"All pink, of course," she says with a slightly perturbed air. "How much have we raised?"

"A thousand dollars for the town. Just think, we are closer to getting the roof on the gazebo fixed. We had these pins left over from Tallulah's dog's gender reveal for her litter, so we thought, why not recycle them for a cause."

"How many puppies could that little thing have?" I ask.

"One, as it turns out. A girl," Cassandra adds.

"Not a bad haul for the town for no cost," Gran says grudgingly.

I want to ask about the ultimate cost—Adam's life. That complaint rises in my throat and begs to be voiced. Also, isn't this insensitive? Why am I the only suspect? Before I can state my objections, a car pulls up and a man gets out. He's got curly hair and glasses. Nerdy author type for sure, but I recognize him right away. Adam's brother, Pete Whitford. Podcaster. He scans the crowd, his glance landing on me. We met once before at a conference. Nothing memorable. A year or two ago. We all had drinks in the bar after the event. Adam was there. Lana also. Nicholas Turner and Marilyn Edwards were there too. So weird that so many of the same players are here today. I suddenly realize I've spent more time with and around Adam than I copped to.

Mack jogs forward, his gaze not landing on me this time, but on The Leach. She puts her hand to her throat and leans into Rusty, taking his arm as she whispers something. He nods and she walks forward, head held high. Jaw tight.

"Is she giving thou dost protest too much vibes?" I ask Phoebe.

"Maybe."

Gran walks over to Rusty to get the scoop. Loving her commitment to the cause as well as her thumb on the pulse of all things Mystic Hollow. It will help, for sure.

Kim's phone pings. "Poison. Interesting," Kim says. "Or at least a toxin."

"Based on?" I ask.

"Prelim results from the autopsy."

"Already?"

"Presence of a toxin shows up almost immediately, but confirmation of the specific type takes a few days." Kim's eyes follow The Leach and Mack, who are having a slightly heated debate as she simultaneously reads the long messages on her phone. "Most people are guessing belladonna." She chews her lip as she thinks. "It tracks."

"How do you know all of this?" I ask.

"My cousin's friend's sister works at the lab in Norwalk that did the analysis. It was supposed to be top secret. But . . . small town."

Small town. Small police force. Small pool of suspects, according to the consensus. I am in trouble. Except I don't know anything about toxins in general and that toxin in particular. "Belladonna? Who has access to that?"

Kim shrugs. "Who doesn't?"

I'm about to ask her if she means because of the witchy trend here or because of the local horticulture, but then Phoebe thrusts her phone in my hand. "I've started a suspect list. The Leach is top of my list. But it doesn't end there."

I hold up my little notebook. "Same."

"Apparently, there are rumors that a few of the women who were angry that he didn't return their affection were in attendance, intending to cause a stir. They were also upset about his flaunting of his wife's death as well as stealing ideas from a woman he critiqued once. It's a whole thing."

"What?" I look at her phone. "WUAA. Women Unite Against Adam."

"The man certainly inspired his fair share of hashtags," Kim says.

We watch as a deputy approaches Gran. Her face turns pasty white then red as she argues with him. She slices the air. "Absolutely not. I won't have you tramping through my garden on a whim."

I jog to meet her. "What's the matter?" I ask.

She ignores me. Takes her phone out, places a call. "Now. Yes."

I get in front of her. "They want to search your house?"

"Not exactly. Not inside anyway."

"What?" Phoebe asks.

My stomach drops. "The garden?"

Gran nods.

"Should we be worried?" I ask.

"It depends on which garden they check." Gran looks down. "Honestly. Who doesn't have a little deadly nightshade growing in their beds? It's ubiquitous. Besides, I told them no. They'll have to speak to your lawyer."

I give her a look. "I have a lawyer?"

"You do now. Sloan Rodgers. Dapper guy. Good dancer too."

"That's great, if we have a dance marathon, he'll be our guy."

Gran laughs. "Yes. I actually came in second with him as a partner one year." Her face gets dreamy. "So light on his feet."

"Gran. Focus," I can't believe I'm having to tell her that. Usually, it's the other way around. "The garden."

"Oh, forget that. Belladonna here is as plentiful as daisies in other places. We all planted it after reading *Practical Magic*. Lavender in the corners of our houses too. Are they going to get all worked up over that as well?"

"Daisies and lavender didn't kill a prominent author."

"Well, there's no way they'd implicate you anyway," Phoebe tells me. "You can't steep tea let alone brew a batch of deadly nightshade. Especially if you had to keep the plant alive long enough to grow berries. Do they know about the wasteland of vegetation you've left behind? About the plant tribunal you'll eventually have to face? I've got receipts."

"Hey!" I say. "Is that a knock on my gardening skills?"

Phoebe gives me a thumbs-up.

"Well, alright then," I say, but I'm not as sturdy as I pretend to be. An insinuation. The townspeople wearing pins implicating me. A sheriff who said I'm a person of interest. I hold the now broken amulet. I could use a little help. "Bookstore?" I say.

"That's an excellent idea," Gran says.

Kim and Phoebe surround me, and I feel protected. Stella hoots. "Are we the new Scooby gang?" I ask.

Blank expression from Kim. Phoebe explains, "Old-people thing."

"I get the reference," Kim answers. "I'm just not sure it's our vibe." She puts a hand on my arm. "But if it makes you feel better, I call Velma. Although, to be honest, I feel like I embody Batman's butler, Alfred, more than anyone else."

That makes Phoebe laugh harder than I've seen in years and despite the very real threat to my liberty, I'm grateful for the magic of this very weird town.

As we enter the bookstore, Gran tells Tatum, "You may go, dear. We are closing for the day. Out of respect. They might need help at the festival if you still want hours."

"I'm good," she says. "I might try to fit in a plunge session if Kiki's is open."

My head whips around. "Does everyone here do those plunges?"

"Most. It's how we keep our healthy glow," Gran says.

Kim does a spit take. Then recovers after Gran glowers at her. "Water. It's essential." She holds up her water bottle as proof.

Phoebe smirks.

"I hate to break up the fun, but we are in dire need of specific supplies." I say.

"On it," Kim says. "What is required?"

"Post-its, colored pens, tacos, and laptops," Phoebe says.

"That's my girl. But did you forget coffee and chocolate? And heavy on the tacos." I hand Phoebe my card and off they go.

Gran settles in the back room of the store. I remember coming here as a kid, hiding in back, reading. First it was *The Chronicles of Narnia*. Later it was *Harry Potter*. Then *Twilight*. I was supposed to help Gran in the store, but she let me read all day, surfacing at the end of a book, too sad to help once it was over. End-of-book depression was a big thing for me.

"Those were simpler times, weren't they, dear?" Gran reads my mind.

"I'm scared," I admit, now that it's just me and her. "They can't think I did this, right?"

"Mack's too smart to entertain that thought for too long. Also, let's break it down. They would need motive, means, and opportunity."

I hold up one finger. "Motive—romantic jealousy."

"No one who knows you would believe that. It took a love spell to get you to even consider meeting him."

"Nobody here knows me, though." I hold up another finger. "Means—the belladonna in your garden, which they will find any moment now."

"Once again, it's hardly a smoking gun. We all grow it. You won't need the Dream Team to get you cleared with such weak evidence."

"Opportunity." I perch my chin on knees that I've pulled into my body. "When could I have given him the spiked drink? I wasn't with him all night."

"That's right!" Gran says. "Plus, if you'd given him a poisonous drink, why would you have to push him? Wouldn't he just naturally pass?"

I drop my feet to the floor. "Do we know how much belladonna is lethal?"

"We could look it up." She takes out her phone, but I wave it away.

"I don't think that's a good idea. Search history."

"Even after the fact?"

"Let's be safe. Surely, we have a book in here that—"

Gran appears in front of me. "I'm not sure that's any better. Maybe we should focus on who else had means, motive, and opportunity."

"A list. Excellent." I open my notebook and write "Suspects" at the top in the center. "Number one . . . The Leach."

"Wonderful!" Gran says. "But what's her motive?"

"Does evil need a motive?"

"Put a question mark there. Means. Also, unknown. Opportunity. She was next to him for a startling amount of time last night."

"Yes!" I do a fist pump.

Gran drags my hands down. "Let's see who else might make the list."

"His editor and agent. Motive? You know, I think he said something about a passion project on his socials. No specifics, I remember that, but just that he was wrapping up his contract and working on something intensely personal that was less commercial. Maybe they didn't want that to happen?"

"The agent or the editor?"

"Either or both," I say as I add their names.

Some of the thoughts I overheard in the authors' room seep in, but there are so many and I can't make sense of them.

"What's up, dear?"

"Before I dropped the amulet, I heard some things that might be clues. Like his editor was definitely angry and also relieved that whatever was going to come out no longer would."

"We're getting somewhere, like one of those detectives in books. So exciting!"

"Playing Nancy Drew might be more fun under different circumstances."

Gran adjusts her expression from excited to serious. She points to the page where I've written Nicholas's name. "That's motive. But means and opportunity?"

I pull up the records from the festival. "We gave everyone bracelets, right?"

"Very popular." Gran nods.

"Well, they weren't just giveaways. They were also to collect data and track movements, etc." The data is complicated. Plus, only specific people had named trackers, but it might be helpful. "Should we give this to the police?"

"Let's vet the information first," Gran says as if she's been involved in murder investigations her entire life.

Kim and Phoebe burst in the front door and make a fast track to the back of the store, their arms full and their mouths moving. "You're missing it!" Bags of take-out food, supplies, and a coffee tray go on the table, and hands pull me outside. There's a crowd gathered around Pete, Adam's brother, who has a microphone.

"He brought a sound system?" I say. "Impressive. I would've thought bullhorn, but the clarity is better."

Phoebe rolls her eyes. "He's a podcaster. He knows about sound."

We spill out onto the street and make our way to the front of town hall in time to see the show.

Pete starts talking. "Adam was my big brother. I am bereft." He pauses. Gets choked up. A young woman in a large puffy jacket with a faux-fur lined hood puts her boom mike down and stands next to him. She moves the hair out of her face and whispers something to him. He waves her away, an annoyed expression on his face.

He must realize he's coming across as gruff, because he corrects his course. "Thank you, Sarah." He clears his throat and starts again. "I am offering a twenty-five-thousand-dollar reward for any information that leads to the arrest of the killer."

Mack makes a disgusted face.

Pete continues. "I know a tip line takes manpower so I am willing to lend the town my resources in the form of assistants and producers from my podcast."

Mayor Racker steps forward, clapping, smile wide. "Thank you so much, Pete. I hereby authorize my entire staff to help with the tips in a rolling work schedule. Laurel?" She calls to her daughter. "Please organize."

"Right." She ducks into the town hall building.

Mack steps in front of Pete. "Let the police handle this. Fairfield County Police Department can help you set up the tip line and reward. Please." He opens his arms and tries to direct Pete to shut down the show.

"Why is Mack opposed to a reward?" I ask Danetra.

She shrugs. "I think it makes for more of a mess to work through. Plus, it gives people who might be suspects access to information that is sensitive."

A thought sparks. If Mack wants to control the flow of information, that must mean I am not the sole suspect. But who does that leave? A wind blows. I hear the noises around me. Mack fighting with Pete to turn his sound system off. The people huddled around the booths, Clayton selling actual bags of popcorn, which would be hysterical if it wasn't so serious. Festive happy sounds primarily but muted by the sadness in the atmosphere.

"Look, I didn't want to say this, but you have a pretty sizeable motive, being the heir," Mack says.

"How could I do it?" Pete asks. "I was three hundred miles away."

"I am waiting for confirmation on your alibi."

A crowd forms behind Pete now. Including some townspeople, which feels strange, but maybe sweet? Pete turns to one of his camera people. "Keep filming. Let's show our fans what happens when a small-town sheriff can't lock down a murder investigation."

"Alright, that's enough of that. You can't do a podcast without a permit and proper authorization from the city council. We're done here." Mack nods to his deputies who confiscate the equipment. "You can have that back when the investigation is complete."

Mayor Racker nods, a sage little smile painted on her face. "It's true. You *would* need a permit."

"Let's talk about this at the station," Mack motions for Pete to follow him. "No one wants to get to the bottom of this more than I do."

Pete follows him, head down. The boom-carrying woman, with the mic raised, and his cameraman, still filming, follow him. Something about the scene feels rehearsed. Pete makes eye contact as he passes, and I get the distinct impression that he wants to speak with me. Good. Goes both ways. I open my notebook and write. Were Pete and Adam close?

"It's a good question," Danetra says, noticing my scribbles. "You should question everyone's motives."

I raise an eyebrow and shoot her a look.

"Except moi, of course." She laughs. Then leans in close. "I heard Pete talking earlier. He said something about Fox N Sox Books—something Adam was going to disclose."

I try not to grin.

She speaks again. "But just don't get too focused on one person. It's not always the most obvious answer. It could be someone hiding in plain sight."

Danetra puts her hand on my shoulder. The warmth paired with the words sparks a memory. Going to the belfry. Catching my breath after the climb. The artificial forest scent. Like one of those horrible air fresheners.

I start to tap my shoulders. I'd done some EMDR therapy after Phoebe's dad left us. It allowed me to open up memories and see things I overlooked at the time. Red flags when it came to her father. Now I use that technique, the tapping, to open up the belfry memory. My back to the staircase. Looking out the window.

The scene below. It all bubbles up inside me. Then something else comes. Breathing. Behind me. I don't turn. I keep looking out the window. Fear. All I feel is fear. Is that Adam? Is he okay? The music from the bonfire. Screams from the crowd—both happy when they won something at the carnival and scared when they come upon Adam. It's like a chord of music, blended, but I know that isn't correct. It should all be separated into tracks.

I don't pay attention to the very soft sounds of someone trying to contain their breathing. Hiding. Someone was hiding. Now that I attune my senses, I feel their presence. Someone was in the belfry when I was, maybe pressed against the wall, waiting for me to descend. Waiting. The glint of metal—maybe that same tin thing in Mack's evidence bag, caught by the tiniest moonbeam, almost like a spotlight.

"It's easy to become overwhelmed in the moment," Danetra says. "It's human."

"Hmm," I hear myself saying, but it feels like I'm far away, floating above the clouds.

"It was an upsetting time. But if you stretch your memory, you may see things you missed at the time. Things that will make this make sense."

I remember Adam earlier in the evening. Drinking kombucha. Someone handed him a cup of it. But am I imagining this? Creating false memories? It feels glitchy. Like I'm almost there but not quite. "Did you see anyone handing him drinks?" I ask.

"I was barely with him," Danetra says, lifting her hand off my shoulder. "But plenty of people were. Who was supposed to be his angel?"

"One of the teen volunteers from the library."

"I remember that. Listen, your mind may have the answer. Be open to receiving information from surprising sources."

I turn to face her, full on. "Thanks," I say, humbled by how kind she's being to me, a relative stranger, and one with a target on her back. I'm not used to this level of support. Nor am I used to letting people help me.

"Of course. One day you may repay the favor," she says.

Gran, Phoebe, and Kim come walking back to me, eyes shining. "The poison was not belladonna," Phoebe says. "Angel's trumpet. Gran doesn't have that."

Angel's trumpet. I know I've seen that somewhere recently. I read it online, I think. Maybe on social media? It's all foggy, but I know I read it and thought about it and looked it up. Which will make my search history look suspicious. Perfect. But really, I'm wondering if I can jog that particular memory and figure out who was talking about the deadly plant that killed Adam right before his murder, because if there's one thing I got from all those nights rewatching *Monk* reruns is that there are no coincidences.

Chapter Twelve

Before we can make it to the bookstore, I get a call from a number I don't recognize, so I let it go to voicemail. It's Adam's brother. He wants to meet up. I let Phoebe hear it.

"Interesting," she says. "Already cleared by the police?"

"He was doing a live event yesterday," Kim says. "I checked it."

"Ironclad alibi. Sometimes those are the most suspicious, if you believe the detective shows," Phoebe points out.

"True, but I'm wondering how that plays in real life. He wants to meet now. At a bar outside of town. Smart," I say. "Prying eyes and all."

"Small town," Kim nods.

"Can you guys do the closing ceremonies without me? Say I have migraine or am in police custody?" I wink so they know I'm joking. Mostly.

"Sure. But what about your tacos?" Phoebe kids. She shows me her taco haul from Mike's Tacos.

My hand goes to my stomach. The bag announces best tacos in Mystic Hollow and then "ask about our tater tot tacos." "What kind of metric is that, anyway? It's not like we're known for tacos in the Hollow, are we?"

Phoebe's hand lands on my shoulder. "Whatever helps you sleep at night. Oh, and don't leave your drink alone with him . . . or your food. Hold your water, missy."

"Maybe I should just grab one for the ride?"

"We'll save you some," Phoebe says. "Kim says they're better cold, anyway."

Kim tries to keep her face neutral, but gives me a thumb's-up.

Collusion!

I race back to Gran's house, grab my keys, and head out to the Our Little Secret Bar, aptly named and known by locals as the best place for clandestine meetings. Is Pete a local or does he just have good sources?

There are five cars in the parking lot as I pull in. All SUV types except one white pickup truck. I don't know what car he's driving or if he took an Uber, so that doesn't give me much information, other than it's not going to be crowded.

When I get inside, the hostess asks, "Veronica?"

I nod.

"Follow me." She leads me into the back room away from the pool tables and the bar. There are a few booths and a large table that looks like it's used for big parties. It's pretty dark so it would be hard to see anyone unless you really tried. Also, there's only one person seated.

Pete stands as I get closer, but I wave for him to sit. "I'm glad you came," he says.

The waitress returns with a highball glass of what looks like Coke and Jack Daniels for him. I remember that was his drink, so that tracks. "What will it be?"

Is it weird that I don't want anything that is already opened? Do I really believe he paid the waitress to drug my water? I'm losing it. But I do feel the need to be careful.

"Um, I think I'll just have some sparkling water. Pellegrino if you have it."

"I do. Anything to eat?"

My stomach betrays me.

"Let's share a pizza," he says, and that feels about as safe as I can get since he'll be eating from the same dish.

"Perfect."

As soon as she leaves, he looks me straight in the eyes and says, "I didn't do it. I didn't pay anyone to do it to him. I am not going to poison you."

I laugh. "Was I that obvious?"

His turn to smile. "Yup. But I get it. You don't know me. I mean, not really. One night in a bar basking in the shadow of my brother's wild success does not make a relationship."

The waitress brings my Pellegrino, twists it open and pours it over ice. Hmm. I decide even if he poisoned me, he'd be implicating himself, and now that we are speaking, it seems unlikely.

I take a sip. "So, you and Adam weren't close?"

"Ha!" he says. "Not exactly. He aggravated me on the regular. First, he stole my girlfriend—his wife, the one who died, was dating me before he took her."

"Wow. That's harsh."

"Adam looked out for Adam always. When Marie died, the way he mourned her was even worse than when he took her." He takes a healthy swig of his drink. "And the flock of women who fell for his . . . marketing ploy. It was disgusting. I told him so many times."

"You didn't feel his public mourning was authentic?"

He laughs like I'm the most naïve person in the world. "Are you kidding me? He stole everything. My girl. The plots for all of his books—derivative. And then the branding idea straight from that cheesy movie—*Sleepless in Seattle*."

It takes me a moment to let that sink in. "You're not saying that Adam didn't love Marie, are you?"

"No. Of course he did. It was impossible not to love her. He gets no credit for that." He swipes the air.

"His books were all highly commercial."

"Yes. But all modeled after other books. The first one was based on *Tell No One*. The second based on *Presumed Innocent*. He switched the roles and flipped the script, but none of them were his ideas. In fact, his agent and editor, at the very beginning, fed him ideas—why don't you write the same premise but set it somewhere else."

"Agents do that?"

"This agent did. And this editor. He told me about it. Cried one night about how vacuous it all was. How he wanted to write his own stuff. Even if it didn't sell that well. He was tired of being their show horse."

"Why would they do that?"

"Word is they needed a big hit and his backstory with Marie made him super sympathetic. Everyone wanted to see him succeed. That fueled sales. The rest, as they say, is history."

"If he was going to pivot to a passion project, how would they have taken it?"

The smile he gives me is a crocodile one, jagged and sorrowful. "He had already fired his agent. Had turned in his last book and told the editor he was out. He had finally grown a backbone and some humanity."

"How do you know this if you weren't close?"

"He met with me before meeting with Marilyn. Said he wanted to honor Marie's memory and he was going to stop the circus. He was going to write a book about a man who goes to the ends of the earth trying to find a fabled resurrection stone so he could be with his wife again."

"Wow."

"I don't know the details, but his eyes lit up when he talked about it. Said he'd take it to a small press when he was done with it. Let the masses decide for themselves if his writing was worthy. If his story was good. And he apologized to me. For Marie."

The pizza arrives, and we spend the next few minutes eating in silence. Finally, I say, "Who do you think would do this?"

"I don't know. He told me he had some dirt on Fox N Sox Books sales practices. Really awful ways they are controlling the market. He had proof of tampering with bestseller lists. He agreed to come on my podcast and reveal all he knew. It was going to be glorious."

I let that sink in. "Wow. So many motives right there. But if he had receipts, as the kids say, where were they?"

"He wouldn't show me until the podcast. Was worried I'd leak them first, I guess. Always had to have his due."

"Would you have?"

A pirate smile this time. "Maybe. It was fair. But he said he had them somewhere safe and would make them available when we needed them. We. He hadn't used that pronoun in years." He takes another large drink. "I was hopeful that we could mend fences. Maybe even work together. After our parents died, we were all we had."

"I'm so sorry."

He wipes his eyes. "I get access to his phone records in three days. Have already filed the paperwork as his heir. I know he kept ideas on his phone. So maybe there will be something there. After that, I need to access his accounts and find out where he was storing his stuff."

Suddenly, I get worried. "If someone killed your brother to hide knowledge that you will get access to in a few days . . ."

He nods. Points at me. "Bingo. The clock is ticking."

I go silent.

"You gotta crack this case or I'm a goner." He mimes having a heart attack. "No pressure."

"Me? Why not Mack? The police?"

He shakes the ice in his glass and then extracts the remnants of his drink. "I do not feel they are as motivated as you are."

"Why is that?"

He leans against the booth. "Let's see." He holds up one finger. "Scene of the crime." Another finger. "Romantically spurned."

I scoff.

He holds up one more finger. "You ran the festival where he was killed and therefore had access to all of the people, places, and things."

"It seems like a frame job. Mack will see through that."

He drains the rest of the drink and sets it down on the table. "I'm sure you're right. But if not, I'd find a good lawyer."

"Ouch," I say. "I thought we were actually getting along."

He softens his look. "Sorry, love. I'm mourning the loss of my brother. I don't have the bandwidth to be a decent human being right now. Catch me in a few years. But believe this—whatever I find, I will be making public immediately on my podcast. So, until then, I plan to stay hidden." He hands me a phone. "How you can get to me."

"A burner phone?" I ask. "Did you really just hand me a burner phone?"

"I use them all the time in my business. People don't like to be tracked. Feels like that would be smart in this current environment. Yeah?"

I nod. "I guess."

He holds up his own flip phone. "My number is already in it." He points. Calls from his phone. It jumps in my hand. "Or just redial."

I'm still staring at thing in my hand that feels like a bomb ready to go off when he throws a bunch of money on the table and leaves before I can get myself together and follow him. Did the person next in line to be murdered just hand me the only way to reach him via a sketchy phone? Does that make him a suspect? Or does it mean he's smart to be scared? All of a sudden everything feels more menacing than before. The secluded meetup place. The patrons at the bar. I walk a little faster to my car, check the back to make certain no one is in there, and lock it the minute I close the door. If Pete was trying to scare me, he succeeded. Or maybe he's just being smart and careful. Either way, I've got to keep track of all of this somehow because I am beginning to feel overwhelmed. I imagine Kim saying, "To the Batcave."

Chapter Thirteen

I make it back to the Hollow in time to join the closing ceremonies. There's a small bonfire lit between the library and the town hall. People are milling around and the gang's all here. The mayor, The Leach, Mack, Danetra, an older woman standing next to her that I haven't met yet, Kiki, Cassandra Fetterly, Tallulah, Lana, most of the other authors, Phoebe, Kim, and Gran.

A warmth fills me as I approach my girls. A hoot alerts me to Stella's watchful presence. *Thanks, Stel,* I think.

"You just missed the eulogies," Gran whispers. "Informal ones, I mean."

"Where are Marilyn and Nicholas?"

Kim leans in. "Just left."

"Mack didn't question them?"

"He did, but he couldn't hold them."

I almost ask how she knows this, but I don't bother. Small town. "Who else did he question?"

"It's easier to say who he didn't question," Kim says. "That would be me, Gran, Phoebe, and Tallulah. Just for the record."

"Interesting," I say.

"How did your thing go?" Phoebe asks.

"Later. How were the tacos?"

Phoebe does a chef's kiss. "If they aren't the best in New England, I don't know which are. They should have named this place Foodie Hollow."

"Mike's is insanely good," Kim offers. "Got a write-up in a *Bon Appetite* article. Sometimes, when he's sick of tacos, he switches to other things. One time it was all different versions of shepherd's pie. Another time it was curries."

"Good to know." I take a breath in. "I thought they didn't want to do this bonfire too far from the fire department."

"Since the bonfire was cut short last night, they thought they'd tone it down and allow for a smaller one here," Gran says. "We had an emergency business community meeting."

Something about that feels wrong. Why did Gran get this invitation to the committee and not the other one?

"How?" I ask.

"How what, dear?" Gran asks.

"How were you notified about this emergency meeting?"

"Text and email. The usual way." Gran takes a sip of what appears to be hot cocoa. Adult version. She hands it to me. I inhale its promising scent. Tia Maria. Love that in my coffee as well.

"Why didn't you get the invite to the meeting that allowed The Leach to head the committee?" I ask after taking a sip of the heavenly beverage.

"I don't know. You're right. I should have been invited."

"That feels intentional," I say. "Collusion. And not in the cute way that you and Phoebe do it."

Phoebe blows me a kiss.

"It's not like I could have blocked it. Weird to intentionally leave me off, don't you think?"

"Yes. But maybe it's a pattern. Something to think about in terms of the bigger picture."

"Agreed. Everything matters. Everyone's a suspect," Gran says, laying her hand on Phoebe's hair. "Except maybe these two."

Phoebe puts her hand under her chin and poses as if to show how innocent she is. That makes me laugh, which is something I desperately need.

We watch as the last of the speakers steps away. The theme is how great a man, writer, friend, client Adam was. I can say that my limited interaction with him did not leave me with warm fuzzies nor did it trip any internal alarms. Without interference from Phoebe and Gran's love spell, no way I would have gone to meet him, but if all of these amazing things about him are true, why did someone kill him? Twice. I mean, the term *overkill* most likely applies here. From what I've read about angel's trumpet, it is highly poisonous, especially to someone like Adam who had asthma, which was well-known since he always had his inhaler with him. If someone poisoned him, why also push him from the bell tower?

I take out my notebook and write a note about overkill.

Danetra leans forward. "I want to introduce you to my grandmother, Callie Underhill. She came in for our little festival."

A slim brown-skinned woman with gray curly hair to her shoulders shakes my hand. "Pleasure to meet you. I guess I missed the fireworks, though."

"Where are you from?" I ask.

"I live in Massachusetts. Salem." She does a little laugh. "It's not as witchy as one might think, but there's definitely history there."

"Oh," I say, not wanting to break witchy etiquette, as it were. "Do you . . ." Gran shoots me a withering stare which I ignore as I revise the end of my thought. "Also do taxes and costumes?"

Gran nods.

"Goodness, no. I'm a baker by trade. I have a muffin shop there. For a second, though, I thought you were going to ask if I dabbled in the craft."

I hold up my hands. "Nope. Not my business."

"Please," she laughs, a warm one that stretches to her eyes, which light up with amusement. "Who doesn't? I'm sure I don't know anyone who doesn't rely on magic of some sort. Lucky shirts for sports. Crystals hanging from rearview mirrors. Tonics to restore health." She holds up her cup in homage to that. "People here don't like to discuss it openly, but I think that's silly."

"Come on, Noni, let's get home. It has been a looong day."

"Okay, dear, but before I go, I want you to know I'm rooting for you. I can tell you've been through some things. Life is like that. But this town has a way of healing some people." Before she leaves, she flashes the inside flap of her coat. There's a pink pin. She winks and then is off.

Gran tugs on my arm. "Maybe we should retire also. Chinese take-out sounds good?"

"Perfect. You grab that and we'll grab junk food. Meet you at home," Phoebe says.

"La La's has the best chow mein," Gran says. "But I think we'll need some kombucha for clear thinking. Meet you outside?"

Before I can answer, Gran has stepped into the Magic Bean. I expect there to be a long line for takeout, but it only takes a few minutes to take our order, pack it, and charge my card. Before I leave, the hostess shows me her pink pin. "Thanks," I say, although it does feel a bit unseemly. Shouldn't we all be rooting for Mack to crack this case? Then again, I am not opposed to people rooting for my name to be cleared.

I exit the restaurant and find Gran waiting, two large tumblers filled with grapefruit kombucha. "I found out something interesting from Rusty, dear. Will tell you when we get home."

The walk back to Gran's is relaxing. It's six o'clock, and I've been on the go for twelve hours. There's so much to do tonight still, and I feel like I'm racing the clock, but also, how much do I have in the tank? Will I conk out after I have a full belly?

Phoebe and Kim beat us home, and they rush out to help us with the bags. I finally get a sip of that kombucha, and I admit, it's really good.

"It'll perk you right up," Gran says. "It's a miracle, really."

Kim grabs paper plates from the cupboard and helps Phoebe assemble the feast. At our old home Phoebe would be upset about using paper products, but tonight she's too focused to care. Excited about this puzzle we will solve together. Hopefully.

We sit in the living room on the couch, TV trays for Gran and me, the coffee table and lap pillows for Kim and Phoebe.

"I started a spreadsheet," Phoebe says, making her computer screen mirror onto the large screen TV. "It's got a list of suspects, a place for means, motive, and opportunity, and a summary of whereabouts and proximity to Adam."

"Means, motive, and opportunity, huh?" I shoot Gran a look. Colluding. Again.

"It's a very good spreadsheet, dear," Gran reminds me, nodding toward the screen. "We need to figure this out."

Mu shu vegetables is Phoebe's favorite, but it's hard to eat and work, so Kim takes over in between bites of vegetable lo mein and sesame tofu.

Phoebe narrates. "So far we have categories of suspects—writers, fans, business associates, family, and miscellaneous."

"Who's in miscellaneous?" I ask.

"Nobody yet. It seems like a throwaway category, but we can't be certain that our killer came from one of those other categories since they are aligned with intrinsic motivations. Like so," she nods to Kim, and the spreadsheet becomes a graphic that dumps the categories into different motivations such as writing ambitions, business impacts, romantic aspirations, and, of course, miscellaneous.

"There's so much information." I mime my brain exploding. "I can't process it all."

"That's what the spreadsheet is for, dear. Let's start with the suspects," Gran advises.

"Okay. First up, Almira Leach," I say.

"Not 'The Leach' this time?" Gran asks.

"No. I think that monicker should be saved for informal use only." I stab a dumpling and bring it to my mouth. Kim slides the dipping sauce toward me. I stand, finger up, and go to the fridge to get the mayo. Kim shoots me a questioning look.

Phoebe says, "Mom took a class on how to make dumplings, and they mixed soy sauce with mayo as a dipping sauce and now there is no saving her from herself."

Kim nods, seeming to take the information in for further consideration. "Noted."

Once my sauce situation is settled, I continue. "Pete said that Adam had information about the deceptive business practices used by Fox N Sox Books to curry favor for certain authors."

"Is that enough to kill for?" Gran asks. "I mean, big-box stores have halfway rigged the bestsellers list for years. There was even that scandal where an author did it herself by ordering five thousand copies of her books from stores all over the country."

"It seemed like it was something more scandalous. Illegal. Like maybe a pay-for-play situation."

"Still. Not to play devil's advocate, dear, but it's just a job. Almira doesn't own Fox N Sox Books. She's a businesswoman and she may even be ruthless, but honestly, that doesn't seem to be enough motive to me."

I nod my head reluctantly. "I agree. I mean, what *would* be a motivation for murder?"

"I think it would have to be very personal. Especially considering the way it was carried out. Poisoning his drink. That feels personal, doesn't it? Then following him up the tower and . . ." Phoebe wrinkles her nose. "There would have to be very passionate feelings even if not of the romantic variety."

"Okay. Next. We have Pete. His brother. They had a falling out. A big one." I dip another dumpling, then chase it with the kombucha. "Adam stole his girlfriend and married her. He then, according to Pete, used her death to catapult his career. There's that and he stole every idea he ever wrote about from other books. Oh—and here's something interesting—Adam met with Pete to tell him that he was giving all of that derivative stuff up to work on a passion project. And he fired his agent and parted ways with his editor."

"Phew! That was a lot, dear."

"Let's break it down," Phoebe says and Kim types. "Pete has a motive that is emotional and passionate."

"But he has a solid alibi. Was filmed doing his podcast five hours from here. Also, he was making up with Adam, supposedly, and Adam was going to help out with his podcast to make it more widely known."

"Well, investigating your brother's murder would make for a fantastic podcast," Kim offers.

"True. And who was that girl from UMass with him today? Who else in his crew could have been involved?"

Kim adds slots for those to be named later. "Was it UMass? I think Amherst."

"Oh yeah. I always mix those up."

"Because UMass is in Amherst," Kim says.

"Exactly."

"Maybe Adam isn't the only one in their family who mined tragedy for fame," Gran says.

"True." I take another sip of Kombucha. "We also have the editor and agent who only recently agreed to attend the festival."

Kim brings up the entries for Marilyn and Nicholas. She updates their possible motives. "If Adam dumped them, that might be enough to get them fired up."

"There was something about that from this morning. Someone in that authors' room didn't want their livelihoods to be affected by his decisions. That could be Marilyn and/or Nicholas. Plus, there's something else. A word that is lighting up ideas in my mind."

"What word?"

I stand and shake out my hands. "I don't know. It's close. I just can't get it. It's on the tip of my tongue. Well, the tip of my brain." I rub my head.

"I'm not sure that's going to work, Mom," Phoebe says.

"Let's keep going," I put my hands together. It's a way of centering my energy. Something I used to do in yoga. Why don't I do yoga anymore? All of a sudden, a long-forgotten yoga series comes back to me. "I'm so distracted. Get me back on track, someone. Please."

"How about the other authors?" Phoebe asks. "Jealousy driving some of them mad?"

I think about Dan and Lana specifically. Even though I can't remember exactly what they were thinking, "I don't get the feeling that their emotions were jacked up enough to commit murder. Besides, they know that even with Adam gone that doesn't help them. If their books weren't getting big advances or print runs, eliminating one author wouldn't change that."

"I agree," Gran says. "It wouldn't solve anything, and career jealousy as a motive in and of itself? I don't buy it. Especially since it was premeditated."

"How ubiquitous is angel's trumpet?" I ask.

Gran shoots me a smirk. "It's a good word, isn't it? Ubiquitous."

We used to do this when I was growing up—try to one up each other with cool words that were underused. "So? Angel's trumpet?"

Kim starts a search. "Well, if we lived in a tropical climate like—"

"Florida," I finish. "Okay. Do people grow it here?"

"In greenhouses on purpose. Or at botanical gardens or universities."

"Do we have a geographical mapping of the participants and attendees?" I ask.

"Not yet. But we will," Phoebe says.

"What about the Women United Against Adam people?" Kim asks. "Do we have names?"

Phoebe takes the keyboard and toggles through the spreadsheet. "Three ladies who identified themselves using that hashtag on socials planned to attend the festival and confront him. They are Karen Sanders, Marla Cope, and Randi Versa. They attended his keynote but according to all of the information we were able to suss out did not approach him. They did post parts of his keynote, mocking his humblebrag approach."

"I'd say those are low on the list. What about those rumors that he stole someone's work? According to his brother, that may be possible," I say.

"We could use one of those stylometry programs. Happy to look into that," Phoebe says. "But we are kind of all over the place, Mom."

"Did you get any information from the amulet, dear?" Gran asks me.

"Yes, but it's been such a long day, it's jumbled. I wish I'd written it all down."

"Hear me out," Phoebe says, "before saying no. I remember there's a memory spell in the book. Maybe we could get in there," she points to my head, "and sort all of that out."

I surprise myself by saying, "I think that's an excellent idea."

"Should we get some well-earned rest?" Gran asks. "After all, you have been going since six this morning."

"Strange," I say, "this kombucha seems to be bringing me back to life. Is it like an energy drink or something?"

"Nope. Just water, the fermentation thingy, flavors, and carbonation," Gran says, her eyes darting to the floor.

Kim shoots Phoebe a conspiratorial glance.

Before I can jump in and demand answers, Gran shouts out orders to pack up the leftovers. When she goes to start the car, I stop Phoebe. "What gives?" I ask.

"I'm sure I have no idea what you're talking about," Phoebe says.

"You do too. The kombucha?"

"I've always been a fan of fermented cultures and the drinks they produce. Plus, I think hydration is super important. You know that."

"Yes," I nod sagely. "That sounds like you."

"Come on, let's get you to the bookstore before you go yumpy," Phoebe says, backing out the door.

"An Uncle Vernon reference? Classic. Hey, why didn't you name Stella Hedwig then?"

"Not everything is about *Harry Potter*."

"You're correct. Now, call your owl and let's fly."

"Funny, Mom. Not."

I race to the car, pushing her out of the way, and call shotgun. I am tempted to celebrate until I remember I'm driving.

"Well played, Mom. Let's hope your conjuring is better than your jokes."

"Murder is no laughing matter," I tell her.

"Certainly not with you at the wheel."

I put my hands over my head. "Burn!"

Phoebe leans forward and says to Gran, "Maybe ease her into the kombucha next time?"

Gran shrugs and we're off. True, we are off to solve a murder. A murder of someone I once admired. But, also, I feel a connection to this place, to my girls. To whatever magic exists not only in the kombucha (apparently) but also in that wonderful bookstore and the life we are building here. Also, what *is* in this kombucha? Another mystery to solve.

Chapter Fourteen

There are huddles of people walking around town but not as many as I would expect on a Saturday night. The festival crowd has mostly emptied out with a few stragglers holed up at the inn. I am no longer in charge of the authors or other dignitaries, officially, and that's a relief.

The last person we see before turning into the back parking lot of the store is Mack. He's still in his sheriff's uniform but stands in the doorway of the diner. When he spots me, he does one of those corny sarcastic salutes.

"Still on the job, I see." I return the gesture.

"He just finished questioning all of the authors," Kim says. "Small town," she offers before I can ask. "Tomorrow he's supposed to bring in more Mystic Hollow people. I guess since we are easier to get."

"Has he set his sights on anyone yet?" I ask, all of a sudden beholden to this seventeen-year-old.

She looks at her phone and scowls. "Not that I've heard."

"Do we know who he specifically questioned?" Phoebe asks.

"Should be pretty easy to find out." Kim opens a note on her phone and starts a list. Number one, find out who the sheriff questioned.

We open the door, and Kim turns on the light at the back of the store.

Concern starts to crawl inside me. The way Mack looked at me just now feels as if he suspects me. Or is that just the way the uniform makes most people feel?

"I think we need to know more about angel's trumpet." I'm now accustomed to commanding my troops it seems, as Kim nods and Phoebe starts her own set of notes on her phone. "Is that a toxin you can buy online or do you have to cultivate it yourself? Once you've made tea out of the leaves, how stable is the potion? Does it have a half-life? How do you transport it?"

"We're on it, Mom."

"Thanks."

Stella arrives in sync with us, and I am amazed by her constant vigilance, but this time she doesn't come inside the store, just perches on a tree like a sentry.

The lights inside the store flicker.

Gran's hand falls on my shoulder. "She's glad we're here. She wants to be useful."

I hope Gran's right. "We could use all the help we can get," I say, hoping to curry favor.

"I'll set up." Kim goes behind the counter and lifts the heavy tome from its current resting place. Next, she lines up the bell and lights the candle. Phoebe sits on a stool, flipping through pages.

"I thought you just had to ask," I say, not meaning to sound confrontational, but I guess my nerves are showing because my voice strains.

"You sound like the dad from *Poltergeist*," Phoebe says.

"Ew. I definitely don't want to give those vibes."

"Say you're sorry, then," Phoebe says.

"You're sorry, then," I say.

"If you two are done . . ." Gran pushes my hands away and puts hers on the outside of the spellbook. "Show us a memory spell." The pages turn until they open to a two-page spread. There is a recipe of sorts. Lists of things we need. A bowl. A mirror. An amulet. Some mint tea.

"Is that weirdly specific? Mint tea? Not lavender?"

Gran puts her hand on mine. "Mint is for reclaiming lost memories. Lavender is for calm thoughts and safety."

"Right," I say, as if I should have known that, even though I'd have no way of knowing any of that.

"It says to use an amulet from your past that will open doors to your memory." Phoebe wrinkles her nose. "But nothing from your past links to this crime. I'm not sure what to use."

Stella hoots but stays outside.

"Nothing?" I ask the owl through the window.

"I guess not," Phoebe says. "Which is weird. Since she gave us this one to begin with."

"Hear me out," Gran says. "If this amulet," she holds up the amulet I used this morning, the one Stella gave us to begin with that is now slightly mangled, "helped you this morning, it is now part of the memories you need to unlock. It's already been formatted for this project, so to speak."

Phoebe takes the amulet in her hand. She lets it dangle, the crushed face swinging in the ambient moonlight. Stella raises her wings like she did the first time when she gave it to us. "I think that's a yes," Phoebe says, her eyes brimming with pride for her owl.

"Does Stella look proud also?" I ask. "Can an owl look proud?"

"Honestly, Mom, you are astounded by the weirdest things."

"So, am I right? Is she proud of us?" I give Stella a thumbs-up.

"Owls do not show human emotions. That is such a species-specific construct." Phoebe places the amulet on the book in the designated area. Stella watches her, then lifts her wings again. She holds up her orange foot—the one that held the amulet to begin with.

"Did you see that . . . she held up her foot . . . she *is* giving us a thumbs-up."

Phoebe places her hand on my shoulder. "Mom, shall we . . ." She gestures to the book.

"Yes, of course." I look around and find all three of them giving me pathetic looks. "Do not pity me," I tell them. "I'm as ready as anyone else."

Phoebe starts chanting in Latin again.

"How do you suddenly know Latin? Feeling inferior!"

"Just what we need for the spell. Shh."

Kim translates, "We ask the goddess of the east to join us. We ask the mirror to amplify our power. Mint and honey make the tea to return my memories to me." She ducks under the counter and retrieves a small electric teapot. "I drink them in."

A cup is brought to my lips. I swallow the minty liquid as a wind blows through the store, leaving the scent of the springs behind it. I feel it climb my nose, the smells of my childhood. Memories do flood through me, but they are not memories from earlier today, they are memories of an earlier time. I must be ten years old or close to it, with my hips deep in the springs, the breeze making me turn away from it, to close my eyes. The feeling of peace and complete understanding fills me until I am so happy I could burst from it. I hear my grandmother next to me.

"Do you want go in, dear?"

I didn't. I wanted to stay exactly where I was. Where everything in the world seemed to make sense. Finally. All the things that felt out of place slipped magically together to create the puzzle of my life. I was where I was supposed to be. Doing what I was supposed to be doing. I'd never felt that way before. Or since.

Then the feelings change. I'm not in the water. I'm inside. Voices surround me but not just Gran's. Also Phoebe's and Kim's. I feel a liquid drip down the front of my mouth and inhale the scent of mint. I hear myself speaking. The phrases I heard in the authors' room along with my thoughts on who might have said them. I can't make my mouth stop talking. I can't make my eyes see what's in front of me. I can't stop the feeling of spinning as the words float out of my mouth.

Gran says, "Are you getting this, girls?"

"Recording to transcribe later."

"Good. Good."

Two other voices. Muffled but in the background, commenting on the information, mostly, and sometimes agreeing with it.

Finally, like a top that spun out of control, I crumple to the ground. Hands fall on me. I hear chanting of some sort. Is that Danetra? "It's okay, love. We've got you."

"Let's give her some of this," Kiki's voice now, I'm sure of it.

"We got it all, Mom. You did great."

I have no idea what they got, but I do know I have a splitting headache. Throbbing. My stomach roils. Migraine. A doozy.

"Let's get her home," Gran says. "The poor dear overdid it."

"I'll close up," Kim says.

"Angel's trumpet," I say. "I heard that somewhere before. Or read it."

"It's okay, Mom. You gave us a lot already. Let's just get you home."

Home. Gran's home. My home. Phoebe's.

As they load me into the car and then unload me into the house, I hear Stella's hoots nearby. She sounds alarmed. I give her a thumbs-up and the hooting stops. Am I dreaming? I think I'm communicating with my daughter's owl, who is also her familiar, apparently.

Part of me believes I'll wake up in my bed in Florida with the hurricane raging outside and find out I really just hit my head and dreamt it all à la *Wizard of Oz.* The lightning bolts that shoot through my mind are different colors—technicolor! But I know those are from my own mind. From my headache.

An ice pack is placed on my eyes and I let myself drift in the sea. That's what my bed feels like now. The ocean.

"We pushed her too hard, Gran," Phoebe says.

"She'll be alright. It's been a long day."

"Too much kombucha," Phoebe says.

"The mint will help," Kim says. "It always does."

Isn't Kim supposed to be closing the store? A heavy blanket is laid over me, and it feels so good to be weighted down even if I feel seasick. As I start to fall away, I see Adam as he walked toward the stage last night. As he strode, he looked ahead of him, a smile on his face. Until. Until. Until . . . his expression changed. He saw someone. Someone he didn't expect to see. Someone he didn't like. Then he rearranged his expression back to the frozen smile and took the stage.

I want to yell at him to stop. To not go to the tower. To not drink anything that isn't from a sealed bottle. To not accept our invitation to speak to begin with. Whoever did this used premeditation. They knew he was going to be at the festival ahead of time so that they could plan his demise.

They knew he'd be here. He didn't know they would be. Interesting.

"Now sleep," another voice tells me. It's soft and husky and somewhat familiar. "I gave her some of the antidote."

"Not too much?" Phoebe asks, her voice full of concern.

"Just enough, angel. Your mother will be just fine."

It's a weird thought to have, but I feel like that's Callie's voice, Danetra's mother, but that can't be since she left earlier today. Still, it's a warm association, and I let that comfort me as I fall asleep.

Chapter Fifteen

The sun pierces my eyes directly through my closed lids, or at least that's how it feels. My tongue feels two sizes too big for my mouth. I'd already become accustomed to whatever magic was in that kombucha potion, and I believed, fervently, that it would stave off this feeling.

A glass of water is by my bed. Gran's work, I'm sure. Along with two aspirins. I take them and down the entire glass. A fresh ice pack also awaits. Migraines are the worst. Gran knows how to take care of them. I lie back, the ice pack over my eyes and let the aspirin and water do their trick. My mind is fuzzy but calm. Which is weird for my usually overwrought brain. I'll take it.

A feeling of complete peace embraces me. Like last night in the bookstore when we did the spell. It's like there are many versions of me, and each one inserts new nuggets of information through cobwebs. The memory spell. Phoebe speaking Latin. Kim translating. The taste of mint.

I was talking. Saying things I heard in the authors' room. Then I spun and spun and the world kept spinning with me.

"Mom?" Phoebe's voice.

I was in the springs. I remembered that. After I remembered all the things that were said in the authors' room.

"You've taken her too far back," a voice said. Whose voice? What voice? "I'll call my mother."

"Mom?" Phoebe sticks her head in my room. "Gran told me to bring you juice."

I pry the ice off of my eyes. "Who was here last night?"

"Um. You, me, Kim, Gran. You okay?"

"More people. I remember more."

Phoebe sits on the edge of my bed so gingerly; it touches me how careful she's being. I do feel like a porcelain doll, to be honest. Close to shattering. "Well, the spell was pretty trippy. You were spinning. And you remembered so many things and then . . ."

"Then?"

"Then we brought you home."

"What's in the kombucha?" I ask, drinking the juice.

Phoebe laughs. "Just spring water. Magical spring water. Funny, right?"

"We're laughing at magic now?"

"Not all magic. Just that in kombucha it will revive you. Wake the dead, they say." Phoebe puts her hand to her mouth, stage-whispering. "Otherwise, it's just the normal SCOBI. Symbiotic colony of—"

"Spring water?" I ask. "Like from the magical springs?"

"Yes."

"Don't have any. Not until you're twenty-one. Promise me."

"I promise."

"Wake the dead?"

"There was much debate about that. Nobody believes it would really revive an actual dead person. But they did decide it hyped you up too much and made you too vulnerable to the spell we did and sent you too far back."

Something about all of that feels important. I finish the juice. "I'm going to shower."

"No offense, but you could use it." She pinches her nose. "I'm going on a coffee run."

"You are my favorite child."

"I am your only child."

"That I know of."

"You know that's not actually a thing, right? A woman can't not know she has a child."

"Maybe I knew and forgot."

"Well, if you did, I've got the spell for you."

"Shoo," I say. "You're bothering me, kid."

"Now you sound like a comedian from the fifties." But she leaves the room or almost does. She peeks her head back in. "We're going to figure this out," she says. "I've been working on the things you told us last night. We plugged everything into the spreadsheet. And I'm going to do the stylometry thing, but I need work that we 100 percent know was Adam's."

"Since he supposedly lifted some work, that might be a challenge." Another memory bumps up against my mind. Dan, his critique partner from before either of them had been published. When I was in a group, we handed out pages or sent them ahead of time. "Oh. Wait. I might have a lead."

"Good. Gran is making cranberry orange muffins with vegan butter."

With thoughts of coffee and muffins fueling me, I manage to wobble to the shower and shove my body underneath the warm stream. I turn it to scalding hot and that's when the memories surface, full on. I hear the snippets of conversation, hopefully caught by my scribes and organized. But almost none of it amounts to motive for murder.

I go back to that. What primal urge makes you want to kill another person? Greed? Lust? Revenge? Self-preservation? Maybe that, most of all. Or protecting someone else.

With these lovely thoughts, I wash myself fully, then step into the steamy bathroom. I used to love doing this when I was young. How foggy the mirror got. How close the steam felt. Like a hug. You don't get this in Florida. Even on those few days in the winter when the temperature dips below fifty, the steam always dissipated before I wanted it to.

Now I pull on yoga pants and a sweatshirt and make my way downstairs. I pass my dollhouse. "Is this where breakfast is served?" I ask the kitchen table diorama.

"In here, dear," Gran says. "Still feeling a little loopy, are we?"

Phoebe opens the door, hands me coffee. "Hot Americano with pistachio foam."

"Not anymore." I take a sip of the glorious stuff. Then I spot a bag of tacos in her hand. "What's this?"

"Magic hangover food." she says. "I got Mike's to make some for you."

"How do you already know the town's fast-food owners well enough to ask for special favors?" I grab the bag and head into the kitchen.

"It's a gift," Phoebe says.

Gran sits at the table, the muffins already plated. I open my tacos. They smell greasy and spicy and insanely good. At the first bite my stomach recoils, but then it settles.

"I called Sloan Rodgers. He's going to meet you downtown for this morning's questioning session."

I look at the clock. It's eight-thirty. Still so early. "Mack wants me for questioning?"

Gran takes a sip of her coffee. "Yup. Called first thing. I told him you need time to get beautiful."

"Stop." I take the second taco out of the bag. A spicy tater tot one. Yum. "I need to get in touch with Dan."

Toggling through my emails to him pre-festival, I am hit with a wave of nostalgia. Critique groups are sacred places. Some are fantastic, filled with writers who are better than you are, ideal for your process. But then, everyone seems to grow. Other critique groups are filled with people who will never be published. Who have learned to nitpick and are not elevating their craft. I wonder what Dan and Adam's group was like. Were they the only two standouts? Did that cause rifts? Could one of his old critique partners be angry enough to kill him?

"What are you thinking about?" Phoebe asks as she inhales another taco.

"Do we know where Dan came in from?"

Phoebe checks her list. "He lives in Florida but is here for two events. Ours and a multiple author signing at Fox N Sox in Hartford next week."

"I wonder what would get him to meet with me."

"We could do an author spotlight for him at the store next month. Keep the buzz going. His new book seems to be doing well out of the gate, but fall-off seems just around the corner, poor dear."

I hand Phoebe my phone. "Use your salesy knowledge to pitch a meetup at Our Little Secret Bar today. Tell him I'm paying."

"That matters?" Phoebe asks.

"Oh, yes. A midlist author having to float himself for a week between events? He's looking for free food for sure. Trust me."

I finish my coffee and drink some water. My stomach feels good, but a bite of cranberry orange muffin might be just the finale my meal needs.

"Honestly," Gran says. "Your stomach. It should be studied."

"Now to pick the correct outfit for a mug shot. What are we thinking?"

"I have always liked you in blue," Gran says. "Brings out your eyes."

Phoebe nods. "Wear your hair down, I think. A ponytail seems too overconfident."

"Hm." I say. "I shouldn't be too confident. Is this like dating tips for the *Victorious* girls?"

"Please," Phoebe says. "As if the *Victorious* girls would be in this pickle."

"Women kill all the time, have been doing so for ages. Agatha Christie was famous for using poisons in her books because women were the ones who prepared the food."

Phoebe considers this. Then says, "True."

"But did the person who poisoned the victim then follow them to the tallest building in town and then push them out of a window? Our killer showed unwavering commitment."

"Maybe that's not why they followed him there. Maybe they wanted to push him as a symbol of bringing him down," Phoebe says. "It could speak to the reason behind the murder, more than a simple poisoning."

"Maybe." I stop at the doorway. "All things to consider." I point to my head. "When I get back, I want to see that spreadsheet of the brain goo you downloaded from me last night."

"It'll be ready and waiting for you."

"Perfect. And by the way, I think I'm going with a power color like red or orange."

"Careful, dear, orange is no longer the new black, and it will get him visualizing you in prison gear." She slashes the air. "I think black or red are best."

"But I love my orange sweater. It's my favorite."

Phoebe comes up behind me. "Upstairs and change, you. I'll drive you to the station."

"Exactly what I was hoping my teenage daughter would be doing in our new town."

"If you see it, you can be it," Phoebe says. "What? That was part of our Wellness Wednesdays at my old high school. A mantra for every occasion."

"What's the mantra if I'm to do jail time?"

"I believe we have to turn to Martha for that one. It's a goodish thing."

"Goodish?"

"She did five months like a boss. Started a garden in jail."

"I am not likewise gifted. But maybe I could do a book club."

"You'd finally have the time."

I can't follow that one up, so I simply go into my room and change. I go with the blue sweater. I read once that blue invokes feelings of loyalty and truth. I hope Mack sees it that way.

Chapter Sixteen

We pull up in front of the police department. Mack catches my eye and makes a motion with his fingers to park. He's in his civvies, and I take that as a good omen. Or maybe that's just Sunday in Mystic Hollow.

By the time we make it into the station, Delores is there, ready to usher me into an interview room. "Your lawyer is already here," she says. Then to Phoebe, "She can call you when she's ready."

Phoebe shoots me a look like she doesn't want to leave, but it's up to me to be strong. "It's just like when you didn't want to leave me in kindergarten," I say.

It works. She laughs. "Um. Pretty sure you got that backwards."

"Wanna do a selfie?" I ask, holding my phone over my head.

"You're messed up," Phoebe says. "Call me." She puts her hand by her ear imitating that famous call me later song.

I don't have an amulet with me. Nor do I have any religious medal or a saint's blessing. What I do have is the truth. I did not do this.

An older man in a suit comes forward. "Sloan Rodgers. Pleasure to meet you."

I take his hand. The grip is strong. I know that's a major trope—strong man with a strong grip makes you feel secure, but it's one of those truisms that still holds. I feel better being supported by this man immediately. "Veronica."

He opens his palm, ushering me forward even though all I want to do is sit on the floor and refuse to move. This won't help me, so I make my feet move forward. Mack comes in. Now he's got his uniform on. This time the shirt fits well. I look at the buttons that are lying flat now, and smirk.

"Is something amusing you, Mrs. Blackthorne?"

"Nope. But it's Miss Blackthorne."

Delores comes in with a tray of coffees and some donuts. Mack makes a face. "There is no reason not to be kind," she says.

Mack waves his hand around. "Well, murder might be a reason, but sure, please help yourselves." He opens a file and slides a piece of paper toward my attorney. "Search warrant. For her phone. For her computer. For her house."

"She doesn't have a house."

"I have included her grandmother's house in the complaint."

Sloan looks over the document. "Judge Watson? You're taking this out of district?"

"I thought given the nature of this town, I needed to contain the information to outside sources."

"Ah," Sloan says. "Very smart. Are you officially naming Veronica as a suspect? I need to inform Alice."

"Did you just call my grandmother by her name? Do we need to have a 'what are your intentions' talk?"

Sloan blushes. Puts his hand over mine. "I've known your grandmother for many years. Was one of her suitors many years ago. Before your grandfather beat me to the prize."

"This is so touching, but can we get on with it?" Mack says. "Unless I'm interrupting an episode of DNA dilemma where we find out that Sloan here is really your grandfather?"

Sloan shakes his head. "That was unseemly, Mack. Even for you."

"Yes. I'm the unseemly one. A man is dead and she's making jokes, but I need to take a course in social graces. Got it."

"Maybe just a quick refresher from one of those HR continuing education providers . . . like the ones you make your employees take every year," I say.

"I need to remind you that annoying me may not be in your best interest."

"I often don't do things in my best interest. It might be the ADHD."

"Will that be your defense?" Mack asks, and I realize once again I've opened my big mouth and made it harder for my attorney. Awesome.

A knock on the door. Mack stands up. He takes a folder with papers in it, flips it open, and nods.

"Just like in those TV cop shows," I say. "I wish I had popcorn."

Mack shakes his head. "I am indeed naming her as a suspect. I'd lock her up right now if I could, but our jailer is off for the weekend and I am assuming you will guarantee her appearance in court on Tuesday."

Sloan gives him a look.

"We missed the window for tomorrow."

"Like one of those Amazon buy within this time period to promise delivery tomorrow!" I can't stop myself.

"You could save me the time by confessing. That's also very much like those television dramas," Mack continues. "Then we can meet to arraign you and put this to bed."

"I didn't do it."

He slides a picture that's been enlarged across the desk. "From your socials. It's you and Phoebe in the botanical gardens in Miami."

I look at the picture. Man, I look gaunt. "Do I look sick here?" I ask. "But what am I supposed to notice about my field trip with my daughter?"

He shoves another picture across the desk. A closeup of the plant behind us. "Angel's trumpet."

Then another photo of my hands. With white gloves on. "That's doctored. I've never worn gloves on a field trip. Phoebe would have disowned me."

"I assume you have the original for our review?"

"On her phone."

He slides more records across the table. "That's means."

"Motive?" I ask.

"He was your mentor." Another photo from a conference. The one from the Miami bookstore. "You were obsessed." One from the bar that night after a conference with Pete and Adam and me.

"You clearly don't know my lack of a love life. On purpose!" I hold up one finger in protest. Sloan eases my hand down.

"Then there's the matter of the stolen work. Did you steal his or did he steal yours? Either way it's motive."

I hold up my hand and do a motion like it could go either way. I realize a typical person might not jest during these circumstances, but it's my only coping mechanism. "I feel like it's important to determine who is the filthy thief as well as who is the bloody murderer, don't you? I mean . . . it speaks to motive, no?"

"You suggested the meetup at the belfry."

"He wanted to be like *Sleepless in Seattle*." I almost put a hand over my mouth. Did I just admit it was romantic? Damn, my impulsive tongue.

"We'd like to do a DNA test," Mack says.

"To prove he's my daddy?" I ask.

Sloan shakes his head.

"You don't mean . . ." I stare at my phone at the picture of Phoebe. No.

"Her father is unnamed."

"I didn't even meet Adam until after Phoebe was born. Well after."

"So, let us take a sample."

"You will not go near my daughter with your swabs." I slash the air a little too dramatically, maybe, because Mack flinches.

"It's not like I was going to hit you. Stop flinching!"

"I didn't flinch," he says.

"Yes. You did. You are a big flincher and soon the entire town will know it."

"I'll need copies of all of the reports," Sloan says.

Delores sticks her head in. "April called. She's got a fire on one of her burners."

Mack jumps up. Points on his way out. "Stay in town."

I put my hands in the air. "Yes! I've got jailhouse bingo now!"

Mack makes a disgusted face as he rushes out.

Sloan laughs. "Your grandmother said you had an offbeat sense of humor. Let's head to the bookstore and discuss."

* * *

Phoebe and Gran are waiting for me in the back of the store. Kim is nowhere to be found. "She's got a paper due in gov class tomorrow," Phoebe says.

Right. School. I realize I may have dropped the ball on parental oversight recently. Not that Phoebe's ever needed me to help her manage her workload. "Do you . . ."

"I'm all set," Phoebe says. "Except for my final read through of *The Tempest.* Amateurs."

"Let the other kids catch up," I quote the father in *Chitty Chitty Bang Bang.* We are a family full of pop trivia references.

Sloan starts us off. "Well, he's naming her a suspect. An arrest is pending. They are executing a search warrant for the bookstore and the gardens outside both the house and the store. It's a very weak case."

"What about the search warrant being issued from an outside judge?" I ask.

"Yes," Sloan says. "That is very encouraging. And smart. Mack may make a mean cherry pie, but he's also a very good lawman. If he wants to control the flow of information that means he doesn't trust people in town. Which means he either is open to other suspects or he thinks you had help."

"I've been in town for two minutes. Who would likely want to help me murder someone?"

Sloan doesn't answer. Instead, he says, "Mack may be a good lawman, but rest assured, I'm just as good of an attorney. I spent twenty-five years as a defense attorney. You are in good hands."

Gran looks at Sloan. "What can we do?"

"Well, for one, we need to verify these pictures from your phone."

"Those are fake. I never wore gloves on a field trip in Miami. Sheesh." I give Phoebe a look.

I expect her to back me 100 percent on that. Instead, she chews her lip. "Except that one time."

"What one time?"

"You stuck your hand in a fire ant hill and didn't recognize the biting sensations until after they bit your entire hand. Then you wouldn't wear Band-Aids because they gross you out, so you said you'd wear white gloves like the lady in the *Columbo* episode where she gets poison ivy on her hands, which implicates her in the crime."

"Oh, the makeup magnet one. Man, *Columbo* was definitely feminist. Ahead of its time. So many lady execs. So many female murderers."

I'm on a roll and there's no stopping me, until Phoebe says, "The photo is real, Mom. That's not good."

"But we have an explanation," I say. "The ant bites. Band-Aids are gross. The *Columbo* episode."

"Well, it's still a stretch. All circumstantial. No one saw you push him to his death. No one saw you poison his drink," Sloan says. "That will be our defense."

"I don't like that term. Our defense," Gran says. She shudders. "It's too real."

"It'll be okay," Sloan says. "Let's keep a low profile until Tuesday. Alice, always a pleasure. Nice to meet you, Phoebe and Veronica. It seems I have some work to do."

"Would you like a piece of rhubarb pie?" Gran asks.

Sloan puts his hand over his stomach. "I'm afraid I need to get busy."

"I can pack it to go."

"I wouldn't turn that down."

Phoebe shoots me a look like she is so enjoying this.

I wait until he leaves before launching my attack on Gran. "He was your suitor?"

"That was a long time ago, dear."

"Gross," I say.

"I think it's nice Gran had an admirer."

"Tell that to my grandpa. Only you can't because he's dead."

"I'm not certain that was the burn you intended," Phoebe says.

"I realize." I point to her phone. I start to pace. "Where are we with the spreadsheets and such?"

"Coming along, actually. I do need those samples of Adam's writing. Any news from his critique partner?"

I check my emails. Dan answered. *Sure, let's meet up. See you at five.*

"Yes, actually. Gotta run. While I'm gone, look at who interacted with Adam during the festival."

"On it."

"And do your homework!" I say. "Also, I want an accounting of everything Adam drank last night. I'm sure the police have already asked this, but I want our own records."

"Good thinking, dear."

"I also want a full understanding of the mystic springs and their effects."

"Why, dear?"

"I just have a feeling that's a part of this. I mean, the man did die in Mystic Hollow. Was he immune to the magic? Or was he on the receiving end of bad woo-woo?"

"Nobody practices black magic here, dear. It's all light and love and a bit of energy and rejuvenation. I swear."

"How do you know?"

She looks down. "That book club I told you about. It might tend toward magical practices."

"Interesting. Okay. So do they all dabble?"

"Yes."

"May I have a list of names?"

"Goodness, no. It's anonymous."

"Like Alcoholics Anonymous?"

"Same principle."

"May I attend?"

"Not yet, dear. First things first. Let's get you cleared from a murder charge and then get you up to date on the witchy practices of the town. Deal?"

I don't really have a leg to stand on, so I say, "Deal. As long as you get me another kombucha. Only a little less potent this time."

Gran smiles. "It'll be done."

Chapter Seventeen

It's my second trip to this out of the way bar in two days. Luckily the waitstaff are not the same and I am able to slip inside unrecognized. I'm not sure if I should be worried about making a habit out of visiting this bar, but it's a small town, and gossip could also tip our hand.

Dan is waiting for me in the back, a highball glass already in front of him. He shakes the ice and drains the drink, holding it up for the waitress to refill. I wonder how many he's already had. I also wonder how he'll get back to wherever he's staying. Driving is out of the question.

When I sit down, he smiles. "I think we met a few years ago, am I right?"

I don't point out that my email should have reminded him of my name and therefore there is no reason to celebrate his correct guess, but I need him on my side and he seems softened by the booze. For the moment.

"Yes, we did. At the conference in Winter Garden, I think."

"Winter Garden. Great name for a town. I'm always collecting names. You too?"

I hold up my hand to testify. "Guilty."

The waitress ambles over. “What can I get you?”

“A vodka martini. Olive. Appetizers?” I ask. Laying all my cards on the table, I want him to know I am here to finance a three-course meal if necessary.

“The sampler’s really good,” the waitress offers.

“Perfect. Oh, and bring us one of those big pretzels,” I point to the table across the way.

While we wait for the food, the waitress delivers my drink. I take a sip. Yum. I don’t intend to drink the entire thing, being the designated driver, but a sip or two will put him at ease. I lean in. “How was the festival for you?”

“Aside from the murder it was good.”

“Just so,” I say, tipping my martini glass toward him. “I’m so sorry about Adam. I don’t think I even said that before. It’s hard to lose someone you’ve had in your life for a long time. No matter the relationship.”

“Yes,” he says. “It’s so weird. I told you we started out together. What I didn’t tell you is I found him in a big-box store checking out the ‘how to write books’ section”

I cover my mouth to contain the laughter. “No. That’s so good.”

“And at one point we considered writing a series together. But that was before he hit it big.”

“Do you believe the rumors that he stole someone’s work?” I ask, eyes wide.

“Nah. No way. His ideas were the best part of his writing.” He takes a drink. “No way he needed anyone else’s ideas.”

“Oh,” I say. “His brother said he was always sort of ripping off the plots of old books and movies. That he wouldn’t be surprised . . .”

“His brother’s not a writer. Is he?”

The waitress deposits the food on the table. Another waiter behind her places my drink on the table.

Dan continues. "Pete. He doesn't know how things work. Adam was a fountain of ideas. He kept notebooks filled with them. Too many to write in one lifetime. And in someone else's hands? No guarantee of payoff. It was his take on the ideas that counted. You get that, right?"

"I do. Yeah. Critique groups can get kind of weird about that stuff though, right? One person puts a catcher's mitt in a book and another one has it show up as the character's boyfriend."

"Subconsciously. But that's not theft. Not in a way that would make him worth killing."

"Can I tell you something pretty awful?" I lower my voice, trying to reel him in.

"Of course." He pops a fry into his mouth.

"The police chief. Mack. He has his sights set on me as the prime suspect."

"What?"

"Yeah. I barely knew Adam. Wouldn't benefit from his death at all. But I'm worried. I need to find another lead to throw him off before he's set on this path."

"He thinks you stole work from Adam?"

"Or that he stole work from me. Stupid, right?"

Dan shakes his head. "I don't see it. I mean, if he wrote a blockbuster and it was deemed stolen, yes, but how would you even determine that?"

I force a casual laugh. "I may have a way." I take a sip of my martini. "If I had verified pieces of his original writing." I wave that thought away. "But who could even get their hands on those? It's impossible."

"Maybe not impossible," Dan does his own laugh.

"Hmm?" I rip off a bite of the pretzel.

"I might have some I could send you. But . . ."

Here it comes. His demands. "But?"

"I'd want credit. And afterwards I'd like to be looped in as to the method you used. I may have an idea for a book."

I tap my temple. "Smart. But how do you have samples of his work?"

"We were in the same critique group. Remember? I'm sure I have some of the before he was famous pages."

"Oh my God, that would be amazing!" I lean back. "Who do *you* think did it?"

"I'd be looking at his editor or agent. He was about to torpedo his very lucrative career and take them down with him."

"I heard he parted ways with both of them."

Dan laughs. "The hubris. He wins the golden cup and then refuses to drink out of it."

"Do you think maybe he had a secret lover who found out he was still playing the field?" I ask.

"He never talked about that stuff. He mostly talked about his new passion project. How he was sick of the grind. He wanted to do something special. I feel like it has to do with that, to tell you the truth."

I take a chip, drag it through the artichoke cheese dip. "When's the last time you saw him?" I ask. "Were you guys still exchanging work?"

He takes a swig of his drink. Points at me. "Now that you mention it, the last time I saw him was the last time I saw you. That conference in Winter Garden. Remember?"

"Boy, do I." I hold up my fingers an inch apart. "The closest I've gotten to making it!"

"You got an agent interested, am I right?"

"You have a great memory," I say.

"We keep track. Believe me. Gotta watch our backs from you up and comers."

I laugh. "As if."

"But now that you mention it, he did seem to be getting very friendly with a woman at that same conference. He'd critiqued her work and she'd asked to meet him in the bar after everyone went upstairs."

"Interesting. You remember who?"

"No. But I saw them having drinks together. They were huddled at the table, and I could see his eyes light up as they were talking."

"Any idea what they were talking about?"

"His writing. What else?" Dan takes the last fried mushroom.

I laugh. "She was a fan?"

"Weren't they always? But I did hear her say he should work on what fuels him. Writing was sacred. Blah. Blah. Blah. He waved her away. Said he'd pitched it and nobody was interested. And then the weirdest thing happened. I can't believe I forgot this."

"What?" I'm leaning all the way in now.

"He went to the bathroom, and I swear I saw her look in his phone. He'd given it to her to put her details in it." He clears his throat. "I was going to investigate, but one of the editors asked me to come meet them for drinks. I couldn't turn that down. From where we were sitting, I saw her storm off before he returned."

"That *is* weird. Did he say what that was about?"

Dan looks like he's trying to search for the memory. "I saw him the next day and asked about it. He laughed and said there'd been a misunderstanding. That she'd been upset about some of the critique. That happens, of course, but that's not how it looked from where I was sitting."

"You don't know her name?"

"No."

"You think she was up to something? That she tried to steal his premise?"

"No idea. I just know it looked unusual and after that he became super secretive about what he was working on. Wouldn't even tell me. Who knows what really happened."

"But you said theft wouldn't work anyway."

"Yeah, but what if he stumbled upon an idea? A big one? If he did and he told her, an underling with no connections . . . that could set the stage for meaningful theft."

"There's someone online accusing Adam of theft." I say. "It was one of the reasons some people on the committee didn't want him to be our headliner."

Dan makes an aggravated face. "I hate when festivals do that—pit authors against each other. Headliner. We all bring in fans. Even if Adam brought in more. But that allegation, it sounds to me like someone trying to cover their tracks."

I chew on my nail. "Yeah. Maybe."

Dan's face falls. "I still can't believe it."

"Me neither."

"They really think it's you?"

"Little old me."

"I'll find those samples of Adam's early work for analysis."

I put my hands together. "Thank you. So much."

"In the meantime, keep this on the down low. If someone killed Adam to keep their secret, whatever it is, then you could be a target. Be careful."

"I guess," I say. "You still hungry? We could get entrées or desserts."

"Nah," he says. "I'm mostly tired."

"Let's get you back to your hotel, then. Gran's store will pay for the week for you."

"That's amazing. You don't have to do that."

"Anything to support the next big hit. Early reviews of your next release are spectacular. All authors deserve support."

"Thank you."

"Remember us when you are planning your events!" I say.

He smiles at me graciously. Puts his hand over his heart. "Always."

It never hurts to throw a little marketing love behind an author who has shown up for you. It costs very little, actually, especially for an indie store like Mystic Hollow Books, and it pays in dividends. I just hope it also pays in examples of Adam's verified work.

Chapter Eighteen

Prior to moving here, our Sunday routine was consistent. Breakfast out. Each of us reading whatever we wanted and fully ignoring each other. Some type of activity. It could be a movie. A walk in the park. A trip to the beach. Home by three o'clock at the latest to wind down. Winding down was always my favorite part. It was bittersweet, though, because it meant saying goodbye to spending time together, just the two of us. With no real schedule or commitments.

Since moving to the Hollow, Phoebe and I haven't established a Sunday routine. "I miss our Sunday wind downs," I announce as I walk into Gran's kitchen.

Tatum is manning the store for the day, and Gran and Phoebe are seated at the kitchen table. Phoebe's working on her phone and laptop almost simultaneously. Gran is stirring something on the stove.

"A wind down sounds great, dear."

"I don't see it in the cards," Phoebe says, then goes back to work.

"Oh, you don't?" I ask. "Now you're a card reader? Tell me, oh clairvoyant one, what do you see in our future?"

She points to her wrist as if a watch were there. "Tick tock. We need to get moving on this investigation before your hearing on Tuesday."

I wave her concern away. "Pffft. Let's watch something fun."

"I'm working on something," Phoebe says.

"Homework?"

"Completed on Friday. This is for the case. Did you get that sample for me?"

"Should I worry that my problems have eclipsed yours?"

"Plenty of time for me to have a crisis. I'm thinking mine will be in my mid-forties." She points to her screen. "So, I started mapping out where all the angels were on Friday night. To see who could have access to Adam's drink." She flips the screen so I can see it.

"This is impressive." I point to Adam's avatar, which looks like its operating in one of those zombies vs. plants games. "Can you zoom in here?"

She maneuvers so that the area around Adam is enlarged. "I pulled the data from those bracelets we gave the angels. Plus, the sensor we put in the authors' name tags."

"Click on Adam."

When she does, it tells us that he picked up his lanyard at 5:03. "Three minutes late!" Phoebe exclaims. "He definitely had it coming."

"He spoke at a little after six. So, sometime after that someone handed him a spiked drink. I don't think they would have done that before his speech. Too risky. If he had a bad reaction, we would have noticed and we'd have sent for help. Had to be when he was signing. Can you fast-forward the map?"

"Absolutely." She clicks and drags and we see Adam's avatar signing books. The time stamp is 7:25. "Let's look at the footage around that time."

She pulls up another file with all of the downloaded pictures and videos that were sent to our hashtag. It takes a good half hour to wade through them and land on one that may help. It shows three women posing with one of Adam's signed books. Behind them, he smiles, purposely photobombing. To his left, a gloved hand slides a drink toward him. "Zoom in," I say.

The more she zooms, the poorer the quality of the image until it's so pixilated there is no point.

Gran joins us. "It looks like a woman's hand," she says.

I gasp.

"What?" Phoebe asks.

"It's just so bold."

"Even though we don't have any other information. Wait. Is that from the Magic Bean?"

Phoebe isolates the cup. Moves it to another tabs and enlarges it. "It sure is."

"Kombucha?" I ask. "The magic kombucha?"

"Well, that recipe is usually reserved for Mystic Hollowians."

"That's what we're calling ourselves?" I ask.

"Why not? But back to the point, you can't just get a magic kombucha if you're not one of us."

"Is there anything in the magic kombucha that would show up on a tox screen?"

Gran makes a face. "I shouldn't think so. But I'm no expert.

"Why does it matter?" Phoebe asks.

"Maybe it doesn't. But it might tell us two things." I hold up one finger. "First, whether the person who poisoned Adam was a Mystic Hollow resident and could therefore have access to the special potion. Second, if the kombucha counteracted the effects of the toxin. If it did, and the person who administered the poison didn't know about it, maybe there was a second person. We always said overkill."

"Two people? One from the Hollow. One not." Phoebe mimes her head exploding. "That seems random, though, right? I mean, how would they meet up? Why would they work together?"

"I want to see the transcript of the things I remembered when I was under the influence of magic."

Phoebe loads a sheet, then hands me her computer. I toggle through all of the memories. As I read each one, they go through me like ghosts. I shiver. "The ones about the books and getting promo are obviously Lana and Dan. Although I don't think they are a smoking gun."

"Agreed, dear."

"*Got what he deserved.*" I put my finger to my lip. "Hmm. Could that be the editor or agent? Upset that he was selling them out?"

"Does it feel murderous?" Phoebe asks.

"No. Not really. When I hear it again, it just seems angry. Not enraged."

"*Couldn't have happened to a nicer dude,*" Phoebe reads.

I laugh. "Oh my God, that one's funny. Sounds like a younger author. Half-baked. As in new to the biz."

"If you liked that one, try this one on for size. *Good riddance to bad rubbage,*" Phoebe reads.

"I wondered about that one even as I heard it. Rubbage. What's that?"

"I believe it's a combination of rubbish and garbage, dear. Something the kids are doing."

"Hmm. Doesn't seem to be in the headspace of a murderer, does it?"

"Maybe an ironic one?" Phoebe offers. "My generation is full of that kind of thing."

"Terrible pairing?" I ask. I read the next one. "*Hate her. Hate him.* Who is the her in this situation. Moi?" I place my hand over my heart. "I'm wounded."

"I don't think so, Mom. No matter how much you desire attention at any cost, I think it most likely applies to Marilyn and Nicholas."

"Or Lana and Dan," Gran offers.

"Agreed," Phoebe says.

"*He used people. What an ego.* Not threatening or guilty enough."

"*The deal's sunk now.* That's got to be Marilyn or Nicholas," I say.

"Here we go. Here's something," Phoebe stands up. "*Do they know? Can they tell?*"

"Yes!" I say. Also, "*Stop looking guilty.* I don't know who thought those things, but I can definitively say those thoughts came from different people."

"Let's let that simmer a bit, dear." Gran gets up and goes to the stove. "It's just a theory. Maybe it was one killer who was slightly scattered and chaotic." She casts a glance my way.

"Are you saying if I were to plan a murder, I'd be inconsistent and need to make hasty corrections due to lack of coherent planning?"

"You said it, I didn't," Gran says.

"Are you actually accusing me?" I ask, even though I know she really isn't. Still, it smarts.

"Of course not, dear. Honestly, you are touchy. Maybe go for a walk to reduce the cortisol?"

"What? Did you watch a podcast on that?" I ask. A little snippy.

"She's making eggplant meatballs and lasagna. This woman is a gem." Phoebe goes to Gran and puts her arm around her shoulders.

"Oh no," Gran says.

"What's wrong?"

"I burned the sauce. What's with me?" She holds her head in her hands.

"I burn things all the time," I say. "You're preoccupied. I distracted you. I'm sorry."

"Now there won't be enough for dinner."

I'm surprised she doesn't have any reserves in the freezer or the pantry. Gran is big on canning. She also tends to make big batches of sauce in the summer and freeze a bunch of it. Enough to make it through until the summer crop. I don't press or pry. I just say. "We'll walk into town and get some canned tomatoes. Shake off some of that cortisol."

"But the pins," Gran says. "They're still handing them out."

"Then they will face our wrath," Phoebe says, putting her arm around my shoulder this time. "We are angry."

"Solidarity sister!" I say as we head out the door.

When we are well out of earshot of the house, I say, "That was weird."

"What?"

"Gran never runs out of tomatoes. She freezes a metric ton of sauce and cans even more tomatoes. She either wanted us out of the house or she wanted us to be in town. But for what reason?"

"Interesting," Phoebe says. "She's a regular puppet master, isn't she?"

"Puppets are creepy," I say.

"But your dollhouse is not?" she asks.

"Take that back!" I pick a berry from a nearby tree and throw it at her.

"Very mature, Mom."

"Maybe she is planning a secret rendezvous with Sloan?" I offer. "He seemed very smitten with her."

"Smitten?"

"I stand by my word choice. Or maybe she wants to meet with him to tell him she thinks I'm a goner. Off to Sing Sing for me."

"That's for high profile killers. I think you'd be more local."

We make it into town and to my chagrin, the pins are everywhere. We pass the head of the PTA, Melissa Waters. She's got on a pink one. "Rooting for you, Veronica." She gives me a thumbs-up.

Things take a downturn when we stop at the newsstand. The owner, Guy Rodgers, gives me the side eye as he proudly displays his blue pin.

Phoebe picks up a magazine. Flips through it. Goes to pay for it, then puts it back on the stand. "Trash, that is." she says.

We bust up laughing. It's childish, but it feels good to push back against people who have decided I am capable of murder when they don't even know me. Tallulah is walking her dogs again, and all of them are wearing pink pins. I want to hug them.

Of course, we see Almira, perfectly rolled up yoga mat in hand, enter the store.

"She annoys me," I tell Phoebe.

"The yoga mat?" she asks.

"You noticed it too? Who rolls their mat so obsessively? It's not normal."

Phoebe pats my shoulder. "There, there. Your old yoga mat accident has been long forgotten."

"Obviously not."

"Take solace in the fact that most of the people here will never know you flattened a ninety-four-year-old man with one end of your mat, and then while you bent to check on him, you took out his dog."

"There's a video." I do a face palm. "Why does she have to yoga here anyway?"

"I've never heard yoga used as a verb before, but I like it. And the video has no attribution. No one could find that."

"It's like she's obsessed with Mystic Hollow. Very weird." I shake my head as if I feel sorry for her. "Poor thing."

"Oh boy. Let's get our stuff and get out."

The store is hopping. Like happy hour without the fruity spiked drinks. It's vibrating with people who have no shortage of opinions. Mayor Racker is at the water aisle with The Leach.

I whisper, "I thought she didn't buy bottled water. Ha!"

Almira turns to face me. I guess the whisper wasn't as quiet as I'd hoped. "Yes. That's the real crime here. Plastic water bottles."

The mayor bursts out laughing. She points to her pin—blue. She's supporting Mack. Whatever.

Snippets of conversation hit me as we browse the aisles. "I play pick-up basketball with Mack. I've known him much longer than I've known Veronica," Clayton, the store owner says. "But murder? She seems a little scattered to pull that off. I'm going to do a purple pin, I think."

My fists clench. Phoebe puts her hand on my shoulder. "Easy, Mom. Purple means progress. And he *has* known Mack longer. Plus, they play basketball together. That means something."

"Smarty-pants," I stick my tongue out and move to the next aisle. "Grab Oreos too."

When we get to the checkout, we are fifth in line behind The Leach, Mayor Racker, Danetra (who is wearing a pink pin), and Cassandra Fetterly. My phone dings.

Text from Dan: Sent the pages. Hope this helps.

Me: Thanks!

Dan: I remembered something else about the girl from the conference. She knew you.

Me: From where?

Dan: I assumed from a critique group or something. Her last name was one of those nature names. Rivers. Clifton. Something like that. Sorry I can't be of more help.

Me: Did Adam say what he critiqued for her?

Dan: Nope. He shut down any questions about her.

Me: Curiouser and curiouser.

Dan: Will let you know if I remember anything else.

Me: You're the best. TY.

Dan: Stay safe.

Phoebe gives me a look. I show her the texts. I admit, I'm a little freaked that this mystery woman has some sort of connection with me. But I shrug it off. The writing community is small, but it could still be one of the hundreds of people I've critiqued or who have critiqued me. I pick up a pack of gum from the aisle as we wait. "We can do the analysis now, find out if the motive *was* plagiarism." Then I realize maybe I'm being too outspoken about things I shouldn't be.

The Leach whispers, "Newcomer in town with zero investigative skills versus sheriff who's been here forever and is an actual detective. Hardly seems like a contest. Despite what the TV shows tell us, it takes more than a can-do attitude and a spunky spirit."

Laughter.

Another ding. Then my pocket starts ringing. "Mom?" Phoebe asks. "That's you."

"Oh, damn. Hello?"

Everyone turns to look at me. "Seems that might be a can't do attitude. I mean, if you don't even know when your own pocket is ringing . . ."

"I forgot about this one." I hold up the phone as some sort of proof. Of what, I'm not certain.

"A second phone—that's not sketchy at all," Almira says.

"They call it a burner phone, I believe," answers Mayor Racker. "Criminals, I mean."

More laughs.

I step out of line, wave them away. Put my finger in my ear so I can hear Pete.

"Just checking in. Are you alone?" Pete asks.

"No. I'm at the store. Why?"

"Be careful what you say in public."

I look around. Is he watching me? "You called me!"

"I've been texting you and you haven't answered."

I look at the phone. "Sorry. I'm not good at this . . ." I whisper, "stuff."

"Read the messages," he says and hangs up.

Pete: I didn't find the book in Adam's files. He must have been exaggerating how far along he was. Boastful to the end.

I'm annoyed that this man thinks I owe him my attention or my time, but I do need his help so I type back:

Me: Heard from Dan. He has early pages of Adam's to check for plagiarism.

Pete: Didn't think of that. LMK.

I'm so busy reading my texts and emails that I don't see it's our turn. Phoebe puts the basket down and pays with her card. "No big, Mom. I got this."

It's one of our jokes since I pay her bills anyway. As we are walking home, the sun starts to sink below the horizon. Twilight in the Hollow is a special time. Breathtaking. Magical. Something niggles at the back of my mind about the magic specific to Mystic Hollow. We pass the bakery. The bookstore. The Magic Bean. The tailors. I look back toward the Magic Bean. "Dare we get some more kombucha?"

Phoebe puts her hand on my arm. "Let's try to lay off the stuff for a while. Coffee addiction is plenty for now."

"When you're right, you're right."

My phone dings.

"More men with info for you?"

I read the email from an unknown sender, stopping dead in my tracks. "No." My hand trembles.

"What is it?"

I don't want her to see. I don't want her to know. It's a notification alerting that a video of Phoebe's school incident has been posted on the socials with the caption: "Phoebe Blackthorne's Violent History."

Chapter Nineteen

I'm so angry, I'm shaking, but I also need to table those emotions in order to be here for Phoebe. I watch her face as she reads the email and looks at the video. It changes from ashamed to angry to happy. Happy?

"This is good news," she says as we turn into Gran's driveway.

"Am I missing something?" I stare at the phone, seething. I am seething.

"Mom, this means we are closing in on our investigation."

I stop and face her. "Nothing is more important than you and your safety and your well-being. Nothing. Not me being cleared of a crime I didn't commit. Not anything."

"That's a bunch of hyperbole for you. Mom, you are the queen of the hyper bowl." This is an old joke, a butchering of the word itself and turning it into an event like the Super Bowl. I don't find the humor here. "Of course I don't want this to get out, but also, it's silly to think I am the center of the entire world. I mean, if saving me from embarrassment costs you your freedom and allows the killer to go free, it's not worth it."

"I know you're right, but how damning is the video?"

"Let's go in and watch it together."

Gran steps out of the house with her cane, a harvesting pouch, and scissors. "I'm making rosemary focaccia to go with our meal."

"We'll help," I offer.

"I'm fine, dear, but if you would like to join me, I won't turn down the company."

I expect to head toward Gran's garden beds, but I see they are mostly potatoes, beets, and parsnips—the root vegetables that still grow in the winter before major frosts and snow hits. It begs the question: Where are her herbs? Then I see it—a small greenhouse at the back of the property.

"When did you get a greenhouse?"

"Last summer. You didn't think herbs would grow in the fall without one, did you?"

"I guess not."

Gran is the first one in, so I can't see what she's upset about, but I hear her say, "Oh, dear. How? Who?"

"What's wrong?" I ask. Then I see it. In the back of the greenhouse is a mature angel's trumpet. Next to what I assume is belladonna. "Is that . . ."

"Yup. I think that's water hemlock. The trifecta of murder plants," Phoebe says. "We must be making someone *very* uncomfortable."

Gran takes out her phone. Dials. I can't see who she's calling until I hear her say, "Mack, I think you ought to come to my house as soon as possible and bring some gloves."

Gran doesn't wait for him to respond before she hangs up. Power move, for sure.

"May I ask why you called the cops? Isn't that counterintuitive or at least shouldn't my attorney be present?"

Gran holds up her finger. "Grand idea. They can all stay for dinner."

"I'm not entirely sure we should all be breaking bread together. I mean, this could implicate me."

"Not likely. Let's trust in the process, shall we?" And with that she snips some rosemary and toddles off toward the house.

"Where are you going?"

"I've got to start my focaccia, don't I? It has to proof."

Mack gets here before Sloan, and Gran sends Phoebe to open the door for him. We haven't had a chance to view the video that we are being threatened with, so I tell Phoebe not to mention it.

Phoebe leads Mack into the kitchen, and he takes a seat. He's in his civvies, which I guess should make me happy, but he's got my file with him.

"You want to tell me what this is about?"

"When Sloan gets here. In the meantime, would you like an oatmeal raisin cookie?"

I shoot her a look. Gran bakes a lot of things but not these. "Since when do you bake cookies?"

"Sometimes I make cookies. I had a hankering for some, and they're pretty easy to throw together. Plus, I like that they feel healthy. It's the oatmeal." She takes a bite as if that's proof of her statement.

I can tell one thing—Gran did not make these, and I have no idea why she's lying. That woman has so many balls in the air, she'd make a juggler quit his day job.

The doorbell rings.

I hold up my hand. "I'll get it."

Phoebe comes with me. "What's up?"

"Your grandmother is confounding me. On so many levels."

"Because she made cookies?"

"Did you see a baking sheet anywhere in the kitchen? She doesn't even own one. I've known her my entire life and she has never baked cookies of any sort."

"It's a weird thing to lie about."

"Agreed. Let's table it for now."

"Okay. Cookiegate investigation will start as soon as you are cleared of these charges."

I hum in agreement and open the door and let Sloan in. He's in jeans and a sweatshirt with Hush Puppy loafers and a fedora. "Thanks for coming. Gran is hoping you'll stay for supper."

"Smells amazing. Your grandmother is very persuasive."

We walk into the kitchen, and Sloan nods toward Mack and smiles at Gran. She smiles back. It would be the perfect romcom if my liberty wasn't at stake.

"What are we doing here?" Mack asks.

"Someone planted angel's trumpet and other murder plants," Gran pauses to check in with Phoebe, "That's what you called them, right?"

"Yes, Gran."

"Well, someone planted murder plants in my greenhouse."

"Is that right?" Mack asks. "Let's go see."

Sloan gives him a look as if the two of them have an understanding about what this means. An understanding that is somehow good for my case. I, for one, remain confused.

We head out the back door this time, which is a little closer to the greenhouse but a little harder for Gran to navigate with her cane, so she leaves it behind. Sloan puts out his arm like they do in those old movies where the women and men take a stroll on the promenade. She takes it. "Thank you, kind sir," she says.

I catch Phoebe's eye and mime puking. She waves me off.

"I'm just glad my impending incarceration has rekindled the fires of love," I whisper.

"Could you *be* more dramatic?"

"Did you just use a Chandler inflection?"

"Maybe. *Friends* was a classic."

I put my hand over my heart. "You wound me. A classic. It's not that old."

"If you say so."

The greenhouse is small, so I stand outside with the door propped and watch as Mack puts his hand on his cheek.

"He looks like Columbo," Phoebe says.

"Shh."

"Just needs the wrinkled raincoat."

"Shh."

He takes out his phone and snaps some pictures. Then everyone turns to exit the greenhouse. I hold the door open and follow the procession back inside.

"So?" Gran asks.

"Definitely planted," Mack says.

"Well, of course they were since they're actually plants!" I say.

He shoots me an incredulous look.

Sloan puts his hand on mine. "This helps you."

"I don't see how."

"Sit, dear. I'll make you some tea."

"I don't want tea. I want everyone to tell me what's going on."

Mack flips open the folder he brought with him. Inside he's got large glossy photos of my possessions, my room, and finally, Gran's greenhouse. "These were taken yesterday."

"When you were out, dear."

"See?" Mack says. "There were no murder plants, as you so eloquently put it, in the greenhouse yesterday. Now there are. They are mature plants, and I bet if I pull them out, they will be fully rooted due to the . . ." he takes his finger and makes his nose twitch. "Witchy doings in this town."

"Did you just mock Elizabeth Montgomery?"

"No. I mocked Samantha Stephens. But the point is, if you committed this crime, why would someone have to frame you for it?"

The room starts to spin. Sweat forms on my neck and my forehead. I feel my legs give out. Hands grip me. Lower me to the chair. Hold me upright while Phoebe presses a bag of frozen peas to my neck and Gran fans me.

"Mom?"

"Let's bring her to the couch so she can lie down."

Hands lift me. I feel myself being carried. Even in my fugue state I can tell it's Mack doing the carrying, and I'm slightly mortified. After a minute or two, I start to come around.

"Give her something with salt," Mack advises.

Phoebe races to the kitchen. She puts salt in my hand and I bring it to my mouth.

"Have a little kombucha, dear," Gran says. "It'll perk you right up."

If I'd been drinking something, I would have done a spit take. The casual references to witchcraft are unexpected, to say the least.

"Also, we've received a video threat," Phoebe says.

That makes me bolt upright. "We haven't even looked at it yet."

Mack gives her a look.

"It's about something that happened in Florida. I was in a fight at school and got suspended. I'm not even sure how anyone got a video of it, but whoever sent it to Mom told us to stop investigating."

"Should I be insulted?" Mack asks. "I mean, I didn't get anything threatening."

"Will you be dropping the charges against my client?" Sloan asks.

"I haven't filed them yet, but I'm thinking we should move forward. Just until we find the real killer."

"I'm not certain how comfortable my client is with that. I mean, it will end up painting her in a bad light and she's already new in town."

Mack thinks. "What if I don't formally charge her, but I let it be known that I am leaning that way. You know how things work around here. Small town," he says before any of us can finish that sentence.

Sloan looks at me. Then at Gran. We both nod.

"Mack, will you stay for dinner?"

"I'll take a rain check. I can't let it seem like we are on good terms."

"Right."

"By the way, for a newcomer, you've scored quite a number of pink pins. I should definitely be insulted by that. All of Cranberry Court went pink. Pink!" He stands and heads to the door. Does a stage whisper. "This is just in case." He points to me. "Don't leave town." Then he walks to his car and heads off.

Once he drives away, we all cheer.

"Now, about dinner, Sloan. You suddenly don't have any work to do," Gran says.

"How do you know that?" I ask. "I mean, he may have other cases, Gran."

"I'm retired. Only took this case for an old friend." He winks. "I'd love to stay for dinner."

As they file into the kitchen, I face my daughter. "Why?" I ask. "Why would you tell him about the video?"

"Because I don't want to see you only on weekends. I might need those for future fun times with my peers."

"But Phoebe—"

"It doesn't matter, Mom. I didn't do anything wrong. They ambushed me. I have no clue how someone got that video. If it's up somewhere, maybe. But if it is, who cares?"

"So, you don't mind if I watch it?"

"I'd rather you didn't." She looks at the ground. "It basically shows me shattering the mirror and starting a fire in the trashcan without touching either of those things. Like magic." She does jazz hands.

"Why are you doing jazz hands for this?"

"Jazz hands make everything better, do they not?"

"I guess so. I'm sorry about the video. That must have been really scary for you. I mean the day it happened. But I guess now also because it could get out."

Phoebe looks straight at me. "It was. But I'm not scared anymore. I Harry Pottered that situation. I should be revered." She looks out the window. "And now I have a white owl just like he did, so . . ."

"You're basically related."

"Or married. Sorry, Ginny. But also, Mom?"

"Yes?"

"You were right. Gran is up to something. When I got the frozen peas for your head, I saw a bunch of tomato sauce. She wanted us out of the house for a reason. She sent us to town so she could do something clandestine."

I smile. "Excellent word. Do you think she planted the murder plants?"

Phoebe looks impressed. "No. But cool if she did. I think she had people over, though. There were tire tracks in the driveway before the sheriff got here. At least two cars. You were too busy with the video to notice."

"Curiouser and curiouser," I say. "Let's eat. We'll grill her later."

Chapter Twenty

We sit around the table, enjoying the fruits of a good harvest—Gran used her own tomatoes, which she said she found after we left. Then she put her hand to her head as if she were a silly old woman. Which she's not. I let her play her part while Sloan is here, but I am determined to get answers later.

"Eat up! We are celebrating!" Gran says.

"Hear, hear!"

"Are we sure I'm off the hook?"

"You heard the sheriff, dear."

"How do we know he's not doing a double fake-out thingy? You know, maybe he really believes I'm the murderer, but he's enlisting us to help him find the 'real' one, thereby creating an environment where we'll share information freely that we normally wouldn't? Huh?" I stab an eggplant meatball and wave my fork around.

Sloan turns to me. "What you're proposing is illegal. I mean, if he's charging you, he has to tell you. Plus, he has those pictures of the greenhouse from before and now after. Unless he planted the evidence." Sloan laughs a little. "No pun intended. But there is no way to trick you into cooperating."

"I don't know . . ." I stare at my plate, not even excited about eggplant meatballs anymore. "It still feels dangerous. All of these suspicions. Me new in town . . ."

Phoebe forks a meatball and holds it up. "You have trust issues, Mom. You really need to work on that."

"Where's Kim?" I ask. "She's been gone all day."

"Well, she doesn't live here, does she, dear? And she doesn't work for us twenty-four seven. I think I'll clear the dishes." Gran goes to grab the plates.

Phoebe covers hers, and I do the same with mine. "We're not done."

Gran sits back down. "Honestly. I am a geriatric woman with a cane. No match for you two."

Sloan says, "Shall I?"

"No, dear. Let the girls eat. They've had a tough week."

"Yes, we did," I say, "Also, we have a lot to unpack. Namely," I motion to Phoebe to take notes on her phone by nodding in her direction, which, weirdly, she seems to understand. "Number one, we need to figure out if Adam did steal someone's work, using the samples that Dan sent me and the first pages of the passion project that Pete found in his effects."

Phoebe pumps her fist.

"Number two, we need to figure out who is blackmailing us."

Phoebe shoots me a questioning look.

"The video. Remember. Your violent past." I use air quotes around the worst word in that sentence. How could anyone consider Phoebe violent?

"A timeline," Phoebe says. "When did people start thinking we suspected them? What caused them to try to get us to stop investigating and to literally plant evidence?"

"Hmm. Do we think those two things feel very different, in terms of level of risk as well as methods of implementation, I mean?

Which also leads us back to a team of at least two individuals. Overkill, remember?"

Gran nods.

"And three, we might have to interrogate someone who is usually beyond reproach but has been known as of late to be less than forthright."

"Who would that be, dear?" Gran asks, her chin propped in her hand. Perhaps to look even more innocent.

"Do I need to stay to defend you?" Sloan asks.

"No, I'm fine. I'll just pack your dessert to go so the girls and I may debrief."

"If you're sure." He looks in her eyes, so sweet.

"I am. But you can do something for me, if you don't mind."

"Say the word."

"I've sent you an email with the specific request."

He takes out his phone. "So you have. It will be done."

I pack up some of the wild blueberry and cranberry crumble. "Thank you for everything." I give him a kiss on the cheek, and Gran sees him to the door.

Phoebe says, "Let's eat this on the couch. It always feels special when we have dessert in a different room."

"Growing up, it was brandy in the parlor." I hold up plates of crumble with coconut whipped cream on top. "This is better."

Phoebe elbows me. "What do you think she asked Sloan to do? Nothing rated R. Right?"

"No. Of course not." I look at Gran waving to him from the porch. "Although I wouldn't put anything past that woman these days."

Gran comes in. Sits in her chair, and I realize she's not even keeping her cane with her anymore, now that the obvious limp she had when we got here has progressed to a slight hobble. "Let the tribunal begin."

I hold up my spoon. "Oh no, you don't mess with that hyperbolic description of a family meeting that is way past due."

"Hey. Is Gran the original Hyper Bowl Queen?"

"Apparently. Now, for the questions."

Gran waves her hand to tell me to let them fly.

"First of all, who was here today when you sent us out on a fool's errand?"

"Excellent use of that term, dear." She salutes me with her spoon as she takes a delicate bite of the crumble.

"Well?"

"I might have had some company while you were out, but I had to do something."

"Did you plant those murder plants, Gran?" Phoebe asks.

"No. Also, little known fact, all plants are toxic, by the way. It is their only means of defense." Gran crosses her arms so as to look put out by this line of questioning. "It's not their fault these particular plants are super dangerous."

"Did any of the people you had over plant the angel's trumpet?"

"Of course not. Although it would have been smart if we had, wouldn't it have been?"

"Who was here and what were you doing that you needed us out of the house?" I ask.

"Well, I needed you out of the house precisely because of who was here—my book club."

"You mean 'book club'?"

"No, dear. We do discuss books. I told you that."

"Gran, are you part of a secret coven?" Phoebe asks.

"If I were, I wouldn't be able to answer that, would I?"

"Why did you call them?"

"I wanted to do a protection spell for you, dear. I was worried about you." She dabs her eyes and unlike her other subterfuge, these feelings seem real.

Phoebe rushes to her side and hugs her. "Leave her alone, you monster."

Gran pats her. "It's alright, dear."

"Do you think maybe they planted them on their own?" I ask.

Gran shakes her head. "To meddle in that way would imply they didn't trust their magic and the universe. It wasn't them, I'm sure of that."

"Can we try to nail down a time for the greenhouse caper now?" Phoebe asks.

"Some time between yesterday afternoon and when we found them today," Gran says.

I wave my spoon in the air. "After this is over, we're going to install security cameras."

"Whatever you say, dear."

"We need to figure out if this was a simple frame job from the beginning or if you have somehow become a threat," Phoebe says.

"Those are different things entirely," I say. "Good work."

"If it was a frame job, they must have known you were meeting him in the belfry that night."

"Right. If we are becoming a threat, then they must have just found out that we were zeroing in on the killer. I mean, we *were* talking about it while we were shopping today. But is that enough time to plant evidence and find that video?"

"We don't know if the video is readily available or if they had to hack into the school cameras. That would take more time. I'll check my Insta. See if anyone's posting it there."

"Whoever is doing this is relatively tech savvy. Maybe that points to Pete or any of his assistants?"

"That Amherst girl looked sus. Or just really serious," Phoebe says. "I can figure out who she is and maybe find her on the socials. See if she was staying anywhere near here. People are so sloppy with that stuff."

"Good. Who else is tech savvy?"

"I mean, anyone my age. Honestly," Phoebe says.

"That's true."

A knock on the door makes me jump.

Kim peeks her head in. "Hello. Is now a good time?"

"Timing couldn't be better, actually. But first, are you hungry?"

Kim puts her hand on her stomach. "Starved."

"Come into the kitchen with me, dear. We have a lot to share about our day."

"Excellent." She pushes her black-rimmed glasses higher on her nose. "I may have something also. A friend of mine who does video game design was able to make our model even more user-friendly."

"Weren't you supposed to be doing homework?" I ask.

"I can multitask."

"You know they recently found out that no one can really do everything all at once, much less do it well," I say. "It's a myth."

"Those studies only looked at typical users. Not those with rampant ADHD," Kim informs me.

"You too?"

"Yep!" she says as she and Gran come back to the living room. "These eggplant meatballs are amazing. You should open a food truck."

"Hmm," Gran says. "Maybe we can park it outside the store."

"Can you run the program isolating people aged 18 to 32?" I ask.

"Sure, shouldn't be a problem," Kim says, continuing to eat as we fill her in on our day and our discoveries. Gran slides a bowl of crumble in front of her as I clear her plate.

I can't explain it. I should be upset that someone broke into Gran's greenhouse without our knowledge. Or that they are trying to frame me for murder. But it feels so good to spend time together, all of us, that I just enjoy it for the moment.

Then my phone beeps.

Text from Dan: Did you read the email????

Me: Not fully. Just glanced at it and the pages you sent.

Dan: You have to read it. Adam told his editor about his passion project. So, if the motive was to conceal that someone stole his work and used it as their own, then . . .

Me: Nicholas is in danger.

Chapter Twenty-One

"This is insane," I say as I pace the kitchen.

Gran nods.

I text Pete: Do you know Nicholas?

Pete: Why aren't you using the other phone?

Me: Sorry. I'm terrible at this.

Pete: Call me on the other phone.

I do. He answers. "What's up?"

"According to Dan, Nicholas was aware of Adam's project. He knew about it."

"I'm not following."

"If the motive was plagiarism, Nicholas may be in danger."

"The motive might be something else. It could be unrelated to writing. Although, that's unlikely. It could be a spurned love interest. That seems plausible. Or the info on Fox N Sox Books. Any of the publishers could be implicated. Including Nicholas's house."

"That's true. You're right. It's like they say, when you're a hammer, all you see are nails."

He laughs. "Keep me posted. I'm in Washington now. Got here yesterday. Doing an on-location video at Fox N Sox's offices. If all goes well, it will air tomorrow.

"Aren't you worried?"

"About this killer? I guess if they are willing to chase me to the West Coast, they can have me. The flight out here was awful. I wouldn't wish it on my worst enemy. Anyway, use the burner. Bye."

I send an email to Nicholas Turner.

Please call me ASAP. 911.

No response.

"He doesn't know me that well," I say. "Plus, he gets thousands of emails. Why open this one."

I get a text from a number I don't recognize:

I wouldn't call the cops.

A link is attached. "They sent a video." I show them my phone. "Should I open it?"

Phoebe presses play. It's the video of her at her old school with the girls in the bathroom, only in this one she uses a lighter to light the fire in the trashcan and she smashes the mirror with her backpack.

"I didn't do that, Mom. I swear. Look at the other video. AI. It has to be."

I try to pull up the original video, only it's not on my phone anymore. "It's gone." I show them my phone. "How did it disappear?"

"Spyware. Malware. A virus. Did you put your phone down anywhere?" Kim asks.

I try to think. Did I? I seem to remember something about that.

"Or they could have used Bluetooth if they were near you," Kim offers. "My cousin's an ethical hacker."

"What's that?" I ask.

"They protect people's businesses from hackers who charge huge ransoms."

"How could they alter a video like that?"

"It's not that hard if you have the software.

"Think, think, think," I say.

"Are you invoking Pooh Bear?" Phoebe asks.

"I'm invoking the memory of baby Phoebe invoking Pooh Bear. But either way, I'm hoping it helps." I throw my attention to Gran. "What did your book club decide they would do? Did they offer protection?"

Gran twirls her wedding ring and looks grim. "Their powers in this matter are limited, especially if the killer is from here and has access to the same mystical springs as we do. But they did say that you could seek specific guidance from the Witch of the Forest."

"Who?"

"There is a powerful witch who lives in the forest between our town and Glendale Springs. Sometimes if you ask for her help in the proper way, she'll grant you a wish."

"Like a genie?"

"Hmm," Gran says. "Not entirely, but similar. I'd say she's Jinn adjacent. But you have to be certain of your request before you ask. You only get one wish, if she's even willing to grant that to an outsider."

"First of all, how did I not know about this mythical magical being living so close to you all this time? Huh? Also, I'm becoming an insider."

"Becoming is the operative word," Gran says. "The fact that you are being snarky about our wonderous lady is proof positive that you are not ready to be called an insider, my dear."

"We need to call Mack," I say. "I'm not so desperate as to beg a forest witch."

"The Witch of the Forest. Our Wonderful Lady of the forest, technically," Gran says.

"That's quite a title. Owl. It spells owl. Get it? Is it Stella? Stella, can you help us?"

"I'm not certain that depreciating her is the best way to get on her good side."

I look around. "What? Is she listening, like Siri? Alexa? Which, by the way, Siri is a fine name but using an actual girl's name—Alexa—is going too far. What about all of the Alexas in the world who are going to have to deal with that? It's inconsiderate."

Kim throws questioning eyes my way.

Phoebe puts her hand on my shoulder. "She gets like this sometimes." Then to me. "Do you need to go to a quiet place?"

"I'm not a child," I say.

"Do you need some coffee?" Phoebe asks.

I nod.

"I'll make her an espresso," Gran says.

"It's information overload. And now, apparently, the witch of the east is listening in on our conversations through some kind of AI tool that we've been convinced we need to make us happy, and I'll never be accepted by her."

"You like Alexa. You tell her to play the soundtrack from *Wicked* and she complies," Phoebe says.

"That's true. And *Les Misérables*."

Gran appears with an espresso and her phone. "Calling Mack."

"I wonder if we can still track him," Kim says.

"Mack?" I drink my espresso, contrite now that the caffeine is lighting up the far recesses of my brain.

"Nicholas. You know. We put air tags in their goodie bags. Remember?" Kim says.

"Oh yeah."

"You were just ranting about AI taking over our lives and you actually tracked people with bracelets and QR codes and geo tags and digital business cards and air tags?" Phoebe puts her hand on her head. "Did you take the hypocritical oath?"

One of our jokes.

"Apparently."

Kim takes a look at the spreadsheets to find Nicholas's air tag and pings it. We stare at her phone as it registers.

"Weird. He's in Mystic Hollow," Phoebe says.

I start to get a bad feeling. "Where?"

Kim screws up her face. "I think he's at Kiki's. That's strange, right?"

"Studio or plunge pools?" Gran asks.

"Plunge pools," Kim says, chewing her lips. "According to this, he hasn't moved since yesterday."

Gran calls Mack, and I wave to get her attention. "Tell him to meet us at the plunge pools. Immediately."

* * *

We jump in the car and race to the plunge pools. There's something about this entire thing that seems to be related to water. The storm that got us to move from Florida. The plunge pools. The kombucha made with water from the springs.

Mack gets there just before we do, and he puts up his hand. "You wait here. Let me go in and check it out."

I'm more shocked than I should be as he pulls a gun out of his holster and enters the plunge pool room, the gun raised in front of him. After a few beats, I hear his walkie, he's calling for an ambulance and a team to investigate. That doesn't sound good.

He comes out.

"Is it Nicholas?" I ask.

"Yes."

"Is he . . ."

"Yes."

All of a sudden, I need to sit down. It's not that I didn't think Adam's murder was serious, but now there have been two murders. That's insane. Two people I knew are now dead and someone killed them.

"I'll need to bring you in for questioning," he says.

"I thought I was cleared."

"I believe he's talking to me, dear." Gran gives a wry smile.

Mack opens the door to the backseat of his car.

"Call Sloan, dear," she says. "Oh, and put up the dishes. I hate a dirty kitchen."

"Wait. Why are you taking her?"

"Nicholas was hit by a blunt object before being thrown into the pool. Most likely, based on the shape, a cane."

"So?"

"Her cane," Phoebe says. "It was her cane, right?"

"Someone's cane. We will be dusting it for fingerprints, of course. Although there are some indications that the killer wore gloves."

"Such as?" I ask.

"Nicholas's prints all over the place, and no one else's. That doesn't track, unless, you know, he somehow hit himself over the head." Mack mimes this ridiculous theory. "And then threw himself into the plunge pool for good measure."

"Not buying it.

"You are amazingly astute. Are you certain this is your first murder?"

I am in no mood for his snarkasm, as Phoebe calls it. "You don't think my grandmother could have done this. For one thing, how could she outpower a taller and younger man?"

"The element of surprise is a weapon in and of itself. Now, shall we?" He gestures to the open door of his cruiser.

I push ahead, blocking her path. "Why? Why would she do this?" I am teary-eyed and desperate now. The thought of my poor Gran being sent to prison is too much to bear.

"To protect you? Just spitballing here." He moves me out of the way. "We really need to get her to the station to discuss this. Or we risk contaminating the investigation entirely."

"We'll be right behind you," I tell Gran.

Meanwhile Kim calls Sloan, which is good since I'd have no idea how to find him. I barely remember his last name. Her cane. When did it go missing? Who could have taken it?

Chapter Twenty-Two

Sloan arrives quickly, changed into a suit and shiny shoes. No Hush Puppy loafers for this prison visit. "Thank you," I say, throwing myself at him.

He hugs me back. "It'll be okay, Veronica. I won't let them keep her."

"Can I go in with you?"

"I'm afraid not." He aims himself toward the interview room, throwing a caring smile at us as he knocks.

The door opens and I try so hard to get a glimpse of my grandmother. To no avail. Kim brings Phoebe and me Americanos from the Magic Bean. The sight of the cup lights up memories of the night Adam was killed. A gloved hand giving someone a cup of kombucha. "For Adam," a disembodied voice says.

It's so hard to separate real memories from ones born out of a wish. Is this one of those? Or did I actually hear the murderer put the plan into place?

Phoebe has her laptop out, typing like mad. "I'm updating spreadsheets," she says. Then she hands it to Kim. "Can you do your video game magic?"

With the laptop perched on her lap and her knees pressed together to keep it secure, Kim works on the spreadsheets. We look over her shoulder, which would drive me mad but doesn't seem to faze her. When she's finished, she pulls up the video game app and pushes play. The screen populates with avatars. Most are nondescript, but some have names attached to them. Each of those have a facsimile of the outfits they wore to the opening ceremonies, so they are easy to pick out of the crowd. I see myself, Phoebe, Gran, Mayor Racker, The Leach, Danetra, Rusty, Dan, Lana, Mack, Tallulah, and Kim. Also identified are the Women United Against Adam people with their signs. Nicholas Turner and Marilyn.

"How did you do all of this?" I ask.

"I've taken the data from all of our trackers and superimposed them on the avatars. I've also looked at the pictures of that night and dressed them accordingly."

"Is that what my hair looks like from the back?" I ask.

"Always concerned with the important things," Phoebe sighs.

My hand flies to the back of my head. "Why didn't anyone tell me?"

"This begins just as Adam arrives," Kim hits play, and we watch as a very dramatic reenactment of the opening ceremonies plays out. Complete with Adam's arrival, ascension to the stage, and a replay of his speech.

"This is insane," I say. "Where were you when JFK was shot? We could've used something like this."

"Focus, Mom," Phoebe says. "Does anything stand out?"

"Not yet. Except for my hat hair."

"Noted. No more bucket hats for you. It's beanies all the way," Phoebe says.

"That's all I ask."

Avatar Adam finishes his speech, looks at his phone. Types something. I blush hot. Was that a text to me? "Do we have any data on his messages?" I ask.

"Nope. That's police stuff."

"No way to hack into that?" I ask.

"Mom!" Phoebe looks around.

"What? You think they're recording us? They've got cameras everywhere?" I stare at the corners of the room where a camera blinks at us. Phoebe points to three more. "Okay! I was kidding!"

Kim presses play, and we watch as Adam signs books, Rusty sells hot chocolate, and Gran sells books. "Where's The Leach?" I ask.

Kim moves a cursor to show me. She's in a group gathered around the stage.

"Damn. No access to drinks for Adam there."

"Wait a minute," I say. "Drinks. You said drinks. Rusty was selling hot chocolate and coffee drinks. Not kombucha. How did Adam get a kombucha?"

"Does that matter?" Kim asks.

"It's an anomaly. Anything that stands out might matter." I take out my notebook and add it to the list of questions. "Keep going."

The video game continues. We see avatars file out. Adam leaves. We watch his avatar head for the belfry.

"Can we tell who is also there?"

Kim nods and chews on her lip. "I've already watched it."

"And?"

"Only you show up."

"Well, that's not great." I pause, like the video. "How are these avatars created?"

"Anyone who has an air tag, a bracelet with a QR code, or a digital business card, which we placed in books and on some of the drinks sold, shows up as an avatar. There are a lot of people who were there who did not buy anything. Who were not given a gift bag or bracelet. The unknowns."

"Right. Who were the unknowns?"

"People who did not register," Phoebe says.

"So, Pete would be an unknown?" I ask.

"Yes, but his alibi confirms he was far away when the murder happened," Phoebe says.

"But he has extensive video editing capabilities, and three motives—inheritance, revenge, and future payoffs, a huge boost to his podcast."

"Right. But an airtight alibi." Phoebe pauses. "Which always makes Monk believe they are the guy."

"Or he likes them for it." I smile. "Don't you just love cop TV talk. We have to ask Mack if that's authentic."

"After we spring Gran," Phoebe points out. "Priorities, missy."

"Right. Who else with a motive is one of the unknowns?" I ask.

The door to the interrogation room opens. Sloan steps out. "They're keeping her. The fingerprints match."

"How?" I ask. "They can't."

"She's okay," Sloan says. "Delores is getting her tea and warm blankets. She will be arraigned tomorrow, on Monday. I'm certain she will be released on her own recognizance. She's a pillar of this community."

Phoebe's hands moved me forward. Kim goes ahead to get the car. I am numb. Frozen. How could they take my grandmother? How could they believe she had anything to do with this?

* * *

We are reassembled in the living room of Gran's house. Phoebe lined the table with snacks. Things that are accidentally vegan—Oreos, Fritos, anything made exclusively of chemicals you couldn't name. Stella followed us home and appeared outside the window. Her soft hoots remind me she is on guard.

"Hey, did Stella wake you up last night?" Phoebe asks.

"No."

"She woke me. I just remembered. She hooted and I wasn't sure what was wrong. I opened the window to see if she wanted to come in, but she was just riled up."

"What time was that?"

"Around five in the morning. What are you thinking?"

"I wonder if that's when Gran's greenhouse was compromised. How could Mack believe Gran did this? Any of this? Especially when he agreed I was being framed."

"I don't know, Mom. It doesn't make sense."

"I feel so helpless," I say. "I can't think of her in that cold dark cell. Alone. Scared."

Kim says, "I bet she's got the entire place listening to her stories. They love her in the Hollow. No one will allow her to be mistreated."

"But if she's convicted, she won't stay here . . ."

"Nobody believes she did this, Mom. Mack is just being shortsighted."

"What do you know about the Lady of the Forest?" I ask Kim.

"Some people say she's a myth. Some people believe she's real. No one knows for certain. Although many have claimed to have gone to her in distress."

"Does she always help them?"

"Some. Others leave disappointed."

"Because their claims aren't just?"

"No one knows for certain. But I do believe that she helps as much as she can when she can."

"What does that mean?" Phoebe asks.

"I don't actually know." Kim looks at her hands, and I can't tell if she feels guilty about something or if she's just bummed she can't offer more relevant information. "I've never personally sought her out. There are stories, though."

"About who?" I can almost hear Gran say, *It's whom, dear.* It's so real and so inside my head, it feels like there's an actual connection between us. I let her voice comfort me. *Go to her,* Gran's voice whispers in my head. *Seek her counsel.*

Something about how Kim is acting lights warning bells in my mind. Her words were super specific. She hadn't personally sought her out. But maybe she knows someone who did? Maybe even helped that person? Maybe it was Gran?

"It *is* the new moon tonight," Kim says. "Some people believe her willingness to help follows the phases of the moon."

"Because the moon influences the tides?" Phoebe asks.

"Hmm," Kim wrinkles her nose. "Perhaps. Everything around here seems to be linked to water in some way."

That statement feels right. Everything, including Adam's murder with the kombucha, and now, Nicholas's death in the plunge pools.

"I think we should go to sleep," I say. "Maybe it'll make sense in the morning." I go upstairs; the emptiness of the second floor offends me. Questions line up in my head. Who are the unknowns? Why did Adam get a kombucha instead of one of Rusty's hot drinks? Whose gloved hand slipped poison into his drink? Who framed me? Who framed Gran? Who is the Lady of the Forest? Will she help me? If she's helped Gran before, what did Gran ask for? Was her wish granted?

Everything in my life has led up to this moment. This decision. I've never asked another person for help. I have difficulty accepting help—something my mother and I fought over for my entire life. But I can't help it. I need to do things for myself. Except in this case, I can't help my grandmother without relying on someone else. Maybe many people.

Just like with Phoebe, I would do anything for her. Literally anything. But I will not take Kim and Phoebe with me. Who knows how I'll find this woman in the woods? I have no idea how to even ask for her help, but I do know that the answers to most of life's big questions can be found in books. For me, the question right now is most likely housed in a certain spell book in Gran's beloved store. I think that means something.

I turn off the light and hope for sound sleep. At least a few hours, anyway. I say a silent prayer to whoever is listening to help me and my Gran. Stella hoots outside. It's not the type of hoot that sounds like alarm. I swear it sounds like an acknowledgement. As in she's acknowledging my prayer. If that's true, or even if it's just in my mind, it feels good and right and at this point I will take more of those things. Mostly, the good and right things that will lead to my grandmother's release. She didn't do this. She couldn't have. Mack has to know this. Doesn't he? Doubt creeps in. He hasn't solved a violent crime in his entire career. Maybe he's not up to the task? Maybe he will fall for this shoddy frame job. Maybe he'll call in the state police, who don't know me or Gran and won't give us the benefit of doubt. Could he do that? Well, if he's going to call in backup, so will I.

I don't know much, but I know I will not allow my pride or principles to get in the way of saving Gran. This time, when I close my eyes, I ask whatever entity is listening to show me the way to clear Gran. I swear I hear a voice enter my consciousness as I drift off on what will end up being a very brief sleep. The voice says simply, *It will be done.*

Chapter Twenty-Three

My eyes automatically open three minutes before midnight. I switch off my alarm before it has a chance to go off, hoping to keep my next move clandestine so I don't wake the girls. I check the lunar calendar that I downloaded and just as Kim said, there is a new moon tonight. I bundle up, trying my best to make as little noise as possible since Kim and Phoebe have crashed on the couches in the living room.

Sneaking out the back door with only my phone light to guide me, the night is so black only the stars shine back at me. I try to remember what phase of moon a new moon is, but apparently, it's the phase where it's not visible at all. Good to know. I walk the five blocks to the store and let myself in.

Even in the middle of the night when Gran has been taken from me and I'm scared of everything, I feel relief coming in here. It's where I first found my favorite authors and books. Where I was allowed to be myself. I didn't have to dress up. I didn't have to make polite conversation or any conversation at all, should I crave alone time. Now I feel the welcoming embrace of the store. I feel like I am meant to be here.

I lock the door behind me and head to the front counter. Reaching under it, I find the spell book, the candle, and the bell. It occurs to me that the items I am using were once used to hunt witches. You rang the bell, closed the book, and blew out the candle to signal the end of a witch's power.

"We're taking it back," Kim says, coming from the back of the store.

I jump. My hand goes over my heart, which is beating like mad right now. "Oh my God, when did you get here?"

Phoebe steps out of the hallway. "Before you did, obviously."

I point toward the house. "I thought you two were sleeping . . ."

Phoebe snaps her fingers. "Keep up, Mom. We knew you were coming here and wouldn't want us to accompany you, but you need us, so here we are."

"What are you taking back?" I ask.

Kim says, "The symbolic use of the bell, book, and candle. We decided to embrace the sound of the bell, the heft of the book, and the light from the candle to give power to magic, not snuff it out."

"How did you know I was thinking that?" I ask.

"Phoebe told me after we did the first spell together. She mentioned the movie *Bell, Book and Candle*. Fun romcom. Except they got some things wrong."

"That's Hollywood for you," I say. "Why are you here?"

"You want to call on the Lady of the Forest? I can help with that."

"Because you've done it before. Right? With Gran?"

Kim lowers her eyes. "Perhaps."

"Let me guess," I steeple my hands. "She asked the Lady to chase us up here. She asked for the storm?"

"Not the storm exactly, but yeah."

"Do you think Gran conjured a hurricane?" Phoebe asks.

Kim shakes her head. "No. Of course not. I think she asked the Lady to use the elements that were already in play to convince you to come up here. I think she helped nudge you to do what you might have already been wanting to do anyway."

Phoebe looks surprised, and I'm grateful not everyone was in on this plan. "It worked out, though. I'm happy here, Mom. We're happy here. With Gran."

A tear runs down my face. Another. Soon I am all-out crying. "I don't like being manipulated," I say. "I like deciding for myself. She could have just asked me."

"She did. So many times, Mom."

"I said no because of you, Phoebe. I didn't want to move you."

"I get that." She wipes tears I didn't realize were also streaming down her face. "But maybe this was for the best. For all of us. I thought those kids were my friends at school. They weren't. Turns out I wasn't good at making friends, I guess."

Kim puts her hand on Phoebe's. "I think you make a really excellent friend."

"Me too," Phoebe says. "But, Mom, you and I—we were so stubbornly certain that we were living our best life. Turns out we were wrong. Really wrong."

Stella hoots outside, and Phoebe opens the window for her to fly in and land on her perch.

"I get that." I wipe a tear. "But now Gran is in danger and I feel responsible for that."

"You aren't. The person who murdered Adam is."

"Or the people," Kim says.

"What should I ask the Lady of the Forest for? I know it has to be specific."

"Um . . ." Phoebe looks up. "What about insight?"

"We did that with the amulet and I got to hear everyone's thoughts. Shudder."

"Right. What about solving the murder? Can it be that direct?" Phoebe looks at Kim.

"Maybe?" Kim shrugs.

"What did Gran ask for?" I see Kim hesitate, and I say, "Full disclosure!"

"She asked for the sacred water to guide you home."

"Oh my God, that is so funny." I slap my leg. Bend over. Grab my stomach. Laugh more. "I mean. Wow. Okay. I needed that."

Phoebe joins in on the hilarity. Kim remains cautious. "It's funny, right? We're laughing. That woman can pack a punch!"

Kim softens her look. Smiles. "Yes. She's pretty amazing."

"Okay. I think I know what I want to ask for." I motion to the book. "Do we use this?"

Kim nods. She lights the candle. Phoebe and I hold the book. "It's sad to do this without Gran," Phoebe says.

"She'll be out soon. Okay. Let's see. What kind of spell do we need?"

"Is there a request for a meeting spell?"

"A 'per my last email' spell?" I ask.

Phoebe shoots me a look. Flips the book until she gets to moon rituals.

"Oh," I say, running my hand over the pictures. "These are beautiful. This art is amazing."

"That's the proper attitude. Respect is key, Mom. Or the book will turn you into a frog."

I laugh. Then look at Kim. She shakes her head.

"Or at least make a frog pee on you," Phoebe offers.

Kim makes a face like she agrees with that sentiment. "Possibly."

Phoebe looks at the spell. Our hands fall on the page. Stella hoots. A warm wind blows through the store as Phoebe says the words in Latin. Then repeats the words in English.

"Please, gods of the forest and the moon and the wind, bless us, accept our offerings, and allow us to find knowledge from Our Wonderful Lady of the forest."

The store warms up and fills with the scent of the springs. Kim nods, and Phoebe rings the bell, closes the book, and blows out the candle.

Stella takes off, flies out of the window, which closes behind her.

"Now what?" I ask.

"Now we follow her."

"All of us?"

"I guess?"

Kim offers, "But first, we need to find an offering worthy of our ask."

"What did Gran give?"

Kim smiles. "Her original first edition *Wizard of Oz* book."

"Wow," I say. Then. "Hey, that was supposed to go to me!"

"Get over it," Phoebe says. "What do we have to give?"

"What's important to us?"

"Coffee?" I say.

"Oh my God. The espresso maker," Phoebe says.

"What? No . . ."

I race after her, but by the time we make it home, I realize it's no use. Phoebe's right. We have to give from our heart. "What's she going to do with that in the forest? Does she even have electricity?" My last attempt to keep the most beautiful coffee making machine I've ever seen.

"Stereotype much?" Phoebe wraps her arms around it and carries it outside. We wait as Stella perches in a tree nearby. "Okay, girl. We're ready."

Phoebe pinches my arm.

"Yes. We are." I say. "With our espresso maker. As a gift."

Stella hoots, then takes off.

We follow, and she lets us. It's kind of amazing how this owl is so aware of us that she stops to make certain we are with her before moving on. We go over creek beds and through trails. So deep into the forest that I know I'd never make it out if it weren't for our guide owl. None of us talk, which is weird for us, but we have to concentrate on putting our feet on the ground instead of in puddles.

Finally, we get to a clearing. The stars shine above and even without the moon, I can see her standing there, majestic, tall, and deer-like. "Is she a—"

"Shh," Kim says. "Not now."

A female voice calls. "Just the one," she says. "Just her."

Her voice is gravely and strangely harmonic. It booms as if from one hundred feet away, and yet it also feels like she's whispering in our ears. It is hypnotizing. I take the espresso maker and march forward. My heart pounds in my chest so hard I want to tell it to stop being dramatic. We are simply walking in the woods at night with no moonlight toward an unknown entity. Friend or foe? Whichever she is, she is powerful. As I approach, the air seems to leave not only my lungs but also the space all around us.

She's got a tea set on a long table made of twigs, where she sits in a chair that is made in a similar fashion. She motions for me to sit. I do.

"Is that for me?" she asks about the espresso maker.

"Yes. Yes, ma'am. Yes, my lady." I wonder if I'm supposed to curtsy. "I'm sorry, I'm not sure what the customs are."

"Clearly," she says. "Is this contraption something that means something to you?"

"Yes. Very much."

"Very well. Put it there." She points to the table.

The light is so dim I can't make out much about the lady except that there are antlers coming from her forehead, and her face looks like it's been painted with glistening greasepaint so she's iridescent and so pretty. Her face seems to change from every angle. Like she's a hologram. Only I know that's not likely. She doesn't look human. But she doesn't look inhuman either. I am confused by her appearance.

"Do I know you?" I ask. "You look familiar. I mean, without the antlers and the moss and the . . ."

She cocks her head as if perplexed by my verbal diarrhea, which means she must not know me. "Drink," she says, motioning to the cups on the table. "We must partake together."

I bring the cup to my lips. I suppose given the recent events I should be cautious about drinking from a cup offered by a person or entity I don't know, but for some reason, I feel safe. I drink. It's delicious. "Lavender and honey and a pinch of something else. I can't quite make it out, but it's striking."

"Rosemary and thyme," she says. "And of course, mint. All for improved insight and direction."

"Thank you."

"I haven't agreed to anything yet. I simply set the table for your request. What is it you would like me to grant you?"

I feel my throat and chest tighten. What if I ask for the wrong thing?

She motions for me to speak.

"I would like the ability to solve crimes. To detect criminals."

"That seems like an exhausting job. People steal all the time. They steal joy. They steal love. They steal things. And people. They also kill."

"I want to free my grandmother. And myself. And I want Adam's murderer to be found."

"So you would like to detect the truth?"

"Yes. I think. I mean, what is truth?" I think of all the ways this could go sideways. All of a sudden, this entire thing feels like a trap.

"You're right to be careful." She takes a tiny sip of tea. "Words can often be misconstrued and soon you'd be hit with truth bombs nonstop. You might think you want to detect the truth, but oftentimes lies are gifts the world gives us."

Truth bombs? Whoever this witch is, she's up on the lingo. Still, I need to focus, and I feel like I'm blowing this. Instead of trying to discover her identity, I should be trying to find the right words, but I am left stumbling over how to phrase my request. "I think . . . I would like to detect this criminal. The one who killed Adam and Nicholas."

She nods. "Ah, that is better. Specific. But my powers are strong. Who knows how long they will last. How many things will be affected. Maybe it's better to see what happens. Let it all play out naturally."

I sip more tea. "Now it tastes like Milano cookies. Blueberry pie with ice cream."

"Your powers of detection are improving already," she laughs, and it's a warm and woodsy sound. I'm not sure how a laugh can be woodsy, but it seems like that to me.

"Is this like that Wonka gum that tastes like three different courses? Or the substance in *The Lightning Thief* that makes food taste like his mother's blue chocolate chip cookies . . . or is it something biblical? Manna?"

"My goodness, you like to talk. Listening would help more." She places her hands on my head. My skin warms and my face heats up. I feel an energy thrumming through me. "I will give you the power to analyze the information your mind has already collected. To find hidden patterns. You need that. Clearly."

"Oh my God, did you just Glinda the Good Witch me with the 'you had the power this entire time'?"

Her tone shifts. "Is that an appropriate thing to ask me?" Her eyes go red. Not the pupils or the irises. The whites of her eyes go red. See? I'm already focusing more. And her face? It's a mask. I see that now. I see past the distractions and discover the hard white shell that lies over her features, disguising her completely. Her voice sounds like it's been altered with one of those voice modifiers like they use in *Scream*. Only less creepy.

She places a small rock on the table. It's bright white and makes me think of luxury soap as it is exceedingly smooth and shaped like a perfect heart. I want to bring it to my nose, but I can detect, even from this distance, that it smells woodsy and of eucalyptus. "Is this from Kate McLeod?" I blurt.

"Clearly not. Have you heard of a worry stone?"

"Yes."

"This is like that, only instead of eliminating concerns, it sharpens your thoughts."

"I'm sorry. I meant no disrespect. Thank you for helping me."

The witch stands, and I see that she absolutely towers over me. Her arms cross over her chest. Icicles drip from her antlers, sharp and dangerous.

I point up at her. "Did you just grow?" I laugh uncomfortably. "Or did I shrink? You know, like in *Alice in Wonderland* where the entire perception is a real thing and magic and blah, blah, blah." But as I look her over, I see her boots are extremely platformed. Even more than the Supremes wore! I can't wait to tell Phoebe. I find myself making a big raspberry. I want to stop, but I can't. "What's happening?"

Her hand goes to my shoulder. "I believe your brain is shorting out from the stress." She presses the button on my beloved espresso machine that is not plugged in or filled with grinds to my knowledge. Still, a perfectly steamed cup of espresso waits for me. "I think I saw your daughter give you this when you were scattered."

So she has seen me before! Which means I've seen her. But where?

I drink the espresso, which somehow has an orange peel in it. And a cookie. "This is wild," I say. "A wish and a cookie." I point to her. "Can I leave a good Yelp review for you? Or is there a 'rate my witch' app?"

She lifts my hand with the cup to my mouth to help me drink. "Place this stone under your pillow every night for a month."

"And after that?"

"Who knows. Maybe it takes. Our brains are wonderous things and they seek neural coordination. A still point."

"Like in yoga?" Wait. Is that a clue? Is this Kiki? I stare harder, trying to see behind the masquerade.

She helps me stand. "Off you go now."

"Oh. Okay. Goodbye and thanks for all the wish-es. Get it." I mock slapping my knee. "Like the Douglas Adams book. Only that's fish and I changed it to wish but grammatically speaking I needed to make it plural."

The witch moves me forward, nodding and making an "Mmm" sound. She lifts her finger, pointing it at the path in front of us.

As I head back toward Kim and Phoebe, I want to turn to wave to her, but I sense she's gone and I've got that Bible story in my head that makes me feel like that's a dangerous thing to do. My mind is reeling, and I'm trying to collect all the relevant details because I've now been programmed to do that. As I make my way back, I am sure of two things. One, that the witch went to great lengths to disguise herself to avoid detection. Two, that means she might be someone we know.

Chapter Twenty-Four

The walk back home is weirdly quiet. They don't ask me how it went, and I'm not sure I could adequately describe it. I take in the sounds of the night, the feeling of the path under my feet, and the small drop in temperature that makes me wrap my arms around myself to keep warm.

I hear Phoebe and Kim next to me, but mostly I listen for Stella's hoots leading us out of the forest. I am not distracted by the sound of the wind. It goes in the background. At the forefront is our safety. Years ago, a therapist suggested I try ADHD medication. I couldn't stand the way it made me feel—like my skin was on fire, I was shaky, and my body felt like it was vibrating. But it did make me focus on the important things. This is like that but with no side effects. Cool.

We make it home, and Phoebe says, "Is anyone hungry?"

Kim says, "I could eat."

I don't get sidetracked by the discussion of food. Instead, I focus on a reoccurring question. "When did Gran's cane go missing?"

"What?" Phoebe asks, heading into the kitchen.

"Her cane. She had it yesterday before we went into the greenhouse. Then while Sloan and Mack were here. How could it have gone missing that quickly in order to be used in Nicholas's murder?"

"I don't see how it could've. His air tag had him motionless since the day before, which means he was murdered before her cane was gone. Unless she had more than one?" Phoebe asks.

"Nope. I could barely talk her into getting the one cane. No way she had two," Kim says.

"That sounds like her. So, I guess what we're saying is someone killed Nicholas with a cane that wasn't Gran's and then swapped hers out."

"But wouldn't there need to be evidence on the cane?"

"They said there were fingerprints. Gran's. And it *was* her cane at the murder scene. I can vouch for that."

"It's a puzzlement," Phoebe says. "The window of time between when we saw it last and when it appeared at the crime scene was so short. Who could have stolen it?"

"Well," I say. "You guys keep saying it's a small town, right?" I start, my fingers steepled together like Mack does. "So maybe somebody heard that Mack was coming to investigate the murder plants and used that as an opportunity to run in and grab the cane and run out."

"We really need to get those cameras set up" Phoebe says.

"It seems like a Mystic Hollow resident might be responsible for the frame job. I'm not certain about the murders, though. No one here has a strong motive."

"That we know of," Phoebe says as she serves three plates of the leftover crumble.

"That we know of," I repeat. "Interesting."

"Why are you repeating that phrase?"

"Because there are many things we don't know. Right? Like the whereabouts of the unaccounted people who were not tagged—the unknowns. Those are things we don't know. Just like the motives."

"We can make assumptions about the motives, though," Kim says. "There are supposedly four major reasons for committing murder—other than if you are a psychopath. Greed. Fear of being found out. Fear of losing something like status or money. Revenge."

"Says who?"

"I follow this cozy mystery writer on YouTube," Kim says. "She broke that down once. I found it interesting."

"Right?" Phoebe says. "And super helpful now."

I take a bite of crumble. "I think Gran put lemon zest in this. You can taste it, right? It's lighting up my tongue!"

"Focus, Mom."

"I am. I'm focusing on the lemon zest. And you're right, we can speculate about the motives and the unknown people who were able to fly under our radar. Were there people who made themselves invisible to our detection on purpose?"

"My goodness, Mom, you actually sound more focused!"

"I feel like the scarecrow who just got a diploma parchment."

Phoebe nods. "Exactly."

"It's past one o'clock in the morning. Let's get some sleep. We need to be alert for Gran's arraignment. We can sort all of this out later." I point to where the espresso machine used to be and put my hand to my heart. "We're going to feel that tomorrow."

"Good night, Mom," Phoebe says.

"Kim, you're welcome to stay."

"Already got out the comforters earlier," Phoebe says. "We're camping in the living room."

"Does your mom know where you are?" I ask.

"Absolutely," Kim answers. "Always." She holds up her phone as proof. I guess they share their location.

Location sharing. That's another way to track people, isn't it? As I head to bed, that thought is the last one I have before I drift off.

* * *

The sun breaking through my window is the only alarm I need. It's seven, and the sun is already shining. Part of me wonders if I'd imagined or even exaggerated some of the mystical elements from last night. I asked to be sharper. Do I feel sharper? I look around. Close my eyes. Breathe. Consider. Hmm. Hard to know.

Listening to the sounds in the house, I hear silence. Phoebe and Kim must still be asleep. I take a hot shower, letting the mirror steam up. If I don't feel more focused, I do admit to feeling weirdly optimistic. As I step out of the steamy deluge, my mind starts ordering things for me. First, figure out who follows who and what that means. Second, find out who in the unknowns group are important. Third, figure out which motive is the strongest. Fourth, figure out if there are any weak or fake alibis.

By the time I make it downstairs, I remind myself that we always believed there were two people involved. Overkill and all. But maybe there were more. Does that mean that the women who had beefs with Adam now go to the front of the line? Not really, since they can all be accounted for on the video game depiction at the time of his murder. They have all since left the Hollow to my knowledge, but I make a note to ask Kim and Phoebe to verify that.

"Morning," Phoebe walks into the kitchen.

"How'd you sleep?" I ask.

"Okay. I miss Gran."

"Well, we are going to go get her soon. Why don't you grab a shower, and I'll make my famous Eggo waffles."

"How are they famous?"

"Well, they are famous because I used to make them for you all the time."

She shoots me a look. "You mean you heated them in a toaster?"

"That counts," I say.

"It's toasting. You may as well take credit for Pop Tarts."

"I may just do that. Now, get going. We've got to save Gran."

Kim pops her head in the kitchen. "I'm going to head home to get changed for school. Tell Phoebe I'll pick her up in half an hour."

School. I am a terrible mother. I completely forgot. Phoebe heads downstairs and ambles into the kitchen. "Kim said she'd be back to pick you up for school in a few."

I see her hesitate. "Maybe I should stay home. Help with Gran."

"Nope. I got it. I'll text you when I spring her."

After Phoebe leaves, I sit, nursing my cup of tea since the espresso machine is gone. "Think, think, think," I say, pointing to my head like Pooh Bear. Hey, if it works for an animated stuffed animal, it might work for me. Only, nothing comes.

Sloan texts me the location of the hearing and the time. I have a small window to grab coffee at the Magic Bean before I can see Gran. On my way to my car, Tallulah stops me. "Hey, honey. So sorry about your Gran. I'm sure they'll let her go posthaste!"

"Thanks."

"No way she's a psycho killer. No way." She slashes the air for effect.

"Thanks again."

"Hey," she calls again. "Did Mayor Racker find you?"

My spidey senses start tingling. "When was she looking for me?"

"Yesterday. She was dropping off the cashbox for the festival or something like that."

"She told you that?"

"No. She didn't see me." Tallulah continues walking her dogs. I race to her side.

"Why didn't she see you?"

"Oh." Tallulah laughs. "I was putting in my bulbs. I always do that right before Halloween. Best time." She starts walking again and I race to catch up.

"How do you know she was dropping off the cashbox?"

She laughs again. "I saw her carrying it into your Gran's house. While you and the sheriff and that nice Sloan were in her greenhouse." She cocks her head. "I guess she changed her mind, though, because when she came out of the house, she still had it."

"Did she have anything else?"

"I'm not sure. I was up to my elbows in dirt. You gotta bury those bulbs deep if you want tulips in the spring." She mimes the action, really going for it, as Phoebe would say, and part of me wants to focus on that because it's funny.

"Tallulah, this is very important. Did she see you?"

"No. She was on the phone—seemed distracted to tell you the truth."

I take her hands. "Listen to me really carefully. I need you to promise not to tell anyone else about this. Okay? It's vitally important."

She nods. "You don't want me to tell anyone that I saw the mayor go into your Gran's house yesterday. I suppose I could do that."

"Good. Please. It's so important."

"Is this about the festival?" she asks.

"It's about helping my Gran."

"Well, sign me up for that, sweetie. I am one of her biggest fans."

I hug Tallulah. Then head for the car. "Remember, shh," I hold my finger up in front of my lips.

I call Sloan. "Can we meet before the hearing? I have information that might be helpful."

"They have a little room we can use. It'll be private."

"Perfect."

Waiting for my cup of cold brew from the Magic Bean, I'm surprised that Rusty isn't there. Or maybe I'm collecting things that aren't important again. Must be focused. Coffee will definitely help with that. I'm about to leave when Rusty comes out of the back room. "Hey, you," he says.

I don't think he remembers my name. "Hey, back," I say.

"Great job on the festival." His face lights up. "I made a killing." Then he covers his mouth. "I can't believe I just said that. I'm so sorry."

I wave him away.

"I didn't mean to be vulgar. I know you were friends with him or were dating him or something?"

"No. Not dating. Just a friend."

"Weird. I distinctly heard that you two were . . ."

"What did you sell the most of?" I ask. "Coffee? Cocoa? Kombucha?"

He smiles. "Coffee drinks were very popular as was the cocoa, I guess. I'd have to check." He scratches his head.

"Not a lot of kombucha?"

"Not really. I mean, it was pretty cold out. Sorry about your Gran, also. I heard they locked her up. That's insane. As if she could push a man like that . . ." He mimes the action, then realizes that it might come off as insensitive. He reaches under his counter. "Hey. Why don't you try this brownie. For free. A sample!"

"Thanks, Rusty. About the kombucha, do you remember who you sold it to at the festival?"

"Just sold one. Can't remember who bought it, though. I don't keep those sorts of records. Is it important?"

"No. Of course not. I had some the other day and I fell in love. Where has it been my whole life. Right?"

"Fermentation is super healthful."

I laugh at that. Rusty looks at me expectantly, though, so I smile. I hold up my coffee. "This is the best, Rusty. Better than any other cold brew I've ever had. And believe me, I've had a lot of cold brew."

"It's in the grinding of the beans. And the chilling of the water," he says. "Each step is important."

"Each step," I say. Only I'm thinking more about murder than coffee, but it applies equally, I guess.

Chapter Twenty-Five

I park behind the courthouse, which is just a block south of the library. It's a small building but furnished with all of the important objects, most importantly, a metal detector operated by Delores. She smiles when she sees me.

"Hello, dear. I brought your Gran one of April's most expensive breakfasts, which Mack will have to take out of his budget. She wins. Gran wins. Mack pays." She pumps her fist "Sisters before misters, am I right?"

"Thank you," I say as I put my phone in the bucket and place my purse on a table. "Did she seem okay? My Gran?" My voice shakes a little.

"Yes. Right as rain."

I step through the metal detector. She hands me the bucket with my phone. I take it out and grab my purse.

Sloan steps out of the courtroom and waves a steady hand at me. "Over here, Veronica."

I stumble forward, my heart hammering. "Can we talk in private?"

"Yes. I've arranged to have a meeting room."

"Have you seen Gran?"

"Not yet, but I have secured release on her own recognizance from both the judge and the prosecutor. No problem. She'll be coming home with you today." He pats my arm, then leads me to a room to the right of the courtroom.

It's a tiny room with only enough space for a small table and four chairs, no window. "Are you sure it's okay to talk in here? No one can hear?"

"No one can hear." He pulls out a chair for me. I sit. He sits next to me, his hand on my arm. "You said you had information to help Alice?"

"Alice? Oh, right. Gran. I'll never get used to that." I clear my throat. Drink some more cold brew, using the pause to clarify my thoughts. "Tallulah. Gran's neighbor, Tallulah, said that she saw Mayor Racker at Gran's house yesterday when we were in the greenhouse with Mack. At around the time when Gran's cane went missing."

Sloan puts his hand on his chin. "Ah. Interesting. Did Tallulah say why the mayor was there?"

"She didn't know. Saw her carrying in the cashbox from the event. But I don't know why she was doing that."

Sloan takes a pad from his briefcase and writes Mayor Racker's name on it. He circles it three times. "That's strange," he says. "When was the last time you saw the cane?"

"Just before that. When Phoebe and I got home, she was using it to go to the greenhouse. When Mack and you came out, she didn't use it. She held on to your arm."

"Yes. Just so. Did Mayor Racker see Tallulah?"

"No. She didn't think so. And I told her not to say anything to anyone. That Gran's release depended on it. I made her promise."

"Good. Good. I'll need to meet with Mack to discuss." He takes out a packet of papers from his briefcase. "Alice . . . your Gran wanted me to draw these up." He slides the papers across the table.

"Ownership of Mystic Hollow Books?" I ask. "This is crazy. I can't think about this while my grandmother is locked up."

He nods. "I understand. She asked me to draft these the other day, and she was adamant that I do it posthaste last night. If she is implicated in the murders in any way, shape, or form, Mystic Hollow Books will suffer." He shows me that the store is being transferred to me and Phoebe equally. "You can't profit off of murder."

"You can't think—"

He puts his hand on mine. "Of course not. I believe Alice wants you to have the store regardless. This is just to be certain it happens before she is charged. Which obviously won't happen. Although, I believe if you were going to be charged . . ."

"She'd confess to something she didn't do."

I wipe a tear. Oh, Gran. I think about the store and the magic. What if losing Gran is part of the cost? I push that thought away. If so, it's not worth it. Not by a long shot. If that's the case, I hereby abstain.

Sloan's phone pings. "Alice is ready to be released. They did it all with paperwork. No need for a hearing."

"How?"

"Perhaps new information? I'm not sure. Let's go get answers together." Sloan offers me his arm as he'd offered my grandmother the other day. I take it.

We walk to the station. Gran is waiting for us, all smiles and waves. I hear the tail end of the conversation she is having with Delores over the best way to bake focaccia.

Mack comes to greet us. He shakes Sloan's hand. Nods to me, maybe uncertain if it's safe to extend his hand to me right now. He's not wrong. I am angry enough to spit. I ignore him and hug my grandmother. "Are you alright?"

She waves away my concern. "I'm fine, dear. The mattress was not my bed but not bad."

"Always a trooper," Sloan says.

"Can we go into this room?" Mack says. "I'd like to explain."

"You have a lot of explaining to do." I spread my arms wide. "Miles of it."

"Alright. Let's get you in here."

When the door shuts behind us, Gran turns to me. "We're running a scam."

Sloan looks down. So does Mack.

"What? Are you kidding me right now?"

"We wanted everyone to think I was a suspect. That I was protecting you."

"Wait. I don't understand."

"It's like this, dear. I thought I lost my cane. I took Sloan's hand to go into the greenhouse, but when I got back, I needed it and it wasn't there. Mack saw me looking for it. When it showed up at the scene of the second murder, well, we knew it had been taken and planted there."

"So Alice agreed to a night in a cell in order to give me some time to investigate," Mack says.

"And what have you found out?"

"We found fingerprints on the ice buckets."

"Whose?"

"I am not at liberty to say."

"Mayor Racker's?" I demand. "Hers, right?"

Mack leans forward. "What makes you say that?"

"I have a witness who saw her."

"Who?"

"Why should I tell you?" I cross my arms.

"Because I need to keep your witness safe. We already have two dead bodies. So . . ."

"Yeah, your board is looking pretty gnarly, huh?"

His face turns red. "Who saw her?"

"Tallulah. But she's promised not to say anything."

"Have you met Tallulah? I'll put a unit at her house. They can guard both of you."

I feel strangely touched by his concern. "Wait. You said there were buckets. Not one bucket. Were there two people there?"

"We're not certain. Apparently, Kiki has a fairly open-door policy for her regulars. Two different pools were used between Friday night when Adam was killed and Sunday when we found Nicholas, assuming a Saturday night timeline for his murder. One of the pools was relatively full. When I asked Kiki, she said that means someone most likely used it for an injury to a specific body part. Meaning, they didn't get in all the way. Just dangled a leg or an arm in."

"Who would do that?"

He gives me a look like I should know the answer, but I don't. "No cameras?"

"She doesn't believe in them. Something about being a healer and HIPPA regulations and all of that."

"You don't think Mayor Racker killed Adam, do you?" I ask.

"We need to suss that out."

"The kids use that word in a different way. You might want to catch up."

"You do realize that you insult me pretty much nonstop."

I nod. Take a drink of my cold brew, unconcerned.

"Well, you might want to rethink that strategy," Mack points to his badge.

I laugh. Actually, I do a spit take. "Was that supposed to be threatening?"

He scowls. "It was supposed to remind you to show me some respect."

"Mack, dear, my granddaughter is equally irreverent to any and all authority figures. Including me." Gran puts her hand over her heart to emphasis her point. "But she does have reason to ask about Adam's murder. We don't think Mayor Racker did it," Gran says.

"Is that right? Based on what, exactly?" Mack crosses his arms.

"She has no motive," I say, shooting Gran a warning glance. I am not ready to share resources with the man who locked up my grandmother, ruse or not. Even if she was in on it.

"Her motive is unclear at this point," Mack says. "And I agree that she is unlikely to have killed Adam. But Nicholas? She might be on the hook for that one."

"They have to be connected," I say, more to myself than to the others. "But how?"

"Two murders after a thirty-year draught of violent crimes committed within days of each other. Yeah, I'd say they are connected."

"Do you know what's the connection?"

Mack looks at his hands. Rough ones that look like he uses them for outdoorsy things. More than what he does in either the police station, what with no violent crimes until recently, or the diner when he helps out. Then I wonder why I'm focusing on what activities Mack does outside of his job. I need to focus. Didn't the Lady of the Forest grant me a special ability? I mean, I did give her my espresso maker!

"Not yet. We've run all of her bank accounts—no discernible change. She just paid out a large sum, but then we traced it to her daughter's tuition. And it was exactly the same as the amount she paid last spring and the previous fall. So, no red flags there."

"What about Nicholas? I thought he left the Hollow on Saturday after the festival."

"He did." Mack pulls out a folder. He slides pictures across the table. "Here we have him driving out of town on his way to Maine.

This was taken on the highway from one of those toll cameras." He slides another one back across the table. "This was taken Saturday night at 11:38 *pm*. On his way back to the Hollow."

"What brought him back?" I ask.

"Who brought him back?" Mack asks.

"Right. I mean, who would he even come back for?" I probe, hoping Mack's figured it out.

"Who do you think he'd come back to see?"

I put my finger on one of the photographs. "See this one, when he's leaving? He looks tired but almost relieved." I point to the return trip photo. "Here, he looks animated. Like he's angry and focused."

"I agree. So, we know he wasn't coming back because he left his phone behind or because he missed us. Someone called him back. Most likely the same person who killed him."

"Okay. Brainstorm session. Maybe he came back because he murdered Adam and someone saw him and was blackmailing him," I postulate.

"Maybe," Gran says.

"And we know that whoever called him back planned to murder him and frame your grandmother."

"We know this how?"

"He was bludgeoned with a cane. Then put in the water. The autopsy confirmed it," Mack says. "The time of death is tough to nail down using the usual methods because the cold plunge preserved his body, but we do know it happened between Saturday night and Sunday afternoon."

"Why put him in the cold plunge to begin with?"

"Maybe to disguise the time of death, as I said."

"But why? Eventually it would come out that he returned to town on Saturday night. With those photos you pulled out. Then, disguising the time of death makes no sense."

Mack puts his steepled fingers into that dimple on his chin. It would be cute if he weren't the annoying police officer who locked up my grandmother. "Right. Maybe they didn't know about the cameras and were hoping he wouldn't be discovered until Monday when they planned to have an alibi."

"Maybe," I allow.

"You never said how you knew he was at the cold plunge," Mack says. "Care to share?"

I hesitate.

"If we work together, we have a better chance to crack this thing," Mack says.

"We?" I ask.

"I have no difficulty asking for help when needed," Mack says. Then smirks and adds, "I don't usually need it, but in this case, you have information that will assist in this investigation."

"The jig is up," Gran places her hand on my arm. "Tell him."

Sloan nods.

"We gave some of the participants in the festival air tags. I was trying to see where Nicholas had been during Adam's murder. He wasn't supposed to even attend the festival and he had a motive for killing him."

"Enlighten me."

"Adam had fired his agent and was reportedly stepping away from his editor as well."

"His agent . . ." Mack looks through his notes. "That would be Marilyn Edwards?"

"Right."

"Why is that motive?"

"Adam's books were a gold mine. With him gone, someone could easily ghostwrite the rest of them, and the editor could claim these were stories turned in before his death."

"That doesn't sound legal."

"It's not ethical, but I could see it. Anyway, Adam was also supposedly working on a passion project. He told his brother he was taking that project to a smaller press. That would embarrass both the agent and the editor. It might've even gotten the editor fired."

"That's enough to kill for?" Mack asks.

"You know, motive is the trickiest part of all. What actually is worth killing for? If Nicholas believed his career was over because he and Adam parted ways and a new agent would be representing him and shopping the new breakout project, Nicholas would lose all of his standing in the publishing world. It takes years of servitude, lucky breaks, and a profound amount of sacrifice to get where Nicholas was. To lose his biggest client overnight would not bode well."

More nods from Mack. "If Nicholas killed Adam, why would someone kill Nicholas?"

"I don't know," I say. "Maybe the coconspirator? I mean, we think there may have been two people involved."

Mack grins. "Oh, we do?"

"Overkill," I cross my arms and give him my best Grace Kelly in *Rear Window* imitation, when Grace Kelly tells the detective that she and Jimmy Stewart believe the guy killed his wife.

"Is that right?" Mack asks.

"Come on. Why poison someone and then push them? It makes no sense."

"Maybe this was their first murder," Mack offers. "Mistakes were made." But he grins like he's enjoying this banter.

"I hate to bring it up since I was hoping to query Marilyn at some point, but if it was a two-person team . . ."

"I am having Marilyn brought in for questioning, if that makes you feel better. Although so far she's eluded us. So if you're tracking her . . ."

"I will have to check with my team."

"Posthaste," Mack tells me. "She's either a suspect or she could be in danger."

"Okay, if we're through I'd like to take Gran home."

"Of course. She's free to go."

I go to stand up but then pull a Columbo move. "Just one more thing."

Mack smiles and opens his palm to indicate he is ready to hear my question.

"How did someone leave a fingerprint on the ice bucket? I thought they were wearing gloves."

Mack smiles. "We have technology, we can take glove prints now and analyze them. The fingerprints come through, especially when the hands are wet."

"Mind officially blown." I put my hands to my head and indicate an explosion.

With Sloan's help, Gran stands and we turn to leave when Mack pulls his own Columbo. "Just one more thing, Miss Blackthorne."

"Yes?"

"I'd like all of the records from the festival. Any data you collected on people's whereabouts and movements."

I look at Sloan.

"You'll need a warrant," Sloan says.

"Let's keep this friendly. How about you give me the info and I promise not to arrest anyone close to you in the future without warning you first."

I nod. "I can give you the information from the air tags and the QR codes. Everyone who registered agreed to a release of information prior to receiving their goodie bags."

"Gotta love commercialism," Mack says.

"People do love their merch, and they are staggeringly willing to give up their liberties and protections in order to have a bookmark with a QR code that they will likely toss at the earliest convenience."

"Where is this information located?" Mack asks.

"I'll have my tech crew send it to your tech crew and they can discuss."

"I think that's the new 'my people will call your people' idiom," Gran says. "Isn't that fantastic?"

"Terrific," Mack opens the door for us to leave. "And if any of it helps me clearing this case, I'll do an interpretive dance to express exactly how deeply wonderful I find all of this."

"I'm keeping you to that," I say. Exit lines are my thing.

Chapter Twenty-Six

I want to take Gran home, but she says, "Let's go to the store. We have to do our monthly ordering."

"Are you certain you're up for it? You don't want to rest first?"

"Rest from what?"

"That jail cell must have been rustic, to say the least."

"Ha!" Gran slaps my knee.

"Ow. And what, ha?"

"I didn't stay there. I stayed at Mack's, of course." Gran smiles like I'm a rube.

"What?"

"He waited until the evening staff took off and then squirrelled me up to his apartment. Believe me, though, it is definitely a bachelor pad. No curtains! The color scheme. Brown. Old. Ugly. That man needs a woman in his life." She knows better than to glance at me after she says that.

"Sounds like that man needs a life before he invites a woman into it."

"Don't be so judgy," Gran says.

"Enough about Mack! I'm going to run and get us some coffees at the Magic Bean. Or do you need kombucha? Will they even sell it to me yet?"

Gran shrugs. "Hard to know. Although something's changed in you, dear."

"Something is not the same," I sing. Gran shoots me a quizzical look. "From *Wicked.* 'Defying Gravity'?"

"I know the song, dear. I just wondered how you came to believe you could represent Cynthia or Idina."

"I was doing my own version."

"Back to my earlier point. What's different?"

"Nothing. I am just in dire need of caffeine."

"Well, that's not different. That's about as same as it gets. How about a piece of cake from Connelly's? I could use something light and fluffy."

"I'll get it," I say before making my way outside.

As I walk to the Magic Bean, I start wondering about my newfound ability to analyze information, which cost me our prized espresso machine. It seems to have vanished along with the machine.

"Two cold brews," I tell Rusty once I walk in.

"Coming right up. Oh," he adds ice to two to-go cups. "I started thinking about the kombucha order on the night of Adam's . . ." He does a throat slash motion. "I remembered! Adam ordered that drink himself."

"He did?" I ask, paying for my cold brews. "I thought that was only for Mystic Hollow residents?"

"Well, he heard people talking about it. Said it was famous! So I sold him one that night before he got up to do his keynote. Which everyone says was exceptional compared to past speaking events, so maybe my brew helped him?"

"Maybe. Back to the not being a Mystic Hollowian. I guess, flattery will get you everywhere," I say, laughing, so he knows I'm on his side. "It might even get you some black market brew?"

"I thought I was immune to that, you know? But he was a big deal and there he was, wanting my special recipe. I couldn't say no. And he drank it down right there in front of me. It felt like the best Yelp review ever."

"Just the one?"

"I think so. But maybe . . . I don't usually give a newbie more than one, but now that you mention it, I seem to remember someone else ordering one. I just can't remember who."

"Cheers." I raise my cold brew cup in salute and turn to leave when something stops me. My brain tells me to focus. Something about what he said doesn't add up. "So, he had two of them?" I ask.

"I'm sorry. Two of what?"

It's all I can do not to suggest he meets with the witch in the woods. Which would be unkind. But kinder than me yelling out the word *Focus!* to his face, which I want to do since my brain is actually working full time at this minute. Is it activated by the sip of cold brew? No idea, I just know all my neurons are firing. Still, it would not be nice to flaunt my newfound focus over Rusty, who is actually trying to help me. "Two kombuchas. One before he went on stage. One when he was signing?"

I remember the image we found. The gloved holding the drink.

"Oh my God, how did I forget that?" He shakes his head. "Yes. He sent someone to get it for him, though. I was disappointed because I wanted him to acknowledge that my kombucha helped him."

"Do you remember who got it for him?" I ask.

"No. Mack asked me the same thing, now that you mention it. The kombucha didn't kill him, did it? Was it too strong, two in one night as a mystic springs water virgin?" Rusty puts his hand over his heart.

"No. Of course not. There was something added to it. Poison."

"I heard something about that," Rusty says. "Angel's trumpet. I would have hoped my special brew would have counteracted the effects, but I guess it's not as magical as they say."

I think about that. "I believe it dampened the effect quite a bit. Leading to the need for . . ."

Rusty mimes someone being pushed. Adam.

I start to get dizzy. "Right."

"Anyway, I think it was one of those Andrews boys who ended up giving it to him. I don't remember who ordered it, but when I saw they had it, I was going to step in until they gave it to Adam. They said they were his angel or something."

"That's what we called the kids who were helping the authors. Lots of literary festivals designate helpers and name them angels. They get drinks for the authors. Show them around. Make certain they get to their next event on time. It's fairly standard. It helps the organizers know where their speakers are while making the authors feel like stars."

Rusty nods. "Well, I did water it down a little since it was his first time. It can be a little potent." He mimes a head explosion. I could attest to what he's saying, having recently been a kombucha virgin myself and also having a very strong reaction to it, but I don't think that will help.

"Thanks," I say. As I'm about to push the door open, Rusty calls out to me.

"You be sure to let me know if you ever want one. A kombucha. I figure you're as much as a town figure as Tommy is now. Or Timmy. Or whoever it was that picked up the kombucha for Adam. I wish I remembered, but I was a little overwhelmed. Good job with bringing in the customers. I mean, we sold out all of our mochas. Came close with our macchiatos. But I mean it about the kombucha. You want one? I'll serve you."

"Thanks," I say. "That's sweet."

Rusty blushes.

Once outside, I call Gran. "We need to speak with the Andrews boys. ASAP."

"Can do," she answers. "School just got out. Sometimes they do deliveries for me."

"Like Uber eats?"

"More like Uber reads. Everyone wants things delivered these days. We are a nation of shut-ins."

"Agreed. Heading for cake. Are you sure you don't want a proper lunch?"

"Woof. After the full breakfast they served? April's famous omelet with home fries and juice. Goodness no. Cake and coffee will do just fine. Unless you want lunch?" But she says it with a sort of flirty flair, as if she's insinuating something. "Maybe a little sesh with April to discuss her very single brother?"

"Excuse me?"

"No tone. I'm just thinking you and Mack seem to push each other's buttons. That could be fun."

"Hard pass," I say. "And I will not be discussing my love life with you—especially since it's nonexistent."

"We could do something to make it existent. Say whip up a little Samantha Stephens magic?"

"If you still want coffee and cake, you'll table this conversation."

"As you wish, dear."

"Different movie."

Connelly's is fairly busy. I wait in line behind Cassandra Fetterly. "So glad they let your sweet Gran go," she says. "We do not believe at all that's she's part of this terrible matter."

"Thank you," I say.

"I see you've figured out the Magic Bean/Connelly's combo. We call it the Beanelly. Very popular around here."

I laugh. "Glad I'm fitting in."

"I wouldn't go that far," a snarky voice behind me says. The Leach.

"Thank you for your opinion, Almira," I say. Then give her my back.

"So glad that you and your grandmother are no longer suspects. Or is that just for now?" She laughs. "I've always said there's something strange with her and the store. But I did not have homicidal maniac on my list of adjectives and descripts for either of you. Maybe I think too small?"

I turn and put my hand on her arm. "Oh, Almira, don't doubt yourself. You think just small enough." With that I turn on my heel and place my order. It's all I can do not to celebrate my verbal victory. I only wish Phoebe and Kim could have witnessed it.

By the time I struggle through the front door of the store, I am still celebrating my win, when I stop dead in my tracks. My mother is here. In Mystic Hollow.

Chapter Twenty-Seven

My jaw must drop open because the first thing she says is, "My goodness, can you stop gaping at me like a fish out of water?"

"Huh?" Oh. My mouth is open. Right. I close it. "What are you doing here?"

"Isn't that a lovely greeting."

I rush forward. Struggle to put the snacks on the counter. Straighten up. Do a mental checklist. Am I wearing underwear? Check. Pants that are not low waisted or ripped? Check. A sweater that does not have a low plunging V-neck. Check. A tee that is not graphic in nature? Check. I smooth my hair, happy with my checking of boxes and open my arms. "Mom. It's so good to see you."

"It's nice you can muster a kind word after your initial reaction of shock," she points at me, and not in the good way.

"Don't be silly. I was just surprised is all. Was this a planned trip? Did we know . . ."

"A mother has to plan to see her daughter and granddaughter now? Do you need sixty days' notice?"

"Of course not, Mom. I think two weeks is considered appropriate in most cases."

"How about seeing my mother? Do I need to give notice for that as well?"

"Enough dramatics, Collette. Of course we are happy to see you. It's just that we are also surprised," says Gran from behind the front counter."

"Well, I came as soon as I heard. What have you gotten up to here? Honestly. Murder. Mayhem. Poison." Her hand goes to her heart. "Well?" she looks at me like she did when I wore my Panic! At The Disco shirt to dinner one time.

"It's not like I caused this," I say. "It wasn't my fault. Any of it. Except Adam was here because of me. But even that wasn't my fault. The first keynote dropped out . . ." I stop. "The first keynote dropped out." I swivel to face Gran. "Remind me what happened to her?"

"You are the most scattered person I know," my mother says.

"Gran?"

"Family emergency."

"That's vague, isn't it?"

"What are the two of you talking about?" Mom shakes her head. She looks back and forth between both of us, as if she was watching a tennis match. "Never mind. I've called ahead and had the house in Norwalk opened. I'll expect you all for dinner Friday night."

"Do you need a ride?" I ask.

"Don't be silly. I will not be riding in whatever broken-down heap you're driving these days. Why you refuse to take one of my cars is beyond me. For now, I have a driver outside waiting."

The door opens, and Phoebe walks in. "Why is there a limo outside?" Then she sees my mom. "Grandma!" she rushes forward, arms open.

"Finally, an actual welcome."

I see them hug. I honestly don't remember Mom ever hugging me that way, but I'm glad they have a good relationship. Besides,

I've got the beginnings of an idea in my mind which feels like it's lighting up with information. Finally.

"Do we know when this family emergency cropped up?"

Gran makes a face. "I mean, I think she wrote to us when she was on the East Coast for that other conference." To Mom, "She's an LA darling."

I use Gran's laptop to go on her website and check the events page. "Here it is. Women in Publishing Conference, Brooklyn, New York."

"I'm not certain how that's pertinent, dear," Gran says. "I mean, family emergencies can crop up at any time."

She's right. It seems like it isn't connected, only it also feels like it could have been the first domino in a series of steps that got us to murder and mayhem.

"I don't know. It feels linked somehow. Maybe?"

I click on the conference registration, which says it's closed. Right. Because it's over. This isn't helping me. I need the actual event's page. Or their socials. Meanwhile, I see the colleges listed as participants. No surprises here. We've got NYU, Sarah Lawrence. Amherst. Wellesley. Swarthmore. Yale. Williams. All the usual suspects. Which is a funny way to look at that list, but one of those names tugs at my memory, and I'm not sure which one.

Kim walks in the front door with her laptop in hand. "Hey. Why do I have to turn my data over to Mack?"

"I'll tell you later," I say. "Just the data from the air tags, the QR codes, and the bracelets. Is that easy to separate?"

"Easy peasy lemon squeezy," she says. "It'll just take a few moments."

"You will all come for dinner Friday night. Kim also, if you're free." Mom glances at the cake Phoebe is munching on, the one I was supposed to share with Gran. But I've lost my appetite at the moment. "Judging by the way I see you eating it'll be the only decent meal you girls will get."

"Still such a snob, dear," Gran says. "They can have a little cake."

Mom smiles at Gran. Not unkindly. "You are a wonderful cook, Mom. Although why you won't let me hire someone to do that for you is beyond me."

"I enjoy it."

My mother makes a face. It's that expression that gets me. The snobby expression she pulls looks just like the one someone else did the other day. Entitled. Superior. Condescending. I wonder why I'm focusing on something so small and seemingly unimportant, but my mind, which usually reacts to any information as equally distracting and important, is homing in on this.

Why? If I trust the gift of focus from Our Lady, I should pay attention. So I let my mind drift back. Someone made that face while saying something annoying. I was annoyed. It was before the festival. We were getting set up. Who said it? Then it hits me. Laurel, Mayor Racker's daughter, made that same snotty face when discussing Adam's work. "Not bad," she'd said and I remember being annoyed by that.

"Wellesley," I blurt. "Mayor Racker's daughter goes there."

"See what I mean? Distracted?" Mom says. Then before waiting for an explanation or answer, she primly walks to the front of the store. "See you all Friday. By the way, the store looks wonderful, Mom. You've really spruced."

Gran nods. Smiles back. Then when Mom leaves, Gran says to me. "Why is Mayor Racker's daughter important?"

"I don't know. I just know that Mayor Racker had no motive for either murder. She had no connection to either man."

"That the sheriff can find," Gran says.

"Yet."

"In this world where everyone shares their location and texts and emails, there's always a trail."

Gran nods. "I suppose."

"So, if she doesn't have a motive, who would she protect?" I ask.

"I'm not sure. I don't know her that well," Gran admits. "I mean, she is in our group. I can tell you that much."

"Your book club? That's really a coven?"

Gran looks at her hands. Twists her wedding ring.

"Are you saying she was there the day when the murder plants were planted in your greenhouse?" I ask.

"I wish you'd stop calling them that. The name doesn't seem fair. But no, she wasn't there. She couldn't attend. I remember being annoyed by that."

"That feels sketchy, right? The one person who couldn't be there."

"Maybe." Gran's face brightens.

"We know she most likely planted the cane at least. What I'm really getting at is who would she kill to protect? Or frame someone else to protect?"

Gran and I glance at Phoebe and Kim eating our cake.

"You'd do anything for your kids or grandkids," I say.

"Right, dear."

"Still, we don't know of any connections between Laurel and Adam or Nicholas. Or even Dawn." I scroll through the images from the conference Dawn presented at, when she found out she couldn't attend our event. Women in Publishing. I follow the hashtag and find image after image of Dawn. With a group of coeds. No Laurel. Speaking. Signing books. At dinner. Still no Laurel. Until I get to the very end. The last image. A profile. Silhouette. With a leather bracelet with quartz beads on it. Could be Laurel. I'm not sure. "Kim?"

"Yes?"

"Can you find out who this is?" I point to the profile picture.

"Yeah. May take me a little while, though."

I hand her Mack's card. "Send the data here."

"And the picture too?"

"No. That's just for us. For now."

"Got it." Kim props open her laptop on the counter.

I sit staring at my screen. The picture. "There are no coincidences, right, Gran?"

"If you say so, dear."

"I do." It feels right. "Kim?" I call. She lifts her head. "Can you pull up Mayor Racker's daughter's tracker from the event?"

Kim starts navigating. Her brow wrinkles in confusion. "I don't see her in the reenactment. Are you sure she had one assigned?"

"I thought so, but we only found out she was coming in the day before so maybe not?"

"Everyone who picked up their tracker and wore it for the festival has been loaded into the system. I used social media posts to confirm that the correct tracker was with the correct person and so far, there were no mismatched ones."

I check the spreadsheets myself. "I know she was a last-minute add-on, but wasn't she supposed to have a badge with a tracking device because she was helping set up some of the major events?"

"Until she had that migraine. Do you remember?" Gran asks. When I don't answer, she reminds me. "She was supposed to set up the authors' room and couldn't."

"Hmm." I laugh. "I hate to accuse a fellow migraine sufferer of being a murderer, but that doesn't explain why she wasn't wearing her lanyard with the tracking device on Friday." I pull up pictures from the event. I see Mayor Racker. Danetra. Dan. Marilyn. Nicholas. Adam. All with lanyards. I do a reverse image search of Laurel and find some of her from the festival. "See?" I say. "No lanyard. Why?"

"She must have known they had trackers. Not great for someone planning to murder the keynote speaker."

"Kim?"

"Yes?"

"It appears her lanyard was never picked it up. Is there a way to track where it ended up if it was motionless?"

"Hmm," Kim thinks. "I think so. Do you have the number?"

"Yes. Four, one, three, six, ten."

"Found it. Yeah. It's in this bin at the registration desk. See?" Kim spins the screen so I can confirm.

"Who was working the registration desk on Friday night?" I ask.

"Kiki," Gran says.

"Let's go ask her what happened. Meanwhile maybe we can find out how someone had access to her plunge pools after hours."

"Not so fast. She's teaching a Zumba class right now."

"I've always wanted to sit in on one of those," I say.

"Really?" Gran makes a face like she doesn't buy it.

"I can watch without getting hurt."

"If you say so, dear." Gran grabs a cane and starts walking toward the door.

"Wait a minute. Where did you get that?" I point at the purple and black swirled cane. Much fancier than the one she lost.

"Sloan got it for me."

"Ooooh."

"Cute, right? I saw him drop it off," Phoebe says. "He may have a thing for Gran."

Gran waves the conversation away. "You're obsessed with romance," Gran says.

"I was asking why you need it since you seemed so much better before."

"Oh, that. The plunge pools are helping, but they have a half-life. You have to continue going until you break the cycle of inflammation."

"Is that important?" Phoebe asks me.

"Maybe. Mack asked me to bare my arms when he first questioned me. I am assuming it was to look for wounds from the struggle. If our murderer covered their injuries in the plunge pools they might reappear."

"Why do you think they used the plunge pools, dear?"

"Mack said as much when he was releasing you. He said someone dangled an arm or other body part into the pool. I would imagine our murderer might have sustained some injuries. Also, there was torn fabric on Adam. Like he grabbed for someone as he fell and ripped their clothes."

"What kind of fabric?"

"Pretty nondescript. Brown."

"Okay. So our murderer is not a snappy dresser."

"If I was planning to murder someone, I'd likely dress down for the event," I say. I pull up pictures of Laurel from the event on Friday night. She's wearing an emerald green silky top. I show it to Gran.

"Maybe it was her coat."

"Maybe." I pull up a picture of Mayor Racker. She's wearing a light brown turtleneck sweater that is not the material or color I saw. "Not a match."

Gran points to the blazer draped over the mayor's arm. Brown. Silky. "Curiouser and curiouser."

Chapter Twenty-Eight

Turns out Gran has muffed up Kiki's schedule and instead of Zumba, according to her chalkboard she's leading a "Sing Away Sleep Apnea" group. What we are looking at is wild. A bunch of senior citizens and mid-lifers lying flat on yoga mats singing "Don't Go Breaking My Heart" as a karaoke machine plays in the background.

Kiki smiles as she sees us but waves her hand to keep her singers going. "Hello, darling. So glad Mack came to his senses. No way you could murder someone." To me she says. "I bought a pink pin. Your Gran and I have been friends forever. I could never go blue. Especially after he shut down my other cash cow." She points her cup of kombucha at me before taking a sip. "The cold plunge pools can't operate until Mack releases them. Then I'll have to do a thorough cleansing and . . . it's a big deal."

I don't point out the obvious—that Nicholas's death was also a big deal. Why make this encounter turn ugly? The song switches to what seems like an adult version of "Bingo" as the participants sing their vowels in order. A. E. I. O. U. Kiki leans over. "Now hum." She waves to keep them going. "This class pays my rent for the entire month."

"It certainly seems popular," I say. "We wanted to talk with you about those, actually. The cold plunge pools. Not the classes. Although . . . I might want to try them out. The classes, not the pools."

Gran wrinkles her nose. "Not with your tone deafness. It'll shut these down."

Kiki grabs Gran's arm and they laugh like crazy.

"Focus, ladies," I say. "The plunge pools. Mack said you have certain VIP members who have after-hours access."

"Not officially." The song changes to the one from *The Sound of Music* with the musical scales. "Doe, a deer. A female deer," Kiki sings and the group sings with her. "Use your talking voice now."

They switch to speaking the lyrics in rhythm with the music.

Gran nudges Kiki. "It's okay. She can be cool."

Kiki sighs. "I am not technically allowed to use 'special water' in the pools. They are supposed to be filled with chlorinated garbage." She uses air quotes over some of the words.

"And?"

"Most of the pools are completely standard. We have all of the chemicals available and 'use' as many chemicals required to keep everything above board. So to speak. Just in case we're ever up for inspection."

"And?"

"Some of the special pools are available for members of a certain club or group or what have you. Some of those people are in the position of signing off on inspections. I don't want to paint an ugly picture. It's really all about health and helping each other out. Not an ugly blackmail scenario, although to an outsider it might seem, shall we say, not entirely above board."

Gran nods. "We are a tight knit group."

"And do those members also have keys to your pool area?"

"Well, since they are used during moon rituals sometimes and I'm in bed early most days, it only makes sense . . ."

I don't ask about who is in the group since Gran made it obvious that wouldn't be cool. Instead, I ask, "How do they know which pools are filled with the special water?"

Kiki smiles. "The ones adorned with the tree insignias."

"And does everyone who uses the special pools know they are special?" I ask.

"Occasionally, and I do mean very occasionally, we will help someone's family member or close friend out without their knowledge, per se. But that's very rare."

"The other night, it seemed like someone who was hurt may have used one of your special pools. How would that be sanitary for the next user?"

Kiki makes a face. "Anyone using the pools without my supervision knows to follow their ritual with a chlorine rinse of the pool and to leave it drained so I can be sure it's clean."

"Did that happen the other night?"

"Mack showed me pictures, and based on what I saw, the typical protections were not taken." She drinks more kombucha, her eyes narrowed and her brow furrowed. "Truuuust me. That person better hope Mack finds them before I do. It's sacrilege! And there will be a penalty. Banned for life."

"From your pools or the group?"

"Exactly." Kiki smirks.

"Thanks, Kiki," Gran says.

"Yes. Thanks."

* * *

Gran gives me a look to keep me quiet as we walk back to the store. When we are safely inside, we wind our way through the aisles and all the way to the back room. Gran finally nods as she lowers herself into a chair.

"Oh, Gran, you look like you're in pain."

"I need those pools up and running again."

"What if I get you a kombucha? That'll help, right?"

Gran shrugs. "Couldn't hurt."

"You sit right here. Rusty insinuated that I was almost a Mystic Hollowian. So I should be in."

Kim overhears. Does a throat slash. "He was being kind. You've got to earn your stripes to get the good stuff. I'll go."

"Earn my stripes? That's so unfair!"

"Patience has never been your strong suit, dear," Gran opines.

"Gran, I just remembered something. There was a strong forest scent in the belfry. Like too much aftershave. Or one of those horrible overly scented candles. Does that sound like a spell?"

"Maybe. But maybe Adam just overused. Some men do that."

"I saw him earlier, he didn't smell like that."

Her face screws up like she's upset. "I certainly hope none of my witchy friends are implicated."

"You think one of them did it?"

"Goodness, no." Then she brightens. "Maybe he put it on for your date."

"That's not comforting at all."

"Where's Kim?" Mack's voice startles me, and I twirl to see him standing in the doorway. "She around?"

"Why are you looking for her?" I ask. "You going to question all employees of the store?"

"Just the owners."

Kim comes back in carrying two kombuchas. "I got you one in case you wanted it—"

Mack swivels to face her. "How did you do it?"

She hands over the drinks, remaining unfazed by the lawman. "The program?"

"Yes. It's brilliant."

"I used crowd sourcing and imported it into a video game format. Took a while. Hours."

I shake my head.

"Days," Kim says. "All-nighters. Like the kids do in college."

Mack scowls. "You're in high school. Don't do that." He points to me and Gran. "Should we shut the door? We could use privacy."

"I'll get it on my way out," Kim says as she leaves us alone.

Gran groans and rubs her knee.

"I'm sorry, Alice. Are you alright?"

"I've just been doing too much."

"She needs the plunge pools to reopen. They were doing wonders."

He smirks. "I bet we can work out a deal."

"So, you want points for being a gentleman?" I ask.

"You're being a little rude, dear," Gran says. "Maybe Mack is here to help us."

"It seems to be our thing," Mack smiles.

"It's a bit," I agree. "We're doing a bit."

Gran smiles. "Whatever you say, dear." But she groans some more. She turns to face Mack. "You said something about opening those plunge pools?"

"Yes. I think this would be a good time to share intel. Before someone else gets hurt." He opens a file. "We believe Mayor Racker did not kill Nicholas. Or Adam."

"We agree with that assessment," I say, and Mack motions for me to keep talking. "For one thing, she was nowhere near the belfry when he died."

"Based on?"

"You've seen the video game reenactment of that night. Her air tag puts her near Town hall. And we have proof that she was actually wearing her lanyard before, during, and after the murder, meaning she's accounted for," I say.

Mack smiles. “We got that from the sophisticated intel you provided. By the way, if Kim and Phoebe want to go into the CIA, or other form of law enforcement, they’ve got a letter of rec from me.”

“Thank you?”

He smirks. “Not for your daughter?”

“Not for me to say. What else have you got?”

“Laurel. The mayor’s daughter. She was not tracked in your system.”

I nod. “One of the unknowns.”

Mack looks at me, the question in his eyes.

“Some people who should have been tracked but weren’t. For whatever reason.”

“Talk more about that. Who was supposed to be tracked? And were they aware?”

I laugh. “For legal purposes, yes. They signed a memo of understanding or a presenter agreement or a volunteer agreement. Each of those documents clearly states that geo tags and air tags of some sort would be used and by signing the agreement, they authorized us to collect that information and use it as we deemed necessary. Same thing for use of photos from the event.”

“Are those agreements typical?” Mack asks.

“Becoming more and more so. Of course, if someone were to take issue with a photo they deem unflattering, and they wrote to us, we’d take it down. We’re not monsters.”

Mack pretends to wipe sweat from his brow. “Whew. I was worried my uniform made me look fat.”

I put my hand on his arm. “Only when you turn sideways.”

He laughs. Looks down. Shakes his head. “Walked right into that one, didn’t I? You’ve skirted around the question, were they aware their movements were being tracked?”

"It's in the agreements, but from my experience, most people don't read what they sign. Especially if it's to get the chance to do something they want."

"Okay. So, if I am getting this right, some people—the unknowns—weren't tracked even though they were supposed to be. Who? Besides Laurel."

I open my laptop and look at the spreadsheets Kim sent me with the added category—The Unknowns. "Some townspeople like Kiki, who told us at the time she was too cool to wear a lanyard. The Andrews brothers, who were angels to the authors—Timmy to Adam, Tommy to Dan. Some volunteers who registered to attend but didn't pick up a volunteer lanyard. There are always a few who fall through the cracks."

"Do we know where Kiki was during the murder?"

I swivel my computer screen to face Mack. "We have evidence that she was with Danetra at the Magic Bean. See? A time stamp and everything."

"The Andrews boys?"

"Had long since abandoned their charges and were at the bonfire." I show him a picture of them throwing an accelerant on the fire.

"Those little devils," Gran says, her voice a tad unkind.

"Why are you looking at Laurel?" I ask. "Because of our intel?"

"Not only." Mack sighs. "This is where I share, isn't it? I don't like sharing."

I laugh. "Who would've figured?" Then before he can say anything, I throw my arms wide and say, "Literally everybody."

He leans on the table and folds his hands, a smile that says he doesn't mind the teasing, might even like it. All of his mannerisms show that we are equals. That puts me on guard. He is trying to ease my mind, but it has the opposite effect. I've got the gift of focus now. And I can see through his act. His Columbo.

I clear my throat.

Mack says, "We don't think Mayor Racker killed either man."

"So you said."

"We don't believe she worked with anyone to kill them either, due to absence of a clear motive for either murder. We do think she tried to frame you, Alice, for Nicholas's death."

"What motive could I have?" Gran has her hand on her heart now.

"The same one Mayor Racker has. Protecting someone you love. She showed us her hand by projecting her fears on someone else."

"Why does that someone have to be Laurel?" I ask.

"The mayor's husband is in a nursing home. He couldn't have done it. She has no other children. Her friends on the council are not worth going to jail for. Her daughter is."

I can't argue with that, and also, I believe he's shown us all of his cards.

Kim walks into the room, laptop in hand. "May I borrow you for a second?" she asks me.

I stand, follow her out.

"That profile photo is Laurel. For sure. I mean, technically, it's 99.5 percent accurate. But . . ." She shows me the readout of the program she used.

"This program is vetted?"

"Yes. But I put it through three separate ones to be sure."

"Great work. Now do your schoolwork before your mother comes in here and demands you quit."

Kim smiles and retreats.

I rejoin the conference. "It's Laurel," I tell the sheriff about our suspicions concerning our previous keynote speaker, as well as the partial photograph.

"You think Laurel did something or said something to Dawn Nightengale so that she'd bow out of the festival in order to bring Adam to Mystic Hollow?"

"It's a theory."

Phoebe walks in the room. "The stylometry program confirmed all of Adam's work is his own." She pantomimes dropping a mic, then leaves. "Doing my homework," she calls over her shoulder.

Mack shakes his head. "I can't hire them?"

"Are you trying to poach our best workers?" I cross my arms in faux outrage. "Feeling superior!" I put my hands over my head.

Mack takes out his phone and calls someone. "Open the plunge pools. Tell Kiki she may clean them and get them back up again." He hangs up. "Okay?"

I nod.

"Why were you looking at plagiarism as a motive?" Mack asks.

"Pete told me Adam stole ideas all the time. That his writing was derivative. There have also been allegations online to the same effect."

"But that's not true?"

"Apparently not. Dan was in an early critique group with Adam and had samples of Adam's original work to use as a source to compare with his other work. It checks out. Adam may have been a lot of things, but he didn't plagiarize his work."

"You think someone plagiarized his work?"

"I would normally say no, but . . ."

"But? How would that even be possible?" Mack asks.

"Dan said there was this woman at a writer's conference in Florida about two years ago."

"It's always in Florida," Mack muses. Then catches himself. "Sorry. Go on."

"Being off topic is my thing," I say, feigning indignation. Mack scowls, moving his finger to indicate I should keep talking. "Anyway, there was someone Dan thought might have been a student who was dining with Adam after the conference. Things got heated—not in the romantic way. Adam was excited about his passion project, and he had been talking about it during the entire conference. He was upset because his agent wouldn't consider it nor would his editor. They didn't even want to see it."

"Does that make sense?"

"In publishing, yeah. He was a big name. He needed to keep producing the same type of books to satisfy his readership as well as his editorial team and literary agency. People laugh about that kind of thing out of wishful thinking. Apparently, it was really weighing on him. Anyway, this woman who sat with him encouraged him to tell her about the book. Apparently. Then, when he went to the bathroom, she picked up his phone and looked through it, hoping to find something of value."

"This is your area of expertise. Play it out for me."

"He meets a young student who has the potential to be the next big thing. She steals his greatest idea since he told her he wouldn't be using it anyway. She uses it to land a prestigious award and start a literary career, but the story or book remains obscure. Their print runs are in the hundreds. And they still have remainders."

Mack smiles. "Is this how you plot?"

"Kind of."

"So, plot this all the way out. You are a young writer hoping to make a mark. You know Adam is open to rendezvous. So you seek him out hoping he will help you . . ." Mack motions for me to take it.

"Which is ridiculous because there's little he can actually do for your career. But you're young. You're hungry. Maybe a little bit ruthless. Because us writers? We're all like reality TV show contestants."

He nods, his smile growing, like he's impressed with me.

I continue. "You hit the jackpot. Adam confides in you about his million-dollar concept. Maybe he even lays it all out for you. He leaves something out, though. The key to it all. And when he goes to the bathroom, you grab his phone, see if you can find any additional details. The point is, you are blown away. So you pitch it to your advisor. Or use it as your thesis. You know it's not going anywhere. Adam admitted it wasn't. He'd never even know you nicked it since it's heading for some obscure journal as a short story, maybe."

"But then he finds out."

I nod.

"How?" Mack asks.

"Publishing is a very small world. Maybe he's at your college doing a workshop. Or at another event with your dean. They get to talking. The dean says they've got this brilliant student with an amazing concept, the kind that could go on to win prizes. And he finds you and tells you he knows. That he's going to report you."

Mack nods. Motions for me to keep talking.

"You beg him for some time to retract it and submit something else. But really, you're planning his murder because you will not lose this prize. You will not lose the glory that comes with being your fine arts program's new little darling. So, you poison him. Just a little bit to make him weak. And you meet him one more time in the tower to beg him to reconsider. You can both win, there are no new stories, yada yada. But he won't. So you push him. And done."

"How do you get the poison in him? He won't take a drink from you. He's too smart."

"Maybe you stay hidden by the festival attendees. Maybe you hope he doesn't see you."

"But how can you be sure he's going to the bell tower? How do you know he'll be somewhere you can kill him without being seen?"

"That's a plot hole right there," I say. "I don't know. But other things also don't make sense, Wouldn't the truth come out about the manuscript, eventually, anyway? His brother was left with all his effects. Wouldn't he go through Adam's things and find the concept and the pitch?"

"You tell me."

"I don't know. It's all so murky. Supposedly, Adam told Pete that his agent and editor wouldn't even listen to the pitch. That's when he parted ways with them. Maybe he didn't write down the pitch anywhere his brother could locate."

"That tracks," Mack says.

"Pete just told me he didn't find any substantial writing, including a pitch that would be worth killing for."

"You're still talking with Pete?"

"Sort of. He's in Washington now, I think he said, filming a segment for his podcast. He redesigned everything to focus on Adam's murder."

"You know who else has a perfect alibi for Nicholas's murder? Laurel."

"Interesting."

"She was on a plane headed to London to study abroad. Left right after the conference to join her cohort."

"That's weird. Right?"

"What?

"She goes to Wellesley, right?"

"Yes. So?"

"They're in the middle of the fall semester. Later than the middle, but not at the end. What kind of semester abroad starts midsemester?"

Mack looks through his phone “It’s not a semester abroad. It’s a residency. And I have the email right here that invited her, dated July of this year.”

“When was the plane ticket purchased?”

“Three weeks ago. According to her mother, she hadn’t decided if she was going to go. Her father is ill and she didn’t want to be that far away.”

“What changed her mind?” I ask.

Mack shrugs. “Mayor Racker didn’t know. She was glad she did, though.”

“He’s ill?” I ask. “Do we have the specifics?”

“Alzheimer’s.”

“So, what happens now?” I ask.

“We keep trying to make a case. Trying to find the loose ends that someone didn’t think to cover.”

“Like?”

“How did the killer know Adam was going to be at this festival if he was added so last minute?”

“I invited him when our keynote dropped out.”

Mack looks through his phone. “Dawn?”

“Right. Adam was a big name and I knew him from conferences.”

“What made you ask him specifically?”

I think Gran recommended it, but I’m definitely not going to say that. “Um . . . a few things, really. He reached out to me the week before to ask me if I’d like to be interviewed for a podcast, so he was front of mind. Also, his new book had just hit the stores, so there was buzz. He was a major draw.”

“Convenient.”

“Am I back to being a suspect?”

He laughs. “Not with the posse you’ve assembled. I’m not ready to go toe to toe with your tech crew.”

I'm not certain I want to lay all of my cards on the table. Mack hasn't entirely earned my trust. I'm not ready to tell him about the tiny little detail I just remembered from Adam's text exchange with me.

Mack snaps his fingers in front of my eyes to bring me back.

"She spaces out sometimes," Gran says.

"Oh. Sorry. I guess I was trying to remember something."

"What?"

"It's eluding me at the moment. Here one sec. Gone the next." My laugh is fake, and Mack looks like he doesn't buy it. Smart man. "How did the person who murdered Nicholas determine he was a threat? If the motive was plagiarism, who knew that Nicholas knew?"

"And when?" Gran asks.

Mack nods like we get it. The way investigations work.

"And if it wasn't plagiarism?" Gran asks.

"Revenge? Spurned love? Monetary gain?" Mack asks.

"That leads back to Pete, who was a thousand miles away when Nicholas died and three hundred miles away when Adam died."

"It's a conundrum," Mack admits. "I noticed you guys exchange words that are underutilized while being very specific and fairly impressive. Did I get all the rules down?"

I feign annoyance. "That's a family game we've been playing. Besides, it's more about using fun words rather than impressive ones."

Mack's phone beeps. "Gotta go."

"What's going on?" I ask.

"Mayor Racker's come in. She wants to confess."

"To which murder?"

"To both."

Chapter Twenty-Nine

When Mack leaves, Kim and Phoebe join us in the back of the store, Kim with her laptop open and ready for our dictates.

"So?" Phoebe asks. "What do we think?"

"I'm confused. Why would Mayor Racker kill Adam or Nicholas, let alone both?"

"I think she killed Nicholas to cover for her daughter. Maybe he saw something. But Adam? That makes no sense."

"We need a timeline."

Kim starts typing. "I'm color coding the events by person."

"Three weeks before the festival, Laurel buys a ticket to London."

"Is that important?"

"No idea, but I feel like we need to focus on when things started happening, like Gran said."

"Thanks for the attribution, dear."

"Great word, Gran."

She celebrates by pumping her fist.

I point to Kim. "One week before the festival, Dawn pulls out."

"When did we know Laurel was coming to the festival?" Gran asks.

"Great question. I have no idea."

"I might," Phoebe says. "Mayor Racker emailed me asking for a pass for Laurel a week before the festival."

"When did Adam reach out to you about doing the interview?" Gran asks.

"Two weeks before the festival."

Kim nods and keeps typing. "When did Adam agree to do the festival?"

"One week before the festival."

"Can we see Adam's social media posts for the past year?"

The usual pics and hashtags celebrating his book release in July. His agent tweeting about his success. Typical industry stuff and doesn't mean anything. "Theoretically, Adam and his agent were kaput by that point, right?" Phoebe asks.

"They'd still do these events together and would continue to post to promote the book."

"But why would they come to the festival to see him? That's not the type of promo that would pay off, not enough for them to deal with him if they were estranged anyway. It's not a big event—no offense."

"That's true. So why did they come?" Gran asks.

"Pete told me he parted ways with them because they wouldn't consider his passion project, so he was going to let them go. In our running theory, Adam tells Laurel about this project at the conference where they met. Theoretically, this is the instigating incident. Our main character, Laurel, has to decide what to do with that information."

"If it was Laurel," Gran interjects.

"Right. Assuming it was Laurel. If Laurel took Adam's idea for her thesis and Adam found out, did that make him revisit the idea? I mean, if it's about to win a big literary prize for Laurel, did that make him move forward with the book, with or without his agent or editor?"

"And is that why they were determined to come to our festival? To talk him out of it?" Phoebe asks.

"Only one way to find out. I'm meeting Marilyn."

Agents are not typically on call for the masses, but I'm pretty sure she'll want to talk. When I draft the email, I put "Urgent About Adam" in the subject line. Then, "Need to speak about Adam. Critical." I hit send and wait. In exactly three minutes and twenty-three seconds she calls me. "When and where?"

"As soon as possible," I say. "You choose where."

She texts me the details. I'm slightly surprised by the location, but it's only a two-hour drive for me so I'm not complaining.

"Tell no one," she says, sounding terrified.

* * *

Mystic Pizza is one of my all-time favorite movies. All-time. I've never actually been to the original restaurant, and I'm trying to be mindful of my mission and not geek all the way out over where we are meeting.

Marilyn is already waiting for me in a booth toward the back, giving her a bird's eye view of the entire place. Smart. As I approach, she waves the waitress away. "I got us one of the original pies plus Coke. Best combination in the world."

I am slightly taken aback since our last conversation was so fraught. She reads my mind because she says, "If this is going to be my last supper, let it be yum."

My response to that is a simple, "Yaaassss."

"You're funny," Marilyn says. "Writers usually are. But almost none of them want to show me that side. You all want us to believe you are so serious. So, worthy." She waves that concern away. "Between us?"

I nod.

"We just want you to write good stuff and be real."

I take a sip of my water. "Good to know."

The waitress returns, carrying our pizza like a prize. She puts it in front of us, sliced and ready for us to devour. Another waitress brings our drinks. "Enjoy."

It's hard not to dive into the conversation, but Marilyn is happily chewing her pizza, making overly dramatic noises, so I let her have this moment. When she finally resurfaces for a drink of soda, I ask. "You said you were scared?"

"Terrified. People are getting murdered."

"Specific people," I point out. Then hear myself making the same noises as I eat my own slice of delicious pizza.

"I am connected to them. Both of them. That's terrifying."

"Adam's brother told us that you guys had parted ways last spring. Is that true?"

Marilyn smiles like she's remembering a good memory. "Adam said that all the time. It never stuck." I take another big bite of pizza, a strategy to keep her talking, and she does. "Agent-author relationships—it's like a marriage. We'd been together for years. And his highly successful books? Those are our children. We are linked together even beyond death. Witness."

I nod. "Who is his heir? Pete?"

"No."

"What?" The air goes out of my lungs. I start to choke. She comes around the table and pats my back repeatedly. Finally, I get my breath back. "I'm good. Thanks. I'm just surprised."

"All of the proceeds from his books go to fund cancer research. That was Marie's cause of death."

"Did Pete know that before Adam died?"

"Yes. Pete gets some subsidiary rights—audiobooks, film. There was some talk of making the books into a series for one of the streaming services, which could end up being somewhat lucrative, but nothing compared to the money that the books themselves generate."

"Merchandizing rights?" I ask.

"To the charity."

"Wow. That's gotta hurt," I say. "When did Pete find out?"

"Last May, when Adam got religion and decided he'd been mistreating the memory of his wife. He brought Pete to the offices and signed the paperwork in front of him. I think Adam meant it as a grand gesture, to let Pete know how much he really had adored Marie."

"How did Pete take it?"

"I'm sure it was a blow. I mean, it wasn't just the money, but the thought that your own brother wasn't going to look out for you? Adam never really understood other people's emotions. We convinced him to go to therapy after Marie died. His inability to connect with other people was creating problems with fans and could have potentially threatened his brand. Ironically, it was during those sessions that he realized how awfully he'd been treating Marie's memory."

"Is that maybe what prevented him from understanding why you wouldn't accept his new idea?"

"Yes, that's right. He was a prolific writer, so he'd churn out three to four books a year. To have a series go on for as long as his did was special. He owed it to his fans to keep that going for as long as possible."

I take a long sip of Coke. "How did he do it?"

"It was astonishing. I'd never met someone who could continue to find new story lines that fit so perfectly with the previous ones. He had a gift. That last one? Werewolves introduced as easily as he did it? It made sense. It felt like it had been there the entire time. It felt intentional. And after a serious bout of writer's block. It was a miracle."

"Writer's block?"

"Adam was so used to having a fountain of ideas, and he was terrified that the source had dried up. I told him it happened to everyone and he should go on vacation or take some time off to reconnect with his inner writer."

"Did he?"

"He took three weeks off. Went away with Pete of all people." She held up her hand like she was testifying. "Went skiing somewhere. Then went to Maui. Returned refreshed. With an idea that would breathe life into the series in a very unexpected way. Said it came to him one day when Pete was out surfing with a ski instructor he'd started dating. Adam was pissed he let her tag along on their vacation but later told me it was just what he needed. Time away. Time alone. And Hawaii's not bad for inspiration."

"I'd say." I think about the books leading up to this one. "But I'm confused. Wasn't the supernatural element in there all along?"

"Yes, but very subtly. The detective was unnaturally lucky. Driven by some outside force. But it was never named or even alluded to. It was below the surface. The book before did introduce a witch."

I search my memory. "The one from the mountains in North Carolina."

"It was far enough removed to be acceptable to the genre, though, and it tied into the characters' discovery concerning their family histories."

"I thought people loved witches?"

"Yes, they do. But we're talking about readers. They get angry if you veer too far, and yet they want something that feels fresh. It's a hard line to walk. Adam walked that line. He introduced a witch in a way that readers readily understood and welcomed. Like old detective shows, sometimes they threw in a psychic but usually made them ineffective or completely fake. He did the opposite. His character was genuine and relatable and real."

"I see."

"Do you? He took tiny steps. First the witch. People were like, unexpected but cool. Sure, we buy it. There are people in real life who identify as wiccans and such. Let's do it. Then he gives us werewolves. Which feels like a metaphor for Wall Street goons but is really just a fresh take. What makes some people high risk, with ice in their blood? Maybe they're not actually people."

"Did you ask how he got there?"

"No. I saluted him. Told him I wanted three more books. It was supposed to be a vote of confidence."

"He didn't take it that way?"

"No. He was fixated on closing out the series and writing this new thing, but what he didn't see was that his new plot line had to be finished."

"Didn't you like his new idea?"

"I told him I wouldn't even look at it or see it until he banked more books for me." She pauses. Takes a sip of Coke. Lifts the cup in salute. "For his fans."

"So you never heard the concept?"

"No. Only the words he used to describe it—dramatic, emotional, sensitive, heartfelt, meaningful." She makes a face. "I told him to put that away until we were able to finish this one out."

"How did Adam take that?"

"He said then he was done with the series and done with me. Then he stormed out like a diva."

"And Pete?"

"He stayed behind. He asked me why I wouldn't consider looking at the concept and putting it under another name. A pen name."

"And you told him . . ."

"That no matter what anyone says, it would pull focus. Readers were used to action-packed supernatural thrillers, not meaningful emotional work. They wouldn't necessarily follow him to a new genre. Adam and I had these conversations before. I told him to deepen the characters in his current series. That way, what he was writing had meaning beneath the surface."

"How did Pete take all of that?"

"He shook his head and left. At the time, I was impressed by his willingness to advocate for the brother who literally just took him out of his will and acted like that was a kindness."

"And now?"

She looks at her pizza like she might take another bite but ends up just pushing it around her plate. "I don't know. It feels a little cold and removed. I wondered at the time what the conversation between Pete and Adam would be like after that meeting. I hoped Pete would talk sense into him."

"Where does Nicholas play into this?"

"I ran into Nicholas the week before, at a book launch for a mutual writer. He told me about Adam's concept."

"And?"

"At first, I was pissed. I thought he and I—Nicholas, I mean—had presented a united front. Nicholas told me that Adam pitched his idea to him. The actual idea. Showed him pages. Nicholas sent them to me. They were amazing. But Adam and I were still not working together. So, we wanted to fix that first."

I let that sink in. Nicholas was in trouble the minute the theft happened because he knew. "So, you know about the passion project also?"

She nods. Her fingers start shaking. "And everyone who knows is . . ." she does a throat slash. "Which is why I'm not eating salad anymore." She takes a bite of pizza. "Although I can't taste this at all right now." Her eyes go wide. She drinks the soda. "Oh, okay. Good. I can taste that. For a second I thought that . . ."

"You thought I put something in your drink? Or your food?"

She waves that thought away. "Nah. Who benefits? You have no skin in the game at present unless you're the mastermind behind all of this." She draws a circle with her hands, illustrating the full extent of the mess we were in.

I laugh. "I don't think anyone would refer to me as a mastermind of anything. My plotting is the worst part of my writing."

Her turn to chuckle. "I can help you with that."

My hand goes to my heart.

She holds up one finger. "If we both live."

"You still haven't said why you were going to the festival."

"We wanted to talk him out of doing the new book. Yet. We wanted to plan an end to the series. Something his fans would accept. We wanted to move the series into other rights. Maybe video games or serialized fiction. Then we'd help him develop the new idea. Make it everything it could be."

Something about that doesn't sit right. The thoughts in the authors' room that I attributed to Marilyn and Nicholas were about how he was going to tank their careers. "Excuse me for being forward, but we're talking about murder here . . ."

"Murders," she corrects me.

"Do you know why Nicholas went back to Mystic Hollow Saturday night?"

"No. He tried to call me. Left a rambling message about losing our rights to the manuscript and he was going to fix that. I thought he was talking about the established series, and I couldn't deal with that conversation. Emotions were running high, of course, after Adam's murder. I kept thinking if we'd gotten there the night before, maybe we could have prevented it somehow."

"Or you could have been hurt as well."

"Isn't there safety in numbers?" she asks. "I mean, that's an adage for a reason."

"In the authors' room, I thought I overheard you saying things that don't match what you just told me."

Her eyes zero in on me, and I feel the heat of her stare causing my neck to sweat. "I think you were speaking with Nicholas. Maybe. It's all a little fuzzy." I wave my hands around my head to emphasize how unfocused I was. "But I thought I heard you say something about him being disloyal and stopping him before he stops you."

Marilyn considers my words. "I can't believe I said that out loud, but who knows. Being around artists, you tend to open up a little. But that wasn't about Adam."

"It wasn't?"

"No. It was about Pete."

"Why Pete?"

"He was threatening to appeal the will, in his bid to be named heir. It would tie up Adam's books indefinitely. I told him I could finagle it so that he could get a bigger portion of the pie, but he wasn't having it. Said he wanted to see any works that hadn't been developed yet. That he should be the executor of his brother's will, despite the allocation of profits, etc."

"Pete?"

"Yeah. And when he drank, which was every time I saw him, he was way too flirty. Aggressively so. Adam said that Marie was fleeing from one such situation with Pete the night she and Adam met."

"Wow," I say. "Pete told me that Adam stole Marie from him. Said Adam was a thief. Did the same with his writing too."

"That's deflection right there. Pete wanted to be a writer. Adam asked Nicholas to rep him, but he could never finish anything. And his writing lacked inspiration or originality. It was banal."

I put my hands on my temples. "This is a lot to process. Pete? Pete? He told me he helped Adam plot."

"He did. Adam told me the same thing. Anyone can plot. Or can be taught how. There are templates. There are outline examples these days. It's the take on the work. That's what makes it good or great or rubbish."

Not rubbage, my mind reminds me. Another reason not to suspect her.

"Pete?" I ask. I think about how he met with me. Played the victim. Said awful things about his dead brother. How I might've been in danger with him since he is now my top suspect. I fan myself. "Is it hot in here?"

"You're just overwhelmed," she says as she slides my Coke toward me. I drink. I need to get in touch with Mack. It's Pete. Not Laurel. Or together, maybe. When I get myself together again, I ask, "Did Pete say anything about having a girlfriend?"

"No. But I tried to limit any and all communications with him. It's not like I was asking him about his personal life."

"So, what are you going to do now?" I ask.

"I've been thinking about that. It's the secret project that is making me unsafe. I have a press conference planned for tomorrow where I'll announce it."

"You're going back to New York?"

"No. Doing it remotely. Not telling anyone where I'm headed. No offense. Not even you."

"I get it."

Marilyn puts cash on the table. Enough for the pizzas and a nice tip. "Get to-go boxes. I believe I'm going to go back to salads." She puts her hand over her stomach. "I forgot how bloated pizza makes me feel." She stands. Opens her purse. Takes out a business card. "Here, so you can reach me. Happy to read anything you have."

"Thanks."

"Yeah." She brushes the hair out of her face. "I've decided I'm living through this mess. Move on. Find a new author to mentor. Send me even a rough draft, and I'll help you plot if that's your weakness. Who knows? I mean, I can't make any promises but . . ."

She's gone before I can answer. The waitress pockets the money and brings a to-go box. I consider not taking the pizza, but know I'd have a lot of explaining to do with Phoebe should I walk away from this opportunity. "I'm coming home," I tell her. "I'm bringing pizza and news."

"Drive carefully, Mom," she says.

We always say this to each other, but the Mom part gets to me. It's not that she doesn't call me Mom or refer to me that way, it's because when she says it this time, it feels filled with trepidation and worry for me.

"We can do a Phoebe podcast, if you want." She means she can talk with me the entire time I'm driving. It's something we do to keep each other awake when one of us is on the road.

"I think I'm okay," I say.

Chapter Thirty

The drive home is harrowing. The rain pours down and my windows fog. My eyes are tired, making it worse. I drink the cold brew I have stashed in the car, secretly wishing it was kombucha. I've become a kombucha junkie. Didn't take long.

I consider taking Phoebe up on her podcast offer, but something about that word circles my brain. Something Marilyn said. Something Mack said. This new ability to focus and see patterns is weird, memories come in pieces and they are reshuffled into something new.

As my mind rearranges the different ways these memories are linked or could be linked, I realize that at the center of this is Pete. Pete did podcasts. So what? I knew that all along. Pete was jealous of Adam. Also not a surprise, since Adam was hugely successful and not good with people. I could see Pete feeling left out. Left behind. Not as important.

Adam could have helped him with his podcasts. Given him connections. A leg up. Lend him some of his cred, at least. But that's not the only connection I'm finding. The online accusations of Adam stealing work. Could that have been Pete? Was he the one who found the video of Phoebe online and posted it?

It all comes down to the when. I call Phoebe. "When did they post that video of you?" I blurt.

"Well, hello to you too."

"I'm on a roll here, let me go with it."

"Okay. I think after we went to the store to get the tomatoes for Gran that she didn't need."

Gran's voice in the background. "Can't a woman forget something. Sheesh."

"Tell her to relax. There's a moratorium on being cranky when a murderer is afoot."

"Nice use of that word, Mom. Very Sherlock Holmes."

"What I was going for. But focus! What were we doing right before that?"

"Um. We were in the store. We bought stuff. Then we walked home."

"Who was at the store? Do you remember?"

"I don't know. I mean, Clayton was handing out pins. Mayor Racker was there. The Leach. Danetra. She was wearing those amazing hunting boots. Yum."

"I thought you were against hunting, dear," Gran calls.

"Of course I am. But I love the look. Feels very old money. British."

"Can we focus, people?" I ask, as I take a wide turn. Headlights coming the other way blind me and I make a noise.

"Mom?"

"I'm okay. Just someone with their high beams on."

"Ugh. Hate that."

"You were saying, dear?"

"I was asking who else was there and what were we talking about?"

"Huh," Phoebe says. "Oh, at the store. That's all I remember. Why?"

"I'm not certain. Hey. I have to go. Need to concentrate."

I hang up before Phoebe has the chance to tell me to be careful. A car whips by me, and skids to a halt in the street my car had just occupied. They do a U-turn and wind up trailing me. That can't be good. Something is definitely up with this one.

My hands grip the wheel so hard I am certain they are white at the knuckles. Like the saying. Which normally would entertain me, but right now I am too busy being terrified to care. I shift forward so I can peer at the road with all of my might. The car is behind me now, beeping their horn, flashing their lights, and riding me as close as they can. I look desperately for a place to pull over or turn off, but there's nothing. I'm shaking. Shaking.

More beeping. The driver's side window comes down and a hand shoots out. Oh my God. Do they have a weapon? Lights from a gas station appear a quarter mile down the road. As I get closer, I see the pumps, as well as a diner attached to it.

I don't know if I should pull over here or not. I do know that the driver will follow me. It's better to face them with potential witnesses versus continuing on this country road where houses are sparse and there wouldn't be any help.

I park next to the diner, under a streetlamp, hoping to deter the other car. It doesn't. They pull up next to me. When the window rolls down, I am amazed to see who it is—The Leach. "Get in the car, hurry," she tells me.

I get out of my car. I'm not going to go with her, but I also don't want to be trapped. My hands up in a surrender position, I back away.

"What are you waiting for?"

I point. "You were trying . . . you . . . you . . ."

"I was trying to help you. To save you." She looks exasperated with me.

Looking around I don't see any immediate danger. "Save me from what?"

"From whom. Did you think I was going to hurt you? Kill you?" She laughs a wickedly funny laugh. "Honestly, you're so dramatic."

The rain pours on me, my hair mats to my head. I've been told by an old boyfriend that I look like a drowned rat when my hair is wet. At the time, I thought he was just a jerk but have since confirmed it for myself many times. None of this matters except I do not want to die looking like a rat. No offense to the furry creatures. The Leach is wearing a trench coat with the hood pulled up, which makes her look impervious to the weather. Damn, that's a great word. I'll have to remember it later to tell Phoebe. Phoebe. My phone rings.

"Why did you stop?"

I hold up my phone. "We follow each other on our phones," I say.

Almira nods. "Of course. Who doesn't?"

"Who doesn't?" I say and answer the phone. "Phoebe, I'm fine. I'll call you back." I hang up.

"What are you going on about now?"

"People can follow each other's locations on their phones. So simple. I can't believe I didn't think of it before." I face-palm.

"You're going to ruin my seats as drenched as you are. Can we please move this along?"

"I'm not going with you."

"Of course you are." She opens the trunk and for a second, I believe she's going to throw me in, but instead she pulls out a towel. "You can sit on this."

I stand there, stupidly staring. "Why are you here?"

Almira ignores me, just opens the door to the passenger side of the car, lays out the towel and turns to me. "Shall we?"

"No. You have to tell me what you are doing. Why should I go with you?"

"Because I'm saving you." With that, she reaches into my pocket, grabs the phone I've got in there, and throws it in the grass. I'm so astonished by her brazen move that I couldn't move if I wanted to. She puts her hand flat on my back and leads me forward, the other hand showing me where to sit. "I think you may be in shock."

"You took my phhhhone," I blurt. "You threw it."

She puts the seatbelt in my hand. "Can you do this or do I need to reach over you to do it myself?"

I blink. Click the belt into place.

"Safety first."

She gets in on her side, seemingly certain I won't fling my door open and leap out. Which, to be fair, I've not given it any thought. She hands me another towel, which I start using on my hair and face.

"You really need to dress appropriately for the weather," she says as she starts the car.

"You threw my phone!"

"Your burner phone. You are holding your actual phone. See?" She points to my hand.

"Oh. Right. Why?"

"Why what?"

"Why any of this?"

"Because you were in danger, and despite our differences, I felt I could help. I have a car. I have my wits about me. Which," she makes a tsking sound, "makes one of us. And I have information you need to figure all of this out."

"Why?"

"There's that question again. I hope when you warm up, some of your sensibility will return. Marilyn sent me. She came to me after meeting with you. She told me about your conversation, and we both agreed you might be in trouble. Especially with that second phone as you called it burning a hole in your pocket." She laughs. "See what I did there?"

"Marilyn?"

Almira reaches into her console and takes out a water bottle. She hands it to me. "Please hydrate. I need you functioning. Marilyn came to me. She told me what she knew. We decided she needed to stay hidden. I helped her with that. Then our attention turned to you."

My hand goes to the door handle. Is this woman threatening me? Am I reading too much into every word she's saying?

She notices my attempt to flee. "Please. I am not here to hurt you. I did not kill Adam or Nicholas, God knows. Mayor Racker is a friend of mine, and she shared some private information with me that I will tell Mack when we get to Mystic Hollow. And since I was reasonably certain you were foolish enough to still be carrying that homing beacon in your pocket, I would find you, rid you of that albatross, and take you safely home."

"Marilyn sent you? To take me home?" It seems unreal.

"Now we've got full sentences at least. Drink your water."

I unscrew the top. Take a sip. It occurs to me after I've downed half of the bottle that this entire deal started with a poisoning. I stare at the bottle.

"Oh, for God's sake. I did *not* just poison you. My goodness, you are paranoid."

"What information do you have for me?"

"I said I had information for Mack. But I guess I can tell you as well. My friend Mayor Racker has confessed to the murders."

"I knew that."

"She didn't do it. Either of them. She is innocent."

"I actually didn't think she did. Why did she confess?"

"To protect her daughter, of course," Almira says.

"Laurel killed them?"

"No. She didn't. She was framed. And the information that was used to frame her was sent to her mother in order to force her to frame your grandmother."

"It was a double frame job?" I ask. "Wow. That's commitment."

Almira laughs.

"A triple frame job, really," I say. "They tried to frame Phoebe also."

"Interesting. If we were playing Blackthorne family bingo, we'd almost have it."

I nod. "Just need my mom."

We drive in silence. My phone rings. Phoebe. "Hey, hon. I'm coming home."

"I know. Just checking."

"Gotta go, hon." I turn to Almira. "Who do you share your location with on your phone?"

"I'm not certain that's any of your business."

"It's a rhetorical question. I share mine with Phoebe. With whom did Adam share his?"

"Interesting."

"His brother was his only living relative and he wasn't in a relationship with anyone at the time of his death."

"That we know of."

"That we know of. But let's say Pete was telling the truth, that he and Adam made up. Marilyn seemed sure that they had, since Pete was looking out for Adam's interests even after Adam took him out of his will."

"That we know of."

"Marilyn said—"

"The will has not been made public. And unless he made those stipulations in his actual will . . . Adam was not great at following through with things. He'd get excited and then he'd flit off to the next thing," she says.

"Interesting. But also, what if he did share his location with his brother? Then Pete would know he was going to the tower. He'd know exactly where he was when—"

"Wasn't Pete out of town when Adam was murdered?" she asks.

"I don't know. I only know he said he'd been doing a podcast at the time. But can't you manipulate time stamps on those things? Make it seem like they are live when they aren't?"

"I'm no expert there."

We pull into Mystic Hollow, and my breath releases. "Where are you taking me?"

"To your store, of course. I believe Mack is waiting for you there."

"That sounds ominous."

"Only if you're guilty."

"I'm not."

"Well, then, good for you."

She pulls into the driveway leading to the back of the store and parks. The rain continues, but it's a drizzle now and it feels less threatening than the storm I just escaped. Am I living *The Wizard of Oz*? Once the car goes into park and she withdraws her key, I clutch the door handle. "Thank you for bringing me home," I say. "It was an astonishingly brave thing for you to do. And now coming in to talk with Mack to help your friend. To give him the information you were telling me about. Amazing."

"Ending a sentence with a preposition. Where did you learn your craft?"

I open my door. "Writing is not the same as speaking, but for argument's sake, apparently it is now acceptable in some cases to end written sentences with prepositions. Try and keep up. Ha!"

"I prefer a more formal and precise use of the language. One is what one writes, after all."

We hurry to the back door of the store only to find the back room cramped with people. My people, specifically. There is also a fair amount of food. Chinese takeout containers. Three pizza boxes. Kebobs. Falafel. And, of course, tacos.

I put my hand to my mouth, feigning shock. "Onto what have I stumbled?"

Almira claps.

Phoebe shoots me a look like she doesn't get the joke.

"I was avoiding the use of a preposition . . . oh, forget about it. I'm so glad to be home."

Mack comes through the door carrying bags of food from the diner.

"Who died?" I ask. "What? It looks like there's enough food for a wake."

"I've seen you guys eat," Mack says. "This is enough for a movie night. Maybe."

"Oh dear," says Gran. "We've run out of tables."

Kim calls out to the store. "We are closing due to a police emergency." Then to us. "We'll move this meeting of the minds out there."

"Won't the customers be upset we are closing early?" I ask.

Kim points to where her watch would be if she wore one. "It's already closed."

"So," I persist. "Who were you speaking to?"

"Nobody." She laughs like she told herself the funniest joke.

Phoebe grabs armfuls of food and takes them out to the belly of the store. Kim follows suit. Mack brings his bags. Gran grabs napkins. I stumble forward, The Leach following. "We've got a lot to discuss," Mack says.

"The kids have school tomorrow," I say.

"Nope. It's a harvest festival holiday. No school."

"Convenient," I say, dipping a fry in ketchup. "Yum. So, who's going to start?"

Gran turns on the big screen she uses for movie days. Phoebe mirrors her laptop. The weirdest thing is, as she pulls up the documents she's been working on, there are keywords highlighted. "Are you guys seeing that?"

"Seeing what, dear?"

"The words that are highlighted. Who did that?"

"Are you sure you're well? There are no highlights."

I step closer. Sure enough, I see words that are highlighted silver with sparkly effects around them. Words like *burner phone* and *overkill* and *frame*. I rub my eyes. "It's been an exhausting night."

Kim takes over and pulls the videos of Pete doing his podcast on the night Adam was killed. "Pete has the strongest motive to date, but he was three hundred miles away when Adam was murdered."

"That's a very specific number," I say.

"He rounded, dear."

"I realize, but three hundred miles would take a long drive. Planes wouldn't even get you there faster. It feels deliberately far. What type of podcast was he doing, anyway?"

"He was reporting on a protest, the dumping of waste in the Chesapeake Bay, from Harbour Place, Baltimore."

I pull that up on my phone. "Ha!" I say.

"Ha?" Mack asks.

"That's two hundred and eighty-five miles."

Gran's hand falls gently on my shoulder. "That hardly seems to make a difference, dear."

"I know. I got excited. What if he put a time stamp on his video? How long was that protest going on?"

"All night. And yes, he could alter the time stamp fairly easily," Kim says.

"Is there any background footage that could provide a more accurate time stamp?"

Kim chews her lip. "I bet I can find some."

"Do that," Mack says. "Where is this chow mein sandwich from?" Mack asks.

I shoot The Leach a look, one eyebrow raised as if to point out that Mack just did the thing she accused me of. Oops, there it is again.

"He's not a writer, is he?" The Leach points out.

"From whence did this sandwich originate?" Mack asks. "Better?"

"Can we return to the matter at hand?" I ask. "The murders. Is this how you usually run your investigations?"

"Someone's cranky," Phoebe says.

"I'm cold and tired and tonight has been a lot."

"There, there," Gran says. "Veronica is right. Let's return to the mission. If it wasn't Pete, then who?"

"Plus, I look like a drowned rat. How come some women can look awesome standing in the rain? If you believe those corny romcoms."

"I didn't think you were a romcom fan," Phoebe says.

"I'm not. I just don't think it's fair. Hmph." I cross my arms. "But let's get back to the investigation."

Mack looks relieved as if he'd take murder over dealing with a diva. "Racker confessed."

"But you know she didn't do it," I say.

"I don't know exactly, but I strongly suspect."

"Dan told us about a student at a writing conference. That feels like the starting point."

"We thought that was Laurel," Phoebe adds.

"Based on?" Mack asks.

Kim brings up pictures of a gloved hand with Adam's drink. Then another picture of someone handing Dawn Nightengale a drink two weeks earlier. The same hand. "They were both with the same person," Kim says. She pulls up a photo of the records of attendance at the event.

I say, "The problem is we are using inductive reasoning here. Laurel may have been at all of these events, but that still does not make her the murderer. We can link her to the drinks, but we don't know if they had been altered yet. We have some of the sequence of the events down but there may be gaps."

"Such as?" Phoebe asks.

"Such as when the killer poisoned the drinks, then gave it to Laurel to hand to Adam. Plenty of people give each other drinks, especially well-known authors with whom the drink givers may want to curry favor."

Mack nods. "Exactly. Circumstantial at best. We need to see who poisoned the drinks. Who had access to the angel's trumpet?"

There are those words again. They ignite a memory, but I can't figure out who said them to me or when. Angel's trumpet. Angel's trumpet. I tip my head.

"What?" Mack asks.

"I've heard of that plant before. Before the murders. And then after."

"Interesting," Macks says. "From a story?"

"Maybe. That feels right."

"Let's keep going," Phoebe says. "Maybe it'll come to you.

"We know it can't be Laurel?" I ask.

"She couldn't have killed Nicholas," Mack says. "She was aboard the flight and on her way well before he returned to town. We have the plane manifest. Images of her at the airport with actual verifiable time stamps."

"But it could have been another student. Or she could have partnered with someone. Pete, for instance."

"There is nothing to trace her to Pete. They were both at the same conference, but that's it. So were thousands of other people.

So were you. Plus, she has no motive. We saw the story she subbed for her thesis. The one that's getting all the buzz, as you all say. It's about a child whose mother leaves her to join a rock n' roll band in the seventies. It's called 'Go Go Gone.'"

"That's a terrible title," I say.

"Agreed," The Leach says. "We'd never shelve that."

Then it hits me. "I feel like we are always asking the wrong questions. With Nicholas's death, it shouldn't only be about the why, but the who. As in, who could get Nicholas to come back to town?" I ask.

"Adam, if he were still alive. Marilyn, maybe, but it seems unlikely. I mean, why here? They could meet anywhere."

"It had to be someone who had something Nicholas needed."

"We've tracked his phone down, and there were some messages that implied urgency, but we don't know who sent those. So far, the sender is untraceable."

"Like the unknowns at the festival."

Mack nods.

"Or the burner phones Pete uses for his podcasts," I say. "I had one—"

Almira interjects. "I got rid of it. It's at the rest stop outside of Mystic. The diner there. I threw it in the bushes."

Mack nods like he already knew that information but still turns his attention to her.

Almira holds up her hand. "Before you get all excited, Nicholas was no fan of mine, nor would I have any information that would get him to drive back here."

"Pete was going to expose you. Maybe Nicholas was part of that?"

"They were going to expose Fox N Sox Books. Not me. If they did, they would have found out I wasn't involved in the pay-for-play scandal anyway. Nicholas wouldn't have come out unscathed from that scandal, though. Pete also never gave me a dirty little burner phone. I wasn't going to flip on Fox N Sox."

"Wait!" I say. "Can you check Adam's phone?"

"Already done," Mack says.

"But did you check the history of who he shared his location with and vice versa?"

Mack's eyes light up. He steps out of the store, but his booming bass can be heard from inside. I hear him give directions. Then he walks back in. "That's a great lead," he says. "But it will take a few days. Phone companies rarely comply with a request like this immediately."

Gran says, "I think we should get you home, dear. You need a hot shower and a warm bed."

"Not going to argue."

"We'll go pick up your car tomorrow, Mom."

"No need." Mack points outside to where a tow truck is pulling my car.

"What? Why?"

"I had a deputy following you to make certain you were safe. He saw the whole scene and retrieved the burner phone. Also, he owns a towing service company, so I figured two birds, one stone."

"Aw. You are nice deep down."

"If you tell anyone, I'll write you up for jaywalking."

"I don't jaywalk. I've never jaywalked."

"There was that time—" Phoebe starts.

"That was an emergency. I had to get to the other side of the street immediately."

Gran throws a questioning look toward Phoebe.

"There was a shoe sale," Phoebe says. "Shh. Not another word until your lawyer is present." She puts her arm around me and leads me toward the door. I want to protest. I want to say we need to clean up the food, but somehow while I wasn't paying attention, it's all been put away or disposed of. Exhaustion starts to creep into me.

"They were Manolo Blahniks. Heavily discounted. And the people on the other side of the street looked like they wore my size!"

"I'm certain there are exceptions to the jaywalking rule under those very specific conditions. Right?" Phoebe prods.

Mack shakes his head.

Gran says, "He's just being a meanie. No jury would convict you."

"As long as they were shoe-loving women like me. I demand a jury of my peers." My hand raised; I am thrust forward into the street where my car is being detached from its tow. The driver hands the keys to Phoebe, who tells me to get in.

Chapter Thirty-One

My bed is the most comfortable thing in the entire universe. I can tell my hair is still wet, but I'm so bundled up that I'm not even cold. In fact, I am impossibly hot. Burning up hot. Feverish?

I feel for the rock under my pillow, the one the Lady of the Forest gave me. I stroke it like a worry stone. The highlighted words and other specific details float toward me, but I'm too tired to make any sense of it. And then I realize I'm dreaming, even before I arise. I'm in a safe place, and I feel myself hug my stomach. No, that's not right. I'm hugging something to my stomach. Both hands wrap around it, and I smile because I'm so proud of it. Proud of me. But there's something else too. Sadness and even deeper—there's anger.

Then I hear a sound. A tinkling?

When my eyes finally open, I hear the sounds of the day around me. No school for Phoebe means she's downstairs with Gran making something delicious. I hear Kim also. And two hoots from Stella lets me know that she's watching over me, even though she's Phoebe's.

I sit up in bed, letting my body adjust to being upright. Yesterday was a lot and I feel like babying myself. The stone is weighty in my hands as I pass it back and forth. Back and forth. My mind wants to focus, but my stomach wins the battle. It rumbles and threatens, and I feel the bed moving under me. When was the last time I ate? Pizza. Mystic Pizza. Right.

I'm both starved and nauseated at the same time.

"Mom?" Phoebe calls. "Is that you?"

"Yeah."

She arrives with an electrolyte packet which she dumps in my water, stirring it before handing it to me. "Watermelon. This will help. Gran's making French toast."

A knock at the door makes me jump. I hear a man's voice. Mack's.

Phoebe's head turns. "Oh, yeah. He called and asked if he could join us. He has questions but says he also has info. You wanna clean up a bit?"

I huff. No. I don't care if Mack sees me disheveled. Although, I smell my arm pits and find I am a bit ripe. "Maybe a tad," I say, pointing at her. "but no starting until I'm there."

"I will hold the line."

The shower does nothing to jog my memory, but it does clear my head. I throw on jeans and a sweatshirt and my sock booties. I make my way downstairs and find Mack standing next to Gran, frying up turkey bacon, eggs, and what I assume are veggie patties for Phoebe.

As I enter the kitchen, Phoebe hands me a steaming cup of coffee.

"It's from the diner," Mack says, "and it's real coffee. Not that hipster cold brew stuff." He leans in closer and puts his hand up in a stage whisper. "Newsflash. You're not in Florida anymore."

I nod. Take a sip of coffee. "This is weird, though, right?" I motion to indicate the cooking competition going on in the kitchen. "Are we fully teaming up? This feels like teaming up behavior. It's like a potluck. Only with teams."

I take a pause in the conversation to drink more coffee. Mack grimaces. "This way the entire town isn't eavesdropping."

"I hate potlucks anyway. You've always got someone who only brings napkins or soda. And someone always makes a weird broccoli and grape salad that actually tastes amazing, but when you ask for the recipe, they get all vague about it and leave out key ingredients."

Phoebe pulls me away from the stove. "You seem hungry."

"I'm right, though. Someone always brings that weird salad that is loaded with mayo and other stuff not suited for a salad. But it is so good, and they never tell you about the toasted pumpkin seeds that make all the difference."

Gran exchange looks with Phoebe as she shows me to my seat. "May I get you some orange juice, dear?"

A tray of French toast appears in front of me. As does a plate of eggs and potatoes and turkey bacon. "Eat," Mack says, a little too bossy for my taste, but also the food smells amazing.

I take one bite of the eggs. One of potatoes. Some French toast. My stomach groans as I fill it.

"I'm glad you're enjoying it," Mack says.

I shoot him a quizzical look.

"You were doing it, Mom."

"I was?" I stare at my plate and my cheeks heat. When I really enjoy my food, I tend to make noises.

"I took it as a compliment," Mack says. "April's the cook, but I like to dabble. Now, let's get down to business. Using the crowd-sourced video clips Kim sent us, we were able to isolate a phone that showed the time of the protest. It was four hours earlier than the time stamp on Pete's video at the harbor."

"So, he could have been in the Hollow in time for Adam's death?" I ask, working hard not to make sounds as I eat.

"Exactly," Phoebe says.

"The burner phone he gave you didn't have any usable intel in it," Mack says.

"Like?"

"We were hoping we could trace it back to other phones. Or that he recycled it and had given it to someone before you that could tie him to the murder. But no dice."

"Isn't that the function of a burner phone?" I ask.

"Sure, but people get lazy. Sloppy. Don't plan well."

"I don't think that's Pete." I face-palm. "I can't believe I'm just remembering this, but one time when Adam was presenting at a workshop, someone asked about his plotting strategies, and he told us that he was garbage at plotting. We all laughed. But he said in the early days he ran all of his plots by his brother. Marilyn also said as much yesterday"

"Only in the early days?" Mack asks.

"Well, they had a falling out and also his agent and editor were working with him, fixing any plot holes."

"I don't get it. If a writer can't plot, why don't they just find someone who can?"

Phoebe laughs. "He fit the suit."

Mack stares at her, clearly not getting the *Brady Bunch* reference.

"He checked other boxes," I offer. Phoebe claps her hands as I distill the entire episode down to its core. "Sometimes the other boxes are more important."

"Like?"

"He was a good story," I say. "I mean his concepts were amazing. His writing was strong. But he, himself, was a good story."

"You mean after Marie died?"

"That's when his career really took off." I take another bite of French toast. "Are you bringing Pete in for questioning?"

"That's the plan. But the timing is the issue. We have motive. Actual multiple motives. And we may have opportunity. But Adam was poisoned with the angel's trumpet before he went to the church tower. Based on the autopsy, it was in his system a full hour before he died."

"And Pete couldn't have been there in time to give it to him," I say.

"None of the videos or pictures taken during the evening's activities showed Pete. I'm not saying he couldn't have avoided being recorded. I'm just saying it's pretty unlikely."

The front door opens. I put my hands out to keep people from talking.

"Hiiii," Kim calls as she walks into the kitchen. Her hand goes straight to her stomach. "I'm starved." She lifts her sling cross-body bag over her head and leaves it on the counter. She washes her hands, then heads to the table. "I've got the drone images for you as well. No Pete."

Gran loads her plate with potatoes, vegie patties, and French toast.

"I did see an SUV drive through town toward the belfry twelve minutes before he was killed."

She shows Mack the image on her phone.

He nods. "We have records of Pete's company renting an SUV. We'll have to check it, of course. Also, guess who Adam shared his location with? The only person—Pete."

"Did Pete share his location with anyone?"

"To be determined," Mack says. "Once we serve this warrant." He points to his shirt pocket.

Phoebe stands to pour coffee refills.

"You brought the big pot," I point to the to-go box of coffee.

"I knew who I was dealing with. So, if Pete came into town in time to kill Adam, who drugged him? Who got him to the belfry?"

I choke on my food.

Phoebe pats me on the back, hard.

Mack shakes his head. "I know he was going to meet you, but was that his idea? Or did someone plot out his demise for him?"

My head cocks. "That makes sense. I mean, the killer would need him to go somewhere remote-ish. And could manipulate him to go there. It tracks."

"Still makes Pete the number one suspect in my book," Phoebe says.

Mack laughs. "Oh, you've got a book now?"

Phoebe laughs. "Apparently, and Pete stars as the lead suspect."

"Noted," Mack says.

"We've said from the beginning it felt like a two-person job. Overkill. Right?" Phoebe adds. "The poison. Plus, the push? Overkill."

"Unless the person who gave him the toxin only wanted to weaken Adam."

"Pete didn't need to weaken Adam necessarily, although it wouldn't have hurt. We originally thought Laurel was a suspect. But . . ."

"Geographically unavailable for Nicholas's murder, at least." Mack takes a sip of coffee. "I do make a righteous cup of coffee, don't I? It's all in the brewing temperature."

"Unless it's cold brew."

Mack grimaces and waves that comment away. "Back to our little problem. If Pete had a helper, who could it be? If it's not Laurel, which we don't think it is. Doesn't feel right."

"Who would Nicholas come back to town to see? Oh my God, is it Nicholas?"

Mack takes a bite of French toast. "This is vegan? I need the recipe."

I clear my throat.

"Maybe?" Mack says. "But didn't he arrive after the murder?"

"That we can verify," I say.

"Motive?"

"The passion project! Maybe Pete has access to it after all. He could have offered it to Nicholas." I wave my fork around. "Oh. Wait. Why wouldn't Nicholas just go through Adam then? I mean, what's the benefit of killing a known entity for an unknown one—all for the same prize."

"The perfect concept," Phoebe nods. "But, didn't Dan say Adam came up with those all the time? He was a wealth of ideas . . . like one big idea tree."

"Yeah. I guess Nicholas was not in on it. No motive."

Mack drinks more coffee. "Well, this was nice. We are waiting on a few leads. Eventually we'll have to bring him in. Hopefully by that time we'll have figured out the rest of the puzzle."

Chapter Thirty-Two

Kim picks Phoebe up for school the next day as I make my way downstairs. My phone rings. Mom.

"What do I have to do to get a moment with my daughter? Murder someone? Or maybe I could just key their car. Rob a store? Is that dangerous enough for you?"

A panicky feeling stabs at me until I look at the face of my phone. "It's only Wednesday. We're coming to dinner on Friday."

"If you make it that long living in the murder capital of America. That's what they're calling it, you know."

"Who's calling it that, Mom? Literally no one."

"There was a write-up in the paper. About how small towns are the new criminal enterprises."

"That might be an exaggeration of epic proportions."

"I'd feel safer if you all moved here. With me. Where it's civilized and you never have to speak with your neighbors. Most times you only see them if they go out of their houses long enough to get the newspaper."

"Don't you and your neighbors have someone to do that for you?" I ask.

"Well, obviously. So, we don't have to see our neighbors. But that's beside the point. I want you and Phoebe and Mom to come stay until the murderer is caught. Promise me."

"You are being ridiculous."

"They say that small towns are not as safe as they used to be. But whatever the cause, there is a dark side to Mystic Hollow. Trust me."

"This was an anomaly. The people killed were not Mystic Hollowians. It's fine."

"I don't like it. You doing clandestine meetings with would-be murderers. Playing detective. Burner phones. It's too much."

My face heats as if I've been slapped. "Where are you getting your intel from, Mom?"

"Wouldn't you like to know?"

"Oh my God. Almira. You're talking with The Leach."

"The Leach? What a horrible thing to call a person. I taught you manners. Now you've become some brute. Florida changed you."

"Is it Florida or Mystic Hollow, Mom? To which unseemly geographical location that is not Norwalk do we attribute my decline? And besides, that's her actual name."

"She's a reputable businesswoman. With exquisite taste."

"How would you know she has exquisite taste?"

"She happened to attend one of the charity events my friends chaired yesterday. An auction. Got a beautiful overstuffed armchair." Mom sighs. "That could have been yours. I would have been happy to buy it for you. To set it up in your old room . . ."

"I have a room at Gran's, Mom. She asked me to come help her. She needs me."

"Is she ill?"

"No. But she needs help with the store. And The Leach is trying to buy it out from under her. Did she tell you that as you two sipped white wine spritzers and braided each other's hair?"

"Who drinks white wine spritzers, Veronica? It's not the nineties."

"You know what I mean. That woman is trying to drive Gran out of business. Don't trust her."

"Maybe it's time to let that dream go, Veronica. Gran could move in with me and we'd—"

"She loves Mystic Hollow. She loves the bookstore. You know that. We'll come for dinner Friday night. And every week if you like. For as long as you are here."

"If you don't know better than to take a burner phone, you have no business investigating dangerous criminals."

I hear the fear in her voice and my heart softens. "You're right, Mom."

"Is the moon blue? I never thought I'd hear you say those words."

"Listen, Mom. I swear I've taken my last burner phone. I hear you. I will be safe from now on. But stay away from that woman. She is not your friend."

"I wasn't born yesterday. I know when I'm being played. Quid pro quo, Veronica."

"You mean prid quo po." That's what I called it when I was little. Made my dad laugh.

Now it's Mom who does. She laughs. Actually laughs. And I feel good about that, except it hits me. Quid pro quo. Whoever was working with Pete was getting something out of it also. But what? If Pete's motives were revenge and monetary gain, what was the other person gaining?

"Gotta go, Mom. I promise to be careful. See you Friday."

I hang up before she can say anything further, then race to Gran. "I've got to talk with Phoebe. How terrible would it be if I text her in class?"

Gran makes a face like she's considering that a parental crime, "I'd say a six. No, a seven."

"Come on, I need to ask her something. I'll go in person."

"That would elevate it to an eight. A nine if you embarrass her and knowing you . . . well."

"Hey!"

"I don't make the rules." Gran drinks her tea. "And if you go in your jammies, there is no coming back from that."

"Oh, right." I rush upstairs, brush my hair and my teeth. I step into jeans and the *Wicked* sweatshirt Phoebe loves. I reach for my standard jacket—cold weather approved—but remember I'm trying to not embarrass my kid, so grab my long faux leather burgundy one. I consider a beanie but decide hatless is best.

Gran smiles. "It won't matter what you wear. Kids have been embarrassed by moms for centuries, dear."

She's right.

"Lip gloss," I put my hand in the air as I escort Gran to the car. "It can do wonders."

"I'm sure you're right, dear."

* * *

We pull up to the school and I park. Phoebe's school in Florida was an industrial looking building. Gray and white with tin roofed covered walkways because it rained so often. Her high school here is an old brick structure that is two stories with a white entranceway that feels charming and inviting. Nothing like mine, which was a super high-pressure college prep school with classmates who had razor sharp smiles.

I hope like mad that Phoebe's experience is different from mine. I think it might be but then remember that video of Phoebe. Of how she was scared by whatever secret power she'd harnessed.

I realize my mind is overly active again. Adam's books and their thematic structure have sunken their teeth into me, making me believe that there is danger all around. Mom's disparagement of small towns didn't help. But as I walk past the peace garden in the walkway with symbols and signs written in different languages, a warmth fills my heart. Appearances may be deceiving, but I feel good about this space.

They call Phoebe to the office, and her face is pale and drawn. "Gran?"

"She's okay." I want to smooth her hair back but wonder how low that would sink me on the parentometer. "We're just going to go to the car for a second. Then I'll send her back," I tell the office clerk. She barely glances up as she types dutifully into her computer.

"You'll have to sign her back in." She waves at the clipboard.

"Got it."

"What's up?" Phoebe asks when we make it to the car. She brightens when she sees Gran. "She's really okay?"

"Yes. Yes. Sorry. It's about the murders."

"What?" her mood skews to fully annoyed. "It couldn't wait?"

"Maybe not. When you ran the stylometry program on Adam's books, did you look at his latest?"

"I'm sure I did."

"The one about the werewolves on Wall Street?"

"It was part of his series, right?"

"Yes. But a departure also."

"I ran the program on the first few chapters."

"Why only those?"

"I matched the sample size of the original work you gave me. Three chapters. So, I took the first three."

"What if you expanded that? For the last book, especially."

"Sure. But it'll take a little while. You taking me home?"

"No. Do it after school."

"I have a substitute next period. I'll see what I can get done."

"Okay. Let's sign you back in." I walk Phoebe to the front office. I'm about to explain there was a family emergency, but the clerk seems unfazed. She points to the paperwork I need to fill out. For reason, I put medical issue. Murder is an issue, for sure of the medical sort. Kind of. If you squint.

After we pull out of the parking lot, Gran says, "What are you thinking?"

"I'm rethinking, mostly. It seems like we got a lot of things right in our suppositions, but our conclusions might be wrong."

"Meaning?"

"I wonder if after all Adam did steal his last book."

"The passion project?"

"Maybe. But also, the werewolf on Wall Street one."

"That would piss someone off. The writer he stole from, for sure."

"The question is, who did he steal from?" I ask. "The answer feels so close. Let's get back to the bookstore. Maybe something will come to us there."

Chapter Thirty-Three

Sometimes when I'm writing, I get stuck and I don't know why. I'll be clicking away, writing five or six pages a day on a work in progress, then it slams to a halt. When that happens the only thing that works is stepping away from the project. Putting it completely out of mind. Clean. Cook. Bake. Walk. Read.

Usually, if I allow my brain to process information without my immediate interference, the solution to the block will present itself. Simply. Elegantly. I'm hoping that will happen today.

Gran works in the back of the store, ordering and arranging inventory, looking at the accounts. I fluff pillows, arrange end caps, dust. I look at the leaky roof, and it's still showing a small spot, but it's vastly improved. I say a small prayer of gratitude, even though I'm not sure which deity I'm addressing.

The bell at the door tinkles. A memory surfaces. Why do I associate that bell with the answer to this puzzle? Tatum is behind the register. She rings up a thirtysomething woman who's toting a baby in a front sling while pushing a toddler in a stroller. It always amazes me how people can handle more than one at a time.

More than one at a time.

Hmm. As in romances? Or books.

Was Adam cheating on his book's due date to the editor in order to work on the new shiny project? Writers do that sometimes. They boast on socials about it, and people laugh and laugh. But maybe Adam was terribly behind. Maybe he took shortcuts?

Phoebe calls. "It's not his."

"What? Are you allowed to call me during school?"

"You're kidding, right? You actually pulled me out of AP Lit where we were studying English poets, by the way, which you know are my favorite, to have me work on this project."

I chew my nail. "I know. I just feel bad that I did it. Guilty Mommy."

"Maybe Guilty Mommy can buy me a video game. One of my favorites just released."

"Ugh. Now you're reminding me you aren't just into British writers of a certain period. What isn't his?"

"The last book. He wrote the first part, and the end, but the middle? It's not his. I can show you the evidence later. The word choices. The way he formatted the sentences. Not his."

"Maybe it was just a really heavy edit?"

"I don't think so."

"Maybe he adjusted his style to suit a new genre or because he was working on something else on the side and it sort of all got jumbled together?"

"Nope."

"It's not his." I consider this.

"What does that mean?" Phoebe asks.

"Not sure. See you after school."

The door closes, presumably with the mom and kids gone, Tatum seems to have gone on to help another customer in the cookbook section, leaving the front counter empty, which triggers something in me. Not a memory, exactly, a reverse memory, maybe. Like I am remembering when the bell tinkled and there was someone at the register and . . . and . . . I can't quite get it.

I grab my purse. Something about a purse. Jingle. Tinkle. What? A purse and the counter. I remember, sort of, standing right where I am. But it was a really long time ago. Maybe when I was Phoebe's age. What kind of memory from my childhood could be connected to this crime? It makes no sense, but the memory itself refuses to either show itself completely or leave. It hangs on, persisting despite everything I'm doing. It has to do with the bookstore, I'm sure of it. But that's not exactly helpful since I've been coming here my entire life.

"Going to get coffee," I call.

Gran sticks her head out. "And cake?"

"A Beanelly it is!"

"You're getting the hang of it, dear. You'll be on the VIP list for the cold plunges soon. Once they reopen, that is."

"Stop patronizing me. I'm not a child," I say. Then, "Sorry. I'm a cranky pants."

"Coffee will help, dear."

"It always does."

I step into the autumn weather that has suddenly turned chilly, almost as if it's purposely annoying me. A huge gust of wind sweeps leaves across the sidewalk, and they land on me. "Gah," I say, clutching my coat. Maybe I won't get a cold brew. Maybe something hot to go with the cake? One stop for me today.

I pass the diner on my way to Connelly's. I guess everyone had the same thought, since there's a line. Cassandra Fetterly stands in front of me, her cane squarely on the ground, gripped by her leather-gloved hands. Driving gloves, the kind with a circle on the back of the hand. It cheers me up to think that someone her age would still dare to be racy. "I like your gloves," I tell her.

"Thanks." Her eyes go to my bare hands. "Aren't you cold?"

"Yes. I thought it would be warmer."

"Cold front," Cassandra tells me. She points to her knee. "My joints never lie."

I wonder why she doesn't do magic plunges like Gran, but she must read my mind because she says, "Kiki's gone out of town while they clean the pools. She's hired an industrial company."

I nod. "Hopefully they'll be up and running soon. As will you."

Behind me there are grumbles. I almost give up on the line and head to the diner for a donut and a regular cup of coffee, but I feel eyes on me. I don't know the Hollow etiquette. Is it insulting to jump out of a line because it's taking too long? Just like I'm pretty sure I'm not supposed to bring up the plunges. Or the witchy book club.

Tallulah bursts through the door, allowing the wind to come in. I pull my coat closed. "You'll never believe it," she pants like she's just run a race.

"Slow down," Sylvester says. "You'll hurt yourself." He holds up his hands as if he has the power to stop Tallulah.

"The Old Candy Shoppe is closed!" Tallulah says. "I've got the girls coming for bridge tonight and there will be no caramel clusters or gummy bears."

"What happened?"

"No idea," Tallulah says. "There's a sign that says family emergency. Will reopen tomorrow."

"Why don't you buy some cookies," Cassandra suggests. "Maybe grab some chocolate-covered espresso beans from Rusty."

"You don't know Bernice. She holds a grudge. I knew I should have bought them yesterday. Who knew Bitsy would close."

"Why didn't she get one of the Andrews boys to run it. Like when she took that fancy-pants trip to Aspen. She doesn't even ski."

"She went to see her daughter," Tallulah reminds her. "Cause her marriage went bust." She whispers the last three words as if they are too horrible to utter. "She was a ski instructor. If you can believe that. Left her husband for one of her students. Some artsy guy according to Bitsy."

"The point is," Cassandra says, "someone could have taken over." She harumphs. "And you would still have your candy for your bridge game tonight."

"I hope everything's okay," I say. Then. Puzzle pieces click together in my brain and I suddenly understand. "Oh. I have to go."

"You don't want your cake?"

"I have to . . ." All of a sudden, the tinkling sound makes sense. I race back to the store just in time to see Phoebe and Kim going in.

I keep my head down, determined, pushing my way forward to the front of the store.

Gran steps out from the back. "Hello?" She waves.

I step behind the counter and start searching on my phone, only my fingers are clumsy in my rush.

"Where's the fire, Mom?" Phoebe asks, then sees my face. "What do you need?"

"Can you look up Carolyn Millner and news article about a short story contest? From around twenty years ago. I was a junior in high school, so—"

"Got it. Then what?"

"It's got her story in it. I want you to compare it to Adam's new book."

Phoebe gives me a look, trying to figure out what it means.

"Please," I say. I can't explain more yet.

"On it," she says, fingers flying over the keyboard.

Kim takes off her sling backpack and slides her tablet out of it. As she does, the charms on her key ring jingle.

"That's the sound." I point. "Or like it. In the genus."

Nobody asks what I mean which is good since I'm not certain I could adequately explain.

"Can you pull up the video with Pete from the day after?" I ask Kim.

Kim loads the video and hits play. I watch. Pete on the stairs in front of the town center. Walking confidently. Angry. Fueled with purpose. His student Sarah by his side wearing her Amherst sweatshirt. Mack. "Again," I say.

She plays it again.

"That girl with the mic. Sarah?"

"Mack wasn't able to find her. Pete gave him her information, but it didn't check out."

"Can you zoom in behind her?"

"I just see a person's shoulder. Their face is blocked."

"What does she have on her purse, the person behind Sarah."

"Charms," Kim says. "You know like people put on their keys. Like I have on my messenger bag."

"It's a thing, Mom," Phoebe shouts from her perch in the reading section.

"Everything old is new again," I say. Then I laugh. Too hard. "Can we see them?" I ask, my head is throbbing now. I push on my temples, trying to contain the ache.

"Mom? I found the story. Copying it and comparing it to Adam's book now. But it will take a while.

Kim swivels the screen to face her. She pinches it, zooming in. Then takes a screenshot. She enlarges the screenshot. "Not super clear," she tells me. Just some charms.

"Charms," I say. "Let me guess—a flower, and skis."

"How'd you know?" Phoebe asks.

"I know why the candy shop is closed," I say. "Call Mack."

"Is closing the candy shop a crime?" Phoebe asks. Then considers, "Although maybe it should be. I was going to get some white chocolate bark later. The kind with the potato chips in it."

"Now I want that too," Gran says. "Pity."

"Call Mack. Please. I remembered the charm bracelet and I saw the skis on her purse charms, but I forgot. She was always so matchy matchy. I hate that."

Gran puts her hand on my arm. "That *is* annoying, dear."

"Please call Mack. Trust me."

"Okay, Mom. Calling."

"Tell him to bring her a coffee, dear. I feel like her brain is short-circuiting."

"I should have known. It was right in front of my face. Actually, she was."

"Let's go into the back, dear." Gran motions for Kim to help me.

"I'm perfectly capable of walking there myself."

"I know, dear."

But I admit that I am floored by my discovery. Shaky. "It was her all along."

"It's okay, Mom."

Mack rushes in, coffee in hand. "What's up?"

"The candy store is closed," I say. It's not what I planned to say, but it's what comes out. Mack slides the coffee in front of me.

"Is she okay?" he asks. "She looks so pale."

I grab his hands. "The candy store is closed."

"The video. Show him the video," Phoebe says.

Kim hits play.

"I've seen that before. A hundred times. What am I missing?"

I drink the coffee, allowing it to scald the back of my throat. I start to feel a little better, so I drink some more. Gran hands me one of the cookies we sell. I take a bite and the sugar hits. The fog in my brain begins to clear. I bite my tongue. "Ow."

"Are you okay?"

I drink more coffee. "Yes. I'm fine. I'm better." I take another sip. I feel the blood return to my face. I take a deep breath. "We were right about most of our assumptions but wrong about the conclusions."

"Meaning?"

"There was a second person involved. The person who blackmailed Dawn to drop out at the last minute, I'm guessing. Then poisoned Adam."

"Okay . . ." Mack says.

"We thought that person was Laurel based on Dan's story about the conference. It made sense that Adam would hold sway over a younger person who wanted to break into writing."

"Right . . ."

"We also thought the motive was about theft. Pete said Adam stole everything. His girlfriend. The ideas for his books. There were allegations of plagiarism online."

"And?"

"Phoebe ran the stylometry program using the original work Dan fed us. None of his work had been stolen. Except . . ."

"Except the last one," Phoebe says.

"I thought you analyzed that one as well?" Mack asks.

"I did. But I initially looked at the sample size we had and ran the program on the first few chapters of the new book only. When I took another sample from the middle of the book, the writing styles did not match."

"Huh." Mack rests his fingers in that cleft in his chin. "Did you run the program on other parts of his other books?"

"Yes. The other ones are his."

"Marilyn said he'd been suffering from writer's block," I say. "Not unusual. We all go through it to some extent and the larger the pressure . . . So maybe he meets someone. A writer, which happens all the time, and stumbles upon writing that blows him away."

"Like?"

"He'd been leaning toward the supernatural in his previous book. He'd hinted at it. Marilyn said she felt his foray into embracing the paranormal was understandable and relatable. She felt like it was the perfect pivot for the series and didn't know many authors who could reinvent themselves midproject like that. Maybe he didn't."

"So, he steals someone's work. How do we figure out whose?" Mack asks.

"She's a writer. Could have met him at a writing event. Then they met up again later. Maybe she was dating him. I could see that."

"Dating who?"

"Either Pete or Adam. I think Adam was skiing in Aspen recently. She lives here."

"Who, dear?"

"Carolyn Millner. She left her husband for one of her students. She was a ski instructor."

"Okay. But a lot of people could have met Adam at a writing event. A lot of people ski in Aspen."

"She was also in Hawaii. Around the same time Pete and Adam were. When Adam was fighting writer's block."

"How do you know it was her, dear?"

"Her charms," I say. Even though I know that doesn't make sense yet. "And the angel's trumpet. That was the toxin she used in that short story. The one I thought was like Agatha's. I can't believe I forgot that. Oh, and that scent. She was always using essential oils and such, like that horrible bug spray her mom made with eucalyptus and lemon balm. I smelled something similar in the belfry that night. I didn't know what it meant, but it pissed me off. "

Mack asks. "Bug spray pissed you off?"

"Not bug spray. The overuse of oils."

"It's cloying," Gran offers. "Especially if you are sensitive to scents. Inconsiderate, for sure."

"Plus, she was so haughty about it. On one of those ridiculous camping trips Mom made me go on with the Scouting Girls. And Bitsy was telling everyone how she made this homemade bug spray. You know how competitive moms get?"

"Is this Bitsy, who is aggressively protecting her child from mosquito bites, we're talking about? Because as annoying as it is, it's not criminal. Or an indication of criminal tendencies. It might just be good parenting?" Mack leans against the doorway.

"Smug parenting."

"I'll give you that."

"Carolyn posted about it on the socials recently. Mom-shaming anyone who didn't do it." Even though she doesn't even have kids. I mean, who joins a moms group when they are childless?"

"Someone who hopes to have kids?" Mack posits.

"People who struggle with fertility join those groups. Or if they join family groups, they lurk. They don't interject themselves in the conversation as if they are an expert. Which she is not. What she is, is someone who believes she should be recognized for her innate superiority. Do they have a name for that?" I turn to Gran.

"A superiority complex?" she shrugs.

"Right. She feels entitled. Smarter."

"I hear what you're saying. It's a profile that fits, but I still don't have a clear path to charging Carolyn with murder," Mack says.

"Start with the angel's trumpet. It was from the old story. The one she wrote where the main character poisoned her husband slowly using angel's trumpet. Remember?"

Gran shakes her head but then nods. "Maybe. It's coming back to me."

"She won that contest. The one I wanted to win. It helped her get into Sarah Lawrence."

"Now it just seems like you've got a vendetta against her, dear."

"Don't you remember that charm bracelet she had that bugged me when we were younger? It had a flower on it—angel's trumpet. The same flower she now also has on her purse."

"What do the charms have to do with it?" Mack asks.

"She was always like that. Using the charms to brag about her life. Look at me, I got into Sarah Lawrence. Look at me, I won a short story contest."

"I don't see how that ties into murder."

"She was so convinced she'd get into the writing program, she bought that charm. When she didn't get in, she moved to Colorado, married an accountant, and tried to get pregnant. Had fertility problems. Went back to writing, although I never knew that."

"How do you know all of this now?"

"The socials. I lurk a bit."

"Okay. But even if she reinvented that story, and brought it to a conference that Pete and Adam were also attending, it still doesn't give her motive. No one can place her at the scene of either crime."

"That small piece of metal that I stepped on that night—it could be a charm spacer. Look." I show him the image of the purse. "These two charms are smashed together."

"We tested it for fingerprints, but it was compromised."

"I bet you didn't test it for essential oils, did ya?"

"Let's maybe not insult the person you're trying to convince," Mack reminds me. "Play it out for me. Or should I say, plot it out."

"Let's say Adam meets her at a conference. He steals her werewolf on Wall Street idea, and then turns it in. She starts a relationship with Pete and tells him what she suspects. They collude."

"Oh, dear," Gran says. "I want to give you points for that word, but I've been on the other side of that accusation."

"Your colluding didn't lead to murder," I say, my hand on her forearm. "And it's said with love when I accuse you and Phoebe of colluding together."

"There's still no evidence," Mack says. "We can look into her. We will, but so far it's just a lot of weird coincidences."

"How about this," I show him the image of the charms again. "Always bragging. This time she's got a pineapple for Hawaii. A flower to represent the angel's trumpet in her story, and skis. Where she went with Pete and Adam. She is so damned arrogant. She's practically confessing. Because she believes she's smarter than literally anyone else."

Mack cocks his head. "That is a profile that is worth looking into."

Phoebe walks in, computer perched in her hand and across her forearm. I always yell at her for carrying her Mac that way, but she's apparently mastered it. Plus, she looks super serious. "Mom. You were right. They match."

"What matches?" Mack asks.

"The parts of Adam's recent book that isn't his matches Carolyn's story from years ago. Same style."

"He takes her style. Her concept. Her writing. He plugs it into his book so he can finish the series and work on what he really wants to work on."

"How could he expect to get away with that?" Mack asks.

"I don't know. It's just what it looks like."

"You're sure about this?" Mack asks.

"About which part?" I ask.

"The murder part."

"Yes," I say. "It makes sense. She was here in town when it happened. I remember seeing her before Adam spoke. He recognized her in the crowd, I think. All of the dates line up. She had motive, means, opportunity."

"I heard the candy store shut down for a family emergency. That's odd," Mack says.

"It is," I say.

"I hope she's not trying to make a getaway." Mack is out the door, barking orders into his phone faster than I can finish my cookie.

A tear runs down my face. "She was in here so many times when I was growing up. She was our customer and a peer. She used to annoy me but still. I feel like I've broken some kind of implied trust."

"She bought a book, Mom. You don't owe her any sort of protection."

"It feels wrong."

Kim pulls up a picture of Carolyn Millner, Bitsy's daughter. She compares it to the girl in the video behind Pete. "It's a match," she says.

Chapter Thirty-Four

Mack leads me into the observation room between the two interrogation rooms.

"It's good to be on this side of things," I say.

"For the moment anyway."

"What's that supposed to mean?"

"With all the caffeine you ingest, who knows what kind of havoc you will wreak."

"That's a myth. Caffeine calms me."

"Sure it does." He hands me an earpiece and puts one in his ear as well. "You'll be able to hear everything through the speakers. Only use this when you want to talk with me. "

"Testing. One. Two. Three," I say.

He covers his ears and then pulls the earpiece out. "I'm right here."

"I was testing it."

"Remember. No talking into this unless you need to feed me information."

"Will she know I'm here?"

"Not if you follow instructions. So, probably." He smiles at me, though.

Phoebe and Kim are next to me, ready to help.

Mack says, "I do not agree with minors participating in this, but your parents gave consent and I could use the help."

Delores comes into the observation room, carrying a tray of coffee and donuts. "Mack's interrogations tend to go on the long side. Better to have snacks."

He shoots her a look.

"What? They aren't even suspects." Then to me. "I never believed you were guilty."

Mack shakes his head.

"The man is too serious," Delores says. She places the tray on the small table in here. "I think we should spruce this space up. So dingy." With that, she leaves, closing the door behind her.

We've got a small night light in the corner and of course the flashlights on our phones.

"Okay. I'll go see if your costar is ready."

Mack opens the door to the other interrogation room. In walk Carolyn and her mother. No lawyer present.

"This is so exciting," I say.

Mack makes a face and I realize I spoke into his earpiece.

"Sorry. Sorry."

He shakes his head.

"Thank you for coming in, Carolyn. Bitsy. You've been read your rights. Do you want an attorney present?"

"No," Carolyn says. "I didn't do it."

"We haven't accused you of anything yet," Mack says.

"But you think I killed Adam. I didn't."

"Do you deny that you were in the belfry that night?"

"No. I was there. But not to murder Adam. To ask him to refer me to his agent or editor. Or to acknowledge my writing. Or give me more money. I was open to any possibility. It was only fair since it was my work that he was getting paid all that money for."

"Meaning?"

"I was his ghostwriter."

"Snap," I say maybe a little too loudly based on how Mack's jaw braces.

"His ghostwriter? Meaning?"

"He paid me to write his books. Or at least finish them when he got bored with them. Men do that. They get bored."

"Revisionist history," I whisper. "But whatevs."

"Tell me how that worked."

"I met Pete at a conference. I couldn't believe he was Adam Whitford's brother. He said he'd introduce us. Offsite so Adam wouldn't have his boundaries up."

"What did he mean by that?"

"He told me that Adam was always on guard around people at those conferences. Pete said if we met on neutral territory, or maybe where I was the expert, Adam might be open to talking with me."

"So . . ."

"So, when Adam was suffering from writer's block, Pete brought him to Colorado and they took ski lessons from me. I told them I was a writer also. They said their next stop was Hawaii. I tagged along as Pete's plus one."

"And?"

"And I showed Adam some of my work. He opened up to me about being stuck on his project. I told him how he could end the series. Switch tracks. I'm really good at plotting. He said he'd pay me to finish the book for him."

"How much?"

"Fifty thousand dollars. See? He was worth more to me alive than dead."

"Damn," I say.

Mack flinches.

"Then what happened?"

"Adam got mad that Marilyn wanted him to write more books in the series. I told him I'd do it. Only this time I wanted triple. Pete told me what Adam made on the sales. Said he'd been his business manager at one point."

"What did Adam say to that?"

"He refused."

"What did you do then?"

"I told Pete."

"Were you and he still together at this point?"

Carolyn flashes the fakest smile ever. "Nope. We'd parted ways romantically. But were still working together on the Adam thing."

"The Adam thing being . . ."

"Pete got a cut of my cut. He told me he'd fix it with Adam. He guaranteed it," Carolyn scoffs.

"What did he say when Adam refused?"

"Pete threatened to expose Adam for having me ghostwrite without telling his editor or agent or fans. But Adam was adamant about not finishing the series. He was just going to walk away from those books. My books. My money. My fame."

"His, you mean."

"His, theoretically. Mine because I wrote it. We had a contract where I wasn't supposed to go public. Adam threatened me with that."

"So what did you do?"

"I asked Pete for help. He told me it was over. Adam held all the cards. With a good PR person he could weather a ghostwriting scandal."

"I'm certain that didn't sit well with you."

"I was pissed. Who were these men?"

Carolyn's face turns red. She slams her hands on the table. Bitsy puts her hand on hers. I'd seen Bitsy do this so many times as

Carolyn was growing up. Calming her. It suddenly occurs to me that Carolyn actually could kill someone who stood in her way of getting the things she felt she deserved.

"Should we get a lawyer, honey?" Bitsy asks. "I think that might be best."

Carolyn throws her mother's hands off of her. "No. I want to finish this. Before you even ask the question, the next thing I did was I told Pete that Adam stole his work."

"Boom!" I say.

Mack must be used to my outbursts because he doesn't even flinch "How did you know that?"

"Adam gave me his files to work from. Idiot." She smirks. "Adam took notes from a conversation he had with Pete outlining Pete's idea."

"How did Pete take that?"

"That landed. For sure. He got really angry. Then he said we should scare Adam a little. That's what we were supposed to be doing that night. Make him feel powerless and get him to concede."

"So, you poisoned him?"

"I microdosed some angel's trumpet. Not enough to kill him. Especially with the magic kombucha. That was my idea." She smiles as if she were pleased with herself. "I knew it would dampen the effect but still make him vulnerable. Loosening him up a bit."

"Without his consent. And without a medical degree or a chemist's education to know how it would affect him."

"I felt confident the microdose would not be lethal. I'd done my due diligence."

"I would like to see your arms," Mack asks.

"Lawyer," Carolyn says. Bitsy stands and walks out of the room.

"Oh my God," I say.

Mack says, "You are free to take a break until your counsel gets here." Then he leaves the interview room and enters our observation room. "What?"

"These donuts are amazing!"

He hangs his head. "Anything else?"

"That was it."

"Now I just have to find Pete," Mack says.

"I might have an idea. Where's Carolyn?"

"I think she's in the restroom. Probably best not to accost her there," Mack says.

"There will be no accosting. Only convincing."

"I've seen your method of convincing. It can be a little forceful at times."

"Are we kidding? Where are my defenders? Girls?"

Kim and Phoebe get super busy packing up the trash—leave no trace is one of Phoebe's favorite quotes from a book she read about a teen who hikes the Appalachian Trail in order to get away from his parents and their expectations. I was just grateful she didn't make me hike the trail in order to reenact some scenes. But in this case, she is obviously using evasive measures. If I weren't the person she was evading, I'd be impressed. Actually, I kind of am.

Without giving them the satisfaction of a response, I beeline to the bathroom.

"Oh, snap. She's going for it," Phoebe says.

I turn and do an exaggerated shushing gesture before walking out.

The door to the bathroom swings open, and I see Carolyn at the sink. When she sees me, she smirks. "Are you a suspect also? Maybe we can get T-shirts or something."

I almost tell her that she and I are not in the same club, but that won't help me. "Mack," I say. "Am I right?"

"He's not even smart enough to figure it out." She leans forward and reapplies her lipstick. "I am not a suspect. I am a witness. Guess they didn't teach him the difference in sheriff school."

"You were there?" I ask, making my eyes wide as if I hadn't just overheard the whole thing.

"Yeah. And I did slip a little drop of angel's trumpet into his kombucha. I figured it would mostly weaken him. No big. That is not murder. He did not *die* from the angel's trumpet."

"That's true!" I say. "You were always a good plotter."

She smiles at me. "What does he think you had to do with it?"

I shrug. "He's been fixated on me this entire time. Thinks Adam stole some of my work and I retaliated. He's all over the place right now."

I can see her eyes go to slits. Direct hit. "No way. That work was mine!"

"Adam stole *your* work?"

She scoffs. "In a way. I mean, he did pay me. I was his ghost."

"Oh my God, are you kidding me?" I am doing my best fawning.

"Yeah," she says. "His last book. The werewolves? That was me. And I tied it into his previous books."

"I met with his agent and she said that was brilliant! And this whole time it was you!" I put my hand on my heart. "Wow."

Carolyn starts washing her hands. Stops to pull up her sleeves. That's when I see the claw marks and redness from being grabbed really hard. "He was angry," she says.

I gasp.

"You pushed him?" I point.

"No. Of course not. Pete did. I didn't know he was going to kill him. Psycho." She makes a face like *Can you believe? Men.*

"Do you have proof that he did it?" I ask.

"I have a video. I turned the camera on my phone on when we got up there. It's trash. You can barely hear and most of the time it's pointed at the floor, but it would be enough to show I did not push him."

"That is so smart." I nod. "You know, I overheard Mack shouting something about not being able to find Pete."

"Yeah, he's probably long gone by now. He had a way to tap into Adam's accounts before the will is read. Just between me and you."

"Wow. Too bad, though."

"About what?"

"Without Pete, Mack may pin it all on you. You said yourself the video is trash."

Carolyn's face changes. "You think so?"

"Do you have a way to get in touch with Pete? To bring him here? Maybe tell him about the video and demand some kind of payoff so you can get away?"

"You are not so bad at plotting, yourself. But no way I want to see that man again. I bet my lawyer can get me off. Or at least carve out a deal, I can write while I'm in jail. It won't be a spa getaway, but it will give me uninterrupted time to write my memoir."

"If your lawyer gets you off for the charges. You can't benefit from murder even if you are an accessory to the fact. Mack told my Gran that when he was going to charge her for Nicholas's murder. If you can believe that."

Carloyn nods. "I'm scared, though. I really do think I'm going to have PTSD from this whole thing."

"What if you didn't have to see Pete at all? I can help with that."

"You'd do that for me?"

"Well, also for me. Who knows who else Mack will try to pin this on if he can't get his man."

Chapter Thirty-Five

Standing in the belfry in the exact place where Adam met his killer, I wonder if this was the best idea after all.

"Can you hear me?" Mack's voice is tight. "I think we should abort the mission."

"No," I say, pressing the earbud in tighter as if that will magically keep me safe. "This is going to work."

I play with the ends of my hair or should I say the wig Danetra supplied me so that my hair looks exactly like Carolyn's. Flippy at the ends and all.

"Stop fidgeting, Mom," Phoebe says. "Besides, your hair is far superior."

Mack hooked up cameras so small you can't even see them, with a feature that lets them go incognito, no light to indicate they are recording. Pretty cool. Phoebe is in charge of monitoring the feed, with Mack's supervision, of course.

"Remember not to turn around," Phoebe instructs as if I were an actor on stage."

I hear Mack's headset saying something about plan B. I hope it doesn't come to that. "Okay. We have drone footage of Orchard Road. He's on his way. Last chance to back out."

"Nope. I've got this."

"We will be with you the entire time," Mack says. "He's parked a block away. We are on radio silence now."

I look down at the area where Adam fell and my heart aches. Poor Adam. Was he the nicest guy? Maybe not. But he didn't deserve that. From his brother. I try to keep my breathing even, but I admit, I'm a little nervous as I hear the door at the bottom of the belfry open.

I breathe in. Breathe out. Two steps. Three. Four. My heart is racing. Ten steps. Twelve. Fifteen. Sixteen. Seventeen. Eighteen. Then he's inside the room with me.

"Well, Carolyn. You certainly took a chance with this little plan of yours, but it won't work."

I stay silent.

"That video is horrible quality. My lawyers will rip it apart in court."

I nod. We know the video is unusable. But when Kim edited it, and Mack used Carolyn's phone to send it to Pete, the accompanying text read that there is much more to the recording and that it was damning.

Pete continues. "What do you want? You want me to say I'm sorry? Because that's all this is. You were dumped. You are a man hater. Everybody knows it. You are a bitter woman."

So far Pete seems to be keeping his distance.

"You know you were in on it," Pete tries.

I shake my head.

"You weren't? How do you know I didn't tape those nights in my apartment when we planned this? I'll tell them it was my idea to weaken him and yours to kill him because he rejected you. He was my brother. Nobody will believe I wanted him dead. Nobody."

I hear his breath caught in his throat. He's emotional. Or scared.

"They tracked my location through Adam's phone. That was a mistake. But I wonder who you share your location with?" Two steps closer to me.

I hold my breath.

"That's all they have on me. Without you sticking your nose in where it doesn't belong. My phone's location. And some emails from Adam to Nicholas proving he was trying to steal my idea. That seems bad. But you know what? Those emails were sent from you. You are all the way in this, love."

Two steps closer. Soon, I'll be able to hear his breathing.

"Why aren't you saying anything? Talk! I don't care if you are videoing. I have a signal blocker on my phone. You won't pick up anything."

Is that true? Can he do that? Does that mean Mack can't see or hear me?

"It was a mistake to give them your phone. You've incriminated both of us. And with no upside since you have no proof that I killed Adam. Unless I admit it myself. Which I'm not going to do. And even if I did, you can't record it! You've lost."

"No, you have," I say, still facing the window.

"You sound weird. Let's stop this. Let's not fight." Hands fall on my arms. "I brought the money." A bag falls to the ground. "You can leave. No one will find out where you are. As long as we don't testify against each other, we will beat this. What say you we team up again?"

I spin to face him. His expressions morph from anticipation to confusion to fear, and finally, to acceptance. "This is a ruse," he says.

"No. It's a trap."

His face contorts. Rage fills his eyes. "You will not stop me. You will not win." He shakes me as he says each word. I hear footsteps coming up the staircase. Mack is coming. I'm safe. "If I'm going down, may as well go all in."

With that he lifts me off my feet and throws me out the window.

* * *

The shock of being shoved out the window freezes me. I'm flying. Speeding toward the ground at a rapid pace. My head is swimming. My eyes tear up. I can't scream or even brace myself. I'm busy scrambling for purchase in the air like a dog who swims on the floor. I am going to hit the ground. Soon.

I tell myself to fall the right way, but I have no idea what that even means. I brace myself. Close my eyes. And then I hit something. Only it doesn't hurt like I think it will. It's slippery, not hard. And bouncy. Bouncy? I'm bouncing. Flying upward now. Is this some kind of magic?

Red and blue lights flash all around me.

"Mom!" Phoebe's voice reaches me on the third bounce. "Mom!"

The big trampoline pillow thing I'm bouncing off of starts to collapse inward and draws me in with it, but it's no longer scary. Most of my falling energy and my flying energy and my landing energy have been swallowed by this big pillow thing. Oh . . . that's what plan B was.

Phoebe scrambles up the side until she reaches me. Her arms go around me and I hear her sob. "He did it. He threw you out of the window."

"I'm okay, Phoebs. I'm okay."

Stella flies by us, giving off a hoot. Men in firefighter uniforms scale the inflatable and help Phoebe and me off. My legs won't hold me so Phoebe props me up, walking me toward the ambulance that is waiting. "You are never going to be bait again, missy," she tells me.

"I promise. But Phoebe, he jammed the signal, didn't he?"

"Yes. But not before we heard his confession. Most of it anyway. And Mack says you can fill in the blanks and testify against him. Although Carolyn's pretty hot about all of this now. She says she's going to testify also."

"We got him?" I ask as someone drapes a warm blanket over my shoulders.

"We got him."

The paramedics take my blood pressure, check my heart, and even my blood sugar. When they've decided I'm mostly well, Phoebe waves to Kim and Gran, who are standing by a squad car. As I head toward my ride home, Mack stops me. "Are you okay?"

"I'll get the heat going in the car," Phoebe says as she runs ahead. Really she's giving me wrap-up time—an expression I made up for when she brings home dates, which hasn't happened yet, but likely will soon.

As soon as she's out of earshot, I say, "Plan B? When did you come up with that nifty scenario?"

"I thought it was best."

"Well, bravo. But why didn't you tell me?"

"I didn't want you to think it was possible he'd throw you out the window."

I look down. "Yeah. That's a tough one. I still can't believe he did that." I hug myself. "It's really cold out." I stomp my feet in an attempt to warm myself up.

Mack puts his arm around me. Walks me the rest of the way to the car. "You're a tough one, I'll give you that, but let's not do this kind of thing again. Straight boring policework from now on."

"Deal. I'm pretty tired."

"Almost being killed will do that to a person."

"Thanks," I say.

"It's my job to keep you and all of the citizens of Mystic Hollow safe."

"Nothing personal?"

"Oh, it's very personal. All of it. This is my town. You are my people."

"Just so."

"Get her home and keep her warm," Mack instructs. "If she shows any signs of shock, call for help right away."

"Should we get you some coffee, Mom?" Phoebe asks.

"I think I've had enough adrenaline for one night."

Mack puts his hand over his heart. "Now I'm shocked."

Sensitive Mack is gone and snarcastic Mack is back. I guess that's good. That means all is well. I watch as they load Pete into the police car, pushing his head down so he doesn't hit it as he gets in.

"Just like TV," I say. "Hey, I have an idea—want to binge watch all the old *Cops* shows?"

"She's fine," Gran says.

"Yeah. We can bet on who's going to act badly and who is going to do bad acts."

"Aren't those the same thing, dear?" Gran asks.

"Vastly different," I say. As the car pulls away and heads toward Gran's house, I catch her up on our system for ranking best actor in a police chase, in a shoplifting arrest, in a traffic stop scene.

"Extra points for pointing long fingernails in the officer's face during a tirade."

"As long as there is a system and reliable method of scoring."

"Are we not civilized?" I pretend-gasp and let my girls' laughter heal the parts of me that were broken in the fall.

Epilogue

We stand in front of the doorway, the large iron gates closing behind us. I hate that sound. It means I'm trapped. It means I'm silenced. It means I'm home.

The door opens, and a slim woman in a gray uniform greets us, taking our coats. I will admit that not having to be responsible for wrangling my outerwear is one of the greatest joys of visiting my mother.

"You're here!" Mom exclaims, arms wide. She is dressed in a Chanel pantsuit, navy blue with gold buttons.

I smooth my sweater and force myself to stand straighter. The least favorite thing about seeing my mother? The inspection I never seem to pass. Although today she doesn't look me over. In fact, she brushes past me and embraces Phoebe. Then Gran. "It's not often I get to have my girls for dinner."

"It smells amazing, Mom," I say as we head inside.

"Celia is a wonderful cook. She's on loan from my good friend Louisa since she and her new husband are on vacation. Although, I might try to incentivize her to stay with me."

"Isn't that poaching?" I pretend-gasp. But I'm really wondering how long Mom is intending to stay. Why would she require a full-time staff?

I'm surprised to see an extra plate. "Who's joining us? You know Kim can't make it, right?"

"Yes, dear. She RSVP'd. As one should."

The doorbell rings.

Mom gestures for us to sit. "Phoebe, we have a special soup for you and a Welsh rarebit for the appetizer. It's straight out of *Gosford Park.*"

Phoebe dons a British accent as she completes a reenactment of that scene. "He's very full of himself. I must say. A vegetarian at a hunting party?" She feigns indignation better than most.

Mom laughs. Then looks up when someone else comes into the dining room. "Ah, our special guest is here."

My stomach drops. Almira Leach. Of course it is.

"Since you all know each other already, this seemed the perfect time to congregate."

I clear my throat. Force a smile. I want to ask my mother to join me in the kitchen, but I know that will just make things worse.

"Good evening. I'm sorry I'm late. Traffic was terrible."

"You are just in time," Mom says as Almira takes the extra seat. "I was just about to ask Veronica to bring me up to date on the arrests made in the Adam Whitford murder."

"As well as the Nicholas Turner case."

The maid serves the soup. "Thanks," I say. She nods.

"My goodness. Small-town life certainly seems to have turned a little grimy, hasn't it?"

"None of what happened had anything to do with small-town life in general or even Mystic Hollow, specifically," I say.

"Well, it had to do with the festival," Almira points out. "And Carolyn."

"That's true." I can't deny that. "It's so crazy, though."

"Did the girl confess?" Mom asks, screwing up her face like she just smelled something bitter.

"Carolyn Millner? Yes. To accessory. She and Pete dated, apparently. She went on vacation with him and Adam when Adam was suffering from writer's block. She offered to finish his books for him so he could write his passion project."

"Interesting. A nice little business. So, what went wrong?"

"Adam's brother found out that he was stealing from him and Carolyn decided she wanted a bigger payday. Adam refused both entreaties. Murder ensued."

"Great word, dear," Gran pats my hand. "Even better summary. It could be a headline!"

"Thanks, Gran. Also, Adam apparently threatened to claim she plagiarized. Get her blacklisted by any future publishers."

Gran looks at me.

"That came out later."

"He did?" Gran gasps. "He had such a kind face . . ."

"Wow," The Leach says. "I knew he was sketchy, but I didn't realize how cruel he could be."

"The strongest defense is a great offense. Right?" Phoebe says.

"Welp, not if that offense gets you murdered."

"So how did they nail them?" Mom asks.

"Is it weird that you're interested in this? I mean, is this even a proper topic of conversation at the dinner table? When I was twelve, I tried to discuss the Tonya Harding incident and was told that was gossip fodder and not appropriate."

Mom sits back as her soup bowl is cleared. "Well, when it affects my daughter, granddaughter, and mother, it is deemed admissible."

"It's okay, dear," Gran says. "Your mother has a right to know."

I brush my hair behind my ears. "Apparently, Carolyn and Pete blackmailed Dawn to get her to withdraw from our festival. To get Adam here. Something about a hazing incident in her past when she was in college. With her sorority."

"That set the stage for murder," Phoebe says in a very dramatized voice.

"You planning your own podcast?" I ask.

"I could do better than Pete."

"The meat of Carolyn's confession came after her lawyer carved out of the deal, for anything she might want to use in future books. You can't benefit from murder, but if you only had intent to weaken—"

"Only to maim or seriously injure," Phoebe jumps in with her favorite quote from Dobby in *Harry Potter.*

I clear my throat. "Excellent reference aside, I'm never going to finish this story."

"Not if you keep meandering around." Mom makes a motion with her butter knife.

"As I was saying, Carolyn admitted to administering the toxin to the kombucha and giving it to his angel to deliver it to Adam to weaken him. Pete set up the meet in the belfry. Where Carolyn attempted to reason with him."

"Didn't work?"

"Apparently not." I clear my throat. "Then Pete pushed him. End of story."

"How did Pete get Adam to go to the belfry. That seems off script." Mom asks.

Phoebe smirks.

I elbow her.

"Veronica, if you'll kindly wrap this up before dessert."

"Pete talked Adam into the entire belfry deal, saying it would be a fun riff on his online nickname. Then Pete faked the time stamp on his video in Baltimore and headed to the festival. He was able to track both Carolyn and Adam using the location tracker on Adam's phone and also the burner phone he gave Carolyn."

"This is why I will no longer be sharing my location with you, Mom," Phoebe says. "Apparently, that practice leads to murder."

"Nice try, missy."

Phoebe shrugs.

"Finish the story," Mom says. "Honestly, you two can't stay on topic to save your lives."

"Or anyone else's," Gran interjects.

"Whose side are you on?" I ask, feigning upset.

"I'm on the side of a satisfying ending," Gran says. "Of the storytelling kind. Proceed."

"Apparently Adam still didn't understand the grave condition he'd put himself in."

Almira makes a face. "In which he put himself."

Mom smiles like she finally has a coconspirator.

I scoff. "Anyway, like I was saying, his brother had discovered another theft—one of Pete's ideas was the basis for Adam's next big thing. His passion project."

"That man really couldn't read people, could he?" Gran says.

"What do you mean?" Mom asks.

"According to Carolyn, Adam thought Pete was going to intervene on his behalf."

"How do we know she's telling the truth?" Almira asks.

"She started recording when she went to the tower. They've got it all."

"So, the mayor?" Mom asks.

"Thought her daughter had been implicated," Almira says, holding up one hand as if in testimony. "She was simply protecting her cub."

Mom nods. "I can understand that."

"So you'd frame someone for murder in order to protect me should you believe I was guilty of murder?" I ask.

"No, no," Almira says. "She never believed Laurel was guilty. She simply was being overly cautious due to the damning information sent to her. Fabricated, of course."

"Any good mother would," Mom says.

I hold up my knife and pretend to stab Almira. "So, if I lose my head and go a little nutty and . . ." I slash the air, "You'd defend my honor and good name?"

"I'd hire a good attorney. And a therapist."

Almira wipes the corners of her lips with such a delicate motion it makes my flailing about with a knife seem even more garish. "The therapist idea might be a good one, Collette. Let's keep one on speed dial just in case."

"What is Welsh rarebit, anyway?" Phoebe asks. "It's not related to rabbit in any way, right?"

I gesture to my daughter. "See how well she changes the subject?"

"it's just cheese toast usually. But for you, we veganized it and made it fancier. Your entrée is going to be a lovely onion tart"

"Smells delicious."

"You know what kills me, though?" I say. "Carolyn was still all smug about it. How she was going to get all this time to write, what with being in jail and all. Like those writers who did the Amtrak thing for a year while they wrote."

"Only, it's jail," Phoebe says.

"Right, but I swear, if she sells something before I do—"

"Oh, look, it's dessert, dear," Gran says obviously trying to distract me, but since it's trifle and that's my favorite, I settle down a bit.

"Don't trifle with me," I say. "Or you'll get your just desserts."

Mom pretends to be annoyed. I take that as a win. A beat too soon because I can tell by Almira's face that she has a snide comment locked and loaded.

"That's a cheap joke, isn't it?" Almira says, wiping her mouth daintily with her napkin. "Although it suits Veronica's style. You know, sort of her own version of popcorn prose. My goodness, you may have discovered a new genre."

"That's good," Phoebe says to calm me down, but honestly, the trifle is already doing that. "You are a literary savant."

"Of sorts," Almira agrees.

With that, the entire table laughs, but it's subdued since it's still my mother's dining room. All the sounds—the laughter at the table, the clinks of the coffee cups on the saucers, the warmth of good company—fill me, hit me. No matter what has happened over the last few months, despite how this phase of my life started, with us outrunning a hurricane, I am home. I don't mean this house, thankfully. But with my people and close enough for an occasional visit to my mother, I silently admit grudgingly.

* * *

After dinner, as Mom walks us to the door, she says. "I think we should make this a weekly thing."

I surprise myself by saying, "I agree."

We walk to the car, silent, full, and happy. Satisfied. When I start up the car, Phoebe says, "Can we stop on the way home and get nachos. And donuts. And cookie dough."

"Of course. That's how I raised you."

* * *

As we pull into Mystic Hollow, I realize I'm home. The feeling of belonging envelops me. "Should we get pie?"

"Why not?" Gran says.

We park and walk into the diner. Mack looks up from the counter. Nods. "Anywhere you like."

We choose a table near the window. April brings mugs and menus. "We want pie," I say

"And ice cream," Phoebe says. "If you've got vegan."

"You know we do. Also made a vegan pie earlier in case you came in," Mack smiles. "Gotta pay my techies."

"He's the baker here," April says. "I can't bake to save my life."

Kim walks in almost on cue.

"You hungry?" I ask.

She puts her hand on her stomach. "Starved."

"Veggie burger and fries," Kim says.

"On the house," April says, laying down the plates of pie with ice cream heaped on top.

I realize my coffee is drained. I take my mug to where Mack is sitting, nursing a green juice. I consider asking him if he's on a diet since I made that eating too many carbs comment but decide against it. Instead, I slide my mug across the counter toward April, who refills it.

"Hey," I say. "Your board is going strong again. Three days in."

"Try not to incite another murder again anytime soon."

"I incited nothing."

He smirks. "By the way, you didn't look like a drowned rat."

"Huh?"

"The other night. You said some guy told you that before. It's not true." He points to his eyes. "It's your eyes. They get even bluer. And your cheeks pink."

I am dumbstruck.

"Guys do that. The kids call it negging. I hate it."

I carry my mug back to the table where Gran asks. "What was that about, dear?"

"Nothing. I complimented his new no-violent-crime board. He complimented my eyes. It's like a business relationship. He makes the pie." I point to the plate. "And the coffee. So I don't see any reason to be hostile."

Mack brings Kim's plate over with a piece of pie for her as well. "On the house. All of it. But if I catch any of you jaywalking . . ."

All eyes zoom in on me.

"They were Manolo Blahniks!"

Acknowledgments

Writing the acknowledgements for a book is usually one of my favorite parts of the process. It's where you get to thank the numerous people who helped bring the book to life. It is the end of a job well done. The victory lap. The raising of the hockey stick as you skate around the rink. I personally love sports metaphors because I am hopelessly clumsy. Anyway, this time, though it was different. I dragged my feet. I couldn't make myself do it. Why? Because this time it was emotional.

I wanted to write a mystery for the longest time. Had tried many times. I sent pitches and pages to my agent, Nicole Resciniti over and over again. For years. None of them landed. She never gave up on me. Not after the first concept, or the second one, or the third . . . you get the idea. Instead, she told me to keep working because she knew I'd get it. It's hard to describe how that makes you feel—to have an agent who believes in you so much even when you don't believe in yourself. I can't thank her enough.

Every book has its own backstory. *Spellbound by Murder* is no different. This story started with a love of family. A strong desire to live out my life in a different universe. A what-if-I-lived-in-New England-universe. What if I ran a bookstore. What if I had unlimited access to all of the types of coffee I love. Plus, kombucha! It may seem like a random compilation of my strange obsessions, but I promise that it all came from my truest self. The part of me that values wish fulfillment and the belief in magic. The belief that was instilled by my first loves—my family and, of course, books.

I remember all of the books my mother read to me as a child. The ones I read myself—thousands of them. Plus, all the ones I read to my children. Books are the thing. They are everything. I remember sneaking books into my classes in high school, sitting in the back of the room and ignoring the teacher as I lived in whatever world the author imagined. Magic. I came home from college to a stack of books for me, curated by my mother because she heard about this one and she thought I'd like it. She was never wrong. Missing my parents is at the heart of my writing. They didn't get to see me land an agent or sell a book. I lost them before that. But believe me, they are in every page I write. Because books are part of where I store them now. That's how sacred writing is to me. So, when I say books are everything, I mean it deep down. The deepest down.

Writing is not an individual sport. It requires the support of many people, all of whom could not be named here, but I'm going to try to do my best not to leave anyone out. First, there is my family. My husband. Our children. Their partners and now, miraculously, their children. The countless times over the years that they watched me struggle through this process, find my feet, lose my bearing, and start over. They never judged or complained that my writing kept me on the periphery of their countless game nights. Which might have been for the best since I'm a fairly competitive. Instead, they applauded when I won and cajoled me when I lost. They are good eggs.

But before my kids and my husband were two people who have always supported me—my brother and sister. They were my first friends. My first supporters. They snuck me into horror movies when I was little which laid the foundation for my love of mysteries and magic. They keep me tethered to our shared history. I count myself lucky for always having them in my corner. I also, of course have their kids and their kids' dogs and their partners to add to my support system. Yay, me. Life is full.

Thank you also to my writing community. To Joyce Sweeney, Jonathan Rosen, Debbie Reed Fischer, Jill Ross Nadler, Faran Fagen, and many, many more people who always see the good in my writing. You need that as a writer—to have people whose writing you respect so much that when they prop you up, you feel proud of your own work. I love you all.

Books don't happen without an editor who believes in them. For this book, that was Holly Ingraham, the person who bought this book. I am so grateful to her. Publishing is a long game. Sometimes editors leave—and then your book's future is in jeopardy. When Holly left Crooked Lane Books, I was worried. Of course I was. Then I met Thaisheemarie Fantauzzi Pérez and I went from anxious to grateful. Thai's editing of this book was meticulous and expansive. She understood what I was trying to do and helped me execute the vision with her constant care and attention. I cannot thank her enough for how she shepherded *Spellbound by Murder* through the editorial and production process. She is good people and fantastic at her job.

That leads me to the team at Crooked Lane Press. I am blown away by the support they've shown me and my book. How they have championed it, giving it the best chance for success. From the cover design by Lucy Rose, and the book designer, plus, the copy editors who made sense of my disordered writing, to the proofreaders and the marketing and promotional team, who have been generous, kind, and effective. Thank you all so much for everything. I am forever in your debt.

To my characters, Veronica, Phoebe, Gran, Kim, Danetra, Stella, and Mack—thanks for being so fun to write.

Finally, to the readers. This book is for you. Every book is for you. Without you, there is nothing.